MAGIC OF BLOOD AND SEA

ALSO BY
CASSANDRA ROSE CLARKE

Our Lady of the Ice

The Mad Scientist's Daughter

Star's End

MAGIC OF BLOOD AND SEA

THE ASSASSIN'S CURSE
AND
THE PIRATE'S WISH

CASSANDRA ROSE CLARKE

1230 AVENUE OF THE AMERICAS, NEW YORK, NEW YORK 10020

Also available in a SAGA PRESS hardcover edition
The text for this book was set in Perpetua Std.
Manufactured in the United States of America

2 4 6 8 10 9 7 5 3

CIP data for this book is available from the Library of Congress.
ISBN 978-1-4814-7641-6 (hardcover)
ISBN 978-1-4814-6172-6 (pbk)
ISBN 978-1-4814-6173-3 (eBook)

This book is dedicated to my parents,
for all their years of love and support

ACKNOWLEDGMENTS

I would like to foremost thank my parents, primarily for not balking when I decided to earn a graduate degree in creative writing but also for all their support over the years, and Ross Andrews, who deserves my utmost gratitude for encouraging me even when I wanted to quit and for helping me through the highs and lows of pursuing a writing career.

My beta reader, Amanda Cole, helped me shape this book from a mess into a story, and our discussions about reading and writing have helped me as much as any class. Bobby Mathews, one of my oldest friends, has watched me develop as a writer and given me encouragement and advice all along the way. Stephanie Denise Brown and Stephanie Scudder propped me up through the six weeks of Clarion West and proved invaluable in their critiques. To all my friends: thank you.

I would also like to thank Dr. Janet Lowery, Dr. Elizabeth Harris, Peter LaSalle, and my instructors at the 2010 Clarion West Writers Workshop, for sharing their knowledge, wisdom, and advice.

A very special thanks goes out to Amanda Rutter, Lee Harris, and all the rest of the team at Angry Robot for taking a chance with their Open Door Month and releasing this book to the world back in 2012. Although Strange Chemistry has since shuttered its doors, Amanda deserves all the accolades for her tireless support of this book and all the books Strange Chemistry released.

Special thanks to my agent, Stacia Decker, for all the work—too much to list!—that she has done to help me, particularly with this series. And thank you to Navah Wolfe at Saga Press for helping the series find a new home.

And finally, I would like to thank everyone who read, reviewed, and wrote to me about *The Assassin's Curse*, *The Pirate's Wish*, and *The Wizard's Promise*. Your support has helped the books with this second chance, and I am eternally grateful for all the love the series has received.

CONTENTS

THE ASSASSIN'S CURSE

CHAPTER ONE

I ain't never been one to trust beautiful people, and Tarrin of the *Hariri* was the most beautiful man I ever saw. You know how in the temples they got those paintings of all the gods and goddesses hanging on the wall above the row of prayer candles? And you're supposed to meditate on them so as the gods can hear your request better? Tarrin of the *Hariri* looked just like one of those paintings. Golden skin and huge black eyes and this smile that probably worked on every girl from here to the ice-islands. I hated him on sight.

We were standing in the Hariris' garden, Mama and Papa flanking me on either side like a couple of armed guards. The sea crashed against the big marble wall, spray misting soft and salty across my face. I licked it away and Mama jabbed me in the side with the butt of her sword.

"So I take it all the arrangements are in order?" asked Captain Hariri, Tarrin's father. "You're ready to finalize our agreement?"

"Soon as we make the trade," Papa said.

I glowered at the word "trade" and squirmed around in my too-tight silk dress. My breasts squeezed out the top of it, not on purpose. I know that sort of thing is supposed to be appealing to men but you wouldn't know it talking to me. At least the dress was a real pretty one, the color of cinnamon and draped the way the court ladies wore 'em a couple of seasons ago. We'd nicked it off a merchant ship a few months back. Mama had said it suited me when we were on board Papa's boat and she was lining my eyes with kohl and pinning my hair on top of my head, trying to turn me into a beauty. I could tell by the expression on Mistress Hariri's face that it hadn't worked.

"Tarrin!" Captain Hariri lifted his hand and Tarrin slunk out of the shadow of the gazebo where he'd been standing alongside his mother. The air was full up with these tiny white flowers from the trees nearby, and a couple of blossoms caught in Tarrin's hair. He was dressed like his father, in dusty old aristocratic clothes, and that was the only sign either of 'em were pirates like me and my parents.

"It's nice to meet you, Ananna of the *Tanarau*." He bowed, hinging at the waist. He said my name wrong. Mama shoved me forward, and I stumbled over the hem of my dress, stained first with seawater from clomping around on the boat and then with sand from walking through Lisirra to get to this stupid garden. The Hariris were the only clan in the whole Confederation that spent more time on land than they did at sea.

Tarrin and I stared at each other for a few seconds, until Mama jabbed me in the back again, and I spat out one of the questions she made me memorize: "Have you got a ship yet?"

Tarrin beamed. "A sleek little frigate, plucked out of the emperor's own fleet. Fastest ship on the water."

"Yeah?" I said. "You got a crew for that ship or we just gonna look at her from the wall over there?"

"Ananna," Mama hissed, even as Papa tried to stifle a laugh.

Tarrin's face crumpled up and he looked at me like a little kid that knows you're teasing him but doesn't get the joke. "Finest crew out of the western islands." It sounded rehearsed. "I got great plans for her, Mistress Tanarau." He opened his eyes up real wide and his face glowed. "I want to take her out to the Isles of the Sky."

I about choked on my own spit. "You sure that's a good idea?"

"Surely a girl raised on the *Tanarau* doesn't fear the Isles of the Sky."

I glared at him. The air in the garden was hot and still, like pure sunlight, and even though the horrors I'd heard about the Isles of the Sky seemed distant and made-up here, Tarrin's little plan set my nerves on edge. Even if he probably wasn't talking truth: nobody makes a path for the Isles of the Sky, on account of folks going mad from visiting that little chain of islands. They'll change you and change you until you ain't even human no more. They're pure magic, that's what Mama told me. They're the place where magic comes from.

"I know the difference between bravery and stupidity," I said. Tarrin laughed, but he looked uncomfortable, and his father was glowering and squinting into the sunlight.

"She's joking," Mama said.

"No, I ain't."

Mama cuffed me hard on the back of the head. I stumbled forward and bumped right up against Tarrin. Under the gazebo, his mother scowled in her fancy silks.

"It does sound like a nice ship, though," I muttered, rubbing at my head.

Captain Hariri puffed out his chest and coughed. "Why don't you show Mistress Tanarau your ship, boy?"

Tarrin gave him this real withering look, with enough nastiness in it to poison Lisirra's main water well, then turned back to me and flashed me one of his lady-slaying smiles. I sighed, but my head still stung from where Mama'd smacked me, and I figured anything was better than fidgeting around in my dress while Papa and Captain Hariri yammered about the best way for the Tanarau clan to sack along the Jokja coast, now that the *Tanarau* had all the power of the *Hariri* and her rich-man's armada behind them. Thanks to me, Papa would've said, even though I ain't had no say in it.

Tarrin led me down this narrow staircase that took us away

from the garden and up to the water's edge. Sure enough, a frigate bobbed in the ocean, the wood polished and waxed, the sails dyed pale blue—wedding sails.

"You ain't flying colors yet," I said.

Tarrin's face got dark and stormy. "Father hasn't given me the right. Said I have to prove myself first."

"So if we get married, we gotta sail colorless?" I frowned.

"*If* we get married?" Tarrin turned to me. "I thought it was a done deal! Father and Captain Tanarau have been discussing it for months." He paused. "This better not be some Tanarau trick."

"Trust me, it ain't."

"'Cause I'll tell you now, my father isn't afraid to send the assassins after his enemies."

"Oh, how old do you think I am? Five?" I walked up to the edge of the pier and thumped the boat's side with my palm. The wood was sturdy beneath my touch and smooth as silk. "I ain't afraid of assassin stories no more." I glanced over my shoulder at him. "But the Isles of the Sky, that's another matter." I paused. "That's why you want to go north, ain't it? 'Cause of your father?"

Tarrin didn't answer at first. Then he pushed his hair back away from his forehead and kind of smiled at me and said, "How did you know?"

"Any fool could see it."

Tarrin looked at me, his eyes big and dark. "Do you really think it's stupid?"

"Yeah."

He smiled. "I like how honest you are with me."

I almost felt sorry for him then, 'cause I figured, with a face like that, ain't no girl ever been honest to him in his whole life.

"We could always fly *Tanarau* colors," I suggested. "'Stead of *Hariri* ones. That way you don't have to wor—"

Tarrin laughed. "Please. That would be even worse."

The wrong answer. I spun away from him, tripped on my damn dress hem again, and followed the path around the side of the cliff that headed back to the front of the Hariris' manor. Tarrin trailed behind me, spitting out apologies—as if it mattered. We were getting married whether or not I hated him, whether or not Mistress Hariri thought I was too ugly to join in with her clan. See, Captain Hariri was low-ranked among the loose assortment of cutthroats and thieves that formed the Confederation. Papa wasn't.

There are three ways of bettering yourself in the Pirates' Confederation, Mama told me once: murder, mutiny, and marriage. Figures the Hariri clan would be the sort to choose the most outwardly respectable of the three.

I was up at street level by now, surrounded by fruit trees and vines hanging with bright flowers. The air in Lisirra always smells like cardamom and rosewater, especially in the garden district, which was where Captain Hariri kept his manor. It was built on a busy street, near a day market, and merchant camels paraded past its front garden, stirring up great clouds of dust. An idea swirled around in my head, not quite fully formed: a way out of the fix of arranged marriage.

"Mistress Tanarau!" Tarrin ran up beside me. "There's nothing interesting up here. The market's terrible." He pouted. "Don't you want to go aboard my ship?"

"Be aboard it plenty soon enough." I kept watching those camels. The merchants always tied them off at their street-stalls, loose, lazy knots that weren't nothing a pirate princess couldn't untangle in five seconds flat.

Papa told me once that you should never let a door slam shut on you. "Even if you can't quite figure out how to work it in the moment," he'd said. He wasn't never one to miss an opportunity, and I am nothing if not my father's daughter. Even if the bastard did want to marry me off.

I took off down the street, hoisting my skirt up over my boots—none of the proper ladies shoes we'd had on the boat had been in my size—so I wouldn't trip on it. Tarrin followed close behind, whining about his boat and then asking why I wanted to go to the day market.

"'Cause," I snapped, skirt flaring out as I faced him. "I'm thirsty, and I ain't had a sweet lime drink in half a year. Can only get 'em in Lisirra."

"Oh," said Tarrin. "Well, you should have said something—"

I turned away from him and stalked toward the market's entrance, all festooned with vines from the nearby gardens. The market was small, like Tarrin said, the vendors selling mostly cut flowers and food. I breezed past a sign advertising sweet lime drinks, not letting myself look back at Tarrin. I love sweet lime drinks, to be sure, but that ain't what I was after.

It didn't take me long to find a vendor that would suit my needs. He actually found me, shouting the Lisirran slang for Empire nobility. I'm pretty sure he used it as a joke. Still, I glanced at him when he called it out, and his hands sparkled and shone like he'd found a way to catch sunlight. He sold jewelry, most of it fake, but some of it pretty valuable—I figured he must not be able to tell the difference.

But most important of all, he had a camel, tied to a wooden pole with some thin, fraying rope, the knot already starting to come undone in the heat.

Tarrin caught up with me and squinted at the vendor.

"You want to apologize for laughing at me," I said, "buy me a necklace."

"To wear at our wedding?"

"Sure." I fixed my eyes on the camel. It snorted and pawed at the ground. I've always liked camels, all hunchbacked and threadbare like a well-loved blanket.

Tarrin sauntered up to the vendor, grin fixed in place. The vendor asked him if he wanted something for the lady.

I didn't hear Tarrin's response. By then, I was already at the camel, my hands yanking at the knot. It dissolved quick as salt in water, sliding to the bottom of the pole.

I used that same pole to vault myself up on the saddle nestled between the two humps on the camel's back, hiking the skirt of my dress up around my waist. I leaned forward and went "tut" into his ear like I'd seen the stall vendors do a thousand times. The camel trotted forward. I dug the heels of my boots into his side and we shot off, the camel kicking up great clouds of golden dirt, me clinging to his neck in my silk dress, the pretty braids of my hairstyle coming unraveled in the wind.

The vendor shouted behind me, angry curses that would've made a real lady blush. Then Tarrin joined in, screaming at me to come back, hollering that he hadn't been joking about the assassins. I squeezed my eyes shut and tugged hard on the camel's reins and listened to the gusts of air shoving out of his nostrils. He smelled awful, like dung and the too-hot-sun, but I didn't care: We were wound up together, me and that camel.

I slapped his reins against his neck like he was a horse and willed him to take me away, away from my marriage and my double-crossing parents. And he did.

All of Tarrin's hollering aside, we galloped out of the garden district without much trouble. I didn't know how to direct the camel—as Papa always told me, my people ride on boats, not animals—but the camel seemed less keen on going back to that vendor than I did. He turned down one street and then another, threading deeper and deeper into the crush of white clay buildings. Eventually he slowed to a walk, and together we ambled along a wide, sunny street lined with drying laundry.

I didn't recognize this part of the city.

There weren't as many people out, no vendors or bright-colored shop signs painted on the building walls. Women stuck their heads out of windows as we rode past, eyebrows cocked up like we were the funniest thing they'd seen all day. I might have waved at them under different circumstances, but right now I had to figure out how to lay low for a while. Escaping's always easy, Papa taught me (he'd been talking about jail, not marriage, but still). Staying escaped is the hard part.

I found this sliver of an alley and pushed at the camel's neck to get him to turn. He snorted and shook his big shaggy head, then trudged forward.

"Thanks, camel." The air was cooler here: A breeze streamed between the two buildings and their roofs blocked out the sun. I slid off the camel's back and straightened out my dress. The fabric was coated with dust and golden camel hairs in addition to the mud-and-saltwater stains at the hem, and I imagined it probably smelled like camel now too.

I patted the camel on the head and he blinked at me, his eyes dark and gleaming and intelligent.

"Thanks," I told him again. I wasn't used to getting around on the backs of animals, and it seemed improper not to let him know I appreciated his help. "You just got me out of a marriage."

The camel tilted his head a little like he understood.

"And you're free now," I added. "You don't have to haul around all that fake jewelry." I scratched at the side of his face. "Find somebody who'll give you a bath this time, you understand?"

He blinked at me but didn't move. I gave him a gentle shove, and he turned and trotted out into the open street. Myself, I just slumped down in the dust and tried to decide what to do next. I figured I had to let the camel go 'cause I was too conspicuous on him. Together we'd wound pretty deeply into Lisirra's residential mazes, but most people, when they see a girl in a fancy dress on a camel—that's something they're going to remember. Which meant I needed to get rid of the dress next, ideally for money. Not that I have any qualms about thievery, but it's always easier to do things on the up and up when you can.

I stood and swiped my hands over the dress a few times, trying to get rid of the dust and the camel hairs. I pulled my hair down so it fell thick and frizzy and black around my bare shoulders. Then I followed the alley away from the triangle of light where I'd entered, emerging on another sun-filled street, this one more bustling than the other. A group of kids chased each other around, shrieking and laughing. Women in airy cream-colored dresses and lacy scarves carried baskets of figs and dates and nuts, or dead chickens trussed up in strings, or jars of water. I needed one of those dresses.

One of the first lessons Papa ever taught me, back when I could barely totter around belowdeck, was how to sneak around. "One of the most important aspects of our work," he always said. "Don't underestimate it." And sneaking around in public is actually the easiest thing in the whole world, 'cause all you have to do is stride purposefully ahead like you own the place, which was easy given my silk dress. I jutted my chin out a little bit and kept my shoulders straight, and people just stepped out of the way for me, their eyes lowered. I went on like this until I found a laundry line strung up between two buildings, white fabric flapping on it like the sails of our boat.

Our boat.

The thought stopped me dead. She wasn't my boat no more.

Never would be. I'd every intention of finishing what I started, like Papa always taught me. But finishing what I started meant I'd never get to see that boat again. I'd spent all my seventeen years aboard her, and now I'd never get to climb up to the top of her rigging and gaze out at the gray-lined horizon drawn like a loop around us. Hell, I'd probably never even go back to the pirates' islands in the west, or dance the Confederation dances again, or listen to some old cutthroat tell his war stories while I drifted off to sleep in a rope hammock I'd tied myself.

A cart rolled by then, kicking up a great cloud of dust that set me to coughing. The sand stung my eyes, and I told myself it was the sand drawing out my tears as I rubbed them away with the palm of my hand. There was no point dwelling on the past. I couldn't marry Tarrin and I couldn't go home. If I wanted to let myself get morose, I could do it after I had money and a plan.

I ducked into the alley. The laundry wasn't hung up too high, and I could tell that if I jumped I'd be able to grab a few pieces before I hit the ground again. I pressed myself against the side of the building and waited until the street was clear, then I tucked my skirts around my waist, ran, jumped, spread my arms out wide, and grabbed hold of as much fabric as I could. The line sagged beneath my weight; I gave a good strong tug and the clothes came free. I balled them up and took off running down the alleyway. Not that it mattered; no one saw me.

At the next street over I strode regally along again till I found a dark empty corner where I could change. I'd managed to nick two scarves in addition to the dress, so I draped one over my head in the Lisirran style and folded my silk dress up in the other. I figured I could pass for a Lisirran even though I've a darker complexion than most of the folks in Lisirra. Hopefully no one would notice I was still wearing my clunky black seaboots underneath the airy dress—those would mark me as a pirate for sure. The dress was a bit tight across my chest and hips too, but most dresses are, and the fabric was at least thick enough to hide the lines of the Pirates' Confederation tattoo arching across my stomach.

I knew the next step was to find a day market where I could sell my marriage dress. I couldn't go back to the one where I stole the camel, of course, but fortunately for me there are day markets scattered all over the city. Of course, Lisirra is a sprawling crawling tricky place, like all civilized places, full of so many happenings and people and strange little buildings that it's easy to get lost. I only knew my way around certain districts—those close to the water and those known to shelter crooks and others of my ilk. That is to say, the places where my parents and the Hariri clan would be first to look. And I had no idea where the closest day market was.

I strolled along the street for a while, long enough that my throat started to ache from thirst. It was hotter here than it had been in the garden district, I guess 'cause it was later in the day, and everyone seemed to have retreated into the cool shade of the houses. I walked close to the buildings, trying to stay beneath the thin line of their cast shadows. Didn't do me much good.

Eventually I slouched down in another shady alley to rest, sticking the marriage dress behind my head like a pillow. The heat made me drowsy, and I could barely keep my eyes open. . . .

Voices.

It was a couple of women, speaking the Lisirran dialect of the Empire tongue. I peeked around the edge of the building. Both a little older than me, both with water pitchers tucked against the outward swell of their hips. One of the women laughed and a bit of water splashed out of her pitcher and sank into the sand.

"Excuse me!" My throat scratched when I talked, spitting out perfect Empire. The two women fell silent and stared at me.

"Excuse me, is there a market nearby? I have a dress to sell."

"A market?" The taller of the women frowned. "No, the closest is in the garden district." I must have looked crestfallen, 'cause she added, "There's another near the desert wall. Biggest in the city. You can sell anything there."

The other woman glanced at the sky. "It'll close before you get there, though," she said. She was right; I must have fallen asleep in the alley after all, 'cause the light had changed, turned gilded and thick. I was supposed to have been married by now.

"Do you need water?" the taller woman asked me.

I nodded, making my eyes big. Figured the kohl had probably spread over half my face by now, which could only help.

The taller woman smiled. She had a kind-looking face, soft and unlined, and I figured her for a mother who hadn't had more than one kid yet. The other scowled at her, probably hating the idea of showing kindness to a beggar.

"There's a public fountain nearby," she said. "Cut through the alleys, two streets over to the west." She reached into her dress pocket and pulled out a piece of pressed copper and tossed it to me. Enough to buy a skein plus water to fill it. I bowed to thank her, rattling off some temple blessing Mama had taught me back when I was learning proper thieving. Begging ain't thieving, of course, but I ain't so proud I'm gonna turn down free money.

The two women shuffled away, and I followed their directions to the fountain, which sparkled clean and fresh in the light of the setting sun. Took every ounce of willpower not to race forward and shove my whole face into it.

I reined myself in, though, and I got the skein and the water no problem. The sun had disappeared behind the line of buildings, and magic-cast lamps were twinkling on one by one, bathing the streets in a soft hazy glow. I could smell food drifting out of the open windows and my stomach grumbled something fierce. I managed to snatch a couple of meat-and-mint pies cooling on a windowsill, and I ate them in an out-of-the-way public courtyard, tucking myself under a fig tree. They were the best pies I'd ever tasted, the crust flaky and golden, the meat tender. I licked the grease off my fingers and took a couple of swigs of water.

I didn't much want to sleep outside—it's tough to get any real sleep, 'cause you wake up at the littlest noise, thinking it's an attack—but I also figured I didn't have much choice in the matter. I curled up next to the fig tree and used the marriage dress as a pillow again, although this time I yanked my knife out of my boot and kept it tucked in my hand while I slept. It helps.

I had trouble falling asleep. Not so much 'cause of being outside, though, but 'cause I kept thinking about the *Tanarau* and my traitorous parents: Mama smoking her pipe up on deck, shouting insults at the crew, Papa teaching me how to swing a sword all proper. It's funny, 'cause all my life I've loved Lisirra and the desert, so much so that I used to sleep belowdeck, nestled up among the silks and rugs we'd plundered from the merchant ships, and now that it looked like I'd be whiling away the rest of my days here in civilization, all I wanted was to go back to the ocean.

Figures that when I finally fell asleep, I dreamt I was in the desert. Only it wasn't the Empire desert. In my dream, all the sand had melted into black glass like it had been scorched, and lightning ripped the sky into pieces. I was lost, and I wanted somebody to find me, 'cause I knew I was gonna die, though it wasn't clear to me if my being found would save me or kill me.

I woke up with a pounding heart. It was still night out, the shadows cold without the heat of the sun, and I could feel 'em on my skin, this prickling crawling up my arm like a bug.

My dress was damp with sweat, but the knife was a reassuring weight in the palm of my hand. I pushed myself up to standing. Ain't nobody out, just the shadows and the stars, and for a few minutes I stood there breathing and wishing the last remnants of the dream would fade. But that weird feeling of wanting to be found and not wanting to be found stuck with me.

Maybe the dream was the gods telling me I wasn't sure about leaving home. Well, I wasn't gonna listen to 'em.

I took a couple more drinks from the skein, then tucked my knife in the sash of my dress and headed toward the desert wall. I was still shaky from the dream and figured I wasn't going to be sleeping much more tonight, so I might as well take advantage of the night's coolness and get to the day market right as it opened.

CHAPTER TWO

The woman from yesterday hadn't lied; the day market was the biggest I ever saw, merchant carts and permanent shops twisting together to create this labyrinth that jutted up against the desert wall. I wandered through the market with my dress tucked under my arm, the early morning light gray and pink. The food vendors were already out, thrusting bouquets of meat skewers at me as I walked by. My stomach growled, and after ten minutes of passing through the fragrant wood-smoke of the food carts, I sidled up to a particularly busy vendor and grabbed two of his goat-meat skewers, even though I do feel bad about thieving from the food vendors, who ain't proper rich like the merchants we pirate from. I ate it as I walked down to the garment division, licking the grease from my fingers. Tender and fatty and perfect. You get sick of fish and dried salted meats when you're out on the ocean.

The garment division was an impressive one, with shop after shop selling bolts of fabric and ready-made gowns and scarves and sand masks. Tailors taking measurements out on the street. Carts piled high with tiny pots of makeup and bottles of perfumes.

It was a lot of options. I knew that I wanted a merchant who wouldn't ask me no questions, but I also couldn't use someone who was the sort to traffic in stolen goods, since I didn't want anyone who might have gotten word from the Hariris to be on the lookout for their missing bride. I decided it was probably safer going the slightly more respectable route, and that meant cleaning up my appearance some.

I snatched a pot of eye-powder and a looking glass from one of the makeup carts and darted off into a corner, where I wiped the kohl off my face with the edge of my scarf—a mistake I realized too late, when I saw I'd stained it with black streaks. I flipped the scarf around and tried to tuck the stained ends around my neck. Then I smeared some of the eye-powder on my lids the way I'd seen Mama do it, a pair of gold streaks that made my eyes look big and surprised. Good enough.

The market was starting to get busy, people walking in clumps from vendor to vendor. I kept my head down and my feet quick, scanning each dress shop as I passed. None seemed right. One I almost ducked into—it was large, a couple of rooms at least, and full of people, which meant my face would be easily forgotten. But something nagged at me to walk on by, and I did, sure as if I had seen my own parents leaning up against the doorway.

I was nearly to the desert wall when a shop—*the* shop, I thought—appeared out of the crush of people. It was tucked away in the corner of an alley, and I only noticed it 'cause someone had propped up a sign on the street with an arrow and the words WE BUY GOWNS written out neat and proper.

The shop was small, but a pair of fancy gowns fluttered from hooks outside the door, like sea-ghosts trapped on land. I went inside. More gowns, some only half finished. The light was dim and cool and smelled of jasmine. No other customers but me.

"Can I help you?" A woman stepped out from behind some thin gauzy curtains. She wore a dress like the one I'd stolen, only it was dyed pomegranate red and edged with spangles that threw dots of light into my eyes. As she walked across the room, the sun splashed across her face. She was beautiful, which set me on edge, but there was something off about her features, something I couldn't quite place—

"Oh, I apologize," she said in Ein'a, which was the language of the far-off island where I'd been born, the language my parents had spoken to me when I was a baby. "We don't normally get foreigners."

Maybe I wasn't as inconspicuous as I thought.

"I speak Empire," I said, not wanting to stutter my way through Ein'a.

The shopkeeper smiled thinly, and I realized what it was that bothered me about her face—her eyes were pale gray, the same color as the sky before a typhoon. I ain't never seen eyes that color before, not even up among the ice-islands.

Something jarred inside of me. I wanted out of that shop. But even so, I unwrapped my silk dress and laid it out on the counter, the movements easy, like I was acting by rote. "I was hoping to sell this," I said.

The woman ran her hands over the dress, idly examining the seams, rubbing the fabric between her thumb and forefinger. She looked up at me.

"It's dirty."

I bit my lower lip, too unnerved to make a joke.

"And it reeks of camel." She glanced back down at the dress, tilted her head. "I recognize the cut, though. It's from court. Last season. How'd you come across it?"

"My mother gave it to me." Avoid lying whenever possible. Always leave out information when you can. Another one of Papa's lessons.

"Hmm," she said. "Looks like it's been through quite the adventure. I suppose I can use it as a guide. Merchant wives tend to be a bit behind on things." She folded the dress up. "I'll pay you one hundred pressed copper for it," she said.

"Two hundred."

"One fifty."

"One seventy."

She paused. Her lips curled up into a faint smile. "That's fair," she said. "One seventy."

Kaol, I wanted out of that store. The haggling went way too easy, and that smile chilled me to the bone. It was like a shark's smile, mean and cold.

She glided off to the back of the store, carrying the dress with her. When she came back out she handed me a bag filled with thin sheets of pressed copper. I slid the bag into the hidden pocket in my dress and turned to leave. Didn't bother to count. Felt heavy enough.

"Wait," said the shopkeeper.

I stopped.

"Be careful," she said. "I don't normally do this for free, but I like the look of you. They're coming. Well, one of them. Him."

I stared at her. She said "him" like it was the proper name of somebody she hated.

"What are you talking about?"

"Oh, you know. Your dream last night."

All the air just whooshed out of my body like I'd been in a drunkard's fight.

"I ain't had no dream last night."

She laughed. "Fine, you didn't have a dream. But you know the stories. I can tell. I can smell them on you."

"The stories," I said. "What stories?" All I could see was the gray in her eyes, looming in close around me. And then something flickered in the room, like a candle winking out. And I knew. The assassins. That boogeyman story Papa used to tell me whenever I didn't mind him or Mama.

"Ah, I see you've remembered." The shark's smile came out again. I took a step backward toward the door. "You're going to need my help. I live above the shop. When the time comes, don't delay."

I tried to smirk at her like I thought she was full of it, but in truth my whole body was shaking, and I was thinking about Tarrin yelling at me yesterday afternoon, trying to get me to come back. *My father isn't afraid to send the assassins after his enemies.* But men'll say anything to get you to do what they want. If Tarrin couldn't charm me onto his ship, he'd try to scare me. Well, it wasn't gonna work.

The shopkeeper tilted her head at me and then turned around, back toward the curtains. I darted out into the sunny street and took a deep breath. The eeriness of the shop faded into the background; out here there was just heat and sand and sun. Normal, comforting. Plus I had money hanging heavy in my pocket. I reached down to pat it. Enough to pay for a room at a cheap inn.

Fear still niggled at the back of my head, though. I hadn't thought about the assassins in years and years.

Papa talked about them like they were ghouls or ghosts, monsters come to take me away in the night. The stories always ended in the death of the intended victim. "They're relentless," he had said one night when I was ten or eleven, my face red and itchy with anger. I'd sassed him or Mama or both, and probably spent some time down in the brig for it too, but by then we were in the captain's quarters. The lanterns swung back and forth above our heads, the lights sliding across the rough features of Papa's face. "You can't escape an assassin." He leaned forward, shadows swallowing his eyes. "Hangings, bumbling bureaucrats, dishonest crewman, jail—those you can talk your way out of, you try hard enough. But this kind of death is the only kind of death."

He always said that when he told me assassin stories—the only kind of death. It was this refrain I'd get in my head whenever I did something bad, like playing tricks on the navigator or trying to read one of Mama's spellbooks without permission. The assassins were blood-magicians in addition to skilled fighters. They lived in dark lairs hidden in plain sight, like crocodiles. They were the last refuge of a coward, of a man too afraid to fight you himself—and that was why they were so dangerous. They gave power to cowards.

As I got older I realized, for all the stories, I ain't never heard of a pirate's out-of-battle death that couldn't be explained away by drink or stupidity. And at some point, I decided the assassins weren't real, or if they were, they weren't interested in tracking down a captain's daughter as punishment for not minding her elders. Or refusing marriage, for that matter.

So that's what I told myself as I cut through the sunlight, back toward the food vendors to buy myself a sweet lime drink. The woman was probably a witch in her spare time, trying to drum up business for her cut-rate protection spells, and the only thing stalking me in the night was some memory from my childhood. A story.

I paid for a room at an inn on the edge of town, not far from the day market. It was built into the desert wall, and my room had a window that looked out over the desert, which reminded me a bit of the ocean, the sand cresting and falling in the night wind. The room was small and bright and filled with dust, although clean otherwise—cleaner than my quarters on Papa's boat anyway.

I stayed in the inn for four days, and for four days nothing happened but dreams. They were the same one as the first night, me wandering around the black glass desert, waiting for somebody to find me, knowing I was going to die. I took to sleeping during the day—though that didn't stop the dreaming none—and went out as the sun dropped low and orange across the horizon, wasting my nights at the night market that was conjured up by sweet-smelling magic a few streets over from the day market's husk. The vendors at the night market hawked enchantments and magic supplies instead of food and clothing, plus spellbooks and charms and probably curses if you knew who to ask. It was a dangerous place for me to go: not 'cause I'd started believing in the assassins, but because you get a lot of scum hanging around the night markets, and the chance of somebody spotting me and turning me into the Hariri clan or my parents was pretty high.

But I went anyway, wearing my scarf even though the sun was down, so I could pull it low over my eyes. I liked to listen in on the sand-charmers who worked magic from the strength of the desert. Mama could do the same thing but with the waters of the ocean, and it occurred to me, as I listened to the singing and the chanting, that I missed her. The most I'd ever been away from her—and from Papa too—was the three weeks I spent failing to learn magic with this sea witch named Old Ceria a couple years back. But that had been different, 'cause I knew Papa's boat would pick me up when the three weeks were up, and Mama'd be waiting for me on deck.

That wasn't going to happen now.

I spent a lot of my time daydreaming during those four nights, too, letting my mind wander off to what I was gonna do now that I wasn't tied to a Confederation ship no more. I knew I had to hide out till the Hariris got over the slight of me running away from the marriage, but once that all settled I'd be free to set out from Lisirra and make my fortune, as Mama used to say of all the young men who set sail with ships of their own. A ship of my own was what I really wanted, of course—what Confederation child doesn't? 'Course, the Confederation won't let women captain, and the Empire ain't nothing but navy boats and merchant ships, but I could always make my way south, where the pirates don't take the Confederation tattoo and don't adhere to Confederation rules, neither.

It was a nice thought to have, and there was something pleasant about spending the early mornings before I fell asleep planning out a way to get first to one of the pirates' islands—probably Bone Island, it's the biggest, which makes it easier to go unnoticed—and then down to the southern coast. The daydreams took my mind off the Hariris, at any rate, and most of the time they kept me from feeling that sharp pang of sadness over my parents.

On the fourth night, I woke up the way I always did, after the sun set, but my head felt heavy and thick, like someone'd filled it up with rose jam. I skipped eating and walked down to the night market, thinking the cool air would clear my thoughts. It didn't. The lights at the night market blurred and trembled. The calls and chatter of the vendors amplified and faded and then thrummed like a struck chord.

I'd barely made it through the entrance gate when out of nowhere I got stuck. I couldn't move. I stood at the entrance to the market, and my feet seemed screwed to the ground. My arms hung useless at my sides. I smelled a whiff of scent on the air, sharp and medicinal, like spider mint. It burned the back of my throat.

And then, quick as that, I was released.

The whole world solidified like nothing'd happened, and I collapsed to the ground in a cloud of dry dust, coughing, my eyes streaming. I could hear whispers, people telling one another to keep a wide berth and muttering about curses and ill omens. I pushed myself up to sitting. Onlookers stared at me from out of the shadows, and I did my best to ignore 'em.

This wasn't Mama's magic, sent out to bring me home—that I knew. Her magic had too much of the ocean in it, all rough and tumble, crashing and falling. You plunged into her magic. This—this was calculated.

I stood up. A nearby vendor had one eye on me like he thought me about to steal his vials of love potion. I stumbled backward a little, coughed, wiped at my mouth. My hand left a streak of mud across my face.

"Hey," said the vendor. He leaned over the side of his cart. I didn't meet his eye. "Hey, you. Don't even try it."

My head was still thick. I stared at him, blinking.

"Go on," he said. "You think I've never seen this trick before? Whoever your little partner is, he's gonna get blasted with my protection spell."

"I don't have a—"

The vendor glared at me. I gave up trying to explain. Besides, I kept thinking the word *assassin* over and over again in spite of myself. The vendor turned toward a customer, his face breaking into a smile, but he kept glancing over his shoulder as he filled the order. Keeping his eye out for thieves, like any vendor.

I coughed again, turned, wanting to get back to the inn, with its coating of dust and its view of the desert. The street leading away from the night market was emptier than it should've been, and quiet too. Halfway down I stopped and eased my knife out of my boot, and then I hobbled along, wishing I could walk faster, or run—but something had my joints stiff and creaking as an old woman's.

The shadows moved.

I froze.

So did the shadows.

I stood there for a few seconds listening to my heart beat and to the distant strains of music floating out of the night market. Papa's old assassin stories worked their way into my head—that old detail about how they moved through darkness and shadows the way a fish moved through water. I loosened my grip on the knife, holding it proper, the way you're supposed to, and dreaded the moment when the shadows would move again.

Nothing.

I slid forward, just a couple of steps in the direction of the inn. That stirred the shadows up. They slid along the buildings like snakes. My body ached worse and worse or else I would've taken off running; instead, all I could do was creep along, my heart hammering and my breath short and my skin cold and hot all at once.

My head cleared.

It happened real sudden, as if a latch had been sprung, and I saw the whole world as clear and crystalline as if I were still at sea beneath a shining blue sky. A man was following me. I whirled around and caught sight of his robes, dyed the color of the night sky, fluttering back into the liquid shadows. I'd no idea what had broken the spell, but I was grateful for it.

"You want to fight me? Come out and fight me!"

My voice bounced off the buildings. Eyes glowed pale blue in the darkness.

My head started going thick and fogged again. The magic crept in. The eyes burned on and on. My fear was a thick coil in the pit of my stomach holding me in place.

It was an assassin.

"Fight me!" I shrieked, and I could feel the hysteria in my voice, like my words were splintering into pieces.

The assassin glided forward, black on black except for the strip of silver at his side. He didn't seem to be in much of a hurry. I forced myself forward, through the magic, and it gave me a pain in my spine that set me screaming, and my scream amplified up out into the starry night, rising up over the buildings, transforming into an explosion of white light that showered sparks and brightness down upon us both.

No one was as surprised as me.

I collapsed onto the ground, but for a second I saw the assassin like it was daytime: the grain in the fabric of his robes, the bump of his nose beneath his dark desert mask, the carvings etched into his armor. He was glaring at me.

"You're from the Mists?" he hissed. The bastard spoke perfect Empire.

"The what?"

The assassin jerked his head around like he was looking for somebody. I wanted to see where he was looking but I also didn't dare take my eyes off him.

"Who are you?" he said, though before I could answer he spat out a word in a language like dead flowers, beautiful and terrible all at once. Then he darted out of the glow of the light and melted into the shadows, all too quick for me to see.

For a few minutes I waited to die.

It didn't happen. The light I'd somehow screamed into existence burned away. I sat there in the street and remembered Papa's stories: they always kill their victims. But he hadn't killed me. He'd just melted into the shadows.

I didn't let myself get too cocky about that, though. Cockiness is useful to fake on occasion, but it'll only get you killed if you believe it. Maybe the man hadn't been an *assassin* assassin, just some hired knife sent by Captain Hariri. But then what about the moving shadows and the fog in my head and his eyes? Ain't no crewman on the *Hariri* able to pull off that trick with the eyes.

And my voice turning into light . . . Ain't no way that was me. That sort of protection spell was basic magic, and I couldn't even get the hang of basic magic back when Mama was trying to teach me.

I shuffled toward the inn, working things over in my head, clutching the knife to my breasts like I was some scared merchant's wife who had no clue how to use the damn thing. Everything was so dark. It took me a minute to realize none of the magic-cast lanterns were burning, and that sent another quake of chills vibrating through my spine.

It wasn't until I was dragging past the empty day market that I remembered the shopkeeper. The woman who bought my dress.

You're going to need my help. Don't delay.

I stopped. The night was quiet and still. I couldn't even hear the night market anymore.

I don't trust beautiful people. But Papa always told me you sometimes got to trust the one person you don't want to trust. "Just be smart about it," he'd say.

Well. I'd managed to avoid the only kind of death. I figured I could be smart about the woman at the dress shop too.

Mama tried to teach me magic, meeting with me down in the belly of the ship after my first menses showed up, but it turned out that I took more after Papa, who's completely untouched: better adept at stealing and sneaking and charming and fighting, all talents borne of the natural world. But unlike Papa, I can at least recognize magic when I see it and when I feel it, and I know better than to mess around with it.

I went to the woman's dress shop straight away, climbing over the day market fence and skittering through the empty streets till I found the sign with the arrow. The woman sat outside the shop eating a honey pastry, a lantern illuminating the lines of her face. She looked tired.

"Good," she said when she saw me. "You didn't delay."

"It was you, right? That's my thinking right now and I want to know for sure." I paused, rubbed at my dry eyes. The woman took a bite of pastry. "Earlier tonight," I said. "When the assassin attacked me."

The woman set her pastry in her lap. "You know that by all rights you should be dead."

"I know it. But you helped me."

She blinked at me.

"Though I can't figure out why."

The woman shrugged. She plucked the pastry out of her lap and finished it off. "Why don't you come inside?" she said. "I can prepare some coffee. I think we both need it."

She stood up and went into the shop. I hesitated. It still seemed too easy to me, her helping me with the assassin. Easy the way it had with the haggling. The woman stuck her head back out into the street.

"You come from pirate stock, don't you?"

I frowned. "How do you know that?"

"Because I looked at you. Don't worry, I won't hand you over to whoever it is you're running from."

"I ain't running from nothing."

"A pirate in the desert? You're obviously running from something." She smiled. "The reason I asked is because the pirates I deal with are so wary, but always over the wrong things. You look at my shop door like it's booby trapped, but you go traipsing through the night market when you've got an assassin tracking you."

I didn't have nothing to say to that, 'cause I knew she had a point.

"Come inside," the woman said. "And I'll help you."

She took me to the back of the store, behind the curtains, and set some water to boiling in the hearth. Steam curled up into the dusty moonlight. I sat down at a low table in the corner and watched her. She didn't spend a lot of time getting the coffee all perfect, the way they do in drink houses, and she didn't ask me how sweet I wanted it neither.

She sat down at the table across from me. I waited until she drank from her own cup before drinking from mine.

"What do you know about them?" she said.

I looked down at the little swirls of foam in my coffee. "They're hired," I said. "They know blood-magic." I closed my eyes. "They're the only kind of death." I felt weirdly safe in this small back room. I wanted to fall asleep.

"Ananna," she said, and at the sound of my name my eyes flew open. My hands turned to fists. The woman gazed at me with heavy-lidded eyes.

"How'd you know my name?"

The woman smiled. "How'd I know you were targeted? I know things."

"Yeah, I wouldn't mind knowing how you knew the assassin was after me too."

She gave me a demure smile.

I scowled, took another sip of coffee, and glanced around the room, trying to find something that I could use to get the woman to talk to me. But there were just dresses and bangles and bolts of fabric. The shop could have belonged to anyone.

"I've fought one of them before," she said. "I won."

That got my attention. I stared at her, trying to figure out if she was lying or not, if she really was a woman who had escaped the only kind of death.

"Don't look so impressed," she said. "Contrary to what you may have heard, they are human."

"What happened?" I asked. "Why would anyone try to kill you?"

"Why would anyone try to kill *you*?" she shot back. "It doesn't matter, really. All that matters is one of them is after you."

"You ain't gonna tell me nothing, are you?"

"Of course not. That sort of knowledge is more precious than gold. But I will help you. I'm not going to risk my life to save yours, mind, but I can offer aid."

I hadn't quite decided if I trusted this offer or not when she pushed her coffee cup aside and slid her hands over the tabletop. Figures rose out of the wood. A little man in a long robe, a girl in a courtier's dress.

"I'm no good at magic," I said. "So don't think I'm facing him down alone."

"But you already did face him down alone." The woman didn't look at me. "And besides, you've got enough magic," she said. "I can see it in you."

"You sure about that? 'Cause believe me, I've tried—"

She lifted her eyes to mine, and I got swallowed up by gray and couldn't talk no more. My ears buzzed and my lungs closed up.

"Quite sure," she said.

"All right. You're sure." My voice came out small and weak, but the woman smiled and the gray all disappeared. The room fell back to normal.

"Tomorrow night," she said. "Go out to the desert. It'll make things easier, to be out in the open."

On the table, the two figures began to move. The assassin's robe fluttered out behind him. The girl—I couldn't think of it as me—took small hesitant steps backward, her hair swirling around her face.

"This is how it's going to go without me," the woman said.

And in one movement, the assassin lashed out with a tiny sword and the girl collapsed on the ground.

I jumped in my seat, my blood pushing violently through my veins. I cursed in the secret language of the Confederation. The woman raised an eyebrow.

"That's not going to happen," she said. "I'm going to give you something. A few things, actually. What they are isn't important."

She raised her hand over the figures. They reset themselves. This time the girl carried four tiny vials in the palm of her hand. When the assassin's robes began to flutter, the girl hurled the vials, small as grains of rice, in his direction. A flash of green light. The assassin was gone.

"Where'd he go?" I asked.

"Elsewhere," the woman said. "A place where he'll never be able to track you." She waved her hand over the table and the figures slid back down into the wood.

"So he'll die?"

The woman stood up, walked to a counter on the other side of the room. She pulled out four narrow vials.

"No," she said. "Don't ask so many questions." She set the vials on the table. "Four ingredients," she said. "Equal parts each. Throw them all at once. Say the invocation. That opens up the doorway. They'll pull him through."

"Who's 'they'?"

The woman didn't answer.

"So why can't you do it?"

She scooped up the four vials and handed them to me. All four fit in the palm of my hand.

"Practice," she said.

"What? You can't do it 'cause of practice?"

The woman glared at me. "I've better things to do than follow you out to the desert. It's enough of a favor giving you the vials at all, let alone two sets. Their contents are rare and very expensive."

I scowled.

She pointed to a clear stretch of wall, empty of any dresses or jars of enchantments. "Throw them there. I want to see if you can open up the portal; the invocation is tailored only for the assassin, so no threat of getting pulled in ourselves. Oh, and I suppose you'll be needing the invocation, won't you." She stood up and glided over to the counter and wrote something down on a scrap of paper, folded it over, handed it to me.

I opened it up.

"I can't read this," I said. I assumed it was another language, 'cause even though I knew the alphabet the words looked like gibberish.

"Sound it out a few times," she said. "I used the Empire spelling."

There was no way this was going to work. Trying to work magic in an unfamiliar language? Taking advice from a beautiful woman with weird gray eyes? But if I didn't, I'd be dead. The only kind of death.

I stumbled over the words a few times, until the woman said, "That's good enough. They'll know what you're saying."

"There's that *they* again. Any reason you ain't telling me who they are?" I didn't like that she wouldn't.

"That's not what you need to worry about." She jerked her head toward the blank wall. "Now say the invocation and throw the charms. Do it all at once."

I took a deep breath. I recited the incantation in my head once for good measure. Then I drew my arm back, stammered out the words, and threw the vials into the air.

They exploded into a corridor of glass-green light, powerful enough that I staggered backward. The air swirled around me, and I thought I could hear a hum, deep and reverberating, coming from the slash of green. Light scattered across the floor of the shop. That corridor of light darkened and widened until it became a doorway. On the other side I saw mist.

Then, slowly, the light faded, growing dimmer and dimmer

until there was nothing left but the doorway, and then that faded away too. I shuffled over to the table and collapsed in the chair. I felt like I'd just been through a thousand sea-battles.

"Now you know why I don't want to do it," the woman said. "It takes all your energy to open a portal like that."

I dropped my forehead to the table. The wood was cool against my skin.

"I have to do that again." The thought left me unsettled. "You sure this is going to work?"

"As sure as I'm standing here before you," she said. "You send him away, and he won't ever come back."

I felt my heart beating in my chest, reminding me I was still alive.

"I suggest you go somewhere to sleep," she said. "Rest. I've got a protection spell on you that'll last until sundown, but I'm not staving him off for another night."

I lifted my head and drained the rest of my coffee, then dumped my cup upside down so I could look at the dregs. Not that I ever remember what they mean. This time wasn't no different.

"Satisfied?" the woman asked. I didn't like the way she asked that. Almost like she was making fun of me.

"Maybe," I snapped.

She laughed. And then she handed me a fresh set of vials and sent me on my way.

CHAPTER THREE

I left the inn at sunset. The four vials were tucked away in my pocket, but I kept my knife out. Even though Papa had partially gotten me into this mess, I hated to think what he would say if I went out there completely unprepared.

I walked across the sand for a long time, long enough that the sun melted into the horizon line and the stars began to twinkle in the unending blackness overhead. The wind pushed my hair away from my face, tangled my dress up in my legs. And I was so scared I kept choking on my own empty breaths. I'd been in battle before. Battles with weapons, though. Battles against people, not ghouls. And even in those battles my skin turned clammy and numb beforehand, even then I had to remind myself to breathe.

I walked long enough that Lisirra was just a chain of lights in the distance. For a minute I wanted to turn back, just drop the vials and run straight to the garden district and beg my apologies.

Suddenly that medicine scent, the one from the night before, saturated the air.

I stopped walking. The wind howled, blowing my hair into my eyes. I clutched my knife in one hand and stuck my other hand in my pocket and waited.

The shadows lengthened, curled, expanded. I whirled around, looking for a pair of glowing eyes, a flick of dark fabric. Nothing.

I wrapped my hand around the vials.

The world was suddenly too big.

And then he was there. I didn't see him, but I felt him, a shiver of cold breath on the back of my neck. I spun around, kicking up a spray of moonlit sand, and shoved the knife into my dress sash.

A flash of skin.

I pulled the vials out, broke them between my palms, and threw the whole thing, blood and magic and glass, in the direction of that skin. I screamed the invocation, the words still clumsy on my tongue.

The light erupted clean and bright. In the desert darkness it was the exact same color as the southern seas. It shot up like a fountain toward the sky. For a few seconds the entire desert glowed green.

And then something happened. The light didn't shower across the sand as it should. It didn't change into a doorway and disappear. It simply blinked out, like a candle between Mama's thumb and forefinger as she said good night, and I was plunged back into darkness and there was the assassin standing in front of me, his eyes—dark tonight, normal, not blue at all—narrowed above his desert mask.

I screamed. I didn't have time to think about the failure of the woman's magic. I didn't have time to think about anything. I just screamed and screamed, and the assassin stared at me with a sword glinting like starlight at his side.

I stumbled away. The sword flashed, sang, cut a long gash in my right forearm. I fell down into the sand. He darted toward me, and I drew up Papa's strength and in one movement yanked my knife out from my sash and implanted it squarely in the assassin's thigh. He stumbled backward, dragging the knife from my grasp, and I thought he looked a little stunned.

No time for thinking, though. I dove forward, grabbed the knife again. He swung his sword down at me and I was able to roll away, sand coating my face, stinging my eyes. I skittered backward across the desert like a crab. I thought the assassin was moving kind of slow for an assassin. Maybe the magic had done something after all. Or maybe he felt sorry for me. That sort of thing happens among cutthroats more often than you'd expect.

The assassin reached into some dark place in his armor and I flung the knife at him, in my panic not taking care to throw it properly. The hilt bounced off his chest. He stopped and looked at me. All I could see were his eyes, but they had a lightness in them that made me think he was laughing, which got me angry instead of scared. I reached over and grabbed the knife, jumped up to my feet, swung my head around, looking for something to use as a weapon or something to use as a trick. Nothing.

Nothing except a weird slithery motion through the sand, black against the black night. Then a pair of narrow white fangs. It was coming up behind the assassin, creeping up close to his ankles, but he didn't take no mind of it. Too busy pulling some murderous enchantment out of his cloak.

I ain't never liked snakes. You don't see enough of 'em on the water to get used to 'em, really, and when I saw this one I shrieked without meaning to and stuck my knife clean through it, 'cause my fear had turned me into a fool who only acted on reflex. Darkness pooled out onto the sand, and the snake flopped a few times and then died.

The whole night went still. I swear it was like the assassin and me were the only two people left in the world.

The assassin said something in that beautiful-terrible language of his. But he didn't try to kill me, which was what I expected. I pulled the knife out of the snake and wiped the blood off on the hem of my dress. The assassin kept staring at the snake like he'd never seen one before. I took this opportunity to attempt an escape, and began creeping back over the sand on my hands and knees.

"Stop," the assassin said, and I froze, sure I was about to die.

Footsteps thudded on the sand. He came and stood beside me, and when I looked up at him, half forcing myself to meet his eyes, he pulled the mask away from his face.

He wasn't a ghoul at all, just a man, like the shopkeeper had said, and younger than I would've expected, though still a bit older than me, maybe by about five or so years. His entire left cheek was scarred, ripples and folds in the flesh as if from a fire or maybe magic. Beneath the scar he was handsome, though, almost as handsome as Tarrin of the *Hariri*, so I didn't exactly relax.

"Did you save my life?" he asked.

"Maybe." I figured in a situation like this, ambivalence is always best.

"Why did you do that?"

I looked at the dead snake and back up at his scarred face. "Seemed like a good idea at the time."

The assassin frowned, and it twisted his face up in a way I found interesting. I waited for him to pull out his sword and slice my throat, but instead he sat down on the sand beside me. He draped his arms over his knees and stared morosely off in the distance.

"I wish you hadn't done that," he said.

"Um . . . I'm sorry?" I waited for a few minutes, watching him. Then I asked, "Are you going to kill me or what?" I figured I might as well get it out of the way.

He looked over at me, moonlight flashing across his dark eyes. I decided I rather liked the look of him, which was a bit of a problem, all things considered.

"No," he said, sounding glum.

"Oh." Relief flooded over me, and anybody with any lick of sense would have picked up and ran back toward Lisirra. Instead, I opened my mouth. "Why not?"

He hesitated. "You saved my life." A pause. "From an asp, of all things."

"That's the dumbest reason I ever heard."

"I'd expect you'd be grateful for it."

"Oh, I'm plenty grateful," I said. "I'm just saying, that's a dumb reason."

"Yes, well, I'm afraid there's more."

I eyed him warily.

"I have to protect you now." The words came out in a rush, like he was embarrassed to say 'em. I woulda been.

"What? Why?"

"You saved my life. That's how it works."

"How what works?"

He didn't answer, just rubbed at his forehead, and I figured this must be some kind of honor thing, like he swore an oath or something. Pretty stupid oath for an assassin, but what did I know? I'd heard about ships in the Confederation with ridiculous rules of honor. Like this one captain who had his crew give a portion of gold to a temple every time they made port in Empire lands. More often than not the temple turned 'em in, so they spent half their time being chased by the Empire navy.

Fortunately, Mama and Papa never much went in for things like that. They always taught me that honor was best defined on a case-by-case basis.

"Well," I said. "I don't require your protective services. I'm a pirate."

"A bit far from the ocean," he said. He glanced at me out of the corner of his bad eye. "Besides, I'm afraid you do. The Hariri clan expects you dead. They'll send someone else."

"Or," I countered, feeling pleased with my cleverness, "you could just tell them you did it."

"They require proof."

"Oh hell." I did shudder a little at that, though. Bad enough they hired someone to do their fighting for them. Demanding proof? Good thing I managed to avoid marrying into *that* family.

We sat side by side without speaking for a while. He went into some kind of trance, and the scent of mint was everywhere and his eyes glowed pale blue like before. Now that I wasn't scared out of my mind I realized they were the color of the glaciers in the northern seas.

While he was in his trance, I sat there and did some thinking of my own. I lucked out with that snake, no doubt about it. If they sent another assassin—and I figured they would, on account of this one screwing up the job—it might be handy to have a bodyguard around. Better still if that bodyguard was an assassin himself. I didn't much want to admit it, but he was probably right about me needing his help.

'Sides, once the Hariris were taken care of, I could ditch him and head off to Bone Island or maybe straight to the southern port cities. His honor wasn't my problem.

After a while, he shook his head and blinked, and his eyes returned to normal, like his soul had come back from wherever he'd sent it. You never know with magic-users.

"How's your leg?" I asked him. Figured it might be good to play at making friends.

"What?"

"Your leg. I stabbed you."

He stared at me. Then he peered down at his leg, spread his hands over the dark fabric of his trousers. Blood on black is too dark to see in the best of times, and even with the moonlight I couldn't make nothing out.

"A flesh wound," he said. "I'll be fine." He paused, tilted his head toward me. "How's your arm?"

"Oh." I glanced down at it. The blood had dried onto my skin, and the wound had stopped hurting sometime in the middle of the fight. "Nothing I haven't dealt with before." I paused. "My name's Ananna, by the way."

He hesitated. I was about to tell him he didn't have to give his name, but then he spoke up. "You can call me Naji."

"Glad I have something to call you," I said. He looked like he wanted to smile, and his eyes kind of brightened, but otherwise his face didn't move.

The wind picked up.

I didn't think much of it, except to duck my head to keep sand from blowing in my eyes. But Naji grabbed me by the wrist and pulled me roughly to my feet. When I looked up my heart started pounding something fierce, 'cause the desert was lit up like it was daytime, light coming from the swirls of sand slicing through the air. When the sand struck against my skin it left a shimmery golden glow, like the pots of expensive body paint we sometimes stole from merchant ships.

"The Hariris?" I said, dazed. Sand stung the inside of my mouth. "Already?"

Naji yanked the mask back over his face, leaving just his eyes. "No," he said. "Find someplace to hide."

"It's the middle of the desert!"

He shoved me away from him, and I stumbled across the sand, almost losing my balance. My eyes watered and my nostrils burned. I pulled the knife out of my sash and clutched it tight, close to my hips, the way Papa taught me. I had no intention of slinking off behind some moonlit desert tree. My people do not hide.

A figure emerged from the swirl of sand and light: a woman dressed in long rippling skirts. Something about her, about the way she moved, seemed familiar—

It was the woman from the dress shop.

She looked a lot grander than I remembered, and even more beautiful. Her hair streamed out in dark ribbons behind her, and her skin glowed with the same light from the sand. Her pale eyes were stones in the middle of her face. I tried to find my voice, to tell her Naji wasn't no threat anymore, but she spotted me and I froze in place.

"You," she said. "Why aren't you dead?"

"What?" It came out barely a whisper. My heart thudded against my chest, anger and confusion spinning out through my body.

The woman scanned the desert. "I should have known better than to send a sea rat out here." Her gaze flicked over to me. "Though you seemed to have so much potential. I really did think it would work."

I realized then that the woman had used me—I didn't know the full of it, but I hated that I'd trusted her enough to let her do it. So I lunged forward, knife outstretched, but she picked up one hand and flicked her fingers and I went flying backward. I landed hard enough in the sand that all the breath slammed out of me, but then Naji was pulling me up to standing. He pressed his face close to my ear, his mask rippling as he spoke.

"If you insist on fighting, take this." And he slipped something into my hand, something rough and dry and so powerful that even I recognized the magic in it, before bounding off to face down the woman.

"Assassin," she hissed, drawing out the word, and Naji reached into his armor, pulled out the same satchel he'd almost used on me. He didn't throw it at her, though, just reached in and pulled out some dark dust, which he blew across the desert, cutting out all the light from the woman's incandescent sand. The desert plunged back into night. The woman's scream echoed through the darkness, and then her silhouette attacked his silhouette, and I blinked a couple times, willing my eyes to adjust.

When they did, Naji had drawn his sword, the blade flashing in the moonlight. And the woman had a sword of her own.

I held up the charm he had slipped me. It was a necklace, a ball of dusty dried-out vines and flower petals hanging off a piece of narrow leather. I slipped it over my neck and immediately I felt protected, impenetrable. Safe.

Damn him! He was sticking to that idiotic oath to protect me. Which meant he was in the middle of a magic-and-sword fight without protection. The charm must have stopped the magic from before, the magic intended to suck him through the portal—now if she tried anything, it would actually work.

I knew better than to jump into the middle of the fight, much as I wanted to. Instead, I looped around behind the woman, keeping myself low to the sand. The woman knocked Naji back with a burst of magic, and as she regrouped herself, I attacked. I shoved my knife into her shoulder blade. She howled, whirled around. Light seeped out of the wound, and a few droplets flung across my face. It was hot on my skin, and for a moment I faltered, not sure what to do about a beautiful lady who bleeds light.

But then she did that flicking motion with her hand again, only this time I stayed put, protected, and in the few seconds before she could realize the secret hanging around my neck, I stuck the knife into her belly. More light spurted out, landing on the sand, on the fabric of my dress.

There were hands on my shoulders, pulling me backward. Naji. He sang something in his language, and the sky ripped open, the stars streaming in the blackness. He wound one arm over my chest and pulled me close to him, close enough that I could feel his breath on the back of my neck. All the wind in the world blew into that gash in the sky. The woman screamed, and her feet lifted up off the earth, light pouring out of her wounds and turning into stars in the darkness, and then she tumbled head over feet through the air and was gone.

The gash sewed itself back up.

Naji let me go. I dropped down to the sand, exhausted, and rolled over onto my back to look up at the sky. The light from the stars was dazzling.

"Who was she?" I asked.

"Stand up," said Naji. "We shouldn't stay here. It's not safe."

"You didn't answer my question." But I got back up to my feet, shaking as I did. The woman's light was still on my clothes and skin and knife, although the glow was beginning to fade. Naji reached over and plucked the charm from my neck, and I felt his touch long after he'd slipped the charm back into his cloak.

"Well?" I said.

"She's from the Otherworld," said Naji. "She's been chasing after me for some time."

I stared at him. "Another world?" I asked. "What, like the ice-islands?"

Naji's head turned in the darkness. He still had on his mask.

"No," he said. "Not like the ice-islands."

I waited for an explanation.

He sighed. "It's a world layered on top of our world. Some call it the Mists."

"Oh, well that clears everything up." But I remembered the woman refusing to tell me where the green-light portal would send Naji. Elsewhere.

"I'll explain it to you later. We need to get out of the desert before the fallout takes effect."

I took fallout to mean the magic-sickness, since even I could feel that prickle in the air that always comes when you use too much magic at once. Mama'd told me stories about how it changes you, since that's all magic is anyway, pure change—she said she knew a dirt-witch who got turned into a pomegranate tree after trying to resurrect her dead husband. And I'd seen clams and ripples of sea-bone sprout out of the side of the *Tanarau* after Mama used magic in battle.

Naji turned, cloak swirling around him, and walked in the direction of the city. And 'cause the air was choking with magic, the sand twisting into figures in the darkness, my own skin crawling over my bones, I followed him.

CHAPTER FOUR

We walked for a long time, the city growing brighter and more distinct on the horizon. Naji didn't talk. I kept trying to think of things to say, and I kept coming up short. Fortunately all that walking warmed me up against the chill of the dusty night wind.

Naji stopped right outside the desert wall, his cloak rippling and casting slinky shadows across the sand. He pulled his mask away and then turned toward me. He looked like he had been in a fight: blood on his face, ragged cuts on his clothing, scratches in his armor. I realized I probably didn't look much better.

"Did you have any belongings in your room at the inn?" he said.

"What?"

"The Desert Light Inn." He jerked his chin toward the city. "Where you were staying."

"How did you . . . Oh." I frowned, wondering if he had ever watched me through the open window without me knowing. "Some spare clothes." I knew better than to tell him about the money. "Why?"

His face got all intense and he said, "I have to protect you. But I'm afraid you shouldn't stay at that inn any longer. We can find somewhere in the pleasure district."

I saw where he was going with this. We could rent a room in the pleasure district and the innkeeper would probably take me for a whore or a mistress and not think nothing of it. Not that I look like anybody's mistress, but you know—there wouldn't be any questions.

If I were just some runaway it'd be the perfect place to hide, 'cause nobody ever looks anybody in the face down there. Unfortunately, the pleasure district was exactly the part of town I might expect to find my parents—or worse, a gang of *Hariri* crewman.

Assuming my parents were still in the city at all.

That thought made me sad. I turned away from Naji so he couldn't see that sadness washing across my face.

"Collect your things," he said. "I'll wait for you in the alley outside the inn." And he started to dissolve, turning into shadows like the ones I'd seen the first time he attacked me. Just like in the stories. He was halfway disappeared when he turned solid again.

"What do you want?" I snapped.

"A word of warning. Don't think you can slip out the back of the inn. I will know."

"What! I wasn't gonna slip out."

"I can track you," he said. "And I can bind you to me if necessary."

"Oh yeah?" I was a little pissed, 'cause I ain't done nothing to make him think I had any intention of sneaking off. Not while the Hariris were still after me, at any rate. "Why didn't you just do that straightaway? Bind me to you?"

"Because it's cruel," he said.

That stunned me, ain't gonna lie. I dug the heel of my left foot into the ground, kicking up a spray of sand, and he gave me a look halfway between a glare and an eye roll and took to dissolving again. I walked through the desert gate alone, although every now and then I caught a movement out of the corner of my eye, as though he was gliding along beside me.

My room was just how I left it: my spare dresses draped over the back of the divan, my money still shoved beneath the loose floorboard under the bed. It was like I'd only been out at the night market, not battling some creature from the Mists and picking up an assassin-protector for my trouble.

Naji was waiting for me in the alley like he said, not as a shadow but as a man, although he'd covered his face again. He looked sinister. At least his eyes weren't glowing.

"You're too conspicuous," I told him. I handed him one of my dresses, folded up to look like a package. "Here, take this."

He didn't. "I've been doing this much longer than you have—"

"I doubt it. Besides, I bet you always worked alone, didn't you? You could slink around in the shadows, no problem. But now that you got me you have to act like a normal person." I pressed the package against his stomach, and this time he touched his hands gingerly against its sides.

"What are you giving me?"

"It's one of my dresses. I don't want to carry it all the way to the pleasure district. Now take off your mask and act like you have a right to be here."

He stared at me. The glow from the street illuminated the little burst of scarring that peeked up from the top of his mask. Then he handed the dress back and turned into shadow.

I cursed under my breath. He had disappeared completely from the alley; all the surrounding shadows lay flat and still and unremarkable. I spent a few minutes juggling my dresses, finally tucking two under one arm and one under the other, before stepping out onto the street. Hardly anybody was out, just a few shopkeepers getting everything ready for the start of the day. I nodded at them like it was totally normal for me to be traipsing through the streets in the dark hours before dawn, heading in the direction of the ocean, alone.

I got to the pleasure district as the sky was turning gray with the day's new light. I ducked into an alley and waited.

Naji materialized a few moments later.

"Now what?" I said. "By the way, I should tell you, my parents might be down here. Wouldn't be up at this hour, but you know."

"Your parents?" He pulled the mask away from his face.

"Yeah, my parents. Kaol, don't you know?"

"I obviously don't."

"I mean, don't you know why you were hired—why the Hariris—"

"I'm not told the particulars," he said, interrupting me. "Only what's needed for my tracking spells. We need to find a place to stay before the sun comes up. You really should rest."

"Is that part of your protection deal? Making sure I get enough sleep?"

He didn't answer, just stepped out onto the street. I hoped he'd pay for the room and I could save my coins for later. That's what Papa would've told me.

Naji stuck his head back into the alley, looking all angry and put-upon, like I was some little kid he got saddled with. I shuffled out to join him. The pleasure district was mostly full of drunks stumbling home for the night. Nobody paid us any mind.

We'd been walking for about ten minutes when Naji spoke.

"Why would your parents be here?"

I glanced over at him. He had his eyes fixed straight ahead. It was like he didn't want anyone to know we were having a proper conversation.

"They're pirates," I said. "I told you."

"You said you were."

We were close enough to the waterfront that I could smell the salt in the sea, and my stomach twisted up with homesickness, not just for Papa's boat but for the ocean itself.

"I grew up on a pirate ship," I said. "Looting and pillaging's all I know."

"How charming. Would your parents take you back if they found you?"

He didn't sound hopeful when he asked it.

"What if they did?" I asked. "What would happen to you? Are you seriously telling me you'd have to tag along, just 'cause of some stupid oath—"

The expression on his face stopped me cold.

"You talk too much about things you don't understand," he told me, his voice low and dark. "Come along. The Snake Shade Inn's this way."

I knew the Snake Shade Inn, but I didn't say nothing. No place in the pleasure district's exactly high class, but the Snake Shade was lower than most of the places there, and my parents generally avoided it when I was in tow. I'd heard stories from the crew, though, mostly about whores they'd met up with there.

So I probably wasn't going to run into my parents, but if Captain Hariri had dispatched any of his men—maybe. A little shiver of fear eked up my spine, and I snuck a glance at Naji, with his mask and his armor and his black clothes, and wondered if I was gonna need his protection again.

All around us, the food vendors were opening up their carts for breakfast. 'Cause it was the pleasure district, there were still drunks dragging themselves around, trying to find a place to sleep off the drinking-sickness. Most of 'em shied away from us, crossing the street and turning their faces away, but I could still hear 'em whispering as me and Naji walked by. It was an uneasy feeling, the way their fear followed us down the street.

Abruptly, Naji reached up and yanked his mask over his face. He didn't falter or stop walking, but the suddenness of his movement set me on guard.

"What's wrong?" I asked.

He glanced at me out of the corner of his eye. "We're almost there."

"That don't answer my question."

"You're not in danger."

"Why'd you put your mask on?"

His eyes darkened and he turned away from me and started walking more quickly, his strides long and brisk. I sighed with irritation and then lagged a little behind him, ambling along, taking my time. He glared at me over his shoulder.

"What?" I asked. "You said I wasn't in any danger."

A peal of laughter broke out from the shadows of one of those narrow Lisirran alleys that run like glass-cracks between the buildings. A man spilled out of the alley, an old Empire sailor from the looks of the rags he wore. He leaned up against the building and guffawed and then said, "Now this is something I never thought I'd see. A little girl hassling an assassin." He laughed again, snorting like a camel, and then took a long drink from a rum bottle.

"I ain't a little girl," I said. Naji just glanced at him and kept walking, although I noticed he stuck his hand on the hilt of his sword. I followed after Naji, though I wasn't too worried—it was just some drunk. What else do you expect down here?

"Why you wearing the mask?" The man tottered forward. "You know you ain't in the desert."

Naji didn't answer, just stared straight ahead. I found myself hanging back a little, watching the whole thing with interest. You live your whole life with pirates, you start smelling when a fight's brewing.

"You don't got an answer for me?" the man called out, stumbling after Naji. "Or are them stories true, that they cut out your tongues?" And then the man grabbed Naji by the upper arm. In one clean movement, Naji had the man laid out on the ground, his foot on the man's chest, the point of his sword at the man's throat. I was pretty impressed in spite of myself.

"No," Naji said, "They don't."

By this point a crowd had gathered, drunks and sailors and sleepy-looking whores. A few of 'em tittered nervously at that, and Naji looked up at 'em, his dark eyes glittering. They looked away.

Then the drunk rolled out from under Naji's foot, grabbed him by the ankle, and yanked hard. Naji stumbled a little but managed to catch himself at the last moment. Even though it was a good sight more elegant than most men could do, I was still surprised by that reminder that he really was just a man.

And then I felt something cold against the side of my neck.

"Oh hell," I said, dropping my dresses to the ground.

"I'll cut your little friend's throat," the man said. "How do you like that?" His hands were shaking and his breath stank, and I stood extremely still, my heart pounding. The giddiness of watching a fight got washed out by the fear of actually being in one. I wasn't aware of the gathered crowd no more—the only things I knew were Naji glowering at me and the coldness of the knife and the drunk pressing his body up against me.

Naji took a step forward. The knife dug deeper into my skin.

"Don't move!" I shrieked. "Please, you'll get me killed!" I tried to make my voice sound as hysterical as I could so the drunk wouldn't notice my hand slipping into the sash of my dress.

"Aw, you ain't gonna help her?" the man said. "Hoping to find someone prettier?"

I jabbed my knife into his side. The man howled and fell away from me and I raced over to Naji.

"Told you I don't need your help."

Naji glared at me. Then he stalked over to the drunk, who was curled up on the street, one hand pressed against his stomach, redness seeping through his fingers. The crowd was whispering again. Naji reached down and dipped his fingers in the man's blood. The man let out a low, frightened moan.

Naji started chanting.

The crowd lurched away, their whispers turning into a terrified babble. Naji's eyes gleamed blue. The man gasped and keened and then his head dropped back and the entire street was full of silence.

Naji gathered up my dresses and my knife and handed them to me. "Come," he said, yanking on my shoulder, pulling me away from the scene.

The crowd let us go.

"What did you do to that man?" I asked. I tried to pull away from his grip but he wouldn't let go. "Did you suck the soul of his body? Why didn't you just kill him normal?"

"I didn't kill him at all," Naji snapped. "He'll wake up in an hour."

We walked the rest of the way in silence. My neck was still bleeding a little from where the knife had pricked it, and I kept wiping at it and looking up at Naji and thinking about the drunk's blood staining his fingers.

When we arrived at the inn, its main room was mostly empty save for a couple of bedraggled-looking whores and a man I pegged as another pirate by the way he was dressed up in aristocrat's clothes. When Naji walked in, all three of them got to their feet and filed out without saying a word. And the innkeeper got the shakes when Naji told him he wanted a room. He kept glancing over at me, eyes all wide with fear. I wondered if it was 'cause he'd heard about the right or 'cause the innkeep was just terrified of assassins generally.

"And . . . and the lady?" he said, stammering. "Will she have her own room?" I wanted to laugh, him calling me a lady when I had blood on my arms and my dress.

"No," Naji said. "She'll stay with me."

The innkeeper went pale, like Naji had just produced the ghost of his dead mother or something. He tried to hand over the key to the room and dropped it on the counter instead. I didn't want to laugh anymore. It occurred to me that if this was how people were gonna act every time me and Naji came into a place—well, I could see that getting to be a problem. Maybe Tarrin would meet some pretty Saelini girl and the Hariris would just forget the whole thing and I could slip off when Naji was in one of his trances. Not that I thought any of that would happen.

Naji finished the transaction and glided over to the stairs. I went up to the counter, leaned over it, and said to the innkeep, "Don't worry, you'll see me again."

The innkeep's eyes twitched from me to Naji, who was leaning against the doorway and looking annoyed.

"He won't do nothing," I said, but the innkeeper shook his head.

"Run," he said, in a hoarse whisper. "Get away. I've seen what his type are capable of—what they'll do to an innocent like you."

I wondered why the guy thought I was an innocent. 'Cause I ain't pretty? I decided to give it up then. I obviously wasn't going to sell the poor guy on my safety.

"Don't feel the need to defend my good reputation," Naji said as we made our way up the stairs to the room, out of earshot of the innkeep. "I don't have one."

"Oh, I'm sorry," I said. "Did you want me to act like your prisoner or something? Slip him a note to send for help?"

"Please don't do that."

"What'd he think you were going to do to me anyway?"

Naji opened up the door to the room. It was smaller than the room I'd had on the edge of the city, and not nearly as clean. I thought of all the Confederation scummies that had passed through here and shuddered.

Besides which, there was only one bed.

"Blood-magic, probably," Naji said, and I shut my trap at that, because I'd just seen how that part of the assassin stories was true, and blood-magic ain't nothing to mess with. Even Mama had warned me off it, before it became apparent my talents lie elsewhere.

"You can sleep on the bed," Naji said. "And you *should* sleep." He gave me a look like he expected me to sass him. When I didn't, he said, "And no, it's not because of the, ah, the oath. It's because I need you alert tomorrow night."

"What for?"

"I have some things I'll need you to fetch for me, so I can determine what we should do next."

He didn't expand on that, and I figured tomorrow I could make a case for our next step to involve convincing the Hariris not to kill me. I was awful tired, to be sure. I'd hardly realized it until we got to the room. Likely still running on the energy from the fight, the way you do during those sea battles that go on for days and days. I collapsed down on top of the bed, not even giving any thought to the last time the sheets might have been washed. And, like any good pirate, I fell asleep immediately.

CHAPTER FIVE

I slept straight on through till nightfall, and when I woke up my entire body ached so bad I could hardly push myself off the bed. Naji was sitting over in the corner, his eyes glowing. I waved my hands in front of him a couple of times and when he didn't so much as twitch I went ahead and peeled off my dress, stiff with sweat and blood and sand, and put on a fresh one. I transferred the bag of coins into my new dress. Just 'cause he was protecting me didn't mean he wouldn't steal from me.

Then I sat down on the edge of the bed and waited for a few minutes. He didn't come out of his trance. "Hey," I shouted. "Sure would be easy for me to sneak out on you right now."

That did it. The glow went out of his eyes and he stood up, unfolding himself gracefully like the fight hadn't affected him at all.

"Not as easy as you would think." He had taken off his armor and his cloak while I slept, and his arms were covered in strange, snaky tattoos the same ice-glacier blue his eyes got whenever he settled into a trance. He didn't say nothing, though I know he saw me looking at them.

He walked across the narrow width of the room, to the rickety old table where he'd draped his cloak, and began to rummage through it.

"I'm hungry."

"I'm sure you can get something downstairs."

"I don't have no money," I said, trying my hand.

"Nonsense." He peered over his shoulder at me. His hair fell in dark ribbons over his forehead, and I felt silly for noticing. "You have a pouch of pressed metal in your pocket."

Immediately, I forgot his hair. "How do you know that?"

He smiled, touched one hand to his chest in the manner of the desertlands, that gesture that's supposed to stand in for an answer you don't want to give. Then he said, "I would like you to go to the night market for me. I'll give you money for that, but I expect you to return with everything I request. And I will bind you to me if I feel it's necessary."

I scowled at him. "You can't go to the night market yourself?"

"No vendor would sell to me." He didn't look at me when he spoke. I got a weird feeling in my stomach, thinking about the inn-keep from the night before, and blood-magic I'd seen Naji perform out on the street. The threat of Naji tying me to him.

"What exactly are you going to do?" I said. "With the, ah, the things from the—"

"Nothing that'll hurt you." He pulled out a stack of pressed metal, gold and silver both, and worth much more than what I had in my pouch. I took a more or less involuntary step forward, trying to see where he'd yanked them from. One glare stopped me.

"And what about the Mists lady?" I asked. "Don't you think she might come back after me?"

"No." But there was a gap in his voice, some information he was leaving out.

"You don't think she's going to try again?"

"Not her, no."

"But someone."

Naji rubbed his head. "They won't come after you," he said.

"They came after me before."

"No, you happened to stumble across them. It's not the same thing."

I watched him, trying to decide if I wanted to tell him that I didn't get the sense that I'd stumbled across anything. I'd almost made the decision to say something when he turned away from me and said, "Run downstairs and ask the innkeeper to borrow some paper and ink."

"You don't need to write it down. I'll remember." I tapped the side of my head. My stomach rumbled.

When I didn't move he glared at me again, and I did as he asked. It was a different innkeep from the one who tried to convince me I was about to die. Too bad. I kind of wanted to reassure the poor bastard, or at least see the expression on his face when he saw I wasn't dead.

The new innkeep gave me the paper and the ink without too much fuss, though he said he'd charge me if I didn't bring the ink down after I finished with it. I waved him off and then bounded back upstairs. The smell of food rolling in from the kitchen, spicy and warm and rich, made my mouth water. That didn't incline me toward screwing around with Naji just 'cause it would annoy him. The sooner he got me his list, the sooner I got to eat.

Unfortunately, he took his time writing it out. He had this special quill that he produced from out of his robes, long and thin and the kind of black that sucks the color out of everything. I sat down on the bed while he puzzled over his list, scratching things out, shaking his head, muttering to himself.

"I'm hungry," I said.

"So am I," he said. "But this is far more important than either of our appetites at the moment." He held the list at arm's length, squinting a little in the lamplight. Then he pressed it up against the wall and wrote one more thing.

"There," he said. "That should be it."

I jumped off the bed and snatched it out of his hand and scanned over his sharp, spiny handwriting. It was all in Empire, and most of the items were plants. Rose petals, rue, dried wisteria vines. Soil-magic stuff.

"Midnight's claws," he said. "You can read."

"Of course I can read." I folded the paper down as small as it would go and slipped it into my pocket. "And why would you give me a list if you thought I couldn't read?"

"I assumed you'd hand it over to the vendors."

"Oh, that's wise," I said. "Let them give me some fountain grass when I paid for swamp yirrus. Whatever that is." I shook my head. "How'd you get your supplies before you met me, anyway?"

"Not from a night market."

I let him have the last word, 'cause I was so hungry I could hardly think straight. I stuck my hand on the doorknob and was halfway to turning it when he roared, "Stop!" like a troop of Empire navymen were about to come bursting through the door. I froze, all my aching muscles preparing for yet another knife fight. But Naji just slouched toward me, the heel of his hand pressed against his forehead. "Curses and darkness," he said.

"What the hell's wrong with you?"

He reached into his robe and pulled out the charm from the battle and tossed it at me. The minute it was in my hands he straightened up.

"I hope that'll stave it off," he muttered, more to the air in the room than to me.

"What are you talking about?"

"Wear that charm." He pointed at my chest. "Keep it on you at all times."

"Why?"

"It's for protection."

"I know what it's for. I'm more curious what it's protection against."

He glowered. "Probably nothing. But I . . . I don't like sending you out alone."

"You sent me downstairs."

"That was different. You were still in the building."

"So? You can look through walls or something? What if someone snatched me when the innkeep wasn't looking?"

"No one was going to snatch you."

"But someone's gonna snatch me at the night market?"

"Probably not."

"But you still need to give me protection?"

"Stop asking questions!" he roared. "I thought you were hungry!"

"I am hungry! I just want to know I ain't walking into a trap is all."

Naji rubbed at his forehead, his eyes closed. "You aren't walking into a trap. As long as you swear to me that you won't take off the charm, you'll be safe."

I stared at him.

He opened his eyes. "I need you to swear it."

"I don't swear," I finally said. "But I'll promise." I looped the charm around my neck. That feeling of safety drizzled over me. I thought the whole thing was off, like I'd just been handed a key to something I shoulda understood, but I was so hungry I didn't much care. I was out the door and into the kitchen before Naji could say another word.

The night market in the pleasure district was a lot bigger than the one where Naji had almost killed me. It stretched from the row of brothels all the way down to the docks, and I could make out the outline of ship sails in the distance, blocking out the sky's bright stars. Vendors crowded onto the street like weeds, shouting at me to come buy their charms and enchantments as I walked past. Mostly love potions and the like. I ignored them.

It took me less time than I expected to gather up all the things on Naji's list. Those plants I recognized—the powdered echinacea, the rose petals, the hyacinth root picked up first, going from vendor to vendor so none of them would ask after what spells I planned on casting.

That left the weird stuff. Like an uman flower. Never heard of that before, and as it turned out, it was extremely rare and extremely expensive, and only grew in a particular swamp in the southern part of Qilar. I had to ask five separate vendors after it, and I eventually got sent to an old man tucked away behind a stand selling vials of snake blood. He was all shriveled up like a walnut, and he peered up at me through the folds of wrinkled-up skin around his eyes. "What you needing a weed like this for?" he asked.

"Magic."

"Don't sass me, girl." But he rummaged underneath his table for a few seconds and produced a plant that reminded me of a body wrapped in burial shrouds. It wasn't like any flower I ever saw, what with its twisted wooden stem, all deformed and grotesque, and its long, fluttering white petals.

"Be careful with her," the old man said. "You can call down the spirits, if you don't know what you're doing."

I thanked him, so as to seem polite, and then tucked the uman flower away in my bag so I wouldn't have to look at it again.

There was one rarity on the list that I did recognize: le'ki, which Mama had used sometimes in the tracking spells that helped us sift out the best merchant ships. I figured I could find that at the stands set up on the docks, and I was right. At the first one I went to, the vendor had a half inch left, dried out and powdered like Naji had requested. Naji only wanted a quarter inch, but I bought all the vendor had, 'cause it reminded me of home, that briny sea scent and opalescent pink sheen, like the inside of a shell.

I'd been half avoiding coming down to the docks, but once I was there, I didn't want to leave. I had everything on the list but the swamp yirrus, and it wasn't even midnight yet. So I followed a dock away from the lights of the city, all the way out to its edge. Boats thumped against the water, that hollow wooden sound I always found so reassuring. Nobody was out but a single dock guard, and he didn't pay me no mind. Not like one person can steal a boat anyway.

I sat down on the pier, the bag filled with Naji's supplies in my lap, my feet dangling out over the ocean. Mama used to tell me the sea had an intelligence all her own, though I'd never been able to feel it like Mama could. I loved the ocean, don't get me wrong, but for me and Papa it was just water, huge and beautiful and strong and bigger than everything in the whole world, sure—but never something I could sit down and chat over my problems with.

When I was younger I'd get up early sometimes and climb to the top of the rigging so I could watch Mama work her magic with the sea. Sometimes she stripped naked and swam in it, and the waves would buoy her around like a jellyfish. Other times she sang and threw offerings from our merchant runs—small things, like a few coins of pressed metal, or a necklace, or a bangled scarf. And the offerings wouldn't float away like jetsam, neither. The sea sucked them down to the depths, leaving a wisp of foam in their wake. Once Mama lowered a jar into the water and scooped that foam up and then drank it down. Three days later, we defeated the Lae clan in a battle everyone, even Papa, thought we'd lose.

Thinking back to my childhood, and to Mama and her magic, and even that horrible battle, I started getting real sad. And I didn't want to be on the docks no more, sea spray kicking up along the hem of my dress. So I gathered up my bag and made my way back to the twinkling lights of the night market. My melancholy left me feeling distracted and confused, and I didn't know I'd taken a wrong turn until I realized I was back in the city proper—not the night market.

I cursed and turned around, intending to follow my steps back to the docks. But the buildings all looked the same in the dim light of the magic-lanterns, and when I started going one direction I was sure it was the wrong way, so I turned and went another—and after doing that a couple times I realized it was hopeless. I was lost, and in a city, unlike the open ocean, it's best to just ask somebody for directions.

Course, all the buildings were locked up tight for the night. I wandered for a while, kicking at stones in the street, fiddling with Naji's charm at my throat. Nothing.

Then I caught the scent of incense.

Incense means a temple, and the temples are always open for prayers and sanctuary. Figured the priestess wouldn't mind giving me directions, neither.

I followed the incense for a few minutes, losing it on the wind and then finding it again, until I came across a little temple wedged up between a key-maker's shop and the office of a court magician. The lamps over the door burned golden with magic, and when I stepped inside, the light had a gilded quality that reminded me of the evening sun. There wasn't nobody praying at any of the portraits, but a priestess stepped out of the archway, her sacred jewelry chiming as she moved.

"You look like you belong to the sea," she said, slipping languidly into the light. Priestesses always talk like that, like everything they say has got to be poetry.

"That's right," I told her. "And I need to get back to it. Can you tell me the way to the docks?"

She gave me a disapproving smile. "You mean the night market?"

"No, I mean the docks. I gotta meet someone there."

"Why don't you ask the gods for help?"

Hell and sea salt. Figured I'd get a priestess who took her duties seriously.

"The gods like to take their time answering, and I need to get back straightaway."

She looked almost amused, but she handed me an incense stick and swept her arm out over the temple. I sighed and followed the line of portraits till I came to one of Kaol, the goddess of tides and typhoons, and the one who's said to watch over pirates. I lit the incense with the little white candle burning beneath her portrait, knelt down, breathed in the smoky sweetness, muttered something about having lost my way, and then stood up and looked expectantly at the priestess.

"Kaol doesn't usually answer requests," the priestess said. "You'd have done better to pray to E'mko." She pointed at the portrait hanging beside Kaol's, and where Kaol's ocean was darkness and chaos, a gray spitting storm and jagged scars of lightning, E'mko's was calm, flat, and dull, his benevolent eyes gazing down on his petitioners.

"Ain't a sailor," I said. "E'mko's for sailors."

The priestess tilted her head at me. "Are you a pirate?"

I shrugged. "I told you, I just need to be down at the docks."

"So you did. Kaol will help pirates." She smiled. "When the prayer finishes, we'll see if she answers."

I sighed again and knelt down beside Kaol's portrait to wait for the incense to burn away—for the prayer to finish, as the priestess had said. I wasn't sure about the gods, since they didn't do much to make themselves known, but Papa used to swear that Kaol always looked out for her children, and that was why a pirate ship could sail through a typhoon unharmed when a navy boat couldn't.

When the last of the incense burned up, I found myself holding my breath, half expecting to hear a voice like thunder telling me the way back to the docks. Instead the priestess took me by the hand and pulled me to my feet and said, "Follow the street until it dead-ends, then turn right. You'll be able to hear the sea."

I scowled at her. "You couldn't have just told me that?"

"I didn't," she said. "Kaol did."

I didn't believe that for a second, but I thanked her anyway and then rushed out onto the street. I'd one more thing to buy—swamp yirrus—and no idea where to find it. Maybe I shoulda prayed to Kaol to help me find that, as well.

The priestess's directions were good, at any rate, and soon as I heard the sea at the dead end, I followed the sound of it to the docks, and then I made my way back to the night market. At the first vendor I came across, I asked after the swamp yirrus, but she shook her head.

"Don't got anything like that, I'm afraid," she said. I must've looked disappointed, 'cause she leaned in close to me and whispered, "There's a new stall down near Lady Sea Salt's brothel. He might have it." She straightened up and tilted her head back toward the city. "He's set up next to a lemon tree, and he usually has a gray horse tied up with his things."

I thanked her and set off. The crowds thinned out some, and a wind blew in from the desert, cold and dry as dust. Everybody seemed to huddle up inside of themselves, even the vendors. But then I spotted the lemon tree, twisted and bent with the direction of the wind. And the gray horse, just like the lady had said. It snorted at me as I walked up.

The vendor had his back turned. The wind toyed with the

fabric of his cloak, and even after I cleared my throat a few times, he didn't look up. Eventually, I said, "Excuse me!" I felt like I had to shout to be heard over the wind.

"Yes, my dear?" He glanced at me over his shoulder. "You look a long way from home."

He said it kindly, but it still left me unnerved. How could some street vendor at a Lisirran night market know my home from anyone else on the street?

"Uh, I'm looking for swamp yirrus," I said. "Lady on the docks said you'd have it."

The vendor turned around, and my whole body froze up immediately. He had the same gray-stone eyes the woman at the dress shop had had. I might've chalked it up to a coincidence except looking at his eyes got me dizzy, like all I could see was that gray.

"Got one left," he said. He gave me a big dazzling smile. "I'll knock the price down some too. Looks like you've amassed quite a collection of supplies there." He nodded at my sacks filled with Naji's stuff.

I didn't say nothing. I couldn't stop shaking. There was nothing sinister about him, none of the warning signs Papa always told me to look out for. Except for those damn eyes.

"This is awfully advanced for someone like you, though," he added. "Someone so young."

"I'm an apprentice," I spat out.

He nodded and turned back to his jars and tins. "Give me just one moment. . . ."

I didn't. I turned and hauled off down the windy street fast as I could, my dress flying out behind me, my hair whipping into my face. The bags of plants banged up against my hip.

I ran till I felt safe, and that meant getting out of the night market completely. I collapsed on a curb outside a drinkhouse, the scent of smoke and strong coffee drifting out into the night. Men laughed over some jangly music. A woman sang an old song I half recognized. I figured Naji would let me have it for not getting everything on his list, but at least I hadn't spent all his money, and I had good reason.

Those gray eyes. I couldn't stop thinking about them, looming clear and steady in front of me, drawing me in. To the Otherworld. The Mists. I couldn't picture it, a world layered on top of ours, but something about the woman at the dress shop and the man at the stall wasn't human. Naji was a bit spooky, but I could see how he was a man. Those two—it wasn't just the eyes. It was the way looking at 'em made me feel like a mouse surrounded by snakes.

CHAPTER SIX

It took some time for my nerves to smooth over, but I dragged myself up to standing and worked my way back to the inn. The innkeep from the night before was at the counter, and his eyes widened when he saw me, and he ducked into the room behind the counter. I was too shaken up to take any joy from it.

Naji was sitting on the bed when I walked in, scrawling out something on a piece of thin-pressed paper. He had his thumb and forefinger pinched against his nose, but once I closed the door he dropped his hand to the table and let out this weird, contented sigh, like he was finally sitting down after a long day's journey. I didn't much know what to make of it.

His tattoos glowed, almost enough to cast light of their own. He went back to writing.

"Did you find everything? You were gone longer than I expected."

"Everything but the swamp yirrus." My throat felt strange when I said it, dry and scratchy.

He didn't stop writing. "Why not? The waterfront night market here is supposed to be indefatigable in its supply of nefarious properties."

It took me a second to realize he was making a joke, but I wasn't in much of a joking mood.

"Well?" He lifted his head and squinted at me. "Why didn't you get the swamp yirrus?"

"I brought you your money." I reached into my pocket and pulled out the last of the pressed gold pieces and tossed them on the bed. Naji stared at them. They glimmered in the light of the lamp flickering on the bedside table. Then he looked back up at me, and I could feel him studying my face, trying to get an answer out of me that way.

I realized there wasn't no reason to lie to him. Not about this.

"The one vendor selling it had gray eyes," I said. Naji didn't react at all, just listened to me. "The same as the woman from before. The one who—"

"So you didn't want to buy from him."

I shook my head. "Gave me the creeping shivers. I'm real sorry. But if a girl don't have her intuition, she don't got nothing. That's what my papa taught me."

"Sounds like a wise man, even if he was a pirate." Naji sighed. "Did the vendor . . . react to you in anyway? Mutter anything? Hum?"

"Act like he was casting a spell, you mean? No." I shrugged. "He did say I seemed a long way from home, which worried me a bit. That was before I saw his eyes. In every other way he seemed normal, like I was just some customer."

Naji nodded. "You did the right thing. They certainly sent him to try to find us." He paused. "I'm glad to see you didn't take off my charm just to spite me. He would have recognized you otherwise."

My hand went up to my neck, to the strip of worn leather. I'd forgotten I was even wearing it.

"I'll take that back now, by the way," Naji said. "I'm going to make you one of your own, so you can stop borrowing mine."

I slipped the charm off my neck and the air in the room felt different, darker, like the lamp magic had started to run out. Naji slipped the charm back into his robe and went back to writing. I hated to see it disappear.

"What did you need the swamp yirrus for?" I asked. "Was it important?"

"Everything on that list was important," Naji said. His pitch quill scratched across the paper. "But I can make do."

I wanted to sit down, but it seemed weird to sit on the bed next to Naji. So I made a place for myself on the floor and watched him write. When he finished, he tucked the quill back into his robes and read over the sheet one last time. Then he started rifling through the bags, pulling out the wisteria vines and the rose petals.

"You don't have to watch me do this," he said, laying everything out on the bed.

Ain't no way I was ditching the inn after the run-in with Gray Eyes at the market, and downstairs there wasn't nothing but drunks and whores, and I wasn't of a mind to deal with either.

"I'd rather stay, if it's no trouble to you," I said.

He glanced at me. The scars made his face unreal, like a mask, but I didn't mind looking at him.

"You might find this unsettling."

I shrugged. Naji picked up the wisteria vine and started braiding the pieces together, threading in the rose petals and strips of acacia leaves. He chanted in that language of his while he worked. The room got darker and darker and his tattoos glowed brighter and brighter. I recognized some of what he was doing as dirt-magic—the chanting over dead leaves and the like—but those tattoos and the darkness weren't like nothing Mama ever taught me.

Naji set the charm down on the bed. He reached into his cloak and pulled out that mean-looking knife from earlier, and then, so quick I hardly had time to realize what he was doing, he drew the knife over the palm of his hand. Blood pooled up in a line across his skin. He tilted his hand over the charm and dropped the blood a bit at a time into the twist of wisteria vines.

His tattoos glowed so bright the whole room was blue.

He stopped speaking and squeezed his palm shut. His tattoos went back to normal. Then the whole room went back to normal, though I could still smell blood, steely and sharp, hanging on the air.

He dabbed at his palm with a handkerchief, not looking at me.

The sight of blood ain't nothing to get me worked up, but the idea of using blood in magic—Mama had told me it was a dark thing to do, and dangerous, though she'd made it sound like blood-magic always used someone else's blood, not the magician's. She always said it was the magic of violence.

"I want to apologize," Naji said. He slid off the bed, the charm resting in the palm of his hand. "I didn't want to bring ack'mora into this—"

"What's ack'mora?"

He looked down at the charm. "What you would call blood-magic. I didn't want to use it, but without the swamp yirrus . . ." His voice trailed off. He shoved the charm at me. "This is for you. Please wear it at all times."

He sounded more formal than usual, like he was nervous. Weird that he should be more nervous than me. But I took the charm from him anyway and ripped a strip of fabric off one of my scarves so I could tie it around my neck. The sense of protection that wrapped around me was warm and thick, like blood.

"I've never seen anyone mix 'em up like that," I said. Naji had walked back over to the bed and was cleaning off the space. He looked over at me when I spoke. His face was pale, drawn, in a way it hadn't been a few minutes ago.

"Mix them up?" he said.

"Yeah, dirt-magic and blood-magic. Uh, ack'mora."

"Yes," he said. "I do combine them sometimes. I learned

some—what did you call it? Dirt-magic?—from my mother."

"You have a mother!" I didn't mean to blurt it out like that, but the idea of him coming from somewhere was too bizarre.

"Of course I had a mother." He scowled and yanked the uman flower out of the bag.

It took me a minute to realize he'd switched into the past tense. "I'm sorry," I said, and I really did feel bad about it. "It's just—you're an assassin, and I didn't think—"

"I had a mother before I went to the Order," he said stiffly. He obviously didn't want to talk about it. "I thought you'd prefer a charm born of the earth and not me, but, well, I had to make do."

I thought that a weird way for him to say it, *a charm born of me*, like he'd hacked off part of himself and handed it over.

"Thank you," I said.

"You're welcome," he said, and he actually bowed at me a little. Not a full bow, just a tilt of the head, but I got real warm and looked down at my hands. I was very much aware of that charm pressing against my skin, soft as a lover's touch.

"This next spell is a bit more involved, I'm afraid." He was laying out the rest of the stuff I'd bought for him, the powders and the uman flower. "I'll be stepping out of myself for some time. I have questions that need answering." A long pause, like he expected me to say something. "You really don't have to stay. It's . . . Well, I'm doing something very rare, full ack'mora—I wouldn't expect . . ." He straightened up, ran one hand through his tangled-up hair. "Though I ask that you stay in the hotel. My . . . oath. I'm not sure what would happen to me if you got caught up in danger while I'm away."

All that talking, and the only thing I could say in response was, "Away?"

He nodded.

"The Mists?"

"Curses, no." He shook his head. "We call it Kajjil—there's no translation."

"But it's a place?"

He stopped messing with the powder vials on the bed and looked me hard in the eye. "I'm not allowed to discuss it with outsiders," he said, and I understood that well enough, being a daughter of the Pirates' Confederation and all.

I used the language of pirates to tell him I understood, which was a joke, because I knew there wasn't no way for him to know what it meant. But he kind of half smiled at me, not with his mouth but with the skin around his eyes, and got to work.

This one was a lot weirder to watch, 'cause it wasn't nothing like the bits of magic I'd dabbled in before. Most of it centered on the uman flower. He spent a while mixing up pinches and shakes of the powders I'd brought him in some big clay bowl that looked like it'd come from the inn's kitchen. Then he set the uman flower on the floor and cast a big circle around it with the powders. The knife came out again, only this time he cut along one of the tattoos on his arm, and he splashed the blood onto the circle, right on the flower like we weren't in an inn.

He said some words and then he sung some words and then he stepped inside the circle, and everything got real screwy.

The room fell dark, first off, even though the lamp was still flickering over in the corner. It just didn't cast no light. Neither did Naji's tattoos, which had taken to glowing as well. It was like the darkness was so thick it swallowed up any kind of brightness.

So all I could see of Naji were the swirls of blue on his arms, and the two blue dots of his eyes. And his singing got louder, and I smelled blood again, so strong it was like I had it running down my face, and I actually wiped at my cheeks, trying to get it off.

But there wasn't nothing there, and after that I only got the medicine scent of Naji's magic, the one like a physician about to do you wrong.

Then the uman flower lit up too, and it started writhing around, and another voice added itself to Naji's, one that was not human. Raspy and animalistic, more like. And the uman flower kept swaying and twisting, dancing like Princess Luni in that old story, the one where she dances herself to death.

Things stayed like that for a while. The singing and the uman flower and Naji's bright eyes. But despite all of it, I wasn't too fearful, even though I knew that made me a damn-right fool. I figured the charm was working, and that's where my complacency came from.

I couldn't say how long Naji was away. It couldn't have been too long because I hardly moved one bit and neither of my legs cramped up. When Naji did come back, it happened all at once. The singing stopped and the uman flower stopped dancing and the light came back into the room. Naji slumped forward onto the floor, knocking the uman flower aside, out of the circle. It skittered up to me and I jumped away from it, not so much out of fear but revulsion. Naji still hadn't moved.

I crawled over to him, stopping just outside the circle, and poked him in the shoulder. He groaned. I poked harder, and then I shook him. The part of my arm in the circle tingled. The smell of his magic was so overpowering, I could taste it in the back of my throat. But at least nothing in the room seemed to be shifting and changing from the magic-sickness.

Naji jerked up, so fast it startled me. He blinked a few times. His eyes were dark again. When he spotted me crouching by the circle he rubbed his head and said, "Don't cross the line."

"I know, I ain't an idiot." I frowned at him. "You all right?"

He nodded, his head hanging low. I scooted across the floor and leaned against the bed. "What'd you find out?"

"Find out?"

"You said you had some questions that need answering."

"Oh." His face darkened for a moment. "It seems we'll need to go across the desert." He stood up, using one hand to steady himself against the bed.

"What! The desert?" I was hoping that he'd seen the Hariri clan wherever he went—not them exactly, but the shadows of them, the way fortune-tellers do. I was hoping that he'd tell me that other assassin wasn't coming after me no more. "I don't want to go to the desert."

"You're in the desert now."

I shook my head. "No, I'm in Lisirra, and it ain't the same thing." I crossed my arms and glared at him. "Why do we have to cross the desert?"

"I need to see someone."

"That's it?" I said. "That's all you're going to tell me?"

Naji glared at me. He looked about a million years old. "Yes," he said. "It's all that concerns you."

"Bullshit!" I stalked across the room, taking care to avoid the circle. I balled up my clothes and wrapped the scarves around them for a strap. I took the protection charm off and threw it on the bed.

"What do you think you're doing?"

"Leaving."

"You can't leave."

I went right up to him, close enough that I could smell the residue of his magic. "Sure can. I got money and my wits and there ain't nothing you can do to stop me."

"There's plenty I can do and you know it."

I didn't have an answer to that, so I stomped away from him, right out the door and into the hallway. I didn't think about what I was doing; it was a lot like when I left Tarrin, honestly. Get the hell out and come up with a plan later.

Naji screamed.

It stopped me dead in my tracks, 'cause it didn't sound like anger or magic, but like he was in pain, like someone had stuck him in the belly. The hallway was silent—nobody stuck his head out to see what was going on.

Then there was a thump and the door banged open. Naji spilled out into the hallway. He cradled his head in one hand, and his skin was covered in sweat. His tattoos looked sickly and faded.

"Ananna," he said, choking it out. "You can't—"

"What the hell is wrong with you?" Part of me wanted to bolt and part of me wanted to get him a cold washrag and a cup of mint tea.

He staggered forward, pressing his shoulder up against the wall. I kept expecting some angry sailor to come out and lay into us for interrupting his good time.

"You can't . . ." Naji closed his eyes, pressed his head against the wall. He took a deep, shuddery breath. "You can't go out there alone, without protection. The Hariri clan—"

"To hell with the Hariri clan. Let 'em send their worst."

Naji looked like he wanted both to roll his eyes and puke. "That's the problem," he said. "They will."

He pushed himself away from the wall and swayed in place. He didn't stop rubbing his head.

"Please," he said. "Come back to the room. You can't leave. I have to protect you."

That was when I figured it out. It sure took me long enough.

"Are you cursed?" I asked.

His expression got real dark. He jerked his head toward the doorway.

"Are you?"

"Get in the room."

I did what he asked. I tossed my dresses on the floor and sat down on the bed. The color had come back to Naji's cheeks, and his eyes weren't glassy and blank no more. He locked the door behind us and started sweeping at the used-up magic circle with his foot.

"Well?" I said. "You are, ain't you? That's why you have to protect me."

He didn't say nothing. The circle was gone, replaced with smears of powders and streaks of drying blood, but he kept kicking at it. The dust made me sneeze.

Naji finally looked at me.

"Yes," he said. Then he turned his attention back to the powders.

I folded my hands in my lap all prim and proper like a lady. Naji wasn't protecting 'cause of some stupid oath. He was protecting me 'cause it hurt him if he didn't.

"When did it happen?" I asked. "During the fight, I'm assuming?" I thought back to that night in the desert, crawling through the sand, flinging my knife at his chest, killing the snake—

"The snake," I said.

Naji stared at me for a few moment. Then he nodded.

"Was it a special snake?"

Naji looked weary, but he shook his head, his hair falling across his eyes. "It was just an asp, in the wrong place at the wrong time. But I suppose it would have bit me had you not killed it."

"Oh."

He stopped kicking at the circle and leaned up against the wall, arms crossed over his chest. "You saved my life. Now I have to protect yours."

"From the snake?"

"Apparently."

"So what you told me was true," I said. "About having to protect me and all? It just wasn't an oath." I frowned. "What happens if you don't protect me?"

"I imagine I would die." Naji turned away from me and fussed with the robes he had lying across the table. "That's generally how these sorts of curses go."

I didn't have nothing to say to that. I'd accidentally activated some curse when I killed that snake and now we were stuck with each other.

This was why untouched folks hate magic.

"So why are we crossing the desert? Is there a cure?"

That darkness crossed his face again. "I said I don't want to talk about it."

"What about the Hariris? You keen on killing me so bad you're gonna march through the desert just to get to do it? You're out of your mind if you think I'm going with you—"

"I told you we are not discussing this matter further."

There was an edge to his voice, anger and shame all mixed up the way they get sometimes, where you can't tell one from the other, and that shut me up at first. But the more I got to thinking about it, the angrier I became. This was worse than an oath, 'cause oaths can be broken. And I didn't want Naji's curse hanging over my head.

"Well, I think we should discuss the matter further." I stood up. "This don't just affect you, you know. I had plans. And they didn't involve tiptoeing around so some assassin wouldn't get a headache."

Naji glared at me. "There's nothing to discuss. If you try to stay behind with the other sea rats, I'll bind you to me."

"No, you won't."

He stepped up close to me, his scars glowing a little from the faint coating of magic in the room. "All I need is a drop of your blood. And I know I can fetch that easily enough."

I lunged at him, but he'd already whirled away from me and all I did was slam up against the wall for my trouble. He had pulled his pitch feather out and was scratching something across the top of his chest armor, trying his best, it felt like, to ignore me. I leaned up against the wall and watched him. I did still have the Hariri clan to worry about, and if I took sail with even a southern ship they'd probably catch up to me eventually.

"I'll go," I said, as if he'd put the decision to me in the first place. "At least until you take care of the Hariris."

Naji glanced at me. Then he tossed his quill aside, sat down on the floor next to the uman flower, picked it up, and started pulling off its petals in long, thin strips. We didn't say nothing, not either of us. The only sound in the room was a crackle as the petals came off the stem, one at a time, white as ghosts.

CHAPTER SEVEN

Two days later, we left for the desert. It was probably stupid of me, going to help cure a man who had been paid pressed gold to see me dead, but every time I thought about giving him the slip I heard that scream of his from when I tried to leave the inn and felt sick to my stomach. And so it seemed the matter was decided for me. Bloody magic. You'd think they could come up with a curse that didn't have to drag innocent bystanders into it.

Naji got me to buy all the supplies. He gave me a list of a few powders from the night market, but the rest of it was run-of-the-mill stuff, and he wasn't too picky about it. Most of that I stole, creeping into a closed-down day market one night for the food, making off with a couple of water skeins and some desert masks one crowded, distractible morning. I did pay for the water itself, though, down at the well. Felt wrong not to.

With the leftover money I bought a camel. A real strong, fancy-looking one, with soft brown eyes and an elegant, spidery gait. I marched that camel up to the inn the morning we left. Naji was waiting for me in the shadows, his face covered like always. When he saw the camel he looked at it and then he looked at me and then he said, "You bought supplies, correct?"

"I got supplies."

His eyes crinkled up above his mask. I wondered if he was smiling.

We took off, me and the camel marching through the streets

like we were important, Naji creeping though the dark places like a ghoul in a story. He didn't materialize again until we got to the edge of the city and the sun was peeking up over the horizon, turning the light gray.

"We need to head southeast," he said. "You know which way that is? I don't want you wandering off—"

"Don't insult me."

Naji looked at me.

"I'm serious," I said. "It was the first thing I ever learned, how to tell north from south." That wasn't exactly true—I learned east from west first off 'cause it's obvious—but I wanted to get my point across. I jabbed my finger out at the horizon. "There. Southeast. You look at the shadows during the day and the stars at night, assuming you don't got no compass." Which we didn't.

"Or you can cast a spell," said Naji. "That's what I did."

"My way's better." I patted the camel's neck, and he huffed at me like he agreed. "Anybody can do it."

Naji didn't answer. It wasn't too hot yet, but already I had the scarf on over my head to protect me from the sun, and Naji made me put on a desert mask even though it itched my nose. Plus I'd stolen one of those light-as-air dresses before we left, the fabric soft and cool against my skin, almost like sea spray, and thin enough that my tattoo peeked through the fabric. I'd heard how bad it gets once you're away from the ocean. Some of the crew on Papa's boat had told stories.

Still, all the stories in the world weren't enough to prepare me for that trip. The first few hours were all right, but the sun got higher and higher, arcing its way across the sky, and I kept wanting all that sand to turn into the ocean, blue-green and cold and frothed with white. Instead it stung my eyes. My skin poured sweat, and the fabric of my dress only stuck to me and didn't do nothing to cool me off. And my feet ached from walking alongside the camel—we'd saddled him up with our food and water, and Naji said we could take turns riding if we needed.

"And why aren't we walking at night?" I asked him, tottering along in the sand.

"It'll be too dark," Naji said. "I can't risk casting lanterns. Besides, we'll be fine. I usually travel during the day."

"'Cause you're magic. I ain't."

Naji sighed. "You'll get used to the heat." And that apparently was enough to settle the matter.

We stopped to eat and rest a little during the middle of the day. Naji pitched a tent real quick and neat and told me to sit in the shade, which I did without protesting. Then he brought some water—he rationed it out to me, said we had just enough for the trip—and a handful of dried figs. The sight of 'em made my stomach turn.

"Don't drink too quickly," he said. He crawled into the tent beside me and tossed back one of the figs.

I didn't listen to him with regards to the water-drinking and immediately my stomach roiled around, and I moaned and slumped up against the fabric of the tent. Naji pulled me up straight. "You'll knock the whole thing over," he muttered.

"I didn't know this kind of heat existed in the world."

"Have a fig."

I shook my head. Naji sighed. "There's energy in them," he said. "They'll help make the evening walk easier."

"What! This ain't us stopping for the night?"

"Does it look like night to you?"

I didn't bother to respond. The tent's shadow seemed to be shrinking, burning up in the sun. Sand blew across my feet, stuck to my legs.

When we set off again I did feel a bit better. I guess the air was cooler, but as the sun melted into the dunes, the heat still shimmered on the horizon like water, which set me to daydreaming about Papa's boat, first during calm weather and then during a typhoon, wind and rain splattering across the desk, drenching me to the bone. I would have given my sword hand to be stuck in a typhoon instead of creeping across the desert.

Naji finally let us stop for the night after it got too dark to see. He set up the tent again, making it wide enough that we could both lie down. I stripped off my scarf and bunched it up like a pillow.

Naji brought me some water.

"Two weeks from now, we'll be at the canyon," he said.

"Two weeks!" My mouth dropped open. "Two more weeks of almost dying?"

"You didn't almost die." He looked at me. "And surely you've gone on longer journeys? I understand that Qilar alone is almost a month's trip—"

"That's on a boat!" I wished I had something to throw at him. "You ain't walking the whole time and you got the shade from the masts and the spray from the sea—Kaol, have you ever even been at sea?"

He didn't answer.

"I can't believe this," I muttered, cradling the skein of water up close to my chest. "Two weeks in the desert all on account of some assassin who doesn't know how to look out for snakes."

"If you hadn't killed that snake," Naji said calmly, "I would have killed you."

"Oh, shut up." I took a long drink of water. "Are you going to tell me where we're going?"

"I told you, to a canyon."

"Anything else?"

"No." He looked over at me. "Stay here."

"I ain't moving. Gotta rest up for the next two damn weeks."

He disappeared out of the opening of the tent. I drank the skein dry and set it aside and lay back and listened to the wind howling around me and to the camel snuffling just outside the tent. At first I was thinking about how awful the next few weeks were gonna be, and how I was probably gonna dry out like a skeleton in the sun. Then Naji came back from wherever he went, his footsteps crunching over the sand, and then I smelled smoke, and I got kind of drifty and floaty, like I was in the sea. Best part of my whole day.

And then Naji was saying my name, over and over, and shaking me awake. It was completely dark save for a reddish-golden glow just outside the tent, and after a few bleary seconds I realized that Naji was sitting outside, tending to the fire and not touching me at all. My body was just shaking from the cold.

I sat up and pulled my scarf around me, trying to get warm.

"Ananna?" Naji stuck his head into the tent. "Oh good, you're awake. Come eat."

"Why in hell's it so cold?"

"It's night time," said Naji, like that answered it.

Now, I knew it got cooler in the desert at night. Lisirra certainly does. But I felt like I'd spent the night on the ice-islands. So I scrambled out of the tent and pressed my hands out to the fire, keeping my scarf drawn tight around my shoulders. Naji handed me a tin filled with salted fish and spinach cooked down to a sludge. The minute I smelled it my stomach grumbled and I scooped it up with one hand, slurping it off my fingers.

"Be careful," Naji said. "Don't eat too fast."

I thought about what happened with the water and slowed down.

It didn't take me long to warm up, what with the fire and the food. When we'd finished I walked over to the camel, who had folded himself up all elegant in the sand. I scratched him behind the ears and rubbed his neck, and he blinked his big damp eyes at me, and for a moment I felt weirdly content, even if I was surrounded by nothing but sand and sky and scrubby little desert trees, even if I was traveling with an assassin who wouldn't tell me nothing.

But the next day, during the absolute blazingest part of the late afternoon, I started tottering around on the sand, and I couldn't see straight. My head was pounding like I'd been in a fight. The sky kept dipping down into the sand and the sand kept swooping up into the sky, which was so hot it was white, and I couldn't even remember what clouds looked like.

The next thing I knew Naji had his arms around me. I blinked and looked up at him, at his dark eyes and the part of the scar I could see above his mask.

"You're going to ride the camel for the time being," he said.

"What happened?"

"Sun sickness."

He scooped me up, one hand beneath my knees and the other under my shoulder, and I got real dizzy, though if it were from the heat or from him carrying me I don't know. His chest was sticky with sweat, even through the fabric of his robes—he wasn't wearing his armor—and I kept thinking about it later, the way his chest felt against my cheek.

He set me on the camel and pressed one hand against my waist while I steadied myself. He took hold of the camel's rope and tugged on it, and the camel pushed forward.

"I'm sorry," he said, not looking at me. "I should have listened to your complaints about the heat."

I squinted down at him, feeling a little smug and also a little touched that he'd bothered to apologize. He didn't say nothing more about it, though.

• • •

The next morning Naji let me sleep longer, and he made me drink twice the usual amount of water before we set off.

"Did it hurt you?" I asked. He was packing up the tent, folding it over on itself.

"Did what hurt me?"

"When I got the sun sickness."

He finished folding up the tent and shoved it into the carrying sacks. Then he stroked the camel's side, not looking at me, just petting the camel like it was a cat.

"Why does it matter?" he finally said.

I frowned. "I want to know."

I was sure he wasn't going to answer, but after a few seconds, he dropped his hand to his side. "It did, a little, but I caught you before you injured yourself, so it was nothing especially painful. And we had the camel, so . . ." He turned toward me. His face wasn't covered, and it was like looking at him naked. I wondered what it would be like to touch his scar. "That isn't something you need to worry about."

"I don't worry about it," I said. "I was just curious." Although that wasn't entirely true.

That morning's walk came much easier, because of the rest on the camel's back and the couple of extra hours of sleep I got in. Naji had me ride the camel in the evenings, and we carried on like that for the rest of the trip. He didn't seem to need the rest. I figured it was some trick from blood-magic. He didn't offer an explanation, and I didn't ask for one.

The days bled together out there, the way they do at sea, turning into one long day, one long night. Eventually the landscape starting changing. The desert trees disappeared and the sand turned coarser. Our path was littered with little round stones and tufts of bristly brown-green plants.

"We're close," Naji said.

"Close to what?" I was hoping he'd trip up and give me some kind of hint as to where we were headed.

"The canyon."

"And what's in the canyon?"

"A river."

I didn't even care that he was weaseling out of telling me anything important. "A river?" I said. "Water?"

"A river is generally comprised of water, yes."

"Oh, thank Kaol and E'mko both!" I closed my eyes and all the dusty dryness fell away, and I imagined diving into clean hard river water, sloughing off all the grime and filth of travel, a proper bath and not a useless sandscrub—

"We're not there yet."

I opened my eyes. Naji was looking at me with little lines creasing the strip of his face, his own eyes bright and sparkling.

"Are you laughing at me?"

"Never."

I lunged at him with an imaginary sword, and this time he really did laugh, all throaty and raspy, and I wondered what I could do to get him to laugh more.

The travel was easier, now that I knew our destination included a river. I didn't even need to hop on the camel that evening. Naji didn't push it, neither, which I appreciated. As we walked, I started telling him jokes, trying to get him to laugh again. Which he didn't do.

The next day started same as all the others, except I launched into my joke-telling straight away. I was building up to my best one, about a whore and a court magician, and I knew it'd get a laugh out of Naji for sure.

I never got to tell it, though, because the sky began to change.

Naji spotted it first, but he didn't say nothing about it, just stopped the camel and pulled his armor out of the pack. I went on walking a little ways before I noticed—I was trying to work out the best way to tell my joke—but then I realized I didn't hear the whisper-soft footsteps, and I turned around and saw Naji suiting up like he was about to go into battle.

"What are you doing?" I asked.

"Nothing you need to concern yourself with."

"Bullshit!" I stalked up to him, spraying sand and stones, building up a bank of all the best cusses I'd heard in my lifetime, when I saw it. This weird cloud on the horizon, snaky and dark, like ink dropped into water.

"What's that?" I stopped a few feet away from Naji, staring past him, out at the desert. The thing crawled across the sky, long thin strands like a ghoul's fingers. "Don't you dare tell me I don't need to concern myself with it!"

"It's a sandstorm."

"No, it ain't."

"And how would you know?" His eyes gazed at me from the top of his mask. "Do you see a lot of sandstorms out on the ocean?"

"I ain't never seen a sandstorm, but you wouldn't be suiting up if it were."

His eyes dropped away from me.

"Give me your sword."

He slapped the camel's thigh to get it moving again.

"Absolutely not."

Naji walked beside the camel, and I followed behind Naji.

"Then give me that knife of yours. I want to be able to fight, it comes to that."

"You have a knife." He paused. "You stabbed me in the thigh with it, if I recall correctly."

"That knife ain't worth a damn. I want yours."

He sighed. "You realize things are easier for me if you don't fight. If you don't . . ." He tilted his head, like he was searching for the right words. "If you don't put yourself in danger. Besides, it might not be anything troublesome. A fellow Jadorr'a passing through."

"The hell is that?"

"An assassin, Ananna." The word kind of soured when he spoke it. "Someone from the Order. Someone like me."

"Oh yeah?" I shot back, though I did feel kind of bad about not knowing what a Jadorr'a was. "You usually leave a trail big enough to see from Qilar when you're passing through?"

He didn't say nothing. I patted the dress sash I had tied around my waist, where my knife was tucked away, to reassure myself.

Naji was walking quicker than he had earlier—not running exactly, but fast enough it was making me pant. The camel trotted alongside him. I kept glancing over my shoulder to look at the cloud, which was filling up the sky faster than I could track.

"We gotta stop," I said.

"Ananna—"

"What? We do."

He looked over at me, all eyes and mask. I hated that mask.

"Look," I said. "Something nasty's obviously about to catch up to us, and you damn near running like that's not gonna help. All it means is we'll be worn out when we've got to fight."

Naji blinked but didn't say nothing.

"We should rest," I said. "Rest up and face them head on. They probably won't even expect it, if you usually run from a fight like this."

"I prefer to stay on the offensive," Naji said.

"Yeah, and that's why you're an assassin, ain't it, a bloody murderer-for-hire. 'Cause ain't no one ever gonna expect you and so you can fight like a coward or not fight at all."

He flinched when I said *coward*. Not a whole lot. Just a little squint of the eye. But I still saw it.

Then he did something I didn't expect. He told the camel to stay put, and he reached into his cloak and pulled out his knife. The blade glinted in the sun, throwing off sparks of light.

"If I give this to you, will it make you feel better?"

"A little. I still want to rest, though."

He shook his head. "You can't fight them. Not without magic."

"You got plenty of that."

"No." He stood close, bending down so our eyes were nearly level. "Any magic I do, it comes from me, do you understand? It takes a little piece of me with it. I can't simply cast any spell I want, any time I want—I have to give my body time to recover."

I set my mouth into a hard little line so he couldn't see what I was thinking. I felt stupid for not realizing that sooner, what the magic did to him.

"I cast a block over us before we left, but it was weak after the work I did creating your protection charm. You are wearing it, right?"

I lifted the mask away from my neck, showing him.

I was sure he knew I never took it off, but I wasn't gonna say it out loud.

"The black streaks are from the block. It's a warning, not an invitation to engage in battle. The canyon's close, we should be able to get there qui—"

The wind changed.

The whole time we'd stood there arguing the air had been hot and still and dry. Stifling. But then a breeze picked up and rustled the hem of my dress, and it was cold as ice. It sent a chill down my spine like a ghost had reached out and grabbed hold of me.

"Oh no," said Naji, like it was every curse in the whole world.

I was stuck in place, the breeze turning into a wind turning into a gale. All the sweat evaporated off my skin. My scarf unwrapped itself from my head and skittered across the sand, a thin twist of white disappearing into the encroaching darkness.

Naji started chanting in his language, his eyes glowing. I stumbled forward, my legs stinging like they'd been stuck with a million little pins. At least I could move again. Naji shoved his knife at me and then grabbed me by the arm as soon as I'd taken it. He pulled me up to him.

"Please don't fight unless you have to," he said, right close to my ear.

The camel made this horrible noise, a shriek-snort of fear, and galloped off, away from the darkness, all our food and water disappearing into the line of sunlight. I cried out for him to stay, but Naji put his hand on my arm again.

"Let it," he said. "I might be able to call him after . . . after it's done."

"I thought you said it was impossible to win."

"It is," Naji said. "I didn't want to . . . to frighten you." I was already frightened, but I wasn't going to tell him. Still, I pressed myself up against him as the darkness moved closer to us. Something was stirring up the sand. Figures appeared on the horizon. I kept imagining them all to look like Naji, a whole army of Najis, but they didn't.

They looked like ships crossed with enormous insects. And as they lurched across the sand, they let out this creaking noise, metallic and resounding. It made my ears ring. It shuddered deep down into my bones.

"What are they?" I shrieked, close to panic.

"I have no idea," Naji said.

"What!" I twisted myself to look up at him. His eyes were still glowing. "I thought you said—"

"A Jadorr'a is among them," he said. "But the Order does not deal in metallurgy."

Metallurgy. The word kind of lodged in my brain, like I should know what it meant but I couldn't quite grasp it.

The creatures shuddered to a stop. The sand settled. Thick black smoke belched out into the sky, mingling with the inky swirls of darkness from Naji's block. Their skins shone in the few beams of sunlight that made it through, like the side of a knife, like—

Like metal.

"They're machines," I said numbly.

Naji dug his fingers into my arm. "Killing a snake isn't going to save you this time."

Under any other circumstance that would've pissed me off, but I was so busy trying to overcome my panic that I didn't care.

The creatures stood there for a long time, creaking and heaving and letting off smoke. Naji murmured to himself, casting magic.

"Why aren't they doing nothing?" I whispered.

He chanted a little louder. The machines stared us down.

Then, like that, he stopped.

I didn't like not hearing his voice. As long as he was chanting, I felt like nothing could hurt us.

"Can you use a sword?" he said.

"Of course I can use a sword."

He slid his sword out of its scabbard and jabbed the hilt at me. His sword was even more mean-looking than his knife, thick-bladed and curving a little at the end.

"When they attack you, fight," he said.

"Planning on it."

"Try, please, not to get yourself hurt. Don't do anything

foolish." Then he took a deep, bracing breath and walked off.

Just like that. He left my side and walked straight into the smoke, disappearing into the haze. I tried to call out to him, to remind him that he didn't have his knife neither, but the smoke got in my lungs and made me cough.

Then one of the machines opened up, its top peeling away like a lemon. More smoke poured into the air. I promptly forgot about Naji.

I used his sword to cut my dress away above the knee so I wouldn't trip on the skirt. Then I held the sword up the way Papa'd taught me a long time ago.

A figure dropped down to the sand.

A man.

Tarrin of the *Hariri*.

I gasped and faltered, stepping back without meaning to, but I didn't lower my sword. My thoughts felt like poison, turning me to stone out there in the light and smoke of those horrible machines. The Hariris. How long had they been tracking us across the desert? How long had they had this kind of magic at their disposal?

Tarrin was all decked out like a Qilari noble, the long coat and the knee-high boots and everything. He slipped off his hat as he walked up to me, clutching it next to his heart. His handsome face didn't fit the backdrop, all that dark smoke.

"We don't have to fight," he said.

"You sent an assassin to kill me!"

Tarrin's expression darkened. "No, I didn't. My parents did. I warned you."

My heart pounded hard and fast inside my chest. Sweat rolled down my back. I hardly noticed the heat, though. I didn't allow myself to. Part of me wanted to attack Tarrin then and there, just lay into him, even though it wasn't the nicest thing in the world to attack a man not holding out a weapon, but then I remembered Naji told me not to do nothing foolish. Laying into Tarrin, what with those machines backing him up? I wouldn't call it foolish, but I knew Naji would.

"Besides, he hasn't killed you yet," Tarrin said.

"Trust me, I noticed."

Tarrin frowned. "Mistress Tanarau, my parents are willing to give you one more chance. I talked them into it. Father lent me his landships and everything."

"That's what those are?" I squinted up at them, gleaming bright in the sun. Landships? Of all the abominable things.

"Please, just come back with me to Lisirra. We can get married on my ship—the wedding sails are still up—and if you come back as my betrothed, Father will let me fly his colors." He smiled at me, as dazzling as the machines behind him.

I thought about it. I really did. Marriage was still the furthest thing from what I wanted, and I didn't even know what I wanted. But it would have made things easier, to climb aboard one of those creaking monsters and let Tarrin whisk me back to sea, away from the sand and the dry desert heat. There was an appeal to it, is what I'm saying.

I lowered the sword and let it hang at my side. My arms ached from holding it up over my head, and besides, I wanted to seem as unthreatening as possible when I asked what I had to ask.

"Could Naji come with us?"

Tarrin scrunched up his face. It made him look prissy. "Who's Naji?"

"My traveling companion."

Tarrin got this look liked I'd suggested we share a bowl of scorpions. "What? The assassin? Why would he come with us?"

"Look, I ain't too happy about it neither, but I can't just leave him."

"Of course you can."

I frowned. I thought about Naji screaming in pain when I tried to walk out of the Snake Shade Inn. What would've happened if I kept going? That scream was the scream of a dying man.

"It won't be forever," I said. "Just until we can get him cured."

"Cured? What are you talking about?"

"He got this curse on account of me, and until he finds the cure I pretty much have to stay around him. It won't be that big a deal. Just lock him in the brig."

"Are you insane? Do you have any idea what he does?"

"Kill people for money? Come on, you'd do it too if the price was high enough."

Tarrin scowled. "That's not what I was talking about." He lowered his voice. "You haven't dealt with the assassins the way my family has. They're dark. The magic they use—it isn't right. Isn't natural."

"Haven't dealt with them? What do you call walking across the desert for two weeks with one? He wouldn't use magic on your boat, I'm sure of it. Just as long we helped him cure his curse—"

Tarrin crossed his arms over his chest and puffed himself up, like I was some recalcitrant crewman he needed to order down. "I can't have something like that on my ship. The brig wouldn't contain him, not with his magic. We spill one drop of blood up on deck and he'd be commandeering the boat—"

"Yeah, to get a cure for his curse."

"Please, mistress!" He threw his hands up in the air. "Just leave the assassin in the desert."

"Why don't you just let him on board? He ain't as dangerous as you're saying. If anything he'll keep the boat safe."

"You don't really believe that, do you?"

"Course I believe it. Why won't you believe me?"

Tarrin sighed. "It's not that I don't believe you, it's that you're wrong, because you simply don't know what the assassins are like."

"Oh, just stop!" I snapped. "Why would I want to marry someone who won't even listen to me?"

Tarrin's face went pale. "Are you telling me no?"

"I guess I am. Maybe you could take this as a lesson, and treat your next lady with more respect."

"No, no, you don't understand." Tarrin shook his head wildly. "I have to come back with you as my betrothed, or as a corpse. It's the only way I'll get the colors . . ."

I stared at him, ice curling around my spine.

"I have my crew waiting," he said, jerking his head back toward the machines. "Our crew, if you'd just come back with me."

"And if I don't?"

Tarrin's face twisted up. "I want those colors, Mistress Tanarau."

"Well, I want a ship of my own, not yours. So I guess we're at an impasse here." I lifted the sword again.

Tarrin glared at me and reached for his own sword. I never did fight him, though, because light exploded out of the black smoke, a great blinding sphere of it, strong enough that it knocked me back onto the sand and momentarily blinded me. Knocked over Tarrin, too, and he stretched out beside me, blood seeping out from a cut on his head—he'd hit a rock when he went down.

"Shit!" I scrabbled over to him, dragging my sword. He turned his head toward me, blinked his eyes a few times.

"As my betrothed," he choked out, and I saw the movement in his arms that meant he wasn't as hurt as he seemed, that he'd figured me soft enough to come coo over him while he went for a knife. "Or as a corpse."

It happened fast. He jumped to his feet and yanked the knife out from under his coat. But I knew it was coming—it was one of the oldest tricks in the Confederation, and one Papa had warned me against when I was a kid. I plunged the sword into Tarrin's belly. Blood poured out over the sand, and he gave me this expression of shock and dismay and for a moment I just stared at him, shaking. I'd been in sea battles before, but this felt different somehow. It was too close, and Tarrin was someone that I knew.

"I had to," I told him, but it was too late.

I gathered up my courage and whirled around to face the machine, 'cause I knew that, by killing Tarrin, I'd changed everything. And I was right.

First thing I saw was the crew clambering down a sleek metal folding ladder, brandishing their swords and their pistols—'cause of course a fancy clan like the Hariris would have gotten their greedy hands on some hand cannons. Shit.

Second thing I saw was Naji, screaming words I didn't understand, his eyes like two stars.

Third thing was Naji's twin, a man in a cloak and carved armor, galloping through the smoke on a horse as black as night.

Those three things, they were all I needed to see. I lifted up my sword and screamed words of my own, all my rage and fear and shame at having killed Tarrin.

Then I ran into the fight.

CHAPTER EIGHT

The *Hariri* crew were terrible shots with the pistols—it helped that the black smoke crowded in around us, blurring the fight and making everything hard to see. I angled myself toward one of the shooting men, running fast as I could, dodging sword swipes. One man came barreling up to me and I stuck out my foot and tripped him. They never expect that.

A bullet whizzed past my head, close enough I could feel its heat, and I spun to face my attacker. Spotted her just as she was shoving in powder for another shot, and I dove forward, slicing across her leg. She screamed, dropped the pistol. I grabbed it and crouched down in the sand to finish packing off the shot. Stupid things ain't worth the trouble in this sort of fight, honestly.

There was another boom across the desert, another flash of light: a pillar this time, shooting up toward the sky. Everyone hit the ground but me since I was already there, giving me enough of an advantage that I was able to jump to my feet a few seconds faster. I tucked the pistol into the sash of my dress and ran toward Naji 'cause I didn't know what else to do, now that I was matched in my weapons.

A couple of shots fired out but none of 'em hit me. Naji was crouched on the ground next to that black horse. Its rider was gone, and the horse chuffed at the sand. When I got up next to Naji he looked like he wanted to tell me to get away, but I spoke up first.

"We need a plan," I said.

"What?"

The other assassin appeared out of the cloud of smoke, limping a little, and the *Hariri* crew had recovered from the blast and were all aiming right for me, so I pushed myself away and fired the gun into the crowd. Somebody screamed. I threw the gun as far away from the fight as I could, since I didn't have no bullets and I didn't want one of the *Hariri* crew to reload it and shoot me with it. I lunged forward, whirling the sword, knocking at people rather than cutting if I could, and tripping 'em too, and praying to every god and goddess of the sea that not one of those bullets would make contact.

Another blast of light, and we all got flung to the ground again, even me. It knocked my wits out for a few seconds, and when I managed to get back up, some burly scoundrel was on me with a big two-handed sword, and I had to fight him off, plus another lady with a pair of knives. Got myself cut a couple of times, on the arm and in the side, nothing major. But I did wonder about Naji, if that hurt him, if it was hurting him worse than it hurt me.

I managed to get another pistol, same way as the last—by sneaking up and slicing and stealing. But I was getting real tired, every muscle in my body aching, and the crewmen kept coming, mean and devoted, and I kept thinking about Tarrin bleeding out on the sand.

Naji screamed my name.

The sound of it chilled me to the bone, despite the heat from the sun and the battle. I froze in the middle of the melee, sword halfway to some guy's gut, and it took the pop of a pistol a few feet away to get me moving.

He sounded like he was dying.

I pushed off through the crowd, ducking low into the smoke. Naji was sprawled out on the ground, white as death, face all wrenched up in agony. I crouched next to him, pistol drawn. The smoke swirled around us, cloaking us, which was a relief even if it set me to coughing.

"I can't . . ." He gasped, pulling in a long breath. "Help . . ." Blood bubbled up out of his lips.

"Ain't enough time for you to say what you've got to say," I told him and immediately set to looking for the wound. "Where's the other guy? Keep it short."

"Dead."

"That's something." He was bleeding from his chest, from underneath his otherwise untouched armor. A magic-wound. Shit.

A figure pushed through the smoke, sword glinting. I fired off the pistol before he could get close to us. The figure dropped to the sand.

I knew we couldn't stay here, Naji and me. All the magic he'd been using had drained him dry, and me trying to stave off an entire ship's worth of crew just sent him spiraling into more pain.

Think like a pirate, I told myself. *Think like Papa.*

Ain't no shame in running from a losing battle, he told me once. Better that than dead.

"You have to get up," I said to Naji, tugging on him as I did. "You have to get up and get on that horse."

He nodded and pushed himself up about halfway.

The smoke had begun to clear, webbing out, revealing patches of white sky. Revealing more *Hariri* crew. "Hurry!" I said. "I got to fight 'em off and if that hurts you—"

He wasn't standing. He'd dipped his fingers into the blood in his chest and was drawing a symbol in the sand.

"Get on the horse, Naji!"

"Protection," he croaked, and then he started muttering, and his eyes glowed sickly and pale, and the crew was descending on us, and I knew I had to fight. So I jumped to my feet and dove in, ignoring the pain in my body and the ache in the back of my throat that meant I needed water. And most of all I ignored the groans from Naji, 'cause I knew I was hurting him, but what choice did I have?

And then he said my name again. And he was on the horse.

I knew it was stupid, me right in the middle of battle like that, but I could've wept, seeing Naji slumped over that horse's back. I raced over and scrambled up to join him, wedging myself in front of Naji so I could take the horse's reins. Naji snaked his arms around my waist, pressed his head into my shoulder, and I dug my feet in the horse's side.

The horse galloped over the sand. Every part of my body hurt. Naji's breath was hot and moist against the back of my neck, even through the fabric of his mask, and it reassured me, it let me know he was still alive.

I rode the horse out of the smoke and craned my neck back up at the sky. The sun was nestled over in the western corner. Naji moaned something. I twisted the reins, sent the horse running off to the southeast.

Naji moaned into my neck for about five or ten minutes, and when he stopped I realized no one was following us. I halted the horse and turned him around. The desert was empty save for us. The cloud of black smoke stretched out over the horizon, a long ways a way.

"Can't . . . hold this . . . Get to the river." Naji's voice was right in my ear.

I didn't know if he meant he couldn't hold the protection spell or if he couldn't hold on to his life, but I wasn't taking no chances. I set the horse to running again.

"How far are we?" I asked, shouting into the wind and the sand.

Naji groaned and buried his face into my shoulder. Even

through his armor I could tell that his body was hotter than normal.

I rode the horse as hard as I could without having it collapse beneath us. Every time I slowed it down my hands shook and I made myself aware of Naji's breath, waiting for it to stop. But it never did.

The sun set. The protection spell held on. And so did Naji.

And then the landscape started to change. I didn't notice at first, in the gray twilight, but the shrubbery got more and more plentiful—it didn't look so much like a desert no more. The moon came out, full and heavy and fat in the sky, casting enough light to see. Naji's breath was thin, weak. The horse panted and trembled.

I smelled water.

Fresh, clean, sweet water. Then I heard it, babbling like voices, and I couldn't help it, I started to cry. I thought maybe I was imagining it, just 'cause I wanted it so bad.

"Canyon," Naji said. His voice made me jump. "Stop."

I slowed the horse down. The land dropped off not far from us, and I figured the river was down in the canyon, carving its way through the desert to the sea.

"How are we gonna get down?" I asked.

Naji didn't say nothing, only gasped and choked and pressed up against me.

"Stay here," I said, and I climbed off the horse. Naji slumped forward, his head lolling. I crept through the shrubbery till I came to the edge of the canyon. Then I crouched down on my knees and leaned over.

The river was a line of starlight flowing through the darkness. The drop wasn't too far, but I couldn't risk jumping, not knowing the water's depth. And I had to concern myself with Naji and the horse, both of whom needed water. Fortunately the sides of the canyons sloped down pretty gently, and I figured the horse could probably climb down, assuming we did it slow.

I knew I couldn't wait till morning.

Naji was still slumped over the horse's back. His hands were dark with blood, and his blood soaked the back of my dress. I nudged him, and every second he didn't move, my chest got tighter. Then he rolled his head toward me.

"We're climbing down to the river," I said. "You have to hold on. I'm going to lead the horse."

He nodded and weakly threaded his hands through the horse's mane. I grabbed hold of the reins and tugged, and the horse lurched forward. Its whole body was covered in white frothy sweat. I hoped it could make it down to the river.

The climbing was slow but not as difficult as I had thought. Showers of stone and sand fell beneath our feet, shimmering on their way down. Every noise we made echoed through the darkness, and the desert night's chill laid over the sweat and heat of my exertion.

At one point Naji nearly slid off the horse. I caught him and, with a burst of strength I shouldn't have had, shoved him back into place. I grabbed his wrist and checked for his pulse—still there, thank Kaol and her sacred starfish, even though it was faint, the whisper of a heartbeat.

I let myself get in one round of curses and then moved us on our way. Eventually the sand and stone gave way to soft pale grasses, and as soon as we stepped onto flat ground, onto the riverbank, I let out a holler of victory that rang up and down the canyon walls. The horse trotted up to the water and took to drinking, Naji still slouched on his back. When the horse bent down, Naji swung back his head and twisted sideways, and I ran up to catch him and let him down easy on the riverbed. I pulled the mask away, my hand brushing against his scarred skin. He stirred and moved toward my touch, but he already looked like a dead thing. Ashen skin, sunken eyes.

While the horse slurped at the river, I scooped some water in my hand and dripped it across Naji's face, hoping to hell that he'd drink some of it. His lips, cracked and bleeding, parted a little, and I went back and forth, dribbling water a little at a time. Then I cracked open his armor, careful as I could. The inside was coated with blood, and the fabric of his robes was stiff to the touch.

I pressed my hand against the side of his face. His eyelids fluttered. "Naji," I said. "Naji, I need you to wake up. I don't know how to treat you."

He moaned something in his language, words like rose thorns.

"Damn it, Naji, I don't know what that means!" I slammed my fist into the riverbed. Mud ran up between my fingers.

He moaned again, lifted one hand, and then dropped it against his chest, dropped it down to his side. His blood glimmered in the moonlight.

I sat back on my heels and stared at him and thought of wounds I'd treated back on Papa's ship, knife cuts and bullet shots, bruised faces and broken fingers. Ain't never anything done by magic. The rare occasion something like that came in, Mama took care of it.

Mama. I wished she were here now, her and her magic, the magic of the sea, of water—

The river.

I crawled down to the river's edge. Everything was silver and light, cold and beautiful. The horse had wandered off, blending into the shadows. I'd never been able to talk to the water. But Mama had told me you got to want it, and maybe before I never wanted it enough, maybe before I never needed it.

I crawled into the water. The cold cut right through me, made all my bones rattle. Silt drifted up around my bare legs. I closed my eyes, concentrated hard as I could.

"River," I said. My voice ran up and down the walls of the

canyon. It became a million voices at once. "River, I ask to speak with you."

Those were the words Mama had told me a long time ago. And I waited, but the water just kept pushing past my waist, tugging on my dress.

Then I remembered. Mama casting gifts into the ocean. I had to give a gift.

The camel had run off with my money, so all I had left that belonged to me was the protection charm Naji made me and the knife I used to save his life. I threw the knife into the water. Mama always said the water knows the true value of things. And this was a trade, one way of saving his life for another.

I said my request again, louder this time, filling my voice with meaning and purpose, with pain and sorrow. If I let Naji die, my voice said, not in words but in tone, I as good as killed him.

The way I killed Tarrin of the *Hariri*.

This time, the babble of the river fell quiet. The river kept moving, swirling past me, but I couldn't hear nothing. And I knew I had permission to ask my request.

"Naji's dying," I said. "I need to know how I can fix him." I thought about it for a few seconds and then I added, "If there's anything in the river that can help him, please. I would appreciate it." Mama always told me to be polite when you're dealing with the spirits.

A heaviness descended over the canyon, a stillness that made me feel like the last human in the whole world. Then the river began to rise, inching up above my waist to my chest, flooding over the bed, washing over Naji, then under him, buoying him up. From somewhere in the darkness, the horse whinnied.

Then, quick as it flooded, the river retreated to normal.

River nettle. The name came to me like I'd known it all along, even though there ain't no way I'd ever heard it before. I splashed toward the shore, slipping over the stones to get to the riverbed. Naji gasped and wheezed, droplets of water sparkling on his skin. I walked past him, stumbling out into the grasses, feeling around in the dark for something that grew low to the ground, in places where the river flooded during that time of heavy run-off from the mountains. It would be covered in stiff, spiny leaves, like a thistle—

My hand closed around a thick stem, and my palm burned like it had been bitten by ants. This was it.

I yanked the nettle out of the ground, flinging clods of damp dirt across the front of my dress. Then I stumbled back over to Naji, who was panting there in the mud. The sound wrapped guilt around my heart and squeezed so hard it hurt.

"Hold on," I whispered to Naji, smoothing his hair back away from his face, wiping off the water that dripped into his eyes. "I got something to help you."

He gasped and shuddered and I knew he was dying and I knew I had to do this fast.

I used Naji's knife to cut his robes away from the wound. It wasn't like any wound I ever saw—it wasn't a cut or a burn, but a hole about the size of a fist in the center of his chest, like a well, a place of darkness and sorrow going all the way down to the center of the earth. I stared at it for a few seconds, and it seemed to get bigger and bigger, big enough to swallow me whole.

And that part of me that knew what to do, that knowledge that came from the river, told me the wound was hypnotizing me, that it wasn't no hole at all, and I had to concentrate.

I closed my eyes and shook my head and that dizzy feeling went away. When I opened my eyes again I made sure not to look directly at Naji's chest.

I stripped the leaves off the stem, going partially by moonlight and mostly by feel. I didn't fumble or hesitate—it was like I'd known how to do this all along. Then I stuck the leaves in my mouth and chewed on 'em till they got soft and mushy. They tasted like river water, steely and clean, and I spat 'em out in the palm of my hand and pressed the mush to Naji's chest. For a few seconds I was sure that my hand would plunge into the darkness, that I'd fall through that hole and wake up surrounded by evil.

Naji's chest felt all wrong, spongy and decayed and hotter even than if he had a fever, but it was there, it wasn't no doorway to someplace else. I spread the river nettle over the wound. As I worked, I sang in a language I didn't know; the words sounded like the babble of water over stones, like rainfall pattering across the surface of a pond, like rapids rushing through a canyon.

When I finished, all that knowledge evaporated out of my head. I fell backward on the mud and looked up at the stars. They blurred in and out of focus. I wanted to stay up, to watch over Naji to make sure the magic held fast, but I couldn't. I was so exhausted I slipped over into sleep, where I dreamed of water.

CHAPTER NINE

The sun woke me up the next day. It was as hot out there by the water as it had been in the desert, and when I sat up my skin hurt. Face, neck, legs: anything that hadn't been covered up was burned. At least the air felt clean. No threat of magic-sickness.

Naji was gone.

That got me to my feet fast, sunburn or not. There were a few faint footprints headed in the direction of the river. The water threw off flashes of white sunlight, nearly blinding me. But Naji was there, floating out in the middle of the river without no clothes.

Now, I ain't normally a prude about things like that—most pirates are men so it wasn't nothing I hadn't seen before. And I'd had an encounter behind a saloon on a pirates' island in the west, with this boy Taj who sailed aboard the *Uloi*. But because this was Naji, my whole face flushed hot beneath the sunburn and I looked down at my feet. I wanted to go hide in the grasses until he came out and got dressed, but I was worried about him too, so I called out, "You all right?" without looking up.

"You're awake," he called back, which didn't answer my question. I heard him splashing around in the water, and I kept my eyes trained down until he padded up to me barefoot, at which point I had no choice but to look at him.

He'd tied his robes around his waist. His whole chest was covered in the same snaky tattoos as his arms. And though the wound had healed up as an angry red circle over his heart, he was still pale and weak-looking. I didn't think he should have been out there swimming, but I didn't say nothing.

"Are you going to have a scar?" I asked. He didn't answer right away and I realized I'd forgotten about his face. "Um, I mean—"

"Yes, it'll scar." Naji looked down at his chest, ran his fingers over the red, crumpled-up flesh. "I thought you couldn't do magic."

He said it like he was accusing me of something, and I floundered around a bit, trying to find the words. "I asked the river. My mama taught me, or tried to teach me. With the sea. And it worked. It ain't never worked before, but it worked this time."

"Oh, of course. I should have known. A pirate—you'd have an affinity with water." He stopped and squinted up at the lip of the canyon, like maybe he was expecting to see somebody. The Hariri clan maybe.

"You saved my life again," he said, still looking up.

"Yeah, hopefully I didn't just double the curse." The irony of me saving his life a second time hadn't been lost on me. I had killed Tarrin only to make a deal with the water to save Naji. The thought made my stomach twist around.

"I doubt it works that way."

"Well, if it does, then I'm sorry."

He dropped his gaze and looked at me real hard, which made me shiver. "No," he said. "Don't apologize. I didn't mean—" He took a deep breath. "Thank you."

I got a dizzy spell then, and I thought it was because he'd thanked me, even though I knew how silly that was. But Naji caught me by the arm and said, "The magic exhausted you. We'll rest here a day before we go on. You should eat."

"What about you?" I said. "You were halfway to death last night, and you ain't looking too great this morning neither." My vision swam, the river turning into a swarm of light. The insects chittered out in the grasses, so loud it hurt.

"You're right," Naji said. He guided me down to the riverbed. It was nice to sit down. My head cleared. Naji sat down beside me. "We both need to rest." He paused. "I only suggested that because I'm used to this kind of healing. I do it constantly. You, on the other hand . . ." His eyes kind of lit up like he was going to smile, but he didn't. "That was some very powerful magic you performed last night."

"It was the river, not me."

"No, it wasn't."

I didn't say nothing, 'cause I didn't know what he was getting at and I didn't want to ask.

We spent the rest of the day lying out by the river. I caught some fish by stabbing at them with Naji's knife—it was a lot easier than it shoulda been, I guess 'cause I was still in the river's favor. Naji got a fire going and cooked the fish on a couple of smooth, flat stones, and that fish tasted better than anything I'd eaten for the past two weeks. I got to feeling a lot better after that, but it seemed to wear Naji out, and he curled up in the grasses and slept.

I took that as an opportunity to strip down and bathe, scrubbing at my unburned skin with a small handful of pebbles. I rinsed out my dress—hardly more than rags now—and laid it out in the sun to dry. And 'cause Naji was still sleeping, I laid myself out in the sun to dry too.

Kaol, that felt good, like all my muscles needed was the strength of the sun. I stretched my hands out over my head and listened to the bugs and the river and Naji snoring over in the grasses.

Every now and then, I thought about Tarrin of the *Hariri*, bleeding to death on the sand, and it gave me a tightness in my chest that hurt like a flesh wound. I know guilt won't get you nowhere if you're living a pirate's life, but it snuck up on me anyway, no matter how much I reminded myself that he would've killed me first. At least with the *Hariri* crewmen I didn't know for sure if they died or not—that's usually how it is in battle, all that chaos swirling around you. But Tarrin stuck with me, and it wasn't just 'cause I knew the *Hariri* clan would have to take their revenge.

We set off the next morning. The horse was gone—it had wandered away in the night, off to join the camel in the desert. I didn't mind walking, but Naji was still too pale, and he moved slower than normal, shuffling along over the riverbed like an old man.

"It's only a few days' walk from here," he said.

"What is?" I looked at him sideways. "Don't you dare say a canyon."

He didn't answer at first, and I thought about laying in to him for never telling me nothing, but then he said, "Leila."

"Who the hell is that?"

"Someone who can cure me."

"Oh. Right." I stopped and put my hands on my hips. Kaol, why couldn't we have met up with this Leila lady before the Hariri clan tracked us down? I didn't know how much it would've changed things. Tarrin still wouldn't have listened to me. But maybe I wouldn't have killed him, neither. Maybe I could have agreed to go with him and then found some other way out of marriage.

"What's wrong?" Naji turned toward me. He had his robes on normal again, but they gaped open at the chest from where I'd cut them, and he kept tugging them over the wound. "I thought you'd be happy to know we've almost arrived at our destination."

"Happy enough," I muttered.

Naji frowned. "Tell me. It could prove important—"

"Why should I tell you anything? Not like you haven't kept

me in the dark since that night I saved your life—biggest mistake I ever made." I started walking more quickly, and I could hear Naji's footsteps catching up with me.

"Ananna—" he began.

"You really want to know?" Anger pulsed through my body, heating up my skin. Anger at Naji, at myself, and Tarrin for not standing up to his father. "I killed him. I killed Tarrin. He was a captain's son. I know that don't mean nothing to you—"

Naji didn't move.

"But a captain's son is special, 'cause he carries on the ship name. Ain't nothing to hire an assassin to kill a captain's daughter, but a son . . ." I hadn't let myself think about any of this yesterday, and now it was flooding over me like a tsunami. The Hariris would want revenge on me for sure. If they were willing to send an assassin just 'cause I spurned their son I didn't even want to think about what they'd do now that I'd killed him.

I wished my brain would just shut down the way it had yesterday afternoon.

"I do know what it means," Naji said quietly. "To kill a captain's son. I've worked with the Confederation before."

And then he put a hand on my shoulder, which surprised me into silence. I stared at the ridges of his knuckles, at the spiderweb of knife scars etching across his skin. His touch was warm.

"Leila is a river witch," he said. "I believe she can help lift my curse."

"Yeah, figured that out ages ago." I scowled down at the riverbed.

"Even when the curse is lifted," he went on. "I'll arrange for your protection."

His hand dropped away. The place where he'd touched me felt empty.

"Thank you," I muttered, looking down at my feet, my cheeks hot.

"Come," Naji said. "Once we get to Leila's, everything will be fine. You'll see."

Yeah, I thought. *For you*.

But I walked along the riverbank same as before.

We followed the river for three days, and it was a lot easier than trekking through the desert, even without the camel. There was plenty of water and fresh fish to eat, and a lot more to look at. Little blue flowers grew along the riverbed, all mixed up with the grasses and the river nettle that I'd used to save Naji's life a second time, and the walls of the canyon grew taller and steeper the more we walked, until it seemed like the desert was another world away. And those walls were something themselves, stripes of golden-sun yellow and rust-red and off-white. Like the wood on the inside of a fancy sailing ship.

We had to stop quite a bit, though, so Naji could rest. His health didn't seem to improve. He stayed pale despite all the sun, and he'd stumble over the rocks sometimes, and I'd have to steady him. He slept longer than me and hardly ate much of anything. It was worrisome, 'cause I'd no way of helping him out if he got any sicker. There was no way the river would give me another cure, not without an offering—which I didn't have.

On the third day, we came across a house.

It was built into the stone of the canyon wall, with carved steps leading down to the river. There were three little boats tethered next to the steps, plus a flat raft that looked made out of driftwood from the sea. Bits of broken glass and small smooth stones hung from the house's overhang, chiming in the wind.

"Finally," Naji said. "We're here."

"This is it?" We were on the other side of the river from the house. I walked up to the water's edge. The house looked empty, still and silent save for that broken glass.

"Yes. Leila's house." Naji closed his eyes and swayed in place. Everything about him was washed out except for the wound on his chest. "She can help me."

But I got the feeling that he wasn't talking to me, so I didn't say nothing.

"Guess we got to swim across," I said. The water ran slow, smooth as the top of a mirror. Looked deep, though. Naji opened his eyes. He nodded, and then he sat down and pulled off his boots and lashed 'em together with his sword and his knife and his quill, which I was surprised to learn hadn't been packed away on the camel. "My desert mask," he said.

"What about it?"

"Where is it?"

"I dunno."

Naji stood up, his boots and sword and all bundled up at his feet. "You don't know? You took it from me! I would never have lost it."

"Well, you didn't seem all too worried about it before." I honestly didn't know what had happened to the mask. It probably got left behind on the riverbed or knocked into the river proper.

"I didn't need it before."

"Why do you need it now? We still ain't in the desert."

Naji face got real dark, his eyes narrowing into two angry slits. "It doesn't matter," he said, turning away from me. He grabbed his boots and waded out into the water. I followed behind him, sure he was gonna pass out and I'd have to save his life again. The water was colder here, and I didn't know if that was 'cause of the depth or this Leila woman. Probably both.

At the other side of the river, Naji put on his boots, and drew his robes tight over the wound on his chest. Then he knocked on the door.

We had to wait awhile. Whoever Leila was, she sure took her sweet time. Naji knocked again. The glass tinkled overhead and cast rainbow lights all over the place.

"She ain't here," I said.

"Of course she is." Naji leaned up against the side of the house, tugging distractedly on the hair hanging at the left side of his head, pulling it over his scar. "She has to be."

At that moment, like she'd been standing inside listening to us, the door swung open. The woman who stepped out into the sunlight was beautiful. Curvy where she was supposed to be, with thick hair that curled down to her narrow waist. Big eyes and lashes long enough that she didn't need to wear no kohl to fake it. This perfect bow-shaped mouth. I knew immediately why Naji'd pitched such a fit about his desert mask.

Course, I didn't trust her one bit.

"Naji!" she cried, throwing up her hands. "My favorite disfigured assassin! What brings you all the way out here to my river?"

"Don't do this, Leila. You know why I'm here." But he didn't say it like he was mad. In fact, he kept looking at her with this dopey expression I'd seen a thousand times before, on the faces of the crew whenever a pretty lady came aboard. Ain't nobody ever looked at me like that.

Leila smiled and her whole face lit up like the river beneath sunlight. "Of course I do! One impossible curse, one round of spellshot to the heart. Which you seem to be mending up rather nicely on your own."

Impossible curse? My blood started rushing in my ears. Mama had told me about impossible curses once, back when I was still trying to learn magic. They were a northern thing, cold and tricky like the ice. And impossible to cure, of course. Naji had dragged me across the desert for a cure that didn't exist.

I was never going to get rid of him. And standing there by that dazzling river, I saw the life I'd imagined ever since I was a little girl sitting down in the cargo bay unfurl and then turn to dust. I'd killed a captain's son and now I had a lifetime bound to a damn blood-magician.

Curse the north and its crooked, barbaric magic.

"The Order said you could help me," Naji said.

Leila dipped one shoulder and fluttered her eyelashes. I wanted to hit her. I wanted to hit both of them. But then she tilted her head toward the mysterious darkness of her house. "Come in," she said. "Her, too. I don't imagine you'll want her to wait outside. Gives you quite the headache, doesn't it?"

Well. I was starting to think she hadn't even seen me.

"Come on," Naji said, wrenching himself away from the house's stone wall. Leila waited in the doorway, gazing kind of haughty-like at Naji. I didn't want to go in. Course, maybe she really could help us.

I went in.

The house was small and dark and cool. It smelled like the river. Naji sat down at the stone table in the center of the room, and Leila disappeared through the back, calling out as she went, "I've something for that fatigue, Naji dearest, if you just give me a second."

I sat down beside him. Water dripped off my dress and pooled on the floor. I hoped she'd have to clean it up.

Leila came back with a chipped tea saucer and a kettle. She poured hot water into the saucer, and grass-scented steam floated up into the air. I watched Naji drink, waiting for something bad to happen. But he just leaned back in the chair and closed his eyes and let out this long satisfied breath.

"Spellshot's nothing to mess with," Leila said to me, like I'd have any idea what she was talking about.

I glared at her.

She laughed. "Naji, where'd you come up with her? She's so sullen."

I clenched my hands into fists. Naji pushed himself up to sitting and leaned over the table and looked at Leila. "Thank you, I do feel much stronger."

"I heard my river gave you a handout a few days ago." She smiled again, and the whole room seemed to fill with light. Kaol, it pissed me off.

Naji's eyes flicked over to me a second. Back to Leila. "Can you help me or not?"

"Well, it's called an impossible curse for a reason." She leaned against the wall. "But I'll see what I can do. Stand up so I can get a good look at you."

For a few seconds Naji didn't move. Then he ducked his head a little and pushed away from the table. Leila sashayed up to him and walked around a few times as though she was sizing up a calf for slaughter. She moved like water, graceful and soft and lovely. Every part of me wanted to stick out my foot and trip her, just to see her stumble.

"Well?" said Naji, who hadn't looked up once.

Leila stopped. She was only a few inches from him, close enough he could have turned his head and kissed her if he wanted.

She pressed two fingers underneath his chin and forced his head up. She stared at his face for a long time, and Naji didn't say nothing, didn't move at all.

"It's really a shame," she said. "You were such a beautiful man."

Naji jerked away from her, slamming his hip into the edge of the table.

"Leave him alone," I said, jumping to my feet, going for the knife that wasn't there no more. Wasn't enough that he had an impossible curse on him, she had to make fun of his face?

Leila glanced over at me and laughed, which made me feel smaller than a fleck of dust. Naji had sunk into his chair, his head tilted down, his hair covering up his whole face.

"Are you sure she's not the one cursed to protect you?" Leila slunk over to Naji and wrapped her arms around his shoulders and pressed her nose into the part of his hair. "Oh, don't be like that," she purred. "You know I was only joking."

"No, you weren't," I said. I wanted that knife so bad. It weren't so much 'cause of Naji, but 'cause I can't stand a bully, and that's all she was. A bully who got away with it 'cause she was so beautiful.

"Ananna," Naji said. "Stop. She's going to help me."

"If I can," Leila said, her arms still wrapped around Naji's shoulders, her mouth right on the verge of smiling.

That was too much. I stalked out of the house, back out into the sunlight, all the way down the steps leading into the river. Naji's headache be damned. I sat down at the top step and stuck my feet in the water. Fish swam up to me and nibbled on my toes but nobody came out of the house. I didn't expect 'em to.

I stayed out there for a while, until the sun set and my stomach grumbled. I thought about swimming over to the other side of the river and setting up camp. But by now it was too dark to see, and I doubted I'd be able to catch any fish to eat. The air had gotten cold again, and the river was cold, and I kept on shivering out there in my ragged, cut-up dress.

My pride kept me from walking back in the house until it was late enough I figured both of 'em had fallen asleep. I crept back in slowly, pulling up on the door handle so the hinges wouldn't creak. The floors were stone, so my bare feet didn't make too much noise.

"I'm glad to see you came back inside."

I yelped.

Naji was stretched out on a cot in the corner of the room. He pushed up on his arm when he saw me.

"Where's Leila?"

"Asleep, I imagine."

I sat down on the floor beside the cot, drawing my feet up close against me.

"I don't like her," I said, pitching my voice low.

"I'd prefer not to talk about this." A rustle as he rolled over onto his back and pulled the thin woven blanket over his chest.

"She's beautiful," I said.

"I know."

I wanted to slap him for that, but I didn't, 'cause I knew I didn't have no good reason. "It means she ain't trustworthy."

"What? Because she's beautiful?"

"Yeah. Beautiful people, things are too easy for 'em. They don't know how to survive in this world. Somebody's ugly, or even plain, normal-looking, that means they got to work twice as hard for things. For anything. Just to get people to listen to 'em, or take 'em serious. So yeah. I don't trust beautiful people."

"I see." He dropped his head to the side. I didn't look at him, but down at the floor instead, at the fissures in the stones. "No wonder you were so quick to trust me."

I heard the hard edge in his voice, the crack of bitterness. And so I lifted my head. He was staring up at the ceiling.

"You ain't ugly," I said.

He didn't answer, and I knew my opinion didn't matter none anyway.

CHAPTER TEN

Leila didn't do much to sway me over to trusting her those next few days, mostly 'cause she toyed with Naji, not giving him a straight answer one way or another with regards to the curse.

"He needs to rest," she told me that first afternoon. "Before I can examine him to see if I can help." She had come out to the river to gather up a jar of silt and a few handfuls of river nettle. I spent as little time inside the house as I could, and it surprised me that she said anything to me. I hadn't asked after him, although I'd been wondering.

"He's a lot more injured than he lets on," she added, scooping the silt up with her hand. It streamed through her fingers and glittered in the sunlight. "I'm surprised he made it as far as he did."

"I took care of him," I snapped, even though I was trying to hold my tongue.

She looked up from the half-filled jar. "Of course you tried, sweetling," she said. "But you aren't used to that sort of magic." One of her vicious half smiles. "Or any kind of magic at all."

The water glided around my ankles, and I thought about that night the river spoke to me in her babbling soft language, that night she guided me into action.

"By the way," Leila said. "I have some old clothes that might work for you. Men's clothes, of course. You're not going to fit into anything of mine, I'm afraid."

I knew I really wasn't going to hold my tongue against that, so

I slipped off the edge of the steps and into the river, the cold shocking the anger right out of me. I kept my eyes open, the way I always do underwater, so I could see the sunlight streaming down from the surface, lighting up the murkiness.

Naji'd told me Leila was some kind of river witch, but the river didn't seem to play favorites, didn't seem to care about the differences between me and her. It wasn't like Naji. And so I stayed under as long as I could, 'cause it was safe down there, everything blurred, the coldness turning me numb.

Naji did seem to get better. I guess I'll give Leila that. He got the color back in his cheeks, and he didn't shake when he shuffled around the house. The wound was slow to heal, though, despite the river nettle Leila pressed against it every evening. Sometimes I watched them, studying the way her long delicate fingers lingered on his chest. When she sang, her voice twinkled like starlight, clear and bright and perfect. That was when I figured out that she and Naji had been lovers before he got the scar. 'Cause she touched him like she knew how, and he stared at her like all he thought about was her touch.

It left me dizzy and kind of sick to my stomach. At least she never did say nothing about his face again. Not in front of me, anyway.

We'd been there close to a week when Leila announced over dinner that she was ready to talk to Naji about the curse.

"Finally," I said.

Naji kicked me under the table.

"You need to be there too," Leila said.

"Be where?"

"The garden, I imagine," Naji said. He poked at the fish on his plate. All we ate was fish and river reeds, steamed in the hearth in the main room.

"There's a garden?"

"Yes, out back," Leila said.

That didn't make no sense. The house was built into the wall of the canyon, and even if she had stairs leading up to the surface, the surface wasn't nothing but desert.

"Magic," Leila said, and tapped her chest. I scowled. She smiled at me like I'd said something stupid that she found amusing.

I slumped down in my chair and pushed the fish around on my plate, my appetite gone. And I kept doing that till Naji and Leila decided they were finished up, at which point both of 'em filed out of the kitchen, toward the back of the house. I took my time, dawdling till Naji strode back into the main room. I was sure he was going to command me to follow, but instead he looked at me real close and said, "Please, Ananna."

I shot him a mean look, and he watched me for a few minutes like he was trying to think of something to say. I can wait out a silence just fine, so I crossed my arms over my chest and stared right back.

He said, "I went into Kajjil last night and spoke with the Order."

"What does that have to do with anything?"

"The Hariri clan hasn't hired another Jadorr'a. If you're worried that curing me will leave you vulnerable—if this is some pirate's scheme for protection—"

"I told you," I snapped, "I can take care of myself."

"Of course. I just thought that might be a reason for your reticence."

"Well, that don't surprise me none. That you'd think that." I gave him my best glare. I didn't want to think about the Hariri clan. I didn't want to think about Tarrin. "I just don't understand what Leila needs me for."

"She says that she needs your help."

"What?"

"You're part of the curse."

"Yeah, an impossible one. I don't see how I'm gonna make much of a difference—"

The expression on Naji's face stopped me dead. I'd never seen a man look so desperate. It made me aware of my own desperation, that ache that had settled in the bottom of my stomach after the battle in the desert.

"I just don't see what good it can do," I muttered.

"The least you can do is give me five minutes," Naji said.

That was enough for me. I followed Naji to the back of the house, through the dark, dripping stone hallway, past rooms glowing with something too steady for candlelight. And then the hallway opened up, the way corridors do in caves, and there was the garden.

So it was underground. There wasn't no sunlight in the room, though the ceiling had that same weird glow to it as the rooms in the house. And the plants weren't like any plants I'd ever seen: All of 'em were real pale, so pale you could almost see straight through 'em. They wriggled around whenever we walked past, as though they were turning to look at us.

Leila sat in the center of the garden, on a stone bench in the middle of a circle carved into the wet rock of the cave. She had on this floaty white dress that made her look like one of the flowers, and when we walked up she patted the bench beside herself. I let Naji take it. She obviously meant for him to sit there anyway.

"Everyone's gathered, I see." Like we were some big crowd, not three people who'd been living in the same house for a week. "Naji, I'll need you to look at me." That damn smile again. "I know it's hard for you—"

I took a step toward her, my hands balled up tight into fists, and so help me, her voice kind of wavered, and for a minute she actually shut up. Then she cleared her throat and said, "Look at me, and don't move. It's important you don't move."

Then she glanced over at me and said, "I need you over here too. Come along, yes, put your hand on Naji's hand there. No, palm down. Good."

She pulled out a blue silk scarf and tied Naji's and my hand together.

"Now," she said, looking up at me. "You need to stand there and not move your hand from his—"

"I'm tied to him," I said.

"And don't interrupt."

Naji didn't look at either of us while she spoke. He just kept his head down, his hair pulled over his scar.

"Don't give me a reason to interrupt," I said. "And I won't."

That got a glare from her and nothing else. She turned her attention to Naji. Put her hands on his shoulders. Closed her eyes. Hummed. The flowers trembled and shook and danced. Naji kept his face blank, and I wondered what was going through his head. I wondered if he bought it.

'Cause I'd seen a lot of magic those last few weeks, and Leila's humming and swaying didn't fool me one bit. There was magic down here, for sure—have to be, with those creepy flowers—and Leila certainly could work a charm when she needed. But she didn't need to do nothing right now. She was faking.

She carried on like that just long enough to be annoying. I shifted my weight around and tapped my foot and looked at Naji's scar. My hand was starting to sweat from being tied up with his.

And then she stopped. The cave seemed to let out a sigh.

Naji stared at her, and his eyes were so hopeful it almost broke my heart.

"Sorry, dearest," she said. "There's nothing I can do."

"What!" Naji jumped to his feet, his whole body springing tight like a coil. The scarf fluttered to the ground.

I felt like the earth had been pulled out from under me. Nothing she could do. I realized then that I'd been thinking she could help too. I hadn't even recognized the hope for what it was until it got dragged away from me and I felt its absence in my heart. I couldn't let go of that old vision of my future life and the thought of what it was going to be like now.

"What do you mean? Nothing? Not even a charm against—"

"It's an impossible curse," Leila said lightly. "What did you expect?"

"But you said . . . And the Order . . ." Naji threw up his hands and stalked away from her. The flowers shrank away from him, curling up into themselves. "I can't believe this."

I was numb. I figured Leila knew from the moment she opened her front door that she couldn't help Naji, but she strung him along, 'cause—hell, I don't know why. 'Cause she was beautiful and he was all in love with her and so she could. This was why I hated beautiful people. They build you up and then they destroy you. And we let 'em.

"Naji, darling," she said. "I still might be able to help you, of course."

Naji picked up his shoulders a little, although he didn't turn around.

"Liar," I said. It didn't give me the satisfaction I'd hoped for.

She glanced at me as though I were as insignificant as a piece of pressed copper. Then she stood up and glided over to Naji, her dress rippling out behind her. She set one hand on his shoulder and whispered something in his ear. He sighed.

"The impossible curses are all from the north," Leila said. "A northern curse needs a northern cure. Even if it's impossible." She smiled. "Especially if it's impossible."

"What are you saying?" Naji asked.

"I can give you a boat."

"What'd you whisper to him?" I asked.

"None of your business." Leila swatted at me. "Naji, I can give you and your ward a boat and a promise of protection on the river."

"We can take care of the Hariri clan ourselves."

"I'm not concerned about some gang of unwashed pirates."

"What?" I asked. "Who else is after us?"

She twisted around, her hair falling in thick silky ropes down her spine. "The Mists, of course."

The garden suddenly seemed too cold. "What's the Mists got to do with it?" I was trying to sound brave, but my voice shook anyway, at the memory of a pair of gray eyes swallowing me whole. "Why didn't you say anything? I thought it was just the Hariri clan we had to worry about. I mean, you kept going on about us being under protection—" I was babbling. The words spilled out of my throat the way they always do whenever I let my fear get to me.

Both of them ignored me.

"The river will take you down to Port Iskassaya, where you can book passage to the Isles of the Sky."

"Kaol!" I shouted. "The Isles of the Sky!"

Naji and Leila both looked at me.

"I ain't going there," I said. "I ran out on Tarrin 'cause that's where he wanted to take me."

Leila gave me this teasing little smile, but I turned to Naji and said, "You can't really think—"

"It's the only way," Leila said.

"I ain't asking you."

"I agree with her, Leila," Naji said. "You know I can't go there."

"Thank you," I said. Finally, he had learned how to talk some sense.

"Oh, Naji, the enchantment from that charm is so strong I could feel it when you were three days away. They'll never catch you."

"I still don't understand why you'd send me there, of all places—"

"You know as well as I that if you want any hope of breaking an impossible curse, you'll need the magic of the Isles. And besides," Leila gave a bright smile, "it's where the Wizard Eirnin lives."

"I've never heard of him," said Naji.

"He's from the north, from the ice-islands. I studied under him as a child. Long before I met you." She smiled and pressed herself close to Naji and he sank into her like her closeness was a relief. "I've seen him cast impossible curses before. And a cure is only one letter off from a curse."

I snorted and kicked at the powdery dirt of the floor.

Naji gave her long hard look. "It's too dangerous."

"So cast some more spells. Someone as powerful as you . . ." She made her eyes all big and bright. Naji gazed moonily at her. "You'll be fine."

"And what about me?" I said. "Will I be fine? I know what happens when the untouched go to the Isles of the Sky. They get turned into rainclouds and dirt or they get sucked down to the depths and drown over and over."

"You aren't untouched," Naji said. "You healed me by the river."

I glared at him. "Well, I ain't as strong as you, then."

"I have to protect you before I have to protect myself," he said. "Leila is right about the magic—"

"Of course I am," Leila said, reaching over to toy with the curl of his hair.

I couldn't say nothing, thinking about the idea that he was putting my protection before his own.

"It may be my only option," Naji said to me.

"My only option too," I said. "You're not the only one cursed here. And I still don't want to go." But already I knew it might be worth it, if the Isles really could break Naji's curse. They were the place where the impossible happened, after all. It was just that their impossible was supposed to be the sort of impossible that's also horrible.

Naji gave me a sad, confused sort of frown.

"Of course," he said, "no merchant ship is going to agree to sail to the Isles of the Sky."

"No pirate ship, neither," I added. "And that's what Port Iskassaya is anyway, a pirates' port-of-call."

"How convenient," Leila said, "that you travel with a pirate."

Naji pulled away from her and trudged away from the flowers, back over to the center circle. "We need to talk," he said to me.

"Can't argue with that."

He gave me one of his Naji-looks. For a few seconds I didn't think Leila was going to let us leave the garden, but she didn't say nothing when Naji grabbed my upper arm and dragged me back into the dripping dimness of the house.

"Told you she ain't trustworthy," I said. "She's been planning that little performance the whole time we were here. I'd put money on it."

Naji didn't say nothing for a long time. Then he said, and it damn near knocked me over, "You're probably right. I was . . . hoping . . . that she wouldn't play any of her games with me. Not now. Not . . . with everything." He slouched down on the cot and stuck his head in his hands. "I knew she trained in the north, that's why I came here, but I truly hoped—"

"And what did she mean about protecting us from the Mists?"

Naji dropped his hands down to his sides. "Oh, her word is good for that," he said. "She wouldn't do anything to actually kill me."

"That don't answer my question."

"Because the answer doesn't concern you."

"Really?" I said. "Well, in that case, this curse of yours don't concern me neither. So if you don't mind, I'll be on my way." And I slipped off my charm and headed toward the front door.

"Ananna!" Naji jumped up from the cot and grabbed me again. I wasn't really going to go. I ain't so heartless I'm gonna let someone be struck down with pain on account of me. Even if that someone is a murderer and a liar. Hell, murderers and liars used to sing me to sleep.

I yanked my arm away from him. "Look, you want me to go with you to the Isles of the Sky—and I can kinda see how maybe it's not the stupidest idea in the world, all things considered, even if it's definitely up there—but if you really want me to go, you have to be straight with me. You gotta tell me things."

"Tell you things," he said.

"Yeah. You know how you didn't tell me who Leila was, or what we'd find here in the canyon? Or what that black smoke was when the Hariri clan attacked?" I glared at him and after a few seconds he nodded. "Well, no more of that."

"I know what 'tell you things' means."

"Sounded like you were asking. Keep in mind that if you want to barter passage on a pirate ship, you will need me. You don't got the cash to buy your way onto one, and ain't no pirate in the Confederation's gonna let a blood-magician on board without some kind of leverage." I jutted my thumb into my chest. "Which is me. So if you want to go on with your secrets, that's fine, but you can expect to wait out the rest of your days in Port Iskassaya."

Naji got that flash of a smile around his eyes. I was too worked up to care.

"I think that sounds like a deal," Naji said.

"Now why the hell should I be worried about the Mists attacking us?" Kaol, even saying "Mists" sent the creeping shivers up my spine.

"Someone in the Otherworld wants me dead," Naji said. "They'll have no fight with you, but they want me. It's a long—"

Leila appeared in the doorway, that white dress swirling around her ankles. She had her cruel smile on, teeth shining in the lamplight. Naji stared at her the way he did, his face all full of longing. Then he turned back to me.

"Let me tell you on the river," he said.

"Fine." So he didn't want to talk in front of Leila. "But if I don't know the whole story by Port Iskassaya, I'm gone."

Naji's eyes crinkled up again. Then he stuck out his hand. I shook it.

CHAPTER ELEVEN

Leila lent us the largest of the boats that had been tied up out front. It had a newly patched sail and a rope net for fishing. I didn't want to trust that boat, but as much as it pained me to admit it, I knew Naji was right when he said Leila didn't want us—or him, anyway—dead.

She gave us a basket filled with salted fish and some of the river reeds we'd been eating. I never wanted to look at another river reed again, but I accepted the basket anyway. She also produced a bundle of black cloth for Naji, which he unfurled into an assassin's robe. Leila had cut up his old robe when we first got here, for patching sails and blankets, and he'd been wearing the same cast-off men's clothes I had the past week.

"Where did you get this?" he asked.

"Surely you remember, dearest." Leila winked at him, and Naji looked down at his feet.

"I'm afraid I don't have anything for you," she said, hardly turning her head to look at me. I resisted the urge to make some rude gesture at her. "Oh, and Naji dearest, I put your armor down below."

"Thank you," Naji said, lifting his head. They regarded one another for a few seconds longer, and I turned away and set to fiddling with the ropes so I wouldn't have to look at them.

And then we took off. Port Iskassaya was a three-day trip downriver, according to Naji. (Leila'd told him, of course, though he don't know nothing about sailing.) When we arrived we were to release the boat the way you would a camel—I thought of our own camel and wondered if he was still trotting through the desert weighed down with our clothes and money and food—and it'd make its way back up the river to Leila's house. Magic again.

Naji moped that first day, leaning against the railing and looking out over the river. He hadn't bothered to change into his robes yet, and his hair fluttered around his face so that he looked like a prince in a story. I tried to busy myself with the work of sailing, but the ship took care of herself, and after a while I was so bored I leaned up beside him.

He glanced over at me but didn't say nothing.

"You miss her, don't you?"

He kept staring out over the water and didn't answer. The sun was sinking into the canyon, throwing off rays of orange and red, turning the water silver. I don't know why I asked him that. It was like I wanted him to say something to hurt me.

"You don't miss someone like Leila," Naji said, after enough time had passed that I figured he'd no intention of answering. "You merely feel her absence."

"That don't make sense."

"It's hard to explain. She's always played games, but it got worse after—" He stopped. "It doesn't matter. I only came here because I was desperate. I hardly see her anymore." He leaned away from the railing. "Thank you," he said. "For coming with me to do this."

I was a little sore from hearing him talk about Leila, so I just dipped my head and said, "I told you. I don't want you hanging around me none, either."

"I'll find a way to repay you," he said. "When it's done. You'll be compensated."

I didn't like the way he said that, like I was some hired hand.

"I promise," he said.

I didn't respond, just left him there, muttering something

about needing to check on the rigging. And he didn't say nothing when I walked away.

I wished there was more for me to do on the ship, so I could throw myself into working and not spend all my time brooding. Mama would have called it the doldrums, but those always came when you'd been at sea for months and months and you were missing civilization so bad you're almost willing to fling yourself overboard and try to swim to land. And it wasn't the river that was causing my trouble anyway.

The second afternoon, Naji came out on deck and called my name. I was up in the rigging—not working or nothing, just sitting up there watching the walls of the canyon slide by. I hung on to the rope and leaned over and watched him clomp around, swinging his head this way and that.

"Look up!" I called out.

He stopped and then tilted his head toward the sky, shielding his eyes from the sun. "How'd you get up there?"

I shrugged and then swung down on the rope, crisscrossing through the rigging, until I landed on deck, a few feet away from him.

"I owe you an explanation," he said.

"I thought you forgot. I was looking forward to ditching you once we made port."

He shook his head. His expression was soft, almost kind, and I wondered what he would look like if he smiled properly. Even with the scar, I bet it was nice.

"All right," I said. "Let's hear it."

"You remember the woman from the desert and the shop? The one who gave you the spell to banish me to the Otherworld?"

"I thought she was dead."

"No. I sent her back where she came from."

"But she bled all over—"

"They don't die," Naji said. "It's not something I can explain—just know that they aren't human."

I crossed my arms over my chest. This was a lot to work through in my head. I'd seen sirens before, and the merfolk too, but you can kill 'em easy as you can kill a man. No wonder I got cold thinking about the Mists.

"So what'd you do to her?" I asked. "That got her so pissed?"

"I didn't do anything to her," he said. "She serves someone in the Otherworld, one of the thousands of lords constantly clamoring for power. I severed some of her master's ties to our world."

"What?"

"I killed some of the children he planted here. They weren't children when I killed them," he added, since I must have looked appalled. There are lines that shouldn't be crossed. "They were attempting to rub bare the walls between worlds, in a move to gain power in the Mists. It's complicated, but . . ." His voice trailed off. "He was willing to sacrifice our world to gain power in his."

The air was real still. The only movement came from the boat as it sliced through the river water.

"Oh," I said. "You saved everybody. The entire world." I gave him a little half smile, even though it was weird to think of him as a hero. "I gotta admit, I'm impressed."

"Don't be." Naji frowned. "I was hired to do it. I didn't know who the targets were. In fact, I didn't understand the implications of what I did until much later, when she first attacked me."

I leaned up against the rigging and thought about everything that happened these last few weeks, everything that happened before Naji went from my would-be killer to my protector.

"You don't need to worry about it," Naji said, looking all earnest. "But that's why Leila offered us her protection against the Otherworld. Because—"

"Just as long as we're on the river."

"What?"

"She only offered her protection as long as we're on the river." I crossed my arms in front of my chest. "And don't lie to me. You said yourself you were putting my protection ahead of your own."

Naji sighed. "Fine. I'm worried the Otherworld will use you—the curse—to get to me."

"Put me in danger, you mean? So you'd have to come and save me?"

"More or less. Although really, you don't need to worry." Naji shrugged. "I've seen you fight. You could hold your own against any monster of the Mists."

I turned away from him, embarrassed. The water glittered around us like a million slant-cut diamonds. The sky pressed down, heavy and bleached white with heat. "Thanks for telling me all that," I said. My words came out kinda slurred like I was drunk. "I appreciate you treating me like a partner."

"You're welcome."

I nodded out at the river, and that was that.

We sailed into Port Iskassaya at dawn, the air crisp from the night before. I was up at the bow of the ship, watching the city emerge out of the pink haze of the morning and thinking on how I didn't much want to leave the river for the sea, for the Isles of the Sky.

Naji came up from down below all decked out in his assassin robes and his carved armor, with a new desert mask pulled across the lower half of his face.

"That don't look dodgy at all," I said.

Naji sighed. "Ananna, these are my clothes. I feel comfortable in them—"

"I was talking more about your mask."

His eyes darkened. "I'm not taking it off."

"I know. I'm just saying."

I sweet-talked the bureaucrat at the river docks into letting me and Naji set the boat for free. "We'll only be here half an hour," I said. "Won't be no trouble to you."

The bureaucrat gave me this long hard look. "I'm giving you twenty minutes. You ain't back by then, I'm letting her loose."

I smiled at him and gave a little salute, and me and Naji went on our way. I figured he might cut the boat free or he might not, but whether or not Leila got her boat back wasn't something I was gonna concern myself with.

Naji got real quiet, quieter than normal, as we made our way through the port town, which wasn't nothing more than some drinkhouses and brothels and a few illegal armories tucked away in the back alleys. He stuck close to the buildings, weaving in and out of shadow. Soon enough we were getting stink eyes from busted-up old crewmen who ain't got nothing better to do than sit out drinking that early in the morning.

I'd been to the Port Iskassaya sea docks only once before, when I was a little girl. It ain't a major port, as it's surrounded by desert and the river don't go nowhere of interest, but somebody built it two hundred years back and since the merchants didn't want it, the pirates claimed it instead. Mostly folks use it as a place to stop off and refresh supplies before they head out to the open sea.

I made Naji go skulk off in the shadows—which he did without question, no surprise there—while I wandered up and down the docks, looking for the right sort of boat to take us out to the Isles of the Sky. Which ain't any kind of boat at all, when you get down to it.

I'd tried to make myself look as much like a boy as possible, though my breasts don't exactly bind easy. For one, the Hariri clan would be looking for a girl, but also it's usually easier to talk your way on a ship if you're at least trying to pass as a boy. Most people ain't that observant.

I made my way through the docks as quick as I could, keeping my eyes on the ships' colors. I'd already decided against trying any Confederation ships since I didn't want word to get back to the Hariris, so my tattoo wasn't gonna do much good. As it turned out there weren't any Confederation ships at port anyway, but I did spot a couple of boats that obviously weren't entirely on the up-and-up.

The whole time I was looking I was thinking about whether or not I really wanted to go through with it—it couldn't be that hard to tell Naji no one was willing to take us aboard. Maybe we could just spend out our days in Port Iskassaya, swapping stories with the sailors down in the drinkhouses. Given our last trip in search of a cure, taking to port might prove more fruitful than sailing out to the Isles. At least that way there wasn't no chance of the curse turning out worse than before. I mean, we were heading for the source of magic. That's not something you can just trust.

But I patrolled the docks anyway, partly 'cause I promised Naji and partly 'cause I wanted my life to go back to normal. And after about twenty minutes I had two possibilities lined up: a busted-up old sloop that looked about a million years old, and a nice-looking brigantine with a crew that seemed to hail mainly from Jokja and Najare and the like in the south, all those strings of countries not bound by the Empire. I decided to try my luck with the Free Country ship, the *Ayel's Revenge*. Pirate's intuition, assuming it hadn't rusted out with disuse and bad decisions.

A few of the crew were sitting on the dock next to the ship, drinking rum and playing cards. I strolled up, acting casual, and one of 'em, a guy with a mean squint I could tell was mostly faked, jerked his chin up at me.

"You ain't a boy," he said.

"Leave her alone, Shan." It was the one woman at the table, and the one who looked like she had all the brains besides which.

She lay down her cards and looked up at me. She had dark brown skin and wore her hair in locs that she tied back with a piece of silk ribbon. There was something calm and intelligent about her expression, and I liked her immediately. "Ignore him," she said to me. "I assume any girl dressed like a boy either needs all the help she can get, or none at all. Which is it for you?"

"I need passage," I said. "So probably the first."

"Passage? To where?"

"Wherever you're going."

She gazed at me appraisingly. The guys at the table shuffled their feet and exchanged glances with one another. I could tell they didn't want me around, but I knew their opinions weren't the ones that mattered.

"We're headed to Qilar," she said. "I suppose it's as good a place as any, for someone who doesn't know what they want."

One of 'em, not the squint-eyed one, muttered something about always playing captain. The woman ignored him.

"What can you do?" she said.

"My parents had a boat a bit like this." I nodded at the ship sloshing in the water. "Not quite as big, but I spent my whole life on her, and I know the rigging ain't that different." I squinted up at the ship's sails. "I know a bit of navigation, too, and I can hold my own in a fight, if the need arises."

"I hope the need won't arise." The woman smiled.

"One more thing," I said, trying to figure out the best way to say this. "It ain't just me. I got a . . ." I didn't know what to call Naji, exactly. I couldn't say assassin. "A ward, with me."

"A ward?" The woman raised an eyebrow. "Where is she?"

"He," I said. "He's back at the inn. He won't be no trouble, though. Keeps to himself."

"I take it he's not as knowledgeable as you?"

No point in lying. I shook my head.

The woman sat for a minute, nodding a little to herself. Then she stood up and held out her hand. "I'm Marjani," she said. "Come back here in three hours. Bring your, ah, ward. I'll talk to the captain."

"Ananna," I said, touching my chest. "And thank you."

"Don't thank me yet." But she gave me a smile and I had a feeling it was going to work.

I left the docks and ducked into the alley where I'd left Naji. He materialized right away. Funny to think that trick once scared me witless.

"I think I found something," I said.

"Really?" His brow wrinkled up. "They agreed to go to the Isles of the Sky? That seems too simple . . ."

I kept my mouth shut.

"Midnight's claws, Ananna. We can't simply wander from ship to ship—"

"Sure we can," I said. "That's exactly how you do it."

"I don't think—"

"You don't know," I said. "'Cause this ain't your world. It's mine. They're heading to Qilar, probably to Port Idai, and if there's anywhere in the high seas you'll find someone crazy enough to sail to the Isles of the Sky, it'll be in Port Idai." I glared at him. "I ain't just delaying the inevitable, you know."

Naji's eyes were black as coals and hard as diamonds, but he didn't protest further.

I decided to kill those remaining three hours down in the Port Iskassaya shopping district, where you'd find the few respectable types who lived out here. I ain't too fond of pickpocketing, but I figured *some* money was better than none.

Naji wasn't too happy about us splitting up again, but I yanked back the collar of my shirt and showed him the charm he'd made me.

"I'll be close by," he said.

I rolled my eyes at that. "You let me go to the docks without any fuss."

"And I could barely move from the headache it gave me."

I looked down at my hands. There were a million ways to respond to that, but I didn't want to say none of 'em.

The shopping district was crowded, which was good, though I really needed women's clothing to make this believable. I was a little too off as a boy. But I pulled some old tricks I learned from one of the crew of Papa's ship, this fellow who'd had a birthmark up the side of his face that made the usual sort of pickpocketing difficult, and after two hours I had a pocket full of coins and another full of jewelry. I scuttled out of the shopping district quick as a beetle and went down to the waterfront, where I found a dealer who didn't ask questions about how a young man-or-woman like myself wound up with a fistful of ladies' baubles.

When I walked away from the dealer, the shadows started squirming and wriggling. The sun was high up, right overhead, so Naji didn't have a lot to work with, just the dark line pressing up against the buildings and a few spindly tree shadows. I ducked into the first alley I could.

"I've never seen a more commendable bout of thievery," Naji said, rising up out of the darkness.

I smiled real big and handed him the pouch of coins from the dealer. He tucked it away in his robe.

"Keep that on you," I said. "Assuming they let us on the ship. But until we know the crew, it's best to not leave money lying around."

"As you wish."

"Also . . ." I took a deep breath, 'cause I knew he wasn't going to like this. "You have to take off your mask."

He got real quiet. "Why?"

"Because we need 'em to trust us enough to let us on their boat. You covering up your face like that, it's a sign of bad intentions."

"I usually have bad intentions."

"Well, you don't now, and even if you did, you'd still have to take off the mask."

Naji didn't say nothing.

"Look, ain't nobody on that boat's gonna care about your face."

Naji's eyes narrowed.

"You never wear it in front of me. It ain't like Leila's around."

I knew I probably shouldn't have said that, but he didn't answer, didn't react at all. For a few minutes we stood there staring at each other, sand and heat drifting through the alley. Then he yanked the mask away and walked out into the sun.

When we arrived at the Free Country boat, the cardplaying crewmen had all cleared out, and the ship rose up tall and grand against the cloudless sky. The sea, pale green in the bright afternoon sunlight, slapped against the docks.

"This is your ward?"

I turned around and there was Marjani with some big barrel of a man in the usual flamboyant captain's hat. He had his eyes plastered on Naji, who scowled and crossed his arms over his chest.

"Yeah," I said. "This is Naji."

"I was expecting a little boy," Marjani said.

"He acts like one sometimes."

Marjani laughed, and Naji turned his scowl to me.

"What business do you have in Port Idai?" the captain asked.

I spoke up before Naji could say anything to screw us. "Meeting with an old crew of mine. We got separated in Lisirra after a job soured. Got fed bad information. You know how it is."

"He part of your crew?" The captain jerked his head at Naji.

"No, sir. Picked him up after my own crew'd left me for dead."

"Bet you're not too happy 'bout that."

"Not one bit."

The captain kept his eyes on mine. "And so why exactly is he accompanying you?"

"He's got some history with my old first mate." Thank Kaol, Naji kept his face blank. "Needs to have words with him, you know what I mean."

The captain laughed. "What kinda history?" he asked, turning to Naji. "It about a woman?"

"It usually is," Naji said.

The captain laughed again, and I knew we had him. Tell any grizzled old cutthroat a sob story about a double-cross and a broken heart and he'll eat right out of your hand.

"Well, if he don't mind sharing a cabin with the rest of the crew, I guess we can spare you."

Naji blanched a little but didn't say nothing.

The captain nodded at me. "You can work the rigging, yeah? That's what Marjani told me."

"And anything else you need me to do. I grew up on a boat like this." And did I ever miss her, the sound of wood creaking in the wind, the spray of the sea across my face as I swung through the rigging—but I didn't say none of that.

The captain grinned, face lighting up like someone had just told him there was a merchant ship sitting dead in the open sea. "Exactly the kind of woman I like to have on board."

I ain't gonna lie, after weeks of following around Naji, not knowing what was going on, it felt good to hear that.

CHAPTER TWELVE

Marjani accompanied me and Naji on board the ship while the rest of the crew was setting up to make sail. She led us down below to the crew's quarters, all slung up with hammocks and jars of rum and some spare, tattered clothes. Naji wrinkled his nose and sat down on a hammock in the corner.

"I know what you are," Marjani said to him.

All the muscles in my body tensed. Naji just stared levelly at her.

"And what is that, exactly?" he asked.

In one quick movement, Marjani grabbed his wrist and pushed the sleeve of his robe up to his elbow. The tattoos curled around his arm.

"Blood-magic," she said. "You're one of the Jadorr'a." I curled my hands into fists, ready to fight. Marjani glanced at me like she wasn't too concerned. "The crew doesn't know," she said. "They wouldn't recognize you. They're all Free Country, and we've got our own monsters to worry about. I only know because I studied Empire politics at university." She dropped Naji's arm.

"You went to university?" I asked. I'd talked to a scholar once, after we'd commandeered the ship he'd been on. He hadn't been nothing like Marjani.

"Are you going to tell them?" Naji asked.

Marjani set her mouth in this hard straight line. I was sure we were about to get kicked off the boat or killed or probably both.

"Why are you here?" she asked. She stuck her hand out at me. "Don't you answer. I want to see him say it."

Naji stared at her.

Don't screw this up, I thought.

"Revenge," he said. "As Ananna told you." His lips curled into this sort of twisted-up sneer. "Even the Jadorr'a fall in love sometimes."

A long pause while we all watched each other and the boat rocked against the sea. And then Marjani laughed.

"That's not what I heard," she said.

"Yes, I can imagine the sorts of things you heard, and I doubt very many of them have much bearing in reality."

Marjani laughed again, and shook her head. "Of all the things I thought I'd see. And no, I'm not going to tell the crew about you." She turned away from Naji, who immediately slumped back against the hammock, pressing his hand against his forehead. When she walked past me, she grabbed my arm and leaned into my ear.

"You should keep a close watch on him," she said in a lowered voice. "Once we get out to sea."

"I'm right here," Naji said. "I can hear everything you're saying."

"Good," Marjani told him. "You can get used to it. These sorts of whispers'll happen a lot more once we've been on the water a few weeks."

"Pirates gossip like old women," I said.

"When they get bored, they stir up trouble," Marjani said. "And you look like you'd be trouble if you got stirred up."

Naji didn't say nothing, but his face got real hard and stony.

"We'll be fine," I told her. "I'll keep 'em off him."

"I'm willing to help, but I can only do so much. I've got my business to attend to."

"You don't gotta do that." I paused. "But I'd—we'd both—appreciate it. Anything you can spare."

"I can take care of myself," Naji said.

"I'm sure you can." Marjani walked to the ladder and stopped there, turning to look at him. "But don't you dare cast blood-magic on this ship. They may not recognize you, but they'll recognize that. Trust me. It'll get you and your friend killed. And probably me for bringing you on board."

Naji glared at her for a second or two, but then he nodded. "Thank you."

"Don't," Marjani said. "Just keep to yourself till we get to Port Idai. That's all the thanks I need."

She gave me a quick, businesslike nod and crawled up on deck.

We set sail that evening, off into the sunset like a damned story. Naji came out on deck and leaned against the railing. I was up in the rigging, yanking at the rope to line up the sails properly when I spotted him down there, his black robes fluttering in the sea breeze. He didn't look happy.

We made it out to the open ocean not long after that, and the water was smooth and calm as glass, bright with the reflections of stars. The captain and the first mate brought out a few bottles of rum and everybody sat around drinking and telling stories and singing old songs. Some of 'em I knew, and some were Confederation standards that'd had the words changed, and some I'd never heard before. Like this story Marjani told, about an ancient tree spirit who fell in love with a princess. He turned her into a bird, so they could be together, but then the princess flew away, 'cause she didn't much love him back, and she flew all the way out across the sea, to an island where there wasn't nothing but birds, and she was happier there than she'd been as a princess. I liked it.

Then one of the crewmen started talking about the Isles of the Sky. He leaned in close to the fire so that his face didn't look human no more, and he told a story about an old captain of his who'd had a friend who got blown off course and winded up in the Isles. That friend had sailed between the different islands, his crew growing gaunter and gaunter until they were nothing but moonlight and old bones. The friend escaped 'cause he made a deal with the Isles themselves, but after he came back to Anjare all his thoughts were wrapped up in the Isles, 'cause the spirits were far trickier than he was.

Naji sat off in the sidelines all this time, shadows crowding dark around him. I got a couple of shots of rum in me after listening to that Isles story, to try and forget that was where we were headed to, and I slunk over to him and sat down. Everything was bright from the rum and the music, though Naji managed to swallow up some of the brightness just by sitting there. I thought of his pitch feather quill.

"You know any stories?" I asked him.

"No."

"Really? None at all?" I wanted to press up against him the way Leila did, but not even rum gave me that much courage. "Don't they tell stories back at the Order?"

Naji's hair blew across his forehead. "You aren't allowed to hear those stories." He pushed at his hair like it was some kind of spider crawling on him in his sleep.

"Why not?"

"Because they're sacred. Darkest night, do I really have to explain this to you?"

That stung me, and I slid away from him, and drew my knees up under my chin. Somebody brought out this old falling-apart violin and took to playing one of the old sea-dances, the one that asks for good fortune on a voyage.

We sat side by side for a few minutes while the crew spun out music and light in the center of the deck.

"Ananna," Naji said. "I have actually dealt with pirates before. With alarming regularity, in fact."

"I know." I said it real soft, and he leaned over to me like he cared what I was saying. "I just want to help you is all."

His eyes got soft and bright. I wanted him to smile.

"That's very kind," he said. "I don't have a lot of experience with kindness, but I . . . I do appreciate it."

I blushed. "And I wish you wouldn't be so sore with me all the time."

He blinked. The music vibrated around us, all shimmery and soft. Nobody was dancing.

"I'm not sore with you," he said.

I guess it shoulda made me feel better, but it didn't. The song ended and another started up. Another sea-dance, and still nobody was dancing. Maybe since they weren't part of the Confederation, they didn't know the steps. Or maybe they just didn't care. It took me a few seconds to recognize the melody without the dancing, and I realized it was the song asking for luck in love. On Papa's ship the crew had interpreted it as a prayer against brothel sickness.

"This ain't right," I said. "Nobody dancing."

Naji glanced at me out of the corner of his eye. His brow was furrowed up like he'd been thinking real hard about something, and I hoped it was me but knew it probably wasn't.

I jumped up and bounded back into the light. It took me a few seconds to remember the steps: a lot of kicks and jumps and twirls, but once I got it down the crew started hooting and hollering and clapping out the rhythm. Then this big burly fellow got up and started following along, and damn if he wasn't lighter on his feet than me. And the next sea-dance started up, asking for victory in battle, and I was laughing and spinning and any darkness Naji might've slipped into me disappeared—at least for a time.

Things fell into a routine quick enough; they always do, once you're out at sea and the novelty of departure wears off. I got all caught up in the routine, though, 'cause it'd been so long since I'd been on the open ocean—the movement of the boat beneath my feet, and the smell of rotted wood and old seawater and sweet rum. You don't realize how much you miss something till it comes back to you, and then you wonder how you went so long without it.

I tried not to think on Naji's curse too much. Didn't want to remind myself of the overwhelming possibility that it really was just impossible and my time on the *Revenge* would be my last time on a ship at all.

Captain put me on rigging duty 'cause I could scamper up the ropes easier than a lot of the men, even though by lady standards I ain't exactly small. By the end of the first week my palms had their calluses back, and I'd gotten to know some of the crew. I liked 'em well enough, even though they teased me and tried to embarrass me with crude stories and the like. Course, I had a few stories up my sleeve that made *them* blush.

One afternoon, when we'd been out on the water for about a week and some days, a couple of the crew told me about Marjani.

"Some big shot noble's daughter down in Jokja," Chari said. He was old and weathered and knew the ropes. "Went to university. Ran off when her father wanted her to marry some second-rate Qilari courtier."

It was noon and we were eating lunch up in the rigging, some hardboiled eggs and goat's milk cheese and honey bread, all the fresh stuff that only lasts a few weeks.

"She don't like people to know," Chari went on. "Afraid they'll hold it against her, or somebody'll find out and send her back."

I didn't say nothing, 'cause I figured it's none of my business what parts of their past people want to leave behind.

"Nah, she just don't want people thinking she's a stuck-up bitch. Too bad it didn't work none," said Ataño, who wasn't much younger than me and always out to prove something. Chari threw a handful of crushed-up eggshells at him and told him to shut up. That set me to laughing, and Ataño gave me a look that might have melted glass had I not gotten used to Naji's constant scowling.

"What about you, sweetheart?" Chari asked. "You got a story?"

I knew he really wanted to hear Naji's story. I wasn't giving it to him, not the fake one and sure as hell not the real one.

"Born under deck and grew up like you'd expect," I said. "Don't need a story to know that."

Chari leaned back thoughtfully while Ataño glowered and picked eggshells out of his hair.

"Ananna!"

It was a woman's voice, and there was only one other woman on board the boat. Marjani.

"What we get for talking about her," Chari muttered.

I leaned over the rigging and waved, wondering what she wanted with me.

"I need to speak with you!" she called out.

Ataño made this kind of grunting noise under his breath. I ignored him and swung down, going through the possibilities in my head: Naji had screwed something up. Marjani was gonna blackmail us. The captain was gonna toss us in the open ocean.

"You said you'd done some navigation before?" she asked soon as my feet landed on the deck.

I stared at her. "A little." It was the truth: Mama'd showed me once or twice, but Papa liked to do most of the navigation himself.

He kept saying he'd teach me once I was older, but then they tried to marry me off.

"Good enough. Come on."

I followed her down below, even though I still wondered why she needed my help.

We passed some crewmen sitting around telling fortunes with the coffee dregs. Marjani kept her head up high, the way Mama used to, and nobody said nothing to her. She had that same don't-mess-with-me expression Mama used to take on, the one I practiced in the mirror when I was younger and sure I'd get a ship of my own someday.

The captain's quarters on the *Ayel's Revenge* were nicer than what I was used to, brocades and silks hanging from the ceiling, with big glass windows that let in streams of sunlight. Flecks of dust drifted in the air, glinting gold. Marjani walked right through them.

"I'm having some trouble with a rough patch on the map," she said, stopping in front of a table. The map showed the whole world, the ocean parts crisscrossed with lines and measurements. Marjani pointed to a little brooch pin stuck in a patch of ocean right where we needed to go. The jewels glittered in the sunlight.

"Sirens," she said. "They move around, but I threw some divinations last night and it looks like they're staying put for the time being."

She looked up at me expectantly.

"Sirens?" I blinked. "You mean this really is just about the navigation?"

She stared at me for a moment before collapsing into laughter. "What, did you think I was dragging you down here to chase rats?" She laughed again.

"I thought you'd told on me and Naji."

Her face turned serious. She shook her head. "I told you I

wouldn't. No, I just . . ." She looked down at the map. "Nobody on this ship knows anything. Well, the captain does, but he spends all his time on deck swapping rum with the crew." She rubbed at her forehead. "I feel like a wife."

"Well, I don't know much, just the bit Papa taught me . . ."

She waved her hand. "I know. All I wanted was someone who'd understand when I tried to talk my way through it."

"Oh." I frowned. "I guess I can do that." In truth I was excited, though I tried not to show her. Knowing navigation gets you one step closer to being a captain.

She smiled at me, and I wondered how I ever thought she was gonna toss me and Naji overboard.

"So," I said. "Sirens."

"Have you ever dealt with them before?"

I shook my head. "Papa would always make a wide berth."

She gave me a weird look then, and I added, "Same with my last captain. Liable to lose your whole crew."

"That's what I was afraid of. But over here's Confederation territory, the *Uloi* and the *Tanisia*," she tapped a spot on the map, "and they've both got a major beef with the captain. And this direction," another tap on the map, "will take us too far out of our way." She looked up at me. "Suggestions?"

"I don't got any." I frowned at the map. "My last captain, he'd probably have gone through the Confederation territory." I didn't mention that's 'cause he was Confederation. "A risk of a fight versus the guarantee of delay or the sirens, you know? But he liked to fight too."

"Not sure about fighting," Marjani said. "We have too much—" She stopped and glanced at me real quick out of the corner of her eye, and I knew she was talking about the cargo.

Marjani messed with the map some, tracing an arc around the

sirens, up close to the northern lands. Something shivered through me—but I doubted Marjani was taking us anywhere close to the Isles of the Sky. She ain't stupid. And as much as I wanted Naji to cure his curse, I wasn't sure I was ready to face the Isles just yet.

So I watched Marjani work, trying to memorize the movements, the way she used her whole arm as she worked, the little scribbles she took down in her logbook. Her handwriting was curved and soft and learned, and it reminded me of the calligraphy I saw in this book of spells Mama used to keep on her. Not plant spells—something else. Alchemy. She never talked about it.

"It's the only way," Marjani muttered. "Up north. Curses! Captain's not going to be pleased." She looked up at me. "It'll take us over two weeks off course. Nearly three."

"We got the food for it?"

"We can make do."

I shrugged. "Well, if you don't wanna fight and you don't wanna lose half your crew to drowning, that's probably the only way." I shivered again, but Marjani didn't seem to notice.

"I might be able to shave it down." She wrote some figures in her logbook, crossing them out, scrawling in new ones. When she turned her attention back to the map, I asked if I could take a look.

"At my notes?"

I felt myself go hot, but I got over my pride enough to nod. "I always wanted . . ." My voice kinda trailed off. Marjani handed the logbook over to me.

"Wanted to learn navigation?"

I nodded.

"It's not terribly hard, once you know the mathematics behind it."

"Most mathematics I ever learned was how to count coins." I wanted to ask her about university, but she was frowning down at the map again. I ran my fingers over the dried ink of the logbook, reading through her scratched-out notes, all those calculations of speed and direction and days lost.

"I might have time to start teaching you," she said, interrupting our silence. Her divider scritch, scritch, scritched across the map. "Especially with this detour."

I looked hard at the logbook.

"I'd like that," I said. "I'd like that a whole lot."

That night, Naji emerged from the crew's quarters and slunk up on deck. The wind was calm and favorable, pushing us north toward the ice-islands, out of the path of the sirens. The captain had issued the orders to change directions that afternoon, and the crew had scrambled to work without so much as a grunt of complaint. I wondered what would've happened if Marjani had issued the order. Or me.

"Something's different," Naji said, sidling up beside me. I was standing next to the railing, looking out at the black ocean. "We aren't going in the same direction."

"You can tell that?"

"Yes." He frowned. "We were going east, now we're going north. Did you manage to convince them to take us—"

I smacked him hard on the arm. "Are you crazy? Don't say that out loud!" Nobody was near us, though. The crew kept clear of Naji, though they sure saw fit to gossip about him whenever he was hidden away belowdeck.

"And no," I said. "We're still headed for Port Idai. But we're having to detour on account of some sirens."

"Sirens?" Naji stared out at the darkness. "I hate the ocean."

That made me sad. Sure, sirens are a pain in the ass, but how could he not see all the beauty that was out there—the starlight leaving stains of brightness in the water, the salt-kissed wind? I wanted to find a way to share it with him, show him there was more in the world than blood and shadow. The ocean was a part of me—couldn't he see that?

Of course he couldn't. He barely saw me half the time, plain and weatherworn and frizzy-haired.

"How far north is the detour taking us?" he asked.

I shrugged. "A couple weeks out of our way."

"That's not what I asked."

I looked over at him. His face was hard and expressionless. "I ain't sure," I said. "Not so far we have to worry about ice in the rigging."

Naji frowned. "Are you wearing that charm I made you?"

Course I was, though my wearing it didn't have nothing to do with protection. Still, I nodded.

"Good," Naji said. "Don't take it off."

I knew there was something he wasn't telling me, probably something about the Mists, and as much as Naji claimed to hate the ocean he sure seemed content to stare all gloomy at the waves.

"It ain't so bad," I said.

"What isn't?"

"Being out here." I glanced at him. "I know something's got you spooked, but I'm safer here. Ain't been in danger once. So there ain't been no hurt for you."

The wind pushed Naji's hair across his face, peeling it away from his scar.

"You haven't been attacked, that's true." He sighed. "But you spend all day scampering among the ropes like a monkey."

"That hurts?" I was almost offended. I've been messing about in ship's rigging since I was four years old. It's about as dangerous as walking.

"Not really," Naji said. "I get a headache sometimes." He looked at me. "But you could fall."

"In fair weather like this? Not a chance." I frowned. The water slapped against the side of the boat, misting sea spray across my face and shoulders. The ocean trying to join in on your conversation, Mama always told me. It's her way of giving advice.

Naji let out a long sigh and wiped at his brow with his sleeve. "I'm going back to the crew's quarters."

"Wait."

He actually stopped.

"Listen," I said. "First off, it ain't healthy for you to stay down below so much. You're gonna get the doldrums faster'n a bout of crabs in a whorehouse. Second . . ." I groped around for the words a bit. "Marjani's gonna teach me navigation, but I don't know none of the math."

"All right," he said. "What does that have to do with me?"

The words hit me like one of Mama's open-hand slaps. "Because," I said, faltering. "You . . . you're educated. I thought you could . . ."

He was staring at me, only his face wasn't stony and angry no more.

"I thought you could help me." I looked down at my feet, my face hot like we were out in the sun. "Marjani's so busy, you know, and I thought—and you spend so much time by yourself."

"Oh." He took a step or two closer to me. He was close enough that I got these little shivers up and down my spine.

"It'd give you something to do," I said.

"Yes." He paused, and I lifted up my head to look at him. He had his eyes on me. They were the same color as the ocean at night. "Mathematics was not my strong suit, I'm afraid."

"You still know more'n me."

"I suppose I do." He took a deep breath. "I would be happy to help you, Ananna."

"Really?"

He nodded.

I hugged him. Just threw my arms around his shoulders without thinking, like he was Chari or Papa or one of the *Tanarau* crew. I realized what I did quick enough, though, when he stuck his hand on my upper back all awkward, like he wasn't sure what to make of me touching him. I pushed away, dropped my arms to my side. "Sorry," I muttered.

"Your enthusiasm for learning gives me hope for the future," he said. "We can start now, if you'd like. You don't seem to be . . . working."

"I'm the daytime crew." I squinted. "I thought you wanted to go down below."

He took his time answering. "Well, the air up here is much more pleasant."

"Yeah, never was clear how you could stand the smell."

He looked like he wanted to laugh, but 'cause he's Naji he didn't.

"We'll need something to write on. And some ink."

"I'll ask Marjani." The whole night seemed brighter now. Naji wasn't glowering no more, and I was about to learn something neither Mama or Papa'd ever saw fit to teach me proper.

Naji nodded at me, and I ran off to the captain's quarters to find some ink and scraps of sail.

CHAPTER THIRTEEN

Marjani taught me the basics of navigation in the evenings, mostly, after mealtime when the bulk of the crew was up on deck drinking rum and watching the sun disappear into the horizon line. It was a lot of measuring and taking notes, and at first she just had me work off the records she took so I could learn how to do the calculations. And Naji gave me practice equations during the day, when there wasn't no sailwork for me to do. He came up on deck and everything, and we sat near the bow of the ship while I worked through them.

The crew ignored us the first few days, just went about their business like we weren't there. Then Ataño picked up on us and took to swinging down when I was working, asking me what I was writing for but staring at Naji while he asked.

"Ain't none of your business," I told him, scribbling with Naji's quill. It didn't work no magic for me. Wouldn't even tell me the answers to the equations.

"I dunno, looks like you're charming something." He dropped to his feet and squinted at Naji. "You know magic, fire face?"

"Ananna's learning mathematics," Naji said.

Ataño howled with laughter, too stupid or too intent on acting the bully to notice that Naji hadn't answered his question. My face turned hot like it had a sunburn, but I kept scribbling 'cause I wanted to learn navigation more than I wanted Ataño to like me.

"The hell?" Ataño asked. "That's even better'n the idea of her writing spells." He laughed again.

"Don't you got deck duty?" I muttered. It was hard to concentrate on the equation with him standing there gaping at me.

"You can't tell me what to do," he said.

"She will once she learns navigation," Naji said, "and you're serving under her colors."

I stopped writing, embarrassed as hell but also a little bit pleased that Naji thought I could be a captain someday.

There was this long pause while Ataño stared at Naji. "She ain't never gonna be my captain."

"Yes, that's probably true," Naji said. "Since I doubt she would require the services of someone as incompetent as you."

I bit my bottom lip to keep from laughing, but then I noticed Ataño staring at Naji with daggers in his eyes. Naji didn't seem to care much, but it occurred to me that we probably shouldn't be stirring up trouble when we were riding on this boat as guests.

Fortunately, the quartermaster stomped up to us and cuffed Ataño on the head before he could say anything more. "Get your ass to work," he said to Ataño, before fixing his glare on me.

"Doing something for Marjani," I said real quick, which was what she'd told me to say if any of the other officers caught me practicing. The quartermaster wrinkled up his brow, but he nodded and sauntered off.

"You shouldn't have said that to Ataño," I told Naji. "You made yourself an enemy just now. You see his eyes?"

"I'm not afraid of children."

I frowned and started working real hard on the next equation so Naji wouldn't see my face. The ink blotted across the sail.

"You're pressing too hard," Naji said.

"I ain't a child," I muttered.

"What?"

"Ataño's the same age as me." I didn't mean to tell him but it came out anyway. "And I ain't a child."

Naji stared at me. I stared back as long as I could but Naji was always gonna win a staring contest. I dropped my gaze back down to the equations. They looked like scribbles, like nonsense.

"You're the same age as him?" he asked.

"Uh, yeah. Seventeen."

This long heavy pause.

"Hmm," Naji said. "I put him at thirteen."

"Oh, shut up. You did not."

"Well, I'd put him at thirteen by his actions. Thirteen or seventeen, it doesn't matter. He can't hurt me." He hesitated. "I won't let him hurt you—"

"Oh please." I tossed the quill and sail scrap down to the deck. "You think I'm scared of Ataño? You really think—"

Then I saw that sparkle in Naji's eye and knew he was laughing at me.

"See?" he said. "Now you know how it feels."

I glared at him for a few seconds. He looked so pleased with himself, but he also looked kind of happy, and that was enough for me to turn my attention back to my equations. I was happy too, about finally learning navigation, and the possibility that I could become an officer on a ship, which was the first step to having my own boat. And there hadn't been any whispers about the Hariri clan, either. I was starting to see my future again.

As long as I didn't think about the Isles of the Sky. As long as I didn't think on how Naji's curse was an impossible one. 'Cause I knew that just 'cause I could see my future again, that didn't mean it was going to happen.

• • •

After a while, Naji started coming with me to my lessons with Marjani. He didn't ask—of course he didn't ask—but he did show up at the captain's quarters one evening after dinner looking sheepish. Marjani had me perched over the maps with a divider, tracking a course from Lisirra to Arkuz, the capital city of Jokja, where she told me she had been born. She'd asked me my birthplace but I just said Lisirra, 'cause the stormy black-sand island where I'd been born wasn't even on the map. And then Naji was banging on the door, asking to come in.

"I hope you don't mind if I join you," he said. "But I find the crew . . ." He hesitated. Marjani looked like she wanted to laugh.

"A pain in the ass?" I offered.

"Tiresome," Naji said. He tugged at his hair, kind of pulling it over his scar, and I frowned, wondering what the crew had said to him.

"I have to go with Ananna on this one," Marjani said. "But you can sit in here if you want."

Naji settled down in this gilded chair in the corner and watched me and Marjani work without saying nothing. It took me a while to chart the course from Lisirra to Arkuz—I was using some calculations Marjani had given me, from an old logbook. I felt like I'd taken way too long to get it done, but when I finished Marjani looked sorta impressed.

"Nice work," she said. "You're a quick learner." She smiled. "You would've done well at university."

That made me real happy, 'cause nobody had ever said nothing like that to me before.

"Yes," Naji said. "She would have."

Marjani glanced at him. "Where did you attend?"

"In Lisirra. The Temple School."

"Oh." She flipped through the logbook and handed it back to me. "Lisirra to Qilar," she told me. "Go."

I sighed like I was annoyed, but really I thought the drills were fun. Marjani turned to Naji. "The Lisirra Temple School," she said. "That's a school of sorcery, isn't it?"

Naji nodded and said, "I didn't study ack'mora there, if that's what you're asking."

"I'll admit I was curious." Marjani smiled. "I've no ability for sorcery, myself. I studied mathematics and history. At the university in Arkuz."

"I've been there. It's lovely."

"The city or the university?"

"Both."

It was like they were speaking a whole other language. Universities and history and sorcery. I wondered what I would've studied if I'd got to go to university. Piracy's probably not an option.

"I've been to Arkuz," I said. "We sailed up the river into the jungle to trade with some folks there."

"Really?" said Marjani. "I always hated the jungle. You never know when it's going to rain." She leaned over the map. "Oh, good work," she said.

"I've got it?" I'd been so wrapped in listening in on Marjani and Naji's conversation that my hands must've kept on working while my brain lagged behind.

"You've got it," Marjani said.

After that, Naji came to my lessons about every day, I guess 'cause he and Marjani had bonded over both going to university. He didn't have a lot to offer in the way of navigation, but he and Marjani would tell me about other stuff they'd learned, like all these weird stories about the different emperors over the years, or how to calculate the volume of an empty container without having to fill it with water first. It was fun.

Then Marjani got me to start helping her with the true

navigation, the navigation that was taking us around the sirens and three weeks out of our way and, as far as me and Naji were concerned, delaying the trip to the Isles of the Sky. One morning she called me down from the rigging and handed me her logbook and a quill and the sextant.

"I need measurements," she said. "You know how it works. Get going."

The crew stared at me while I stood there fiddling with the sextant. Marjani trotted off to speak with the captain up at the helm, and I felt real conspicuous with everybody's eyes on me. But then I lifted up the sextant and peered through it up at the sky and the whole boat fell away.

I stopped doing as much work in the rigging after that, since Marjani had me taking measurements for her every day. Seems that charting a new course on the water's a bit risky, as you're creating a new path in addition to the usual work of checking where you are in the water. But we stayed on course, still moving up toward the north and to the east, and Marjani said it was partially 'cause I helped her. I didn't necessarily believe that, mind, though I suppose I had no reason not to.

One afternoon I crawled up on deck to make the usual round of measurements and noticed immediately that something was off. There were a lot of voices shouting and yelling, but it wasn't about rigging or wind or none of the usual complaints. At first I thought we must be under attack, that some tracker from the Mists—or worse, the Hariris—had followed me and Naji all the way to sea. Immediately my heart started pounding and I went for the knife at my hip. Which I still hadn't replaced. Stupid. I needed to ask Naji for his knife or nick it off him while he slept.

But then I realized I didn't hear the clank of sword against sword, or the pop of a pistol. And nobody'd sent out the call to arms, neither. It was just yelling. And jeering.

And my heart started pounding all over again.

I raced across the deck to where Ataño and a couple of his cronies were crowded around the railing. Naji was there too, staring at them stone-faced. Ataño said something I couldn't make out, on account of the wind blowing in off the waves and beating through the sails, but he pushed up the skin of the left side of his face until it snarled the way Naji's face did sometimes and his cronies laughed like it was the funniest thing they'd seen in a year.

Me, I felt like someone had punched me in the stomach.

"Fuck off!" I screamed. All three of 'em turned toward me and I took off running. Half the crew was up in the rigging or clustered over on the other side of the ship, not participating but not doing nothing to stop it neither.

And then Ataño was flat on his back, Naji crouched on his chest with his sword at Ataño's throat.

I stopped dead in my tracks.

Naji made this hissing sound through his teeth and pressed his sword up under Ataño's chin. A trickle of blood dripped onto the deck, glistening in the sunlight. Ataño whimpered, his eyes clenched shut.

"Look at me," Naji said in a voice like an ice storm.

Ataño opened his eyes.

"This is the last time you will ever look at my face. If you see me coming, look the other way. Because if you look at me again, or speak to me again, I'll make sure your face comes out worse than mine."

Nobody on deck was moving. Even the wind had stopped. In the silence, all you could hear was Ataño's pitiful little moans.

"Do you understand?"

"Y—Yes," Ataño said.

Naji pulled his sword away. Ataño scrambled backward, his

head twisted over to the side, looking everywhere but at Naji. His cronies stumbled after him.

Naji wiped the blade of his sword on his robe.

And like that, the spell broke. A couple of the bigger crewman bounded across the deck and grabbed Naji by the arms, pulling him into a lock, though I could see that Naji didn't have no intention of fighting back.

I could see that if Naji had wanted to fight back, both of those crewman would've been dead.

And anybody else he wanted too.

When he'd attacked Ataño, he'd covered close to five feet so fast I hadn't seen him move. He hadn't even moved that fast during the fight in the Lisirran pleasure district—this time, I hadn't seen him go for his sword, or even noticed the twitch in the arm that meant he was thinking about it. One second he'd been standing there like a victim, the next he could've slit Ataño's throat before anybody knew what was happening.

The two crewmen dragged Naji down to the brig, and all I could think about was that night in the desert, and how he hadn't done what he just did to Ataño—to me.

The brig smelled like rotten fish and piss and the air was thick with mold. Saltwater dripped off the ceiling and down my back as I made my way over the dank floor. I had Naji's desert mask tucked into the pocket of my coat.

He was curled up in the corner of his cell, sitting with his chin on his knees. His eyes flicked over to me when I came in but he didn't say nothing.

I stared at him for a minute, his hair all tangled up from the sea wind, the lanterns illuminating the lines of his scar. Looking at it I got this phantom pain in the left side of my face.

"They take your knife off you?" I asked him.

He shook his head.

"Can I see it? I'll give it back."

Naji stared at me.

"C'mon, I ain't gonna do nothing bad."

He reached into his cloak and then there was a *thwap* and the knife wedged into the wood of the ship a few inches from my head. I was real proud of myself 'cause I didn't even blink, though I did see him go for it this time—something told me it was 'cause he wanted it that way. I yanked the knife out of the wall and walked up to the lock on the bars. Shoved the knife into the keyhole and wiggled it around like Papa'd taught me. When the lock clicked I snapped it open and stepped into the cell with Naji.

"I brought your desert mask," I said, pulling it out of my pocket and dangling it in front of me. Naji didn't move. I started thinking this might've been a bad idea.

But then he took the mask away from me and straightened it out on his knees.

"You sure it won't look suspicious?" he asked, his voice full up with sarcasm, and I looked down at my feet, shamed.

"I'm sorry." My voice kinda cracked. "I didn't think—on Papa's ship they would never—"

"Forget it." Naji pulled the mask across his face, hiding his scar. "Of course you're correct, the young men on your father's ship never once jeered at a disfigurement. Upstanding citizens the whole of them, I'm sure."

I didn't know what to say. My face got real hot, and Naji kept glaring at me.

"You have no idea what it's like," he said. "To look like me. To be what I am on top of that—people think I'm a monster."

"I don't." But I said it so soft I'm not sure he heard me.

I wanted to get out of the brig. I wanted to run up on deck till I found Ataño so I could pummel the shit out of him. Instead, I sat down next to Naji, the floor's cold damp seeping up through the seat of my trousers. He didn't talk to me or look at me, and the air was heavy with his anger and I tried to think of a way to fix it. I couldn't come up with nothing.

After a while, Naji said, "I'm sorry."

The sound of his voice made me jump.

"I'm sorry I was cold with you," he said. "I don't think it was your fault."

"Oh. That's good." I chewed on my lower lip and looked at the pool of scummy seawater that had collected over near the bars. "I tried to stop it—"

"I know you did."

We sat for a few moments longer.

"Can I ask you a question?" I said.

"Depends on the question."

"It's not about—"

"Just ask it, Ananna."

I took a deep breath.

"You could've killed Ataño and been down below before anybody saw you. I ain't never seen a man move as fast as you."

Naji didn't say nothing.

"I get why you didn't kill him, that's not my question. But . . ." I forced myself to look over at him. "Why didn't you do that to me? Before I started up the curse and everything? In the desert? You could've laid me out faster'n a jungle cat. I know there was a protection spell but it must've worn off by then, 'cause you did cut me and all . . ."

My voice kinda trailed off. Naji stared straight ahead.

"It's true," he said. "There wasn't a protection spell on you in the desert."

"Then why . . . ?"

Naji took his time answering.

"Because," he said. "I didn't want to kill you."

I stared at him. My heart was pounding all fast and funny, and I felt like I'd forgotten how to speak.

"Ananna! Get the hell out of there before the captain comes down and sees you."

Marjani. I jerked up in surprise, banging my head against the back wall. Naji glanced at me but didn't ask me if I was all right or nothing. His voice kept echoing around in my head: *I didn't want to kill you.* I'd no idea what to make of that.

Marjani pushed the cell door open and stood there expectantly. She didn't say nothing about Naji's mask. I handed him back his knife, and once I'd stepped out she slammed the bars shut. The clang of metal against metal rang in my ears.

"Crew's saying you move like a ghost," she told him, leaning up against the bars.

Naji didn't reply.

"Fortunately, the captain doesn't believe in ghosts."

"He ought to," Naji said.

"Is he gonna toss Naji overboard?" I asked.

"The captain?" Marjani looked at me. "No."

Over in the corner, Naji didn't even stir.

"Ataño's a worthless little shit," Marjani said. "But it seems he's done more work in the past three hours than he's done in the past three days, so—the quartermaster's happy." She smiled. "Captain's letting you out tomorrow morning."

"Wonderful," Naji said, though he didn't sound like he meant it. "Curses and darkness, I want off this ship."

"Well, it's four weeks till Qilar. You've got a while. Whispers are gonna be worse. You need to remember that you're here on the captain's good graces. You're lucky he's not a superstitious man."

Naji lifted his head a little. "No, I'm lucky he has a navigator clever enough to dispel any residual belief in ghosts and ghouls."

Marjani didn't say nothing, but I could tell from the way she tightened her mouth that he was right.

CHAPTER FOURTEEN

Whatever magic Marjani worked on the captain held fast; he released Naji at sunup the next day. I filched a knife off the cook when he wasn't looking and made sure I was down in the brig when it happened, tucked away out of notice in a back corner. Ataño wasn't nowhere to be seen.

The captain had a couple of crewmen standing by with a pair of pistols each, all four barrels pointed at Naji's forehead.

"I see any hint of magic," the captain said as he unlocked the cell. "Any hint of weirdness, I'm tossing you out to sea."

He didn't say nothing about tossing me off the boat along with Naji, but then, I can't kill a man in less than a second.

"I understand," Naji said. He'd kept his mask on but his words came out clear and even.

The captain nodded like this was good enough and pulled the cell door open wider. The crewmen kept their pistols trained on Naji as he strolled up to the ladder. Naji glanced at me when he walked past but didn't say nothing. The captain stopped, though.

"What're you doing down here?" he asked.

"Checking up on my friend."

The captain chuckled. "Ain't gonna hurt him, little girl. Not unless he pulls a knife on me."

"He won't." I shifted my weight from foot to foot. "'Sides, and with all due respect, sir, I was more worried about Ataño striking out revenge."

The captain roared at that. Even his cannon-men kind of looked at each other and laughed. I frowned at them.

"Ataño ain't gonna cause no more trouble," the captain said. "Can't believe I put a man in the brig for scaring some discipline into that boy." He laughed again and all three of them climbed up out of the brig.

Things got back to normal after that. I kept on working for Marjani, taking down measurements and tracking our course toward Qilar. Naji went back to spending all his time in the crew's quarters, scribbling over the sail scraps left over from my mathematics lessons. I went down there once or twice to keep him company, but he didn't much talk to me, just muttered over his work.

"What're you writing?" I frowned. "It ain't magic, is it?"

"Don't be ridiculous. When I said I wanted off this ship I didn't mean I wanted to be thrown into the open sea." Naji handed me one of the sail scraps. It was a story—an old desertlands story about a little boy who gets lost in the desert and has to strike a deal with the scorpions to make it back home.

"Why're you writing this?"

"I need something to do." Naji leaned back in his hammock.

"Nobody writes down stories."

"They do when they're trapped at sea and bored senseless." Naji hunched over his sail scrap and wrote a little swirl of something. "I hear from Marjani you're plotting part of our course each day."

"Getting us to Port Idai as fast as possible." Not that I liked the idea of leaving the *Revenge*. Any boat crazy enough to take us to the Isles wasn't one I'd want to work on.

Naji stopped writing and looked up at me, all dark hair and dark mask and the little golden strip between them. "I appreciate that." He looked down at his sail scrap. "Although I can't say I'm much looking forward to our second journey north."

"Me neither."

Naji picked up his quill and began writing again.

"You think it'll work?" I asked him.

"Will what work?"

"Do you think we'll find a cure?"

Naji's hand twitched, but he kept writing, and he didn't look at me. "I don't know."

That was not the answer I wanted to hear. I left him to his stories and stomped back up to deck, where Marjani was waiting for me with the logbook and a quill, and things fell back into their routine, ocean and wind and salt and sails.

It felt like the beginning of the end.

A week later, the weather turned.

I was helping with the rigging, 'cause the wind had been strong all afternoon, blowing in from the south, hot and dry and tasting like dust and spice. It had everybody in a mood, especially the more superstitious fellows in the lot, and so there were a lot of charms getting tossed around, and certain words getting uttered. And everybody was drinking up the rum, superstitious or not. I'll admit that my hands kept going to my throat that day, rubbing at Naji's charm.

The wind picked up, and it howled through the sails, flattening 'em out and then billowing 'em up. Water sprayed out from the sea, huge glittering drops of it. Not a cloud in the sky, though, the sun hot and bright overhead.

Crewmen were crawling all over the rigging, and Marjani was up at the helm, throwing her whole body into keeping the ship steady. A big green wave splashed over the railing and slammed into me, and I fell across the deck, hitting up against old Chari's worn-out boot. He hardly offered me a glance as he pulled at the rigging, shouting curses and prayers alike. I scrambled to my feet and grabbed hold of the rope to help him out. The whole thing felt like a typhoon if not for the sun and the weird spice scent on the wind. Maybe it was that noble from the Mists, drawing the worlds together like Naji had said . . .

For a half second, I caught a whiff of medicine, sharp and mean, like spider mint, and I shot back to Lisirra, to the entrance of the night market. The rope slipped out of my hands.

"The hell's your head, girl!" shouted Chari. "Hold on tight if you don't want to get knocked overboard."

The smell of Naji's magic disappeared. *He can't*, I thought, scrambling to pick up the rope. *It has to be the Mists. He can't be doing this. It'd put me in danger—*

And then another wave crashed over the side, and I managed to hold on, and all thoughts of Naji's magic washed away with it. I had a ship to keep afloat.

By then somebody was ringing the warning bell, the *clang clang clang* that meant an attack or a storm or just plain ol' trouble. Seawater showered over us like rain, the salt stinging my eyes and the sores on my hands. Chari turned around and grabbed my wrist and shoved me over to the foremast. "Get up there!" he shouted, jabbing his hand toward the rigging. Water streamed over my face, blurring my vision, but then I saw it: The storm sail had come loose.

"Shit!" I scrambled up the rope, slipping and crawling, my clothes plastered to my skin. The wind threatened to knock me off the rope but I dug my nails into the fibers, clinging with every bit of my strength. The sail flapped back and forth, snapping like a whip, though at least it was dry up here, away from the fury of the waves. I reached out and made a grab for it. Missed. Righted myself. Took a deep breath. Watched the sail and waited for it to snap back toward me. This time I caught the edge and yanked on it one-handed even though the wind had other ideas. My arms shook. My eyes watered. I screamed, trying to gather up the will to do this without dying.

And then I had it. That split second between wind gusts and I had it. I tied the sail back into place, looping the rope with aching fingers.

The boat jerked, tilted, and I fell, grabbing at one of the riggings before I crashed down on deck. I cried out but the wind swallowed my voice right up and no one down below even noticed me.

I kicked out my feet, swinging up like a monkey. The wind kept on howling. I started crawling back down, my arms hating every second of it. Every part of my body ached.

And then I heard this low creaking groan, and I knew they were shifting the boat so we could run with the wind to safety. Under normal circumstances it ain't nothing I can't handle but with the wind and the hurt in my body it was too much. The movement knocked me loose. I managed to hang on with one hand, swinging out over the deck. What with the seawater and the sunlight, everything down there was covered in rainbows.

Then I lost my grip, and I fell.

I woke up and all I knew was the hurt. Pain vibrated through my body, all the way out to the tips of my fingers and toes. My head throbbed. But I was laid out on something soft, a pile of rope and old sails, and I guess that was why my brains hadn't spilt out all over the deck of the *Ayel's Revenge*.

She was moving, at least, soft and smooth, and there wasn't any wind or water splashing over the railing. No voices, neither, only the purring ocean, the occasional snap as the sails rippled overhead. I pushed myself up on my elbows, and when that wasn't the bone-breaking trauma I expected, I forced myself to sit up halfway, my back aching, my head lolling.

The air was cold.

That bothered me. Ain't no reason for us to be anywhere near coldness, not at this time of year, and not where we were sailing. Don't care how bad that storm knocked us off course.

Not a storm, I thought, remembering the sunlight, the scent of spider mint, but I shoved the thought out of my head.

I took another few moments to pull myself up to standing, and then took even longer to recover from it, standing in place and swaying a little. Then I shuffled forward, limping from a twinging pain in my left thigh. We were someplace else. I knew that soon as I came out from the under the shadow of the rigging. The sky was the color of a sword's blade, and the water lapping up at the sides of the boat was dark gray, nearly black, and everything smelled like metal and salt. We were north, up close to the ice-islands, maybe. I'd only been there a few times in my life but I remembered the smell of the air, that overwhelming scent of cold.

A handful of crewmen were bunched up at the port bow of the ship, all huddled together, not talking. Chari was there, and Marjani, her arms wrapped tight around her chest. I limped toward them.

"Hey!" My voice came out strangled, raspy. Nobody turned around. "Hey, what's going—?"

I stopped. We were in sight of land. Way far off in the distance was a line of green, that vivid dark-almost-black green you only get in the north.

And below the line of green was a line of black beach and below that, a strip of gray. The sky. A gap between the island and the sea.

And like that, all the pain in my body got replaced with the icy grip of dread, and I remembered how I'd smelled medicine back during the storm, before I—

Marjani glanced over at me, her eyes widening. "Ananna!" she said. "Oh, Aje, I thought you'd been thrown overboard! I—" She stopped, covered her mouth with her hand. "You look like hell."

I tried to choke out some kind of nicety, something about falling into the rope, something, anything to make her think I had nothing to do with us being within swimming distance of those horrible islands.

Instead, I turned away from her and hobbled over to the ladder that'd take me down below.

"Ananna? What're you . . . Stop, it's flooded—"

"Stay there," I said, 'cause what else could I do? She didn't listen, of course, and came chasing after me, grabbing hold of my arm. Pain shot up through my elbow.

"Let me go! I need to . ." Do what? I didn't want to put it into words.

"Need to what?"

"Naji." It was all I could bring myself to choke out. I jerked away from her and half slid, half climbed down the ladder. Down below the floor was covered in a half foot of dirty water, rum bottles floating by like they might hold some kind of message for me, and scraps of clothing and pieces of dried fish. I splashed through the water, the chill setting my whole body to shaking. Marjani had stopped at the ladder.

"Ananna, come back!" she said. "It's too cold. You'll get hypothermia . . ."

I didn't have the faintest idea what that was, and I didn't care, neither. I pushed my way into the crew's quarters.

The first thing that hit me was that horrible medicine smell, stronger than anything that ever soaked its way into the air of the crew's quarters before. My eyes watered and my throat burned and my skin prickled from all the leftover magic. The ship walls down here were all blood-red, transformed by magic.

And there was Naji, slumped across a hammock, blood trailing down his arms, his skin white as death. Bits of sail floated in the water around him like flower petals, leaving streaks of red in their wake.

He lifted his head when I came in, just enough that I knew he wasn't dead.

I splashed forward and picked up one of the scraps of cloth. His writing was all over it, the ink a brownish-red color, not black like Marjani's ink. It wasn't a story. I stared at it for a long time, not making any sense of those symbols, knowing full well it was a spell. I balled the cloth up in my fist and dropped it at my side. Naji moaned, dropped his head back. My anger swelled up inside me like a wave.

"You son of a whore," I said. "You filthy, mutinous, lying sack of shit—"

Naji tried to say something, but his words came out all slurred, and for a second I wondered how bad it had hurt him when I fell out of the rigging, if his body shattered like it was made out of glass. I hoped so. And then my anger was this flash of white light, hot and searing, and I waded up to him, pulled my arm back, and punched him square in the face.

"Ananna! What are you doing?"

Marjani crashed into the room. I hit Naji again, open-handed this time, and he tried to squirm away from me, shoving his hands between us to block me. I grabbed his wrist, dried blood flaking off on my fingers, and yanked him up off the hammock and punched him again. He slammed up against the wall. And then Marjani had her arms around my waist.

"Stop it," she said. "Stop." She pulled me away from him, dragging me through the water. I strained against her, arms flailing, but it wasn't no use.

"Calm down," she said, over and over. "Ananna, this isn't the time. Calm do—"

She froze in place, staring at the walls, and I wriggled out of her arms and turned to look at her. Over on his hammock, Naji moaned my name.

"Shut up," I told him. My heart pounded up against my ribs and it didn't have nothing to do with the fight.

"The air," Marjani said. "It's all wrong . . ." Then she picked up one of the sail scraps and stared at it good and hard. I stood there with my chest heaving, waiting for her to get angry, as angry as I was. But she only seemed sad.

She looked up at Naji. "You shouldn't have done this."

"You don't understand," Naji said. "The curse—"

"Shut up!" I screamed at him. "You're going to get us killed." I turned to Marjani. "We were always headed for Port Idai, like I said. I never thought he'd do something like this."

"Neither did I," Marjani said. She splashed over to me. "I know about the curse," she said, her voice soft. "He told me."

"What?" I said.

"I tried . . ." Naji gasped. "Tried to save—"

"Get him," she said, jerking her head at Naji. "And come up on deck. And for Aje's sake, play along."

"You knew?" I said. "How long?"

She didn't answer, just made her way out of the crew's quarters, the water splashing up around her knees. I turned to Naji. He'd sat up some, and there was a bruise forming around his eye from where I hit him.

"You heard the lady," I said.

"We are . . . The islands? We're . . . here?"

"Shut up."

I grabbed him by his arm and jerked him up to standing. He

slouched against me. Fine. I threw his arm around my shoulder, and together we waded through the ship's belly. I wasn't screwing around with this. We'd been caught, flat-out. Having Marjani on our side helped, but it wasn't just Marjani who'd caught us, it was everyone. The crew. The captain. If we were lucky we'd be thrown in the brig for the rest of the trip. I didn't think we'd be lucky.

It took us a while to get up on deck, 'cause I pretty much had to push Naji up the ladder. He pulled himself up through the hatchway, Kaol knows how, and then he slumped against the deck, wheezing and grasping for breath. The captain and Marjani were waiting for us, standing side by side with the rest of the crew fanned out behind 'em.

"This true, Ananna?" the captain asked me. Marjani had this right mean look on her face. Play along.

Naji coughed and pushed himself up on his hands. His hair pressed in thick clumps against his face.

"I did it," he said. "Don't blame her."

The captain looked like he wanted to whip out his sword and take care of the problem the old-fashioned way, but instead he just spat at Naji and turned to me.

"Wasn't asking him," he said.

I closed my eyes. All I could feel was my heartbeat, the blood rushing through my body.

"Well?" he said.

"Yeah, it's true." I forced myself to meet his eye. Any of that kindness I'd seen before had disappeared. "I didn't know he was gonna do it, though, or I'd have stop—"

The captain held up one hand, and I shut my mouth. I was shaking from the cold and from fear, wondering what he was going to do to us.

"Blood-magic," the captain said, spitting the words out. "Can't believe you'd bring something like that on board. I trusted you, little girl."

I flushed with shame, but I didn't hang my head. Kaol, was I proud of that.

"Believed that whole damn story you told . . ." The captain shook his head.

"I'm sorry," I said, looking at the captain, looking at Marjani. She frowned, little lines appearing around her eyes.

"Throw 'em overboard," the captain said.

Marjani whipped her head toward him. "Captain, I don't think . . . In this water, that will kill them."

"Good," he said cheerfully.

I about started to cry. I've cried out of desperation twice in my life and both of those times were nothing compared to the mess I was in right now, about to get cast out in the icy northern sea 'cause of a blood-magic assassin with no manner of patience.

Marjani gave me this look of full-up desperation, quick as a flash, and I knew whatever plan she'd made just fell through. I'd never felt so small and vulnerable and doomed.

And then Chari spoke up.

"Sir," he said, stepping forward out of the crowd. "I agree we shouldn't keep this pair of hijacking mutineers on board, but I did see the girl during the, ah, storm and she about near died trying to save this ship."

The captain stared at him. Chari held his gaze. He was the kind of old that commands respect.

"So what do you suggest?" the captain said.

"Give 'em a boat," Chari said. The crew didn't like that, and they all hissed and booed behind him. "Or a piece of plank board, captain. Enough to get 'em to the island."

I wanted to kiss the old son of a bitch, I really did.

"They'll be good as dead there anyway," Chari said. "It's what you'd do if we were down in the south."

Something flickered though my head. Ain't got nothing to lose.

"Confederation rules," I said. "Mutineers are always stranded. Not killed."

Everybody stopped talking and turned to me.

"We ain't part of the Confederation," the captain said.

"I am," I said. I pushed out my chest and took a deep breath. "My full name is Ananna of the *Tanarau*. My father is the captain of that same ship." Then I lifted up the hem of my shirt to show him my Confederation tattoo.

The captain's face got real dark.

"You drew that on," he said. "You're faking me."

"You want to risk it?" I said. I nudged Naji with my foot. "You have any idea what he's capable of this close to death? That's blood-magic's nexus, Captain, death. This close to the other side, he could send a message to my father so quick you'd be dead in a week."

The crew fell silent, so I figured I must have convinced most of 'em at least half way. The captain didn't look too doubtful himself, either.

"I don't want no business with the Confederation," he said. "I could kill you right now and not worry about a thing."

And then Naji started chanting.

It gave me pause, ain't gonna lie. I thought maybe he was working some kind of darkness over there, maybe calling down demons to swoop in and save us. But when I glanced at him his eyes were dark as night, not glowing at all. And I realized he was faking for me.

"You hear that!" I shouted, getting into it. "Speaking straight to my father, he is. You can't kill me now. Neither one of us."

The captain's eyes went wide with fear. Marjani's didn't. She glanced back and forth between me and Naji but didn't say nothing. But the chanting got the crew into a tizzy, and they all backed up against the railing.

"Make him stop," the captain said.

"Can't," I said. "He don't listen to me. If that were the case, we'd still be on our way to Port Idai."

The captain took a few steps back from Naji. "Fine," he said. "You want me to treat you like some Confederation mutineer—Marjani, get them a boat."

"And a pistol," I added. I didn't want to push my luck but those were the Isles of the Sky.

"And a damn pistol." He spat on the deck.

Marjani dipped her head and disappeared over to the starboard side.

Naji stopped chanting and slumped over. The captain took a deep breath and looked relieved.

Then he jerked his head back to the crew and called up a couple of the rougher fellows to drag me and Naji over to the side of the ship, where Marjani was waiting with a rowboat and a pistol and a thinly-hewn rope net that she probably meant to serve as a blanket. The crewmen shoved Naji and me into the boat. One of 'em looked like he wanted to spit on me, but he glanced at Naji and nothing happened.

"Leave," Marjani said to 'em.

They didn't.

"Do what I tell you," she said, pulling out a thin little knife I didn't even realize she carried.

And what do you know, both of the crewmen took off.

She held the knife up to my throat and leaned in close. I could tell she didn't aim to use it, but still. Nobody likes having a knife at their throat.

"Listen," she said, talking real close to my ear, hissing like she was threatening me. "He said something the other day about somebody following him."

"What—"

"He tried to get me to change course. He wouldn't tell me details, but just—be careful." Her face got kind of soft and understanding. "Stay on that island," she said. "And for Aje's sake, stay alive. Keep warm and keep dry. There are ways off every island."

And before I could respond, she turned away from me and cut the ropes holding the rowboat aloft. We crashed down into the black sea. The *Ayel's Revenge* rose up in front of us like a leviathan, and I had no choice but to grab hold of the oars and row us away.

CHAPTER FIFTEEN

The island really did float. Once we'd cleared the *Revenge*, once my arms got so sore I could barely move 'em, I drew the oars back into the boat and drifted along the choppy water, shivering from the cold, from my injuries, from the distracting knot of fear coiling in my stomach. Up ahead the island hovered above the sea, chunks of smooth black stone tapering into points beneath the gray beaches and the trees. In the distance, you could just make out the other islands through the haze drifting off the water.

"Hey." I shook Naji's shoulder. He was curled up on the net and didn't move. "E'mko and his twelve dancing seahorses, you better not be dead."

He stirred, moaning a little. His breath blew out in a white cloud.

"That spell of yours have any way for us to get on land?"

That must have gotten his attention. He sat up, pushed his hair back away from his face. "We're here," he said.

"Of course we're here," I said. "We just got kicked off the *Ayel's Revenge* for it." I frowned at him.

His expression glazed over as he stared at the island. The sight of the damn thing made me dizzy, so I stared at Naji even though I wanted to throttle him.

"Vaguely. I vaguely remember . . ." He dug his hand into his good eye. "I can't seem to keep my thoughts straight."

"Oh fantastic." Figures I'd get stuck with a blood-magician who'd driven himself insane.

Or maybe it was the island, working its magic like in the stories. Changing him, making him forget himself and who he was. I studied the angles of his face, looking for some sign that his bones were pushing out of his skin. He looked gaunter than usual, but maybe it was because of the spell. I hoped it was because of the spell.

"It's cold," he said, and his voice sounded small, like a kid's.

"Not a whole lot I can do about it." We drifted along, the water pushing us toward the island, like it was a normal island and there was a tide to pull us ashore. Part of me wanted to look back, catch a glimpse of the *Revenge* as she sailed away. But I didn't. Water slapped up along the side of the rowboat, spraying us with a cold fine mist. Naji moaned and rubbed his head, and I was still dizzy myself.

The rowboat jerked up, her bow clearing the water in an arc of gray water drops, and then slammed back down.

"What the hell was that?" I shouted. I yanked the oars in even though it didn't do much more than make me feel more vulnerable, the two of us sitting there in the open ocean like that. Naji slumped down, his eyes wide, and mumbled something about being weak.

"Shut up," I said. I didn't hear nothing unusual: just the howl of the wind, the rush of the waves.

The boat jolted again, knocking me forward into Naji's lap. I bit down on my tongue to keep from screaming.

"Ananna," he said.

"We need to get on land." At least on land any enemies couldn't lurk beneath the depths. "Is it safe to row?"

"Don't . . . I don't really know."

"Kaol!" I shoved the oars into the water and pushed us toward the island. We weren't far, almost to the line of shadow the island cast onto the water. I tried to lift the oars up but the left one wouldn't move. I shrieked and let go, and it slid into the ocean without a sound.

I yanked the other oar into my lap and sat very still, heart racing. We floated underneath the island. Dark as night down there, although the ocean water gleamed silver. The boat bumped up against a hunk of low-hanging stone. It was too smooth to be any use for climbing, and besides which, it would only take me to the underside of the island. I didn't have time to try to make some kind of rope throw.

The boat tilted again. Naji gripped the sides and his eyes gleamed like the water.

I had an idea.

"How weak are you? Can you do anything?"

"What?"

"Your shadow thing," I said. "Can you take me with you?"

He didn't answer.

"Naji?"

"Under normal circumstances, I could."

"Naji! There's something in the water!"

Naji didn't answer, and I glared at him in the dark.

"Maybe somebody shouldn't have used up all their energy blowing a brigantine off course. But you wouldn't know nothing about that, would you?"

"It wasn't just the magic," he said darkly.

"Yeah, you put me in a spot of trouble with that wind. Damn near killed me."

"It nearly killed me as well."

"Well, I imagine we're both going to die if we don't get on land." My whole body was tense, waiting for the boat to rock again, but the water stayed as smooth and still as a mirror. "Do your thing."

"My thing?"

"Damn it, Naji! The shadow thing. We're in shadow now. There's shadows up there—have to be, all them trees. So do whatever it is you do to get both of us out of this boat and on that bloody island."

Silence. I sucked in a deep breath. I could barely make out his outline in the silvery shadow of the island.

"This might hurt me," he said.

"I don't care."

He didn't say nothing. I shoved the pistol into the waistband of my pants. Nothing happened.

"Well?" I said.

"You have to touch me," he said. "Well, not just . . . We need to . . . Come here."

And then he reached out his arm and drew me into him. His touch surprised me, and suddenly I wasn't cold anymore.

"We need to be close," he said. "As close as possible."

I slid across the boat, pressing up against his body. He didn't have his armor on and I could feel him, the muscles in his chest and his arms. He smelled like magic and sweat and the sea, but there was something else beneath all that, something sweet and warm, like honey, and just for a moment I didn't feel afraid anymore.

I was furious at him, and I was terrified, but I didn't want him to stop touching me.

Then the shadows started moving around us, slinking like cats. I stiffened, thinking that it was the island and her magic, but Naji tightened his arms against my back and said, "It's fine." I let out a slow, careful breath. Something prickled against my skin, cold and damp. It soaked through the fabric of my clothes. It pressed my hair against my scalp.

And then I couldn't see nothing at all, just blackness. And there was this roaring in my head that scared the shit out of me. But at least I could still feel Naji even though I couldn't see him. I could still smell him, that scent like honey.

And then I smelled soil and pine and rotting wood. We were on the island. It was like I'd opened my eyes and here we were, curled up together beneath a tree taller than any ship I'd ever seen, the sand of the beach not ten feet away.

Naji's arms loosened and he fell with a *thump* against the soil and the fallen pine needles.

This might hurt me. His words echoed around inside my head and I thought maybe he said hurt when he meant kill and I rolled him over onto his back and pressed my fingers against his neck until I felt his pulse fluttering beneath his skin. I lay my head on his chest and listened to his heart beating.

"You're all right," I said, just in case he might've heard me.

A breeze blew in off the sea, biting and cold. I remembered what Marjani told me: stay warm and stay dry. We weren't doing too good on neither count.

And I hoped those woods didn't hold the same kind of monsters as the water.

I pushed that thought out of my head so I could concentrate on not freezing to death. I left Naji lying beneath the tree and picked my way down to the beach. The sand was rough and dark, coarse like Orati salt, and littered with bone-gray twists of driftwood. I gathered some of the driftwood, trying not to think about how it got there, and stacked it in the sand. Then I sprinkled some powder from the pistol onto the wood and fired off the one shot I'd been allowed, wincing as it rang out through the trees, echoing and echoing. Streaks of white erupted from the trees and I slammed down on the sand, fumbling around for my knife—but they were only birds, and they flew off and disappeared into the gray clouds.

Thank Kaol, the shot took. The powder sparked and smoldered and burned. I watched the fire for a while, sitting close enough that the heat soaked into my skin. The light of it made me feel safe.

I walked back over to Naji. He was still passed out. I took off his boots and his cloak and lay them out by the fire to dry. Then I gathered up my strength and wrapped my arms around his chest and dragged him over the pine needles and the sand to the fire. He squirmed a little, twisting his head this way and that. I brought him as close to the heat as I could. He moaned and fluttered his eyes and kind of looked up at me and then at the fire.

He said something, but I couldn't understand it. I sat down beside him and took off my own boots so they'd dry out. I stuck my feet close to the flames. I warmed up pretty quickly, all things considered.

Just once in all that work, I let myself look out at the horizon, to see if I could spot the *Revenge* one last time before she left us. And I did. It wasn't nothing but a few specks of sails against the gray sky, but Kaol, did it ever fill me with despair.

I was dozing on the sand, drowsy from the heat of the fire, when Naji shook me awake hours later. I rolled over and looked at him.

"You're alive," he said.

"Course I'm alive," I snapped. "You're the one who keeps passing out."

"I feel better now."

He didn't look better. Still death-white and haggard. One bruise blossomed out on the unscarred part of his face and another ringed around his eye. Kaol, I got him good.

When he reached up to shove his filthy, clumped-up hair out of his face, his hands shook.

"We need to find fresh water," I said, really meaning I would have to do it, 'cause in his state he didn't need to be traipsing through the woods. "I hope it won't turn us into monsters." I squinted up at the soft gray sky. "Do you think it's gonna snow?"

I'd seen snow once when we sailed to the ice-islands, and I

knew that it was cold as death and not anything we'd want to mess with in our present state.

"It shouldn't," he said, and I didn't know if he was talking about the snow or the water's magic, and I didn't ask.

I sat up best I could—my body was stiffer than it'd been before, like I'd just gone eight rounds with a kraken. "I don't know about you but I ain't too keen on dying." I grabbed my boots and patted the leather. All dry, but also stiff and shrunken. I kneaded at it while I talked. "One of the first things I learned. You get stranded, look for water. Then find a place to protect yourself." I jutted my head at the fire. "I made an exception on account of you getting us stranded in the forsaken north. Figured water wasn't no good if we both froze to death."

Naji closed his eyes and let his head loll between his knees.

"Though I'm also a bit concerned with whatever the hell's following us."

That jerked him back up to full alert.

"It's the Mists, ain't it?"

"The Hariri clan would not have followed us this far without attacking."

I sighed and started kneading at the other boot.

"Ananna, your detour took us through a part of the world where the barriers are thinnest. They'd picked up on my trail while we were out at sea. I was trying to save the ship." He leaned forward. "You must be careful. This place is part of the Otherworld that found its way to our own . . ."

His voice trailed off as though speaking had worn him out. I stared at him with my mouth hanging open.

"Are you kidding me!" I shouted. "You couldn't have told me that earlier?"

"We need to find the Wizard Eirnin."

"Don't ignore me."

"You have no idea . . . I'm utterly incapacitated by this curse . . . If the Otherworld finds me, if they find you—"

"I'll hand you right over! You don't think this curse is hurting me too? Kaol! I should have let you die in the desert."

Naji's face turned dark as a typhoon sky, and I immediately regretted shooting off like that. I didn't really want him to die, curse or no. So I pulled on my other boot and stood up. I hated stepping away from the fire, but it'd gotten big enough that its warmth spread all up and down the beach. I did not want to go into those woods, though, all dark and misty and shivering.

"Stay here," I said. "I'm going to find a stream or a pond or . . . or some dew. Something for us to drink." I glared at him. "You probably need it more than me, and I've fallen out of sail rigging once today."

I stalked away from him before he could say anything, up to the treeline. When I figured I was far enough away I chanced a glance back at the fire, and there he was, yanking on his boots to follow me. Fantastic.

Still, I waited for him.

He leaned against a tree to steady himself.

"You ain't going to make it," I said.

"I'm fine." He wobbled a little in place. "And I'll be worse if you go off on your own. We shouldn't . . . We shouldn't stay too long—"

"Naji, we're stranded here!"

I took off deeper into the green shadows. The air was damp and cold and wrapped around me like an old wet shawl. Everywhere I stepped I made noise, branches snapping, pine needles crackling. But so did Naji, and he was usually as graceful as a Saelini dancer and twice as silent.

We walked for twenty minutes when I heard pattering up in

the tops of the trees, distant and soft. I cursed. All rain would get us was wet—we didn't have nothing to collect it in.

"We gotta head back," I said. "I don't want to lose our fi—"

I stopped. Naji was leaning up against a pine tree, his skin waxy like he had a fever.

"Kaol's starfish," I said. "You look like you're dying."

He moaned a little and rubbed at his forehead. "I'm not sure I can go on. I was hoping the spell would lead me to Eirnin, but . . ." His voice trailed away.

I glared at him, not wanting to think about his spell, the whole reason we were gonna die on a magic floating slab of rock in the first place.

"I used the last of my magic to bring us on land," he said mournfully. "It's run out."

"Good," I snapped. "If only it'd run out when we were on board the *Revenge*." Then I turned and stalked away from him, blood pounding in my ears.

"Ananna! Wait!" I heard the snap of branches that meant he was following. "You don't understand."

"I understand plenty. You stranded us here without any kind of protection." I whirled around to face him. He looked shrunken and old. "That's what you're going to tell me, isn't it? You can't do your protection spells?"

He didn't have to say anything to answer.

"At least you were able to get us on land before the ocean sucked us down." I dug the heels of my palm into my eyes. I was exhausted, and in truth, all I wanted was to lay out by the fire and sleep. But I knew I couldn't. "Give me your sword," I said, "and go back to the fire."

He tried to stare me down, but he was too weak. So he just handed me his sword, nodded, and turned away.

I picked my way through the woods. The rain misted across my hair and the tops of my shoulders and set me to shivering, and the forest pressed up against me, impossibly tall trees and thick green cover and ropy vines. I kept the sword out, although I wasn't sure if a sword could stop whatever creatures the island had hidden.

Every now and then I stopped and listened for the bubbling of a river. But there were just forest sounds, leaves rustling and water dropping off the tree branches and critters scurrying around in the underbrush, and beyond that, a distant chiming sound like some weird far-off music. I didn't trust it. Didn't trust the normalcy of it. That's when magic's the most dangerous: when it feels like the untouched world.

The woods grew darker from the rain, and mist started rising up from the forest floor, gray and cold and wet. I tightened my grip on the sword, trying my best to ignore the panic rioting around my chest. I got a flash of pirate's intuition: I wasn't safe in the forest.

I should go back to the beach.

My left hand peeled itself away from the sword and found Naji's charm still looped around my neck. I thought about him leaning up against the tree, rubbing his forehead, pale from exertion. He was probably in pain now, all on account of me. I wondered if it was keeping him from healing.

But if we didn't have water, we'd die of dehydration within a couple of days. And even magic-tainted water was better than that.

So I kept walking.

After a while, the forest brightened a little, not from the sun peeking out behind the rain clouds but because the trees were different, tall and skinny and pale, with white crystalline leaves that clinked against one another in the wind. This must have been the chiming I heard earlier—this bright, strange forest. I tensed and hoisted up the sword. Nothing about this forest was natural, and yet after a few moments that sense of danger had passed. The forest chimed and sparkled around me, and I was just too exhausted to stay alert.

That was when I heard the faintest murmur of water. It was hard to make out over the chiming, but I listened closely and wandered about, trying to find its source. I don't know how long it took me, but I finally stumbled over a spring bubbling up underneath a big normal-looking pine tree, the water clear and clean-looking. I plunged my hands in and scooped it up to drink without thinking. Water was splashing down my chest when I remembered that I was on the Isles of the Sky, that this water could destroy me.

I fell back and stared at the spring, waiting for something to happen, for something to change. Nothing did that I could feel. And although I still didn't trust this normalcy, I allowed myself a bit more of that sweet-tasting water, and I prayed to Kaol and E'mko to keep me safe from the spirits.

The rain stopped, and I sat beside the spring, listening to the chiming from the trees, half waiting for the mist to form again, to come creeping along the forest floor. But nothing happened. And after a while I started thinking on Naji, thinking on his curse. He cast a spell so strong it wiped out his magic, and we didn't even know if we could cure his curse. Hell, we didn't know if the Wizard Eirnin was even on this rock.

Maybe he'd die out there on the beach and I'd be free of the curse just long enough to get swallowed by the Isles of the Sky.

Maybe I shouldn't have left him alone after all.

So I ripped some strips of fabric off my trousers—they were soaked through with rainwater anyway—and knotted them in the tree branches as I made my way back to the beach.

The fire had burned out, just like I said it would, and the driftwood lay blackened and ashy along the horizon line. Naji was crouched beside the remains, his head hanging in his hands, hair stringy from the rain. He stirred as I walked up to him, but he didn't say nothing, didn't even look up.

"I found a spring," I said.

No answer. I sat down beside him and balanced the sword on my knees and stared at the remains of the fire, trying my best to ignore the dampness in the air.

"A spring," Naji said after a while, muttering down at his feet.

"Yeah. You know. For drinking. I had some and it didn't do nothing to me, so hopefully . . ." I couldn't finish that thought. We sat in silence for a few moments more.

"I'm sorry I said I was glad your magic ran out."

Naji lifted his head but he still didn't look at me. I could hear the waves crashing beneath us.

"It happens," he said, "when I exert myself."

"I know."

Another moment of silence.

"I hope to be recovered enough within the next few days to cast a tracking spell on the Wizard Eirnin, but I don't . . ." He dipped his head again. "I've never run out like this. And with the curse—I just don't know."

I toyed with the hem of my shirt and looked down at the sand. My head felt thick with what he had just told me. Maybe he didn't have to die for us to get sucked into the island's magic.

"Maybe we can find the wizard the untouched way." Not that I liked the idea of wandering the island.

"I doubt we'll be able to find him just by searching."

"Ain't that big of an island."

Naji glanced at me out of the corner of his eye, and even with just that tiny look I caught a glimpse of the weariness and the hurt I'd caused him as I had traipsed alone through the woods. "The size of the island isn't the issue," he said. "I doubt very seriously the Wizard Eirnin will be easily found. Most wizards aren't. Not unless you know where to look."

I didn't have no answer to that.

"I might be able to conjure up a fire tomorrow," he said. "A small one."

"Maybe you should focus on getting better first."

"Perhaps you should show me the spring. You are correct that we'll need water to survive." He sighed. "We can look for food and shelter tomorrow."

"I can look for it to—"

"No." The word sliced through the air, left me colder than any rain ever could. "No. Once was enough."

I didn't need to ask him what he meant.

"I'm sorry," I said softly.

Naji pushed himself to his feet, and I noticed that he was shaking. If it was because of the cold or because of the way he wore himself out or because he was as scared as me, I couldn't say. But I didn't say nothing about him not being able to make it. I didn't say nothing about the spell he cast on board the *Ayel's Revenge*.

We walked side by side as I led him through the woods.

CHAPTER SIXTEEN

That night I made a little tent out of fern fronds and fallen sticks not far from the spring, and I fell asleep to the gurgle of water and the glow of Naji's tattoos as he started healing himself. It was weird sleeping so close to him again, after everything that had happened, and at first I lay on my back and looked up at the pattern of shadows created by the ferns, my hands folded over my stomach so I wouldn't accidentally touch him.

I woke up the next morning covered in ferns and rainwater. The tent had collapsed in the night, probably 'cause of some storm, and Naji was curled up on his side, his tattoos dull and flat against his skin. I pushed the ferns away and peeled off my soaked-through coat and shivered in the cool, damp air. The spring bubbled and churned a few feet away. Naji didn't move.

I shook his shoulder. He moaned and fluttered his eyes.

"Naji?" I asked. "Are you all right?"

He rolled onto his back, shedding a cascade of fern fronds and raindrops.

"Ananna?" he asked. "Where are we?"

"Kaol! You really don't know?" Anger rose up in me and turned to panic. I pressed my hand to his forehead. His skin was hot. "I think you have a fever."

He closed his eyes. I lay my ear against his chest to listen for the rattle of the northern sickness, but his breathing was steady and even.

"Need to rest," he murmured.

"Naji!" I shook him again. He stirred but didn't respond. At least his chest was rising and falling, and his tattoos had taken to glowing again. I stood up and paced back and forth in front of the spring. If he was sick, he needed warmth and shelter. And I didn't much like the idea of us staying in the woods, neither.

So I stole his sword and took off for the beach. The chiming forest was rioting in the pale morning, the trees throwing off glints of light, everything sounding like temple bells after a wedding. I picked my way through those narrow trunks, leaves drifting through the air. They stuck to my skin, and when I tried to wipe them away they shattered and smeared like the spun-sugar figures in a fancy Lisirran bakery.

Still, I made it to the shoreline easy enough. The sand dropped off toward the sea, which churned below the island, frothy and roiling with the wind. I rubbed at my arms to try and take out some of the chill; it didn't work, and so I put my coat back on even though it was still wet. I didn't know which direction to go, which direction would lead me to shelter. All the damn trees looked the same, and the clouds covered up the sun.

I shouldn't have left him at the spring.

But if I'd stayed behind, what could I have done then? Watch him burn up with a fever? Watch him sink into the soil and become part of the Isles?

No. I had to do something.

I trekked along the sand, gathering up the largest pieces of driftwood I could find and stacking them together close to the treeline. The beach felt safer; it was out in the open, which meant it was easier to spot any creatures that might come our way. But I wasn't sure if the tides came in here, and I didn't much want to risk it.

Once I had the driftwood gathered I ventured into the fringe of the woods. I didn't want to bother with fern leaves again, but there really wasn't much I could use in the way of shelter-building. I pulled the sword out of its scabbard and crept deeper into the forest. Here, the light turned a syrupy golden color I didn't trust one bit. Ain't no way the northern sun could give out light like that. But there was a certain type of tree in this part of the woods, one that I hadn't seen before, with trunks covered in a chalky pale white bark that peeled off in long wide strips. I didn't trust it, but sometimes you gotta trust the thing you don't want to.

Course, following that particular bit of Papa's advice was what got me in my current predicament in the first place. I guess it came down to a matter of choices. And I didn't have much of any at the moment.

I stacked the driftwood up into a lean-to against one of the pine trees—those at least I recognized from the ice-islands. Then I wove the tree bark into a sort of roof, which I tied to the driftwood using some twists of old vine.

When I finished, I took a step back and admired my work. I almost forgot where I was. I almost convinced myself I was just on the ice-islands, having the sort of adventure I used to dream about.

But then a wind blew in from the forest, and it smelled like musty damp and magic. I had the sword out before my brain could even figure out if I was in danger or not.

The beach stayed as empty and desolate as always.

I crawled into the lean-to and peered out the opening and through the cracks in the branches I'd left in so we could keep look out. I figured there should be enough room for me and Naji to both stretch out and sleep, and it was high enough that when I was sitting down I could reach up and my fingers would just barely graze the underside of the tree bark ceiling.

Since I'd managed to take care of our shelter problem for the time being, I figured I should look into food. The truth was I didn't trust nothing on this island enough to eat it. Even if the water had turned out fine.

But my stomach was grumbling and I figured Naji was gonna need food if there was any hope of him getting better. So as I picked my way through the forest, back to the spring, I watched for any edible plant that I might recognize from the ice-islands. I didn't find nothing.

When I came to the spring, the ferns were scattered across the ground, and Naji was gone.

All thoughts of food flew out of my head. I had my sword out, my body tense and alert, and I stalked around the spring, stepping as careful as I could.

"Ananna?"

I froze, and then turned around slow and careful. Naji was leaning up against a tree, holding his shirt up like a basket.

"You left," he said. "And you took my sword."

I let the sword drop. "I thought you were dying. And we needed shelter. Real shelter, not leaves." I kicked at the ferns.

"I'm not dying. But the healing is taking a long time." He stumbled forward and I noticed his hands were shaking.

"Should you be wandering around the woods, then?"

"Probably not. But I was hungry." He knelt down in the remains of our tent and flattened out his shirt. A handful of dark red berries and little brown nuts spilled across the ground.

"I know these are safe to eat," he said. "They grow in the ice-islands too."

I scowled, irritated that he'd been able to find something when I couldn't.

"Have some," he said. "I can show you where to collect more."

I picked up one of the berries and sniffed: It smelled sweet as rainwater. I was too hungry to be cautious. I tossed it into my mouth.

Best berry I'd ever tasted. After that first one didn't kill me, I took to shoving the rest of the pile into my mouth. It wasn't enough to satisfy me, but it took the pang away. When I finished, Naji was staring at me.

"I'm glad I ate some on the way back."

"Sorry."

His eyes brightened a little, and seeing it made me feel weirdly happy even though I was surrounded by gloom and magic.

"I made a lean-to," I said.

"Ah, so that's where you disappeared off to."

"I guess it didn't hurt you too bad."

Naji shrugged. "It wasn't as bad as yesterday, no."

"Well, I figured we needed shelter. And fire, too, although I don't know if I'll be able to start one in all this damp." I stood up and rubbed at my arms, trying to work out the chill. "Do you want me to show you? I don't . . . I don't much like staying in the woods."

Naji tilted his head a little and looked at me like he wanted to say something. But he only nodded.

It was slow going back to the beach. Naji stumbled over the underbrush and kept getting caught up in the woody vines that draped off the trees. Although he let me carry the sword, I was on edge the whole time, waiting for something to come creeping out of the shadows. It didn't help that every now and then I'd hear these weird chiming animal calls off in the distance, and the wind had a quality to it that sounded like a woman's whisper. At one point, Naji slumped against a tree, his forehead beaded with sweat. I only just caught him before he collapsed.

"Not safe," he whispered. His face twisted up and he pressed his hand into his forehead. "Not safe. For you."

"What's not safe? The woods?"

He cried out in pain and groped around my shoulders. His fingers were clammy and cold. I peeled the collar of my shirt away. The charm he made me was still there.

"Thank the darkness," he whispered, and he slumped up against me, as if all the air had been let out of him. "I'm sorry I can't protect you better."

The forest was rustling around us, dropping down feathery green leaves, and my breath was coming out fast and short. I knew we couldn't stay here—knew I couldn't stay here. But I wasn't leaving Naji behind.

"Here," I said, shoving the sword at him. "To protect me with."

His fingers fluttered around the handle. He straightened up a little, and his face no longer seemed so drawn and haggard. Stupid curse. It ain't like I don't know how to use a sword.

"Let's run," I said. "To keep me safe."

He stared at me like he didn't understand. But then he said, "Yes, I think that might work."

So we ran.

I ran faster than him, flying over the ferns and fallen tree trunks, but he kept up better than I might have expected, and I guess the running really did count as a way of keeping me safe. We burst out of the forest and the sea wind didn't carry the same cold whispers as the forest wind. I collapsed on the sand, panting, my stomach cramping up from the berries I'd eaten.

Naji knelt down beside me and took a long, deep breath. "Thank you," he said. "I couldn't think straight."

"Yeah, you looked pretty rough." I sat up and twisted around so I was facing the forest. I didn't like having it out of my sight. "You want to see the lean-to?"

I stood up and helped him to his feet, 'cause he was shaking and trembling like an old man. The lean-to wasn't far; I could see it crouched next to the treeline like an ugly gray toad.

"Ain't much, I know," I said. "But hopefully it's sturdier in a rainstorm. I bet it can last us till we find the wizard." I tried to sound sure, 'cause I figured it wasn't too fair to burden Naji right now. But inside I was afraid we'd never find the wizard at all.

I helped Naji crawl into the lean-to. He stretched out on his back and closed his eyes. I hardly had a chance to ask him how he was doing before his chest started rising and falling in the rhythm of sleep.

I took the sword off him and crawled back out onto the beach. I didn't want go too far—I certainly didn't want to go into the woods. We did need a fire, though. Papa had shown me how to start fires back when I was a little girl, since Mama couldn't start 'em with magic on account of her being a water witch. I figured it was safe to burn the wood since nothing had happened with the first fire, plus I'd already built a lean-to out of it, and I'd drunk the island's water and ate its berries without any trouble. And I was shivering so hard too. This time it wasn't just 'cause of the fear.

I wandered down the beach looking for driftwood I hadn't already gathered up for the lean-to. When I got my courage up, I'd dart into the woods and pluck some dead, fallen branches off the ground. Never went in more than a few feet, though. Never went into the dappled shadows.

Stones were easier to come across. They were scattered across the beach in big piles, like someone had come through and set them that way as a message to the gods or to the spirits of the Isles. Part of me hoped it was the Wizard Eirnin, that maybe I'd stumble across him and we wouldn't have to wait for Naji to heal himself. But I never saw anybody. No animals, no birds, no wizards.

The lean-to was glowing when I came back, intense pale blue, a color that made me feel colder just looking at it. I checked in on Naji and the light from his tattoos seemed to overpower his whole body.

Maybe he'd heal quicker than he thought.

I piled up the wood and sat in the sand and struck stone against stone until a spark caught. You're supposed to feed the fire dead dry grass, which is easier to find in the south, so I made do with twigs from the dead tree branches. Luck was on my side. I had the fire going just as the sun, what little of it I could see, was dropping down to the horizon. In what I was pretty sure was the east.

I tried not to dwell on it.

The fire grew and grew as the island fell dark. Naji kept on sleeping, the blue from his tattoos mingling with the orange firelight. I never crawled into the lean-to myself, 'cause I didn't want to leave the heat and light of the fire and so I fell asleep out there in the open.

The next morning, I rolled over onto my back, sand crunching beneath my weight. It was still dark, although whether that was 'cause of the time or 'cause of the rainclouds I couldn't stay. At least the fire was still burning, casting light up and down the beach—

Except it wasn't.

I sat straight up and screamed. The fire was nothing but a pile of dark ashes. The light was coming from me.

I screamed again and pushed myself up to standing and stumbled down to the edge of the island. Streaks of light radiated out behind me, and I froze in place, terrified. The sea crashed and churned beneath my feet. I took a deep breath and held up one of my hands and squinted at it, and I could see bright lines moving beneath my skin, those veins and arteries where my blood should be.

"No," I whispered, because I knew that all those stories about the Isles were true, that I really was turning into moonlight. "No, no." I took stumbling, shambling steps, trying to work through my panic. We couldn't build a boat and live out on the water, and we couldn't stay on land, neither.

Tears squeezed out of the corners of my eyes, blurring my skin's light and turning it into golden dots that scattered across the beach. I stumbled over the sand. The wind picked up, smelling of brine and fish—

"Get away from the edge!"

Hands grabbed me by the arm and dragged me backward, away from the churn of the ocean. I flailed and screamed. It was only Naji, but he was glowing too. Not just his tattoos. All of him.

"We're turning into moonlight!" I screamed.

"No, we're not. You almost ran off the side of the island. Come."

His voice was stronger, the voice I remembered from that night in the desert. He led me back to the lean-to and sat me down next to the fire remains.

"What's going on?" I wailed.

Naji blinked at me. It was unnerving to see him with his bright skin and his dark eyes, the opposite of how his magic worked.

"We're fine," he said. "Do I look like I'm in pain to you? There's no danger. At least as long as you stay away from the edge of the island."

"But the stories—"

Naji reached over pulled the charm out from under my shirt. "It's keeping you safe," he said. "As far as you're concerned, this is just . . . an effect. A courtier's trick." His glow brightened for a few seconds.

"Are you sure?"

"Yes." Naji pushed a piece of my hair out of my eyes. The movement was distracted and careless, but the minute he did it he dropped his hand into his lap and looked away. I felt myself growing hot and I realized that my own glow had brightened and turned a rich syrupy color. "I imagine it was caused by drinking from the spring. In a few days' time I should have enough strength to cast a spell to keep it from happening entirely."

I sighed as my panic mostly disappeared.

"Think of it this way," Naji said. "We won't need to worry about lanterns when we walk down to the spring."

"What! The spring! You said that's what's doing this to us!"

"It's also giving us water. Which we need if we aren't to die. Which I need if I'm ever to be well enough to track Eirnin."

"You seem well enough now," I muttered.

"I'm not." He stood up and held out his hand.

We trudged through the woods, our glow throwing off weird, long shadows that seemed to wriggle and squirm between the trees. Naji had the sword, but I had to stop myself from reaching over and grabbing it from him. I always feel safer with a sword in hand.

The spring was waiting for us, looking as normal as ever. Naji knelt beside it and took to drinking, but I hung back. His glow shimmered across the surface of the water.

"Ananna," he said, "I swear to you that it's safe."

I was thirsty. And I knew I couldn't go without water. What would be the use of coming all this way, just to die of thirst?

"Fine," I said, and I sat beside him and drank my fill.

Nothing happened on the walk back—no whispers on the wind, no flare-ups of Naji's curse. He led me off the path we'd flattened out on our trips to and from the spring to pick some nuts and berries, and I was so hungry I ate 'em without waiting till we were on the beach. This time, they seemed enough to fill my belly. The sun pushed out from behind the clouds and washed out enough of the glow that I almost got to thinking everything was normal.

"We shouldn't stay," Naji said.

"Are you hurting?"

"No. I just don't want to linger."

Stepping out on the beach eased my tension up some, the way it always did. Out in the open, my glow had almost entirely disappeared in the pale northern sunlight.

"The lean-to," Naji said.

"What about it?"

"It's gone."

I stopped in place and squinted down the beach. He was right. All I saw was trees and shadows and sand.

The fear slammed back into my heart.

"Someone knows we're here," I said. "The wizard? He's trying to scare us off?" My voice pitched higher and higher. "He ain't gonna help you after all? We got stranded here for no reason?"

"I don't think that's it." Naji pulled away from me and marched to the place where our lean-to had been. And that's when I saw it: the smear of ashes from our fire. The lean-to had been replaced by an enormous bone-gray tree, twisting up toward the sky.

"Curse this island," Naji said.

I couldn't speak. The best I managed was little gasping noises in the back of my throat.

"It's the magic," Naji said.

"I know it's the magic!" I shouted. "This island ain't nothing but damn magic!" Desperation welled up inside of me. He wasn't never gonna get better and the wizard wasn't never gonna cure his curse and we were gonna die here just 'cause of some glimmer of hope Leila had nestled inside him. "What if we'd been inside?"

Naji turned toward me. Even though the glow was mostly washed out by the sun, his eyes seemed much darker than normal. "We should be grateful that we were not."

I turned away from him and walked over to the fire ashes.

Kicked at 'em with my boot. The tree that had been our lean-to rustled its branches at me and showered down a rain of gray, twisting leaves. Everything about the island was gray. The sky, the sand, the shadows, our home.

I was becoming more and more convinced that the rest of my life would be nothing but gray.

We spent the next few days sleeping in fern tents that I built out on the beach. A storm rolled in one afternoon and soaked through all the wood and our tent, but Naji had gotten enough of his magic back that he was able to build a little fire afterward. It must have exhausted him, though, 'cause he stretched out on the sand afterward and slept, the glow of his skin and the glow of his tattoos fighting it out in the dark.

We always moved our location, and we always used different ferns for the tents. We took different paths to the spring. Naji said that would keep the island from changing too much, though he didn't explain how. At least that was back to normal.

Things fell into a routine. I didn't get used to 'em, but they were at least a routine.

Then one morning I woke up and Naji was gone. The familiar sick panic set in. I was on my feet immediately, tearing the tent apart, screaming Naji's name. A million possibilities raced through my head. Maybe he'd turned into moonlight after all, and I was next. Maybe he'd turned into a fern and I was ripping him into shreds in my fear.

I dropped the fern and I stepped back, almost stepping into the fire. The beach was silent save for the wind and my racing, terrified heartbeat.

"Naji?" I said one last time. All my hope was lost. That wasn't much of a surprise, though, 'cause I really didn't have much of it left.

"Ananna? Are you all right?"

Naji popped up in the shadow of a tree.

"You!" I shouted. "What's wrong with you?"

He blinked at me.

"I thought you got turned into a fern."

"Oh. Oh, Ananna, I'm sorry, I didn't think—"

"You go on and on about how I can't be left alone and then you just leave me here?"

Naji walked up to me. He moved with his old grace, slinking across the beach instead of shuffling. I'd hardly noticed that particular quality was coming back along with the magic.

"I was restless," he said. "I'm sorry. You weren't in danger."

I suppose that was something, but my heart was still beating too fast.

"I have something to show you."

"What could you possibly have to show me? Did your sword turn into a courtier's dress?" I narrowed my eyes at him. "Or did you find the wizard? Did you—"

"No. I'm not that well yet. But I think you'll appreciate it nonetheless."

He turned and headed off down the sand. I followed him because I didn't much want to be left alone again. After fifteen minutes we came across an old falling-apart little shack, set back into the woods, still within sight of the beach.

I didn't trust it at all. "Does somebody live here?" Though I had to admit it looked long-abandoned, the stones in the walls cracked and warped, the thatched roof dotted with holes.

"Look at it, Ananna. But the answer's no, no one lives here. I cast a history spell. A small one, but enough to tell."

I stepped up to the shack's door and nudged it with my foot. Inside, the stone floor was coated with sand and old ashes and the thin, glassy sheen of sea salt. There was a tiny hearth in the back, where Naji had started a fire, and a pile of stone jars and a rotted bed in the corner.

The warmth spread over me, welcoming as an embrace, but I just looked on it with suspicion.

"It's some island trick," I said, turning toward Naji. "It'll be like the lean-to. We'll go fetch water and come back to find it turned into a big pile of stones." I thought about the stones on the beach and shivered.

"It's not. I cast a history spell, remember?" Naji leaned up against the doorway. "It's been here for almost seventy-five years. And the first spell cast on it was one of protection."

"And it's still working?"

"It was very strong magic. Very old magic."

I glowered at him. He stepped inside and the fire flickered against his rotting clothes. "Would I do anything to put you in danger?"

He'd done plenty to put me in danger. He'd dragged me across the desert in the white hot heat. He'd gotten me stranded on the Isles of the Sky. But I'd let him. I'd done it all 'cause I wanted to break the curse as much as he did.

I shrugged and didn't look him in the eye.

"You should sit by the fire. It's a work of magic in and of itself that you haven't gotten sick yet."

"I'm fine."

"Let's not risk it."

I had to admit, the firelight looked awfully inviting. And Naji looked healthy, not in any pain at all. I took one step cautiously through the doorway, and then strode across the shack to the hearth. The heat soaked into my skin, and I sat down, drawing my knees up to my chin. Naji sat down beside me.

"Why'd you do this?" I asked.

"Do what?"

"Find a shack."

"Because we need it," he said. "I don't know how long it will be until I'm fully healed, and it isn't helping that we have to sleep out in the cold every night."

I didn't say nothing, just leaned closer to the fire. Naji got up and paced around the room liked a caged jungle cat.

"I hope the wizard can break your curse," I said, speaking into the fire.

Naji stopped pacing. I looked over at him, and he stared back at me from across the room, the firelight flickering across his scars. But he didn't say a word, not about the curse, and not about anything else, neither.

CHAPTER SEVENTEEN

The shack looked halfway destroyed, but I was grateful for it when a storm blew through later that week, cold driving rain and dark misting winds. There was a hole about the size of my fist up in the roof, and water sluiced across the far wall, opposite the hearth, but me and Naji huddled up next to the fire and stayed dry. Naji kept rubbing his head, though, and I think it might've had something to do with the whispering on the wind. This time I could make out what it was saying: a voice speaking a language I didn't understand.

The next morning, the sun broke through the clouds, sending down pale beams of light that dotted across the beach. It was hard to imagine the storm from the night before and harder still to remember the voice, which seemed more like a dream as the day wore on. I thatched the roof with fern fronds and pine needles, and Naji swept out the inside with a broom I made for him from pine boughs. When we finished, we sat down to eat berries and some pale creamy tuber Naji dug out of the ground. Neither were very satisfying.

"I might be able to catch some fish," Naji said after we'd finished. "I think that may be the reason I'm not healing as quickly as I expected. I don't have enough strength just eating berries."

"We'll need a line. I guess I could make one out of that net Marjani gave us—"

"That won't be necessary." He paused, and the wind blustered in off the beach and knocked the pine trees around. "The island casts enough of a shadow over the sea that I can move through the water that way. I've done it before, in the Qilari swamps."

"How long you been well enough to do that?" I didn't have my usual strength, neither, although I'd thought it was 'cause of the island, or that I was spending energy on glowing.

"A few days."

"What! Then why haven't you done it already?"

"I don't like leaving you alone."

"You've done it before."

He frowned out at the ocean line. "Things were different."

I thought about the whispers on the wind.

"I got my charm," I said.

"I know you do."

"If you don't get us some fish we'll probably both starve to death and then it won't matter if the Mists show up. That's what you're worried about, isn't it? The Mists?"

He didn't answer.

"Hell and sea salt! Naji, you promised me that you'd start telling me things."

"I'm telling you now." He unfolded himself and the wind pushed his hair away from his face. It was cloudy and a bit of his glow peeked through his skin, his scar shining a pale soft white. "While I'm gone, you must promise to stay in the shack."

"Fine. I just hope it won't turn into a tree."

"It won't." Naji frowned, and then glanced over his shoulder at the woods. "Come."

"Into the woods? Why?"

"I need to gather up something." He plodded over to the treeline and then ran his fingers over the greenery spilling onto the sand. He plucked three narrow, shiny fern leaves, twisted them together, and muttered in his language. His glow dimmed for a few seconds, and then he handed me the bundle of ferns.

"Hang this above the door," he said.

I turned the ferns over and over in my hand. They were much heavier than three twisted-up leaves should be.

"Go on," he said. "*You* have to do it."

"What's this to protect me from?" I asked as we made our way back over to the shack. "The Mists or the Isles?"

"They're the same thing," he said.

A chill went down my spine.

I jammed the ferns into a crack above the door, and Naji slipped off his sword and scabbard and handed it to me.

"Stay inside," he said.

"Go," I said. "I'm starving."

He nodded, stepped into the shack's shadow, and disappeared.

He was gone for longer than I expected, not that I knew how long it took to sneak up on fish and catch 'em that way. I got bored and started tossing leaves that had fallen through the hole in the roof into the fire to watch 'em smolder and curl in on themselves. When I ran out of leaves, I stood in the doorway, Naji's sword and scabbard looped around my hips, and stared out at the shadowline along the trees. Nothing. I drummed my fingers against the doorway. Glanced up at the bundle of fern leaves. Thought about Naji telling me to stay put.

Something flashed out of the corner of my eye.

I had the sword out even though my brain was telling me it was only Naji. Except it wasn't Naji. It wasn't nobody at all, just a gray mist that was slinking out of the woods, shrouding my view of the forest, of the beach, of everything—

"Darkest night! Get inside!"

Naji looped his arm around my chest and pulled me backward into the shack. I cried out and dropped the sword in a clatter on the floor. The door to the shack slammed shut with a force that rattled the stones in the walls. I could hear Naji breathing in my ear. He smelled like the sea and like the cold nights of the ice-islands.

"What the hell!" I shouted. "Where did you come from?"

"The water." Naji let me go, and I whirled around to face him. He was as dry as when he left, but he had a big silver-striped fish in one hand, and he didn't look furious the way I expected him to, only tired. "I felt you about to do something stupid. I told you not to go outside."

I slumped down on the floor, my heart pounding. "I was just bored," I muttered.

"Fortunately, they didn't see you," he said, laying the fish out on a slab of stone that was next to the hearth. "They'll only get stronger, though. You need to be more careful." He leaned in close to me, and I stared up at him, dizzy with the rush of my fear, and with something else I couldn't identify. "Promise you won't go out alone."

"You're the one that left me be—"

"Promise."

"I promise. Kaol. I'm sorry I stood in the damn door."

He slid away from me and pulled out his knife. "Midnight's claws, I wish I could heal faster. If only I knew how long I had to keep them from you—"

"Me! You're the one they're after."

He slid the knife up under the fish's scales, his movements quick and assured. If I hadn't been annoyed with him, I might've been impressed. "I'm currently far more protected than you are," he said. "I have the strength of the Order behind me."

I scowled. "Don't cut that fish too thin. It'll burn up in the fire."

He stopped cutting and looked at me. "Would you rather do it?"

"I can do it better than you can."

He pulled out the knife and handed it over like it was a peace offering. Cleaning the fish calmed me down a little. It helped that Naji didn't nag me about the Mists no more, and by the time we had the fish cooking on the fire, I had forgotten about the mist curling through the woods outside the shack. I was inside, I was surrounded by warmth and the smells of real food, I was safe.

The two of us finished off the entire fish. Its flesh was flaky and almost sweet-tasting, and it snapped clean and bright inside my mouth. The best meal I'd had in ages.

When we finished eating, Naji pulled out his sword and started sharpening it against the side of a rock he had brought in from the beach with him. It didn't take him long; he was sure practiced at it.

He held the sword up to the fire. It glittered, throwing off little dots of silvery light.

"You had that sword long?" I asked him. Some people, soldiers especially, make a big deal about their swords, and you can get 'em to talk about the things forever. Never been one for that sort of thing myself. A weapon's a weapon.

"I received it when I took my vows." Naji lay the sword over his knees.

"What kinda vows?" *Celibacy?* I thought, though I didn't say it. Nobody keeps a celibacy vow anyway.

Naji lifted his head. "I'm not supposed to discuss it with outsiders."

"Oh, course not." I picked the sword up by the handle and swiped it through the air a few times. But without the threat of danger, it only reminded me of Tarrin of the *Hariri* and I dropped it on the floor. Naji gave me one of his looks and slipped it back into its scabbard.

"Can I ask you a question?" I said.

"I'm not divulging any secrets of the Order."

"Not even one?"

Naji narrowed his eyes, and I realized he'd probably been joking, in his way. I took a deep breath.

"Why didn't you want to kill me?"

Naji looked away, toward the fire-shadows flickering across the doorway.

"Well?" I prompted. "Or is that a secret of the Order too?"

Naji sighed. He leaned back against the wall. He didn't look the least bit like an assassin, what with the firelight and his seaworn clothes. In truth, 'cause of the scar and his long hair, he looked like a pirate. Even the tattoos reminded me of ocean waves.

"Do you know who the Jadorr'a are?" he asked.

"Assassins."

My answer made him look worn out.

"No, do you know their involvement in the history of the Empire?"

I shrugged. Not much use for knowing history on board a pirate ship.

"They used to prevent wars," he said. "Before the Empire bound together the countries of the desertlands, they were a way to put a cease to the constant fighting between kings. Better to kill one man than allow soldiers to destroy the countryside, raping and burning their way across the desert."

War between countries was something the Confederation didn't much get involved in beyond its own internal squabbling. Though there hadn't been war for a long time, not since I was a little girl, and that was over on Qilar anyway. The Empire had formed long before I was born.

"I don't see what any of this has to do with me," I said.

"It doesn't," Naji said. "That's my point. The Order was always paid for its services, but once the Empire formed, gold lust opened them up for use by any merchant with enough wealth to provide payment."

"Like Captain Hariri?"

"Like Captain Hariri." Naji shook his head. "I joined the Order after my strength manifested itself—after I learned my magic came from darkness and death, not the earth, the way it did for my mother, my brother—"

"You have a brother?"

Naji fixed me with a steely gaze. "My mother sent me away. She said I could harness my darkness into something good, that I could stop the Empire from destroying all the people living under its banners . . ." He laughed, a short, harsh bark. "I suppose I've done that. Once or twice. But mostly it's errand-running for rich men. I despise wealth."

I didn't say nothing to that. *Wealth is power*, Papa always told me. *Wealth is strength*. But I could see where Naji was coming from too.

"So that's why you didn't want to kill me?" I finally said. "'Cause you didn't think it was worth your time?"

Naji looked up at me. "No," he said. "I didn't want to you kill you because I thought it was wrong."

I dunno why, but my face flushed hot at that. Hotter than the fire.

"I won't tell nobody," I said.

"It doesn't matter. No one's going to believe you escaped an assassin."

"A Jadorr'a," I said.

He looked at me again, and I still couldn't read his face none. Not even his eyes.

"Yes," he said. "A Jadorr'a."

And his voice was soft as a kiss.

• • •

I woke up to rainfall pattering across the roof. It was awful hard to tell the passing of days here, on account of the cloud cover and the way the sun didn't always rise and set in the same place. The rainfall was constant, though. It was a shame you couldn't keep track of the days through the rain. All I knew was that I'd heard that soft rustle of rain more often than not.

This morning something was different, though. The shack was lit not by the usual faint golden glow of our skin, but by bright blue light. Light the color of northern glaciers.

I sat up, mussing the pile of pine needles and leaves I used for bedding. Naji sat in the corner next to the fire, his eyes and tattoos glowing. My heart pounded. Was he tracking the wizard? Or maybe he was talking to the Order. Maybe they'd have a way to bring us home.

For the first time since we landed on the island, I felt a dizzying twist in my brain that I half recognized as joy. A pile of berries was lying next to the hearth, and I ate 'em and checked the water jar. It was empty. I cursed and sat back down on my pile of leaves. Figured he'd think to pick some berries but not go fetch some water. And I was thirsty from sleep.

I watched him in his trance for a while, my head leaned up against the stone walls. He didn't move. Not even his chest rose and fell with his breath. It was eerie, truth be told. I'd never watched him this closely during a trance before. I'd always had better things to do with my time.

"Naji!" I said, waving my hands in front of his face. "I'm thirsty."

Naji didn't move, and the light in the shack didn't change.

"If you don't come out of that trance I'm gonna go fetch water myself."

Nothing.

I sighed. His sword was lying across the bed. It wouldn't take long to walk down to the spring, I knew the different paths so well now, and I was in such good spirits I felt invincible. I hadn't even seen any mist in the last week. Hadn't heard no voices, neither.

And I was wearing my charm. It'd protected me from the Mists man in the night market in Lisirra. It'd made him look right through me. Maybe it could do the same with the island.

And Kaol only knew how long Naji would be under.

I scooped the sword off the bed and grabbed the water pot. Naji was wearing the scabbard, so I just carried the sword with me out into the rain. The drops were cold and stinging, the way the rain always was here. Made me miss the warm soft rains that fell across the pirates' islands. But once I got into the thick part of the forest the leaves caught most of the drops, and I trudged over pine needles and crushed ferns, shivering and miserable. My brain started churning up like the sea, thinking on the curse and getting kicked off the *Revenge* and fighting the Hariri clan. I thought about Tarrin, who I'd managed to shove down deep inside me when we left Port Iskassaya. The memory was back now: his breath tickling my ear, how easy the sword had slid into his belly, the heat of his blood spilling over my hands. And it was this sword that had done it, this sword that I'd used to kill Tarrin.

I suddenly couldn't stand the thought of the sword touching me no more, and I tossed it off into the greenery, my chest heaving, my heart racing. I watched it disappear in a spray of ferns, and for a split second I wondered what I'd done. But then my thoughts went elsewhere.

The woods had gone silent.

There's always noise in the world.

But not now.

I stopped and that's when I heard it, that emptiness of sound, like the forest was holding her breath. I got this creeping chill up my spine, and my palms turned cold and clammy, and here I was alone and with no manner of weapon 'cause I'd just thrown it away, and what sort of stupid girl does a thing like that?

A shimmer appeared up ahead, a curl of mist, pale silver and hazy. I took a step backward, trying to figure out the best way to run. I was in the chiming forest, all those skinny trees covered with bone-white bark, weird transparent leaves disintegrating in the rain—

"Ananna of the *Tanarau*."

A woman stepped out of the mist, her body long and thin, her eyes that same eerie silver as the woman in the dress shop. But this was a different woman. The woman in the dress shop had been human enough to fool me; this one had a narrow feral face, her chin too pointed and her cheekbones too sharp. And the silver in her eyes blocked out all the white.

"I don't know who that is," I told her.

The woman laughed. Her teeth were filed into points. "You don't know who you are?" she asked me.

"I know I'm not Ananna of the *Tanarau*."

The woman laughed again, and I knew it was pointless to lie. I wished to the deep dark sea that I had waited for Naji to finish his magic.

"Who are you?" I asked.

She tilted her head and little lights danced in the shadows around her. Whenever I looked at them I felt dizzy.

The woman drifted up beside me. It took me a minute to realize that she didn't have feet, that her skirts ended in a cloud of creeping mist that got up under my clothes, all cold and damp. Those little lights swirled outside my line of vision, and I used all my willpower to keep my sight focused on the bridge of her nose. I knew better than to look her in the eye.

"Surely you know," she said. "You've met my kind before. Harbor. Although she did insist on a fully human body." The woman laughed. "Stupid of her. At least she bled all over your world and not mine."

"That ain't what I'm talking about. I know you ain't human." I took a deep breath and steadied myself. "You know my name. Only seems fair I know yours."

The woman gazed at me for a long time. I stood my ground, even though the mist crept and crept around me.

"You can call me Echo," she said.

"You expect me to believe that's your name?"

"I didn't say it was my name. I said it's what you can call me." She gave me this sly, slow smile that reminded me of a fox. It showed just enough of her teeth.

"So what do you want?"

"Now that," she said, "I'm certain you already know."

"You'd be wrong." A lie, of course. I knew damn well what she wanted.

She stared at me for a long time, like she couldn't decide if I was lying or just that stupid. I could tell she figured either one was a possibility.

"Your companion," she said finally. "The assassin."

"Oh, him." I frowned. "I don't know where he is."

She tilted her head. "Don't confuse me with Harbor," she said. "I've been doing this much, much longer than she. That charm she lent you was one of my own devising. It should have worked. But the assassin had taken precautions I didn't realize."

The woman ghosted her hand along the line of my throat, coming close but never quite touching. I could feel Naji's charm pressing against my heart. "You seem to have taken precautions yourself."

"Figure I can't be too careful, out in the wild."

She drifted closer. Her body gave off cold the way a normal person's gives off heat. She still didn't touch me, though, and I figured I could thank Naji's charm for that.

"You can still help me," the woman said. "It will be of your own accord, and that way is always better. And I would never expect you to work for free."

Her silvery eyes drifted over my face and came to rest on the charm.

"Oh yeah?" I asked. "What would you give me?"

She laughed. "Whatever you want."

"Money? Empire money, I mean, not some worthless Mist coins."

"We can acquire wealth, yes. Human wealth."

I looked past her, to the gray space where she'd first appeared. It shimmered in the trees, a thundercloud that lost its way out of the storm. From where I stood, the Mists were grayness. They were nothing.

"My lord would be pleased if you brought him the assassin," she said. "He would grant you a boon." She smiled. "A hundred boons."

Her hand traced over the line of my forehead. She couldn't touch me, but it was still like walking straight into a typhoon.

And I got these pictures in my head. Me with my own ship, sleek and tall, with sails the color of blood. And that ship of mine, she had a crew that listened to me even though I was a woman, and together we sacked the coasts of Qilar and all the lands of the Empire. The Confederation fell 'cause of me and that ship. All Confederation pirates became part of my armada, and I ruled the oceans, the richest woman in the world. I took lovers more handsome than Tarrin of the *Hariri*, more handsome than Naji. I wielded Otherworld magic that put the seas under my control and gave me power over typhoons and squalls and sunshine and steering winds.

I became the most perfect version of myself, fierce and terrifying and even beautiful.

I wanted to take her up on it. I wanted to wrench that charm off my neck and stomp it into the ground and race through the woods till I found Naji crumpled up in pain in the shack. I wanted to, 'cause on the surface it was the most common-sense thing to do. *Always take the money*, Papa said. You can always double-cross on the deal later if you don't like the terms.

But I also wanted to do it 'cause Naji didn't see me, he would never see me, and for reasons I couldn't decipher, that bothered me.

I wanted to do it. I just couldn't do it.

I stepped away from her, my forehead damp from where she'd almost touched me.

"You liked that, didn't you?" she asked.

"It had appeal, ain't gonna lie." I took another step back, hoping my legs weren't shaking too bad. "But I think I'll leave you to it on your own. You don't need my help."

Echo's eyes turned flat as mirrors. Darkness roiled through the woods. The trees shook. The earth rumbled.

"You can't hurt me," I said, thumping the side of Naji's charm with my thumb. "I ain't afraid of you."

She bared her teeth, sharp and bright, and let out a low, snaky hiss. But I was right. She didn't move to attack. I was protected.

"Protected?" she sneered. "You think you're protected?"

"Course I do. You can't even touch me." I tried not to think about her reading my thoughts.

"Why do you think you threw your sword into the woods?" Her voice was nothing human. She glided up to me, and there was that cold dampness again, but I held my ground. "I can control you, I can force you to lead me to him—"

"Then why don't you do it?"

She snarled, her face twisted and wild. I was not going to flinch. I was not going to run away.

And then something darted out from the underbrush, something swift-moving and black as pitch. A sword flashed. It sliced through the woman and her dark mist, and this time there wasn't any starlight to splatter all over my clothes. She just evaporated. The entrance to the Mists dried up like it'd been left too long in the sun.

I sat down on the transparent tree leaves and the damp ferns.

A branch snapped off to my right. I didn't bother looking over. I knew who it was.

"I told you it was dangerous," Naji said.

"Is she gone?"

"For now." Naji paused. "Thank you."

"For what?"

He stood beside me, his sword hanging at his side. I kept my gaze down on the ground and tried not to think about tossing it off into the underbrush.

"For not telling her where to find me."

I kicked at the fallen leaves, splintering them into shards, digging a ditch in the soil with the heel of my boot. The forest noises had come back, the chittering and shaking and rustling of the rain, the crystalline chiming of the surrounding trees, but the silence between the two of us swallowed all that noise whole.

"I almost did," I said after a while.

"Almost did what?"

"Helped her find you." I couldn't look at him. "She showed me all these things that could happen if I did amazing things. My own ship, my own crew." I stopped, not wanting to remember some future that wasn't ever gonna happen.

Naji got real still. I knew he was staring at me even though I refused to look up at his face.

"Why didn't you?"

"'Cause."

"That doesn't answer the question." The hardness in his voice sliced through the liquid air of the forest. This time, I did look at him. Lines furrowed his brow. His eyes were sunk low into his face. "I can't keep doing this, Ananna, not if there's a chance you might turn me over to the Otherworld. Not if you're going to run away when I explicitly told you . . ." He took a deep breath. "What stopped you? Why didn't you help her?"

"'Cause you're my friend," I said.

All the hardness in his features melted away. "Oh."

"I'm not going to turn you over to your enemies." I stood up, swiping the forest floor off my dress. "So you can stop fretting about that. But I'm thirsty still. That's why I left—you were in a trance and didn't bother to get water."

He didn't say nothing. I started kicking around in the underbrush, trying to find the water jar. I didn't remember dropping it, but that was probably just more Otherworld trickery.

"It's a few feet behind you," Naji said. "Beneath that tree there."

I glared at him and then fumbled around in the wet greenery until I felt the smooth cold stone of the jar. Naji waited for me, his arms crossed in front of his chest, and then we walked the rest of the way to the spring, our silence heavy with our unspoken thoughts.

The spring was waiting for us as though nothing unusual had happened. It bubbled and frothed in its usual place beneath the pine trees. I plunged the jar into the spring, and the water flooded over my hands, cold as ice and reminding me of Echo's almost-touch.

I know that Naji saw me shivering.

CHAPTER EIGHTEEN

Naji paced back and forth through the chiming forest, knocking down tree branches and those sparkling, transparent leaves. I watched him from beside the spring and waited for the thoughts to stop jangling around inside my head.

Finally I got so tired of listening to him trampling through the underbrush that I asked, "So I guess you found out where the Wizard Eirnin is, then."

"Yes." He stopped his pacing, glanced at me, and then looked away. The wind pushed through the trees, and the leaves shimmered and threw off dots of pale light, and the tree trunks bent and swayed. The chiming was everywhere.

"That's it?"

"What else is there to tell?"

I narrowed my eyes at him. He still wasn't looking at me, and I could tell he was leaving something out. He'd done it so much when we first left Lisirra I'd become a master at spotting all his omissions.

"I don't know," I said, "or else I wouldn't be asking."

"The Wizard Eirnin lives in the center of the island," Naji said. "It isn't far from here. That's all I know."

I sighed and refilled the water jar one last time. "Well," I said. "I guess we ought to go look for him." I straightened up and rested the jar against my hip.

"Are you going to take that with you?" Naji asked.

"Course I am. It's impossible to tell east from west on this damned island. Chances are we'll wind up wandering back around to the shack before we ever find the wizard."

"I tracked him," Naji said. "I know exactly where he is." His expression darkened. "Exactly how I knew where you were when the Otherworld attacked."

I shoved past him, jostling water. He didn't say nothing more about the Otherworld attack, and I let him lead me out of the chiming forest and into the darker parts of the woods. The rain had been threatening us the whole time I laid out by the spring, and now it started again in earnest. Naji plowed forward like it didn't even bother him, like he didn't even notice the rain and the gray light and the scent of soil.

We walked for a long time. The rain hazed my vision and filled the water jar to overflowing. The trees crowded in on me, looming and close, and I started wondering if it was the Mists. Echo coming back for one last fight. My hands started to shake.

And then, like that, the trees cleared out and there was this little round house built of stone sitting in the middle of a garden, smoke trickling up out of a hole in the roof.

Time seemed to stop. I forgot about the Mists and about the island. When I saw that house, there was only Naji's curse, which was also my curse. And we'd come so far across the world to get it cured.

This stone-built house hardly seemed capable of that sort of magic.

Naji was already knocking at the front door. I ran through the garden to join him. They looked like normal plants, not the weird ghost-plants Leila'd had growing in her cave. They drooped beneath the weight of the rain.

The door opened up a crack, and a sliver of a face appeared.

Naji didn't say nothing. Then the door swung all the way open and this man was standing there in a rough-cut tunic and trousers. He had that look of the northern peoples, like somebody'd pricked him and all the color had drained out of his hair and skin.

"Well, look who's on my front porch," he said, speaking Empire with this odd hissing accent. "A murderer and a cross-dressing pirate."

I looked down at my clothes, ripped and shredded and covered in mud and sand and dried blood. I'd forgotten I was dressed like a boy.

"So are you here to kill me or to rob me?" the man said. "I generally don't find it useful to glow when undertaking acts of subterfuge, but then, I'm just a wizard."

You know, that pissed me off. We'd traveled half around the world to get to him, and there were monsters chasing us and Naji's curse was impossible to break, and here he was cracking jokes about our professions. I took a step forward, pushing Naji out of the way and spilling water on the porch.

"Mister," I said. "Do either of us look like we're capable of any kind of pillaging right now?"

The man looked like he wanted to laugh. "That one might," he said. "But you look halfway crossed over to Kajjil."

"How do you know that word?" Naji asked.

"What? It's not one of the secret words." The man winked. "Though I know plenty of those, too. You two come on in. I'll fix you something warm to drink, get you a change of clothes."

Naji slumped into the house, and I followed behind, setting the water pot next to the door so I wouldn't forget it on my way out.

It was nice, everything clean and tidy, with simple wooden furniture and bouquets of dried flowers hanging upside from the rafters. A sense of protection passed over me when I walked through the doorway, rum-strong, like the feeling I got when I put on Naji's charm for the first time. I headed directly for the hearth, 'cause there was a fire smoldering in there, licks of white-hot flame. Naji sat down beside me, his hands draped over his knees. The firelight brightened his face and traced the outlines of his scars.

The man hung a kettle over the fire and pulled up a chair. I felt like a little kid again, sitting at Papa's feet while he told me stories. But the man didn't tell no stories, he just leaned forward and looked at me real hard and then at Naji. Then he stirred whatever was in the kettle.

"Are you the Wizard Eirnin?" Naji asked.

"I surely am." The man glanced over at him. "Leila let me know you were on your way. She told me about the curse." His weird pale eyes flashed. "And I've heard your name on the wind's whispers these last few days." He turned his gaze to me. "I see you emerged from your encounter with the Mists unscathed."

I looked down at my hands.

"From what Leila said about you, I wouldn't have expected it."

"What's that supposed to mean?"

Eirnin stood up. "I promised you clean clothes, didn't I? Getting dotty in my old age. Wait here." He strolled across the room and rummaged around in a dresser. I watched him. Naji watched the fire.

"Here we go." He pulled out a long pearl-colored dress, the fabric thick and warm, the edges trimmed in lace, and a gray man's coat and tossed both at me. "You can go change in the back room if you want."

It'd been a while since I wore a proper dress, but really, having any clean clothes was a blessing from Kaol. I ducked into the back room and peeled off my old damp clothes and piled 'em up on the floor. It would've been nice to have a bath before changing into the dress, but I didn't know if I trusted a bath in a wizard's house. Still, putting on new clothes made me feel better, despite everything that had happened—warmer, too, 'cause these were dry.

When I came back into the main room Naji was dressed like a right gentleman, in a white shirt and dark brown trousers, no black anywhere on him. Eirnin handed me a ceramic mug filled with something warm and sweet-smelling. I knew I shoulda been more cautious, but I'd been soaked through and cold and more shaken from my encounter with the Mists than I cared to admit, so I sipped some and it washed warmth all the way down my throat. It was some kind of liquor, sweet like honey but spicy, too. I sat down next to the fire and drank and drank.

"Can you help me?" Naji asked.

Eirnin laughed. "Help you with an impossible curse?" he said. "I don't know. Tell me about it."

Naji looked down at his own mug. "What do you want to know?"

"Anything you can tell me."

The room got real quiet. All I could hear was the fire crackling in the hearth and the rain whispering across the roof.

"You know you're safe here," the Wizard Eirnin said. "I don't traffic with the Otherworld."

Naji tightened his fingers around his mug. The firelight carved his face into blocks of darkness and light.

"I was in the north," he said. "I had an assignment. To track down the leader of a splinter group that had fled there." He sipped his drink. "It was winter. Dark, cold. I had tracked the leader to the settlement of one of the northern tribes. They'd taken him in. I wound up killing some of their tribesmen. I didn't intend to, but the leader had expected me—or someone like me . . ." Naji's voice trailed off.

"So which one of those, ah, accidental deaths got you the curse?" Eirnin asked.

"I don't know. They caught me—the only time I've ever been

caught—and dragged me out into the snow. Everything was white. And then a woman came out of one of the tents. She looked like she was carved out of ice. And she was ancient, older than the mountains.

"She told me that someday someone would save my life. When that happened, she said, I would be indebted to them forever. I would have to protect them."

"I take it that's you?"

Eirnin's question broke the spell of Naji's voice. I jumped about a foot and spilled some of my drink down the front of my dress. Naji didn't look at neither of us, just stared into the fire.

"Yeah, it's me," I said. "I told him he didn't have to, but—"

"Well, it's a curse," Eirnin said blandly. "He can't help it." Then, to Naji: "What happens if you don't keep her safe?"

"It hurts me."

"Care to be more specific?"

"A headache, or a pain in my chest or my joints. It depends on the level of the threat."

I thought about meeting with Echo in the woods, about the cold curling mist.

Eirnin nodded.

"So can you help me?" Naji twisted around and the expression on his face was so desperate that, for a moment, my stomach twisted up in empathy.

"No," said Eirnin.

All the air went out of the room.

"What?" said Naji, and his voice was cold and dangerous, like the blade of his knife.

Eirnin didn't do nothing, though, didn't shrink back, didn't even act like he was scared. "What did you expect, Jadorr'a? It's an impossible curse. You know that. Even that one knows it." He tilted his head at me.

Naji's face twisted up with rage.

"I do know that woman, though, that ice-woman. She's quite traditional. Always casts her spells in the old northern style." Eirnin paused. His eyes flashed again. "The north is different from the hot civilized places of the world. We have different understandings of things. Of words."

No one spoke. The house pulsed twice with the manic energy of magic. I realized I was holding my breath.

"What the magicians of the Empire call an impossible curse is not what we call an impossible curse. A northern curse is not impossible in the sense that is incurable."

Naji leaped to his feet, his body hard and tense beneath his clean clothes. The sword gleamed at his side. "Then why did you say you couldn't help me?"

"It's not my place to cure your curse." Eirnin leaned back in his chair and pressed the tips of fingers together. "If you want to break one of the old north's impossible curses, you have to complete three impossible tasks."

The energy that crackled through the house like lightning died away. But Naji kept his eyes on Eirnin, his gaze strong and sure.

"Do you at least know what they are?" Naji said.

"I do. Smelled them on you the minute you walked through the door." Eirnin smiled but didn't say nothing more.

Naji glared at him. "Well?" he asked. "What are they?"

"Impossible," Eirnin said.

I figured by this point it was taking all of Naji's willpower not to launch at the guy the way he had Ataño. I figured Eirnin knew it too. You could see how he'd have gotten along with Leila.

"Perhaps you'd like to write them down," Eirnin said. "I have parchment around here—"

"No," said Naji. "I don't."

Eirnin smiled. I wanted to hit him myself. "All right. First one: Find the princess's starstones and hold them, skin against stone."

Well. I'd no idea what a starstone was, but I didn't think that sounded too bad. Lots of princesses around. Naji just kept on staring at Eirnin, though.

"Second one. Create life out of an act of violence."

Naji pressed his hands against the side of the mug, his face all twisted up in anger. I waited for the mug to shatter.

"You want to hear the third one?" Eirnin asked.

"You know that I do."

Eirnin smiled. "The third task," he said, "is to experience true love's kiss."

"Seriously?" Naji asked.

"Quite. You'll have to find someone who loves you for who you are." He paused. "And good luck with that, murderer."

Something brightened in my heart, like the first star coming out at night. But then Naji opened his mouth.

"Leila," he said. "She's the only one . . ."

The light blinked out. I got real hot and looked down at my hands.

"Leila!" Eirnin roared with laughter. "That woman has never loved another human being in her entire life, and never will. I wouldn't put all my eggs in that particular basket, if I were you. Which, fortunately, I'm not."

Naji stood up and hurled his mug against the wall. I jumped at the sound of breaking porcelain and twisted my hands up in my dress. I wanted a way to get out of that house without anyone knowing why. And to get away from Naji, the Otherworld be damned.

Naji stalked out the front door and slammed it so hard the foundation shuddered.

"Looks like it's just you and me," the Wizard Eirnin said.

I stood up and straightened out my skirts. Worthless, this old man was. What a waste getting blown out here, away from civilization and people who could actually help us, to some place that used to belong to a nightmare world.

"The stories are true. This place did spawn itself from the Mists." Eirnin leaned forward. He was so pale he looked like a ghost. "They won't hurt you, you know. Not if they think you can help them. Remember that, my dear, the next time Echo comes calling. That's what she called herself today, isn't it?"

I stumbled backward at the sound of her name. "I should go." I hesitated, knowing that you never want to cross a wizard the wrong way. "Thank you for the clothes and the . . ." I waved my hand at the mug. "And for helping Naji. I mean, I wish you could have done more—"

"I'm sure you do." He gave me this weird knowing look that I didn't like one bit. "You be careful out there, little pirate. Things come out of those woods that know how to get at you. The Mist's not the only thing you need to worry about."

I stared at him. "I ain't little."

Eirnin grinned. That was it. I slammed out the front door.

I hadn't been walking long when Naji stepped out of the shadow of a pine tree. I shrieked so loud my voice echoed through the woods. I'd been mired in my own thoughts. 'Cause I was trying not to think about Echo and the Mists, I thought about Naji instead, and the thing I learned in the Wizard Eirnin's house. I'd handed my heart over to him, a damned blood-magic assassin, without even realizing it.

"I told you I don't want you wandering off alone."

"Stop talking to me like I'm a little kid. You're the one who left me."

Naji fell into step beside me. "You left the water jar behind."

"Kaol and her sacred starfish!" I stopped in the middle of the woods, whirled around in the direction of his house. "Damn it, I'm not going back there." I pushed my hair out of my eyes. "At least he gave us something to drink."

He snorted and took off into the woods, paying no mind to the snapping of branches. I trailed behind him. "So now what?" I said.

"We go to the shack," Naji said.

"That ain't what I meant." I ran up beside him. "I mean with the curse. You know a way off the island? You said the Order was protecting you—why couldn't they just bring us both back? Don't tell me it ain't possible, I know the stories."

He stopped. "How did you know?"

"Know what? About the Order?" I almost laughed. "You mean they can actually do that?"

"Of course they can." But then his expression changed. It went from hard and anger to . . . almost sad. "I spoke to them this morning. Magic is strong here. They'd certainly be able to send an acolyte through Kajjil."

Water dripped out of the trees and landed in dark spots on my new coat. "They aren't coming, are they?"

Naji looked at me, and then he shook his head.

I should have known it wouldn't be that easy.

He walked off, his face tilted down to the ground.

"And why not?" I called after him. "They don't want to bother with you when the Mists are on your tail? Or are you damaged goods now that you got that curse?"

He stopped. The wind rippled his hair and his new clothes. When he turned around his face was a mask.

"They wouldn't have rescued you," he said. "They wouldn't risk bringing an outsider through Kajjil."

"Guess I just ruin everything for you, don't I? Give you headaches and keep you from getting rescued—"

"I told them no," he said, "even when I thought—when I hoped—that Eirnin would have cured me."

The entire world suddenly seemed to stand still. Naji and me were statues. The forest was no longer shaking with wind and rain. Even the dripping had stopped. But my heart was still beating, pounding too fast inside my chest, threatening to break me open.

"What?" I whispered.

"Give me your hand," Naji said, and then he walked over to me and grabbed it without waiting for me to move. The shadows crowded in around us. I didn't quite understand what had happened until we were standing in the shadow of the pine trees that grew beside our shack.

"I didn't feel like walking through the woods again," Naji said, and he stalked into the shack, leaving me shaking outside.

"Hey!" I shouted. My voice disappeared on the wind. "Naji!"

He didn't come back out, and so I went in and found him staring at the fire.

"Did you mean that?" I leaned up against the doorway. "About staying with me even if you were cured—"

"Yes." He looked at me over his shoulder. "Close the door, please. The wind will blow the fire out."

I stepped inside and sat down on the floor beside him. The fire crackled in the hearth.

"It was the only decent thing to do," he said.

My heart warmed, and for a moment I thought about leaning over and kissing him on the cheek.

The first impossible task.

"Besides," he said, "the Mists would have snatched you up the moment I left. Even if you didn't give in," and he looked away from me as he said this, "even if you weren't tied to me because of the curse, they would have used you. Somehow."

The warmth in my heart froze over.

"I can take care of myself," I snapped.

Naji fed another stick into the fire.

"I bet I can get us off this island."

Naji didn't say nothing.

"Any Confederation baby knows how to build a signal fire," I went on. "I would have done it sooner but I figured we should get your curse cured first."

"And we still haven't done that."

I glared at him. "You know how to do it now. It just ain't nothing we can do on the island. We'll have to build a bonfire on the beach," I said. "And feed it green wood so it'll let off plenty of smoke."

"It's going to be difficult to keep a beach fire burning here," Naji said. "Because of the storms."

"Long as we keep the fire going in here, we can relight it."

"That's not very efficient." He sighed. "I know a way, but—"

"A way to what? To keep it burning?" I looked at him. "Then why haven't you done it? Why didn't you do it as soon as they told you they wouldn't rescue us?"

The look he gave me was sharp as his sword.

"Kaol," I said. "You like it here, don't you? You like cold rainy islands half out of the world. No wonder you're an assassin."

He opened his mouth. Closed it. Then he said, "Scars don't spontaneously emerge overnight, Ananna. They come from somewhere."

It took me longer than it should've to figure out what he was getting at.

"Oh," I said. "Oh, then you don't have to . . . I can just relight the fire—"

Naji stood up and brushed past me. He stuck a stick into the hearth and yanked it back out with a spray of ash and sparks.

"It's fine," he said, in a voice that suggested it wasn't.

"Naji—"

He walked out of the shack, and for a moment I sat there, not knowing if he wanted to be left alone. The wind picked up and knocked tree branches against the side of the shack, and I thought about how if it wasn't for me he'd be off the island right now, back in the dry fragrant heat of Lisirra. And then I wondered what exactly had happened when he got his scars, if he'd had someone to help him when it all went wrong.

I threw my coat around my shoulders and ran down to the beach.

Naji was set up a ways down from the shack. The bit of fire was smoldering on top of the sand, and Naji was tossing driftwood into a big pile. I gathered up some pine needles from the forest's edge and added them to the driftwood.

Naji looked at me but didn't say nothing, and I didn't say nothing to him.

With the two of us working together, it didn't take long for us to get a good-sized pile. I picked the hearth fire up off the sand. Naji jerked his head toward the woodpile, and I dumped the fire onto it. The pine needles curled up and blackened and turned to ash.

"Stand back," Naji said, his voice a surprise after us working in silence for so long.

He pulled out his knife and pushed up the sleeve of his robe. His scars glowed faintly, tracing paths up and down his arm, undercutting the glow of his skin. He closed his eyes and took to chanting and dug the knife into his skin. The fire brightened, turned a gold color I ain't never seen in fire before. I felt something tugging at the edge of my thoughts, trying to drag me closer . . .

Blood dripped off Naji's arm, splattered across the beach. He caught some of the drops with his free hand. His chanting sounded like it was coming from a thousand voices at once. I wanted to be closer to the fire but I knew I needed to do what he said and stay back.

And then he flung the blood into the flames and there was this noise like a sigh and the fire erupted out so hot and bright that I fell backward onto the beach. It was still bright gold, and figures were entwined in the flames, swirling and dancing, and Kaol help me but I could feel their desperation, like if they stopped dancing my whole world would end.

Naji grabbed me by the arm and yanked me to my feet. He left a smear of blood on the sleeve of my coat.

"Stay away from it," he said. "This is not a cooking fire."

"What'd you do?" I asked.

"Gave myself a headache," he snapped. "From putting you in danger."

I almost said, *It's just a fire*, but the firelight caught on his scars and I thought better of it.

I glanced over at the fire, golden light and dancing bodies, and thought about the assassin stories Papa always told me. How there was no way to defeat them, no way to intimidate them. Funny how wrong stories can be.

Naji led me up the beach, one hand gripping my upper arm. Anytime I tried to look back at the fire he jerked me forward again. When we got far enough away from it he dropped his hand and stopped on the beach. The sea wind blew his hair away from his face, revealing the dark lines of scars. The dark sand stirred around our feet. It was almost the same color as the sky.

"Marjani will be back for us," I said. "I know it."

Naji sighed and folded his arms over his chest. "And what does it matter?" he asked.

"It matters a whole hell of a lot—"

"For you," he said. "I'll still have this curse, whether Marjani comes for us or not. Whether anyone comes for us."

"It'll still matter to me! I'm as much cursed as you are! I have to follow you around and I can't do nothing that I want to do. Can't set up shop on a pirate's island, can't work the rigging on a Confederation ship."

He didn't answer.

"And it's not really impossible anyway," I said. "Isn't that what the wizard was getting at? You just have to complete those three tasks . . ."

Naji turned to me, and I was expecting fury but all I got was this look of sadness that made my heart clench up. "The tasks are impossible," he said. "That's where the name comes from. Three impossible tasks, one impossible curse."

At least one of the tasks isn't impossible.

I almost said it out loud. I almost said, *I'm in love with you.* Even though it didn't make sense, me being in love with him, even though it pissed me off—because he treated me like a kid sometimes and he sulked around when he was in a bad mood and he hated the ocean. But I loved him and if I kissed him then it would complete one of the tasks.

And if one of the tasks was completed, then the other two could be as well.

Naji sat down on the sand, his legs stretched out in front of him. He looked so sad I didn't think I could stand it. After a few moments, I sat down beside him. The sea misted over us, and I could taste the salt in the back of my throat.

"I don't think the tasks are really impossible," I said.

"And what do you know about magic?"

I pushed the sting of that aside. "I saved your life with it."

He didn't answer. I scooted close to him and put one hand on his shoulder. He tilted his head toward me, his hair tickling the tops of my knuckles.

"Marjani will come," I said. "She'll keep her word."

"She didn't actually promise—"

"Shut up. She'll come. And then we'll get a boat, and we'll find the princess's starstones and get into battle after battle until you figure out a way to create life from fighting."

He scowled out at the horizon line. The gray northern light fell around us like rain, and the sea slammed against the underside of the island.

And in the secret spaces of my mind, I imagined true love's kiss.

THE PIRATE'S WISH

CHAPTER ONE

"Do you feel that?" Naji asked.

"I feel cold." I rubbed my arms over the worn-down fabric of my coat sleeves. Me and Naji'd been stranded on the Isles of the Sky for longer than I could keep track, thanks to him throwing the *Ayel's Revenge* off course while we were headed to Qilar, and the weather did a number on my clothes. I planned to march down to the Wizard Eirnin's house to see about getting some new things later today.

"You're always cold." Naji leaned forward and squinted out at the sea, his features twisting from the rough scars lining the left side of his face. We were sitting outside the shack the two of us shared, knotting bundles of pine needles to re-thatch the roof. "No, this is . . . something's on the air. Something disruptive."

"Disruptive?" I tossed my bundle of pine needles on the sand. "The hell does that mean?"

"Are you still wearing your protection charm?"

At that, I gave him a withering look and yanked back my coat collar to show him. "I ain't never taken it off before. Don't know why I'd start now."

He didn't answer, which wasn't much of a surprise. He'd been in a mood the last few weeks—at least, that's what I would guess, I'd stopped keeping track of the days a while back—mostly 'cause him and Eirnin had gotten themselves tangled up in a feud. As near as I could tell, it started when Naji was casting one of his blood-magic spells. He had a whole mess of them going: some to protect us from the magic of the Isles and some to keep me hidden from the Mists, that whole other world full of lords and monsters who kept trying to break through to ours.

Now, he'd been casting those spells the whole time we'd been on the island, ever since he got his strength back, but this *particular* spell had mingled with one Eirnin had going and messed Eirnin's up. Since then, the two of 'em had been at a feud like a pair of noble families in some Empire story.

It went pretty much like this: when his spell failed, Eirnin retaliated against Naji, sending a swarm of droning gnats down to our shack one evening. I managed to get away since they weren't after me, and I sat on the sand and watched 'em swirl in a dark cloud around Naji. Not biting him or nothing, just annoying him. It took almost two days before he dispelled 'em completely using magic, and by that point I was sleeping out on the beach just to get away from the noise. Then Naji marched down to Eirnin's house as soon as he was free from the gnats and cast some kind of long-term binding charm that made it pour rain for six days straight. Eirnin cleared it up, thank Kaol, but who the hell knew what they'd get up to next. Probably ruin my day, whatever it was.

"I don't like this." Naji dropped his pine needle bundle into his lap and stared up at the sky, which was gray and cloudy like always. His sleeves were pushed up to his elbows, revealing the swirl of tattoos on his skin. "Stay close to the shack for the next few days."

Well, blood and saltwater. There went my trip to Eirnin's house. And I really wanted some new clothes.

"Does your head hurt?" I asked.

Naji glanced at me. "No," he said. "It's just . . . as a precaution."

"Right. A precaution." I nodded. If his head didn't hurt, then that meant the curse wasn't activated and I wasn't in danger, which meant I could sneak off while he was fishing, like I'd planned to originally. "Is it . . . it's not the Mists, is it?"

"The Mists?" Naji shook his head. "No. This is different. Something with the island."

I shivered. Course, his magic had kept us free of the side effects of living on the Isles of the Sky for a while now.

"Something's changed," he added.

"Something's always changing on this damn island," I said. "The trees, the path in the woods—the freaking *sunrise*." I finished up the last of my pine needles. "There, done. I'll thatch up the roof while you're fishing."

Naji blinked at me, then pushed aside his own pine needles. "Maybe I shouldn't—"

"What? No! I'm starving. And, last I checked, fish is all we got to eat."

Naji sighed. "Stay in the shack."

"I'll stay *on* the shack."

"Ananna, you know I can't concentrate when you do that."

I frowned at him. "I ain't gonna fall! How many times I got to tell you—"

"As many as it takes." He stood up and dusted the sand from his own clothes, which were worse off than mine, hanging in tatters around his arms and legs. Eirnin was only willing to trade clothes with me. "If I feel the slightest suggestion of pain," Naji said, "I'm coming back to the island. Fish or no."

I slumped up against the shack. "Fine. But we're cooking that fish before I thatch the roof. Don't blame me if it rains."

He didn't say nothing, only unhooked his scabbard from around his waist and tossed it to me, then stepped into the shadows of a pine tree and disappeared. I wrapped the scabbard around my hips, the sword a reassuring presence at my side.

For a moment I stood there on the sand, listening to the wind and the sea. Off in the distance the bonfire flickered golden. I didn't look directly at it. Naji'd set it alight after we visited Eirnin for the first time, and it was a terrible, magical thing. Blood-magic. Sometimes Naji would go out at night and stand in the fire's glow, and the next morning he would wake up with dark circles under his eyes. It must've been draining him, bit by bit. I grew up around magic, though I can't do it much myself, but Mama's magic never hurt her, never kept her up at night. But then, she didn't do blood-magic.

At least the fire stayed lit even through the worst of the thunderstorms, and hopefully someday someone would see it. I still hoped that somebody would be Marjani, who'd tried to save us from being marooned in the first place. The captain didn't listen to her reasoning, but she'd leaned in close to my ear that moment before the rowboat dropped me and Naji into the sea and told me there was a way off every island. I trusted her to find it. The memory was one of the things keeping me going day to day.

I gathered up the pine needles and carted them into the shack, dumping them in a pile in the far corner from the fire. I knew Naji well enough to know that climbing on the roof would really hurt him—that damn curse, thinking me scrambling up on the roof was somehow a danger. His curse was that he had to protect me from harm. As far as I can tell, it was a bit of a joke from the northern witch who cast it after Naji went on a mission to her village. He's an assassin, a member of a secret order called the Jadorr'a, and he was hired to kill me once. I accidentally saved his life, and now, thanks to that curse, I had to listen to him nag me every time I wanted to get some work done.

Course, he *had* said the disruption, or whatever it was, hadn't activated the curse at all.

Which meant I should be able to make it to Eirnin's house and back before he returned from fishing.

Now, Naji would know where I'd been, but maybe I could cajole Eirnin into getting me some clothes for Naji. It'd be tough, but I was willing to clean out his hearth again.

I didn't have nothing better to do anyway.

So I double-checked my charm—still there, hanging on a loop of fabric, just like I'd shown Naji earlier—and set off into the forest with Naji's sword at my side. The woods shimmered in the gray sunlight. It was cold, the way it always was, but walking helped warm me up some.

It took me shorter than last time to make it to Eirnin's house. I noticed that with him. Each time the path seems to shrink, and I don't know if it's magic or if it's just 'cause I know my way better. Tough to say with wizards.

Whatever the reason, Eirnin's house appeared quicker than I expected. The garden was blooming, big red and orange flowers bobbing a little in the breeze. The air crackled, like a storm was about to roll in from the ocean.

Something disruptive.

I touched my charm again. After so long on the island I knew danger didn't have to look like what I expected. Naji would probably tell me to turn and run back to the shack, but then, Naji wasn't right about everything all the time. Much as he liked to think otherwise.

So I walked up the stone pathway, my hand curled tight around the sword, and kept watch for anything out of the ordinary: shadows moving through the trees, or a curl of gray mist. I prayed I wouldn't see the gray mist.

I didn't see nothing.

I knocked on Eirnin's door. No answer. A chill rippled through me, but then, Eirnin had been known not to answer if the mood didn't suit him. I knocked again, and then shouted, "Eirnin! It's me! I'm here about some clothes!"

Nothing.

At this point, the dread was pooling in the bottom of my stomach, and the forest seemed full of sneaking terrors, though I couldn't see any of them outright. Part of me wanted to turn back and the other part of me didn't want to go anywhere near the woods.

I pounded hard on the door, and this time, it creaked open.

I stopped, lifted the sword a little. A scent like flowers drifted out from inside the house. Dead flowers. Rotting flowers.

"Eirnin?" I called out, nudging the door open further. I stepped inside, sword lifted. It was dark. The air was colder than it was outside, as cold as the ice storms in the north, and it felt wrong somehow—empty, hollow.

When I stepped into the main room, the darkness erupted. Shapes poured out of the dead hearth, dark shadows that slid and undulated along the walls. Moaning filled up the room, the moaning and wailing of a thousand echoing voices. I couldn't move. The darkness slid around me, thick and oily, smelling of decay and magic.

And then a pale figure moved into the room, transparent and glowing. A ghost.

It looked at me, and although its face was stripped of humanity, like all ghosts, I recognized its features immediately.

"Eirnin," I said.

The ghost opened its mouth and a stream of ululating syllables poured out. It was the language of the dead. I'd heard it once before, when a sea-ghost boarded Papa's boat and tried to pull us all under.

I screamed and found the strength to break through the hold of the angry magic that Eirnin had left behind when he died. I raced out of the house, swinging my sword through the thick shadows. They shrieked when I cut them, and their cuts splattered spots of darkness across my hands and arms.

I burst out into the garden. The forest had stilled. Behind me, I could hear the rattle and screams of creatures in the house, and I didn't stop to contemplate on what had killed Eirnin. I just ran. I ran out of the garden and into the woods, and I wasn't even out of sight of the house when I slammed into Naji's chest.

"I told you to stay at the shack!" he roared, dragging me to my feet.

"I'm trying!" I shouted back.

He dragged me into the shadow of a tree, wrapped his arm across my chest, and melted us both into shadow.

A heartbeat later we stood at the edge of the forest, the beach flowing away from us to the edge of the island. Naji slumped up against a nearby pine tree, and for the first time I noticed how pale and waxy he was, and my heart twisted up and I had to stop myself from running over to him and throwing my arms around his shoulders.

"I didn't take off the charm," I said.

"I see that." Naji closed his eyes and let out a long breath. "You realize what that was, correct? What you felt the need to stumble into?"

"Eirnin's dead." I sat down at the doorway to our shack. "I saw his ghost." I didn't have a lot of love for Eirnin, truth be told, but the fact that he was no more for this world gave me the shivers.

"What were you doing at his house?"

"Getting new clothes."

Naji glared at me.

"I was gonna try and get some for you!"

His face softened a little at that. "I did warn you."

"No, you didn't. You said something on the island had changed. And what in hell does that mean?" I kicked at the sand. "What was all that stuff, anyway? You know what I'm talking about, right? The shadows pouring out of the hearth—"

"It was his magic, released when he died." Naji straightened up and stepped away from the tree. He looked better, which was something of a relief: it meant I wasn't in danger no more. "It has to burn away before it's safe to go back to his house. Which could take months. I don't know. Years, maybe."

"What killed him?"

"I've no idea." Naji frowned. "Perhaps you should stay in the shack for the next few days. Until we figure out the cause—"

"What about you?" I said. "Why do I got to be locked away like some princess in a story?"

Naji glared at me. "You know why."

I turned away from him, fuming. His damn curse.

"Ain't fair," I muttered.

"None of this is fair," Naji said, and he stopped pacing long enough to collect his sword. "There's a fish in the shack waiting for you to clean it."

That was something, at least.

Naji gave me a dark look. "You might as well get used to it."

"What, fish? Trust me, I'm plenty used to fish."

"No," he said. "Letting me protect you."

"We've had this conversation before." I turned away from him and stepped into the shack. A huge flat halibut was laid out next to the hearth, a single glassy eye staring unseeing up at the ceiling.

"And yet you act as if it's the first time you've heard it every time I remind you that you need to stay safe."

I pulled out my knife—another gift from Eirnin, although this was, admittedly, one he hadn't known he'd given me—and shoved it up under the fish scales. Naji didn't think his curse could be broken, 'cause he had to complete three impossible tasks in order to do so: hold the princess's starstones skin against stone, create life out of violence, and experience true love's kiss. Thing was, I knew at least one of the three, the last one, wasn't impossible at all. 'Cause I loved him. I loved him more fiercely than I'd loved anyone. But he didn't love me back, and I ain't one to embarrass myself needlessly.

Naji stepped into the shack behind me and shut the door.

"Maybe we should concern ourselves with figuring out who killed Eirnin," I said, fish scales sticking to my hands.

"Maybe we should," Naji said.

But neither of us got to talking.

I spent the next day or two in the shack, like Naji asked. He strung up strands of tree vines and red berry leaves and muttered his charms while I sulked in the corner and watched him. Just 'cause I was in love with him didn't mean I wasn't gonna resent him for locking me away like I was useless, or that I wanted to spend every moment of the day hanging around him.

Course, I understood that if he hadn't locked me away he would hurt, a pain in his head or his joints, but I still didn't think I was in as much danger as he believed. Just as long as I stayed away from Eirnin's house, right? And there was no way in the deep blue sea I'd go back there.

Those two days were boring as hell, which was exactly what I expected. Naji left to go fetch water or to catch fish and gather berries for us to eat. I sat in the doorway, my knife balanced on my knee, and tried not to look at the bonfire.

By the third day of imprisonment, I was going batty.

"You ain't seen nothing!" I said to Naji, after a week had passed. He'd let me sit just outside the shack that day, and though the air was colder than usual the sun had managed to burn away most of the clouds. "I ain't seen nothing, neither. Probably Eirnin's heart just gave out. He was old."

Naji glanced at me. "His heart didn't give out."

"How do you know?"

"I went to his house."

"What!"

"The day after you found him. I wanted to ensure I wasn't being overly cautious." He looked at me pointedly. "I'm not, by the way."

Despite my irritation, a little prickle of fear trembled down my spine. "What do you mean?"

"I mean," Naji said, "I spoke to his ghost."

I shivered and wrapped my arms around my knees. "Nobody speaks to ghosts."

"The Jadorr'a can."

I knew he was gonna say that. Any pirate would tell you attempting to learn the language of the dead is a grave mistake—about as grave a mistake as sailing to the Isles of the Sky.

Naji had a long history of ignoring pirates' wisdom.

"Well?" I asked.

"He was killed by a monster."

"A monster?" I frowned out at the ocean. "What sort of monster? He couldn't have been more specific?"

"The dead rarely are."

I slumped up against the side of the shack. "You're never gonna let me out again, are you?"

"Not until I determine where the monster is and how to destroy it." Naji glanced at me. "Thank you for understanding."

There was an undercurrent of warmth in his voice that made my toes curl up inside my boots, and I looked away from him, over at the beach curving into the forest. I knew I should speak, but I didn't know what to say, so I muttered something about knowing how much it hurt him. As soon as I spoke I was overwhelmed by that secret I carried, the potential power of my kiss. That happened sometimes. I just got to thinking about it at the wrong moments.

Naji stood up in a shower of sand. "The sun's going behind the clouds," he said.

"Oh hell."

"But it makes it easier for me move through the woods. We're running low on berries."

"And running high on monsters. Maybe you could see about taking care of that nonsense first?"

Naji's eyes brightened a little, and he said, "I plan on doing that, as well."

I usually liked it when his eyes brightened like that, but today it annoyed me, like my having to spend days in the shack was amusing to him.

"I guess I have to go inside."

"If you want me to actually accomplish anything, then yes."

I sighed, stood up, and did as he asked. The air already felt stale. At least the sun was gone. Nothing worse than wasting those few precious moments of sunlight inside.

Naji hung up a pine cone charm in the doorway but didn't leave his sword, which cheered me up a bit, since it meant he might actually have plans to hunt down this monster. I still had my doubts about a *monster* monster, some beastie roaming the forest. It seems like we would have seen it already. The Isles certainly threw enough horrors our way in those first few days we were stranded, before Naji had his powers back in full—all those eerie overnight transformations, trees into stones and stones into sand, or the time Naji and I were suffused with a strange glow. But not once did the island resort to a proper monster.

I stretched out on the nest of ferns I used for a bed and stared up at the ceiling. This was, I had discovered, the most entertaining way to pass my time. Trying to count the number of damn pine needles I'd used to thatch the roof. I got up to fifty-seven before I gave up.

The sky had turned darker since Naji left, and I could smell the rain on the air, waiting up in the clouds to fall. I sat up, mussing my pallet a little, and paced around the shack once or twice. Then I went to get a drink of water.

The bucket was empty.

"Damn him!" Naji always forgot to fill the bucket. Some Jadorr'a trick of never having to drink anything, apparently.

I scowled and kicked at the bucket. It clanged against the floor. I wondered how long till Naji returned. If he was just gathering berries, it probably wouldn't be long, but if he was off monster hunting—

How dangerous could it be for me to walk down to the water spring?

I mean, before Eirnin dropped dead in his house I'd gone down to the spring a couple times a day. I'd never run into any trouble. The two biggest dangers had been the Mists and the island itself, and Naji's magic kept us protected from both. Why wouldn't it protect me from some island monster?

And I had my knife, which I could throw well enough if necessary.

And nobody ever died from a headache.

I picked up the bucket and slid it into the crook of my arm. Then I walked over to the door and peered out.

Thickening clouds, a deserted beach.

He probably wouldn't even know I was gone.

I reached up and touched the charm for good luck, and then I stepped outside.

I made it to the spring without incident, which left me feeling more than a little smug. The woods were still and the sky thick with the threat of rain. Nothing moved but me: no shadows, no creeping curls of mist, no beasties watching me from the trees. Even the spring seemed calm, nearly stagnant—just a few faint gurgles let me know it was still running.

I dropped the bucket into the spring and took a long drink. It tasted steely and cold like always. Then I filled the bucket to the brim and stood to walk back to the shack.

Something small and sharp zipped past my head, so close I felt the swish of air from its movement, and impaled itself into a nearby tree. I dropped the bucket, water sloshing over my feet and legs, and slammed against the ground. I was tense and ready to defend myself, but at the same time I couldn't help thinking: *Damn it, Naji was right.*

I scanned the glimmering light-shadows of the chiming woods.

Nothing.

Real slow, I reached back for the knife. My fingers wrapped around the handle. Every muscle in my body was ready for a fight.

"Stop right there, *human*."

I stopped. The voice wasn't like any voice I'd heard, not even from the people of the Mists. It had a rhythm like bells, rippling and cascading, fabric fluttering in the wind, high and chiming. Oddly feminine.

"And kindly remove your hand from your weapon."

I obliged, sticking my hand back under my chest. Everything was so damn still. My lungs didn't want to work.

"Who are you?" I choked out. "You from the Mists?"

Laughter filled up the forest, a deep resonant clanging like the bells on the clock tower of the Empire Palace.

"I'm afraid not, girl-human. I am very much a part of your world."

The monster.

I pushed myself up on my hands, moving as slow as possible, listening for the zip of another dart. I leaned back on my heels, keeping my eye on the woods.

"You gonna let me see you?"

"Perhaps. Are you a friend of the wizard-human?"

"The wizard-human? Uh, you mean Naji or Eirnin?" Sometimes playing dumb is the best course of action.

"Naji? I do not know that name. But Eirnin—aye, that's the one I speak of."

"I know him," I said, not wanting to commit myself as his friend or foe. Who knew with monsters?

A branch broke off in the chiming woods, and I tensed up, ready to grab for my knife.

"That does not answer my question."

"Well, I don't know him *well*, not well enough to say—"

Another dart zoomed past my head. I ducked back down.

"I ain't seen him but a couple times!" I shouted into the dirt. "He gave me some clothes and helped my friend out with his curse—well, not helped exactly, more told him what to do next—and other'n that he might as well not exist to me."

The speaker didn't give me an answer. I kept my head down and tried not to let on how scared I was.

For a second I wondered about Naji, if he was hurting real bad, if he was coming to save me.

I wondered how pissed he was gonna be.

"So you have no loyalties to the wizard-human?"

"Ain't got no loyalties to anybody," I said, even though I knew it to be a lie even as I spoke.

A shadow rippled across the forest, and I heard footsteps, the crackle and snap of a figure moving over the fallen leaves of the forest floor.

"You may sit up, girl-human. I will not shoot again."

I ain't so stupid as to take someone on her word for a claim like that, so I moved slow as I could, inching up a little at a time. I was halfway up to sitting when I caught a glimpse of the creature speaking to me, and it took every ounce of willpower not to curl back up into a ball.

The speaker was a manticore.

Now, I'd seen a manticore or two before, locked away in cages, and those were frightening enough. But I ain't never heard one speak—I didn't even think they could. And this one was bigger than the caged ones, only about a foot shorter than me, even though she stood on four legs instead of two.

She padded up close to me and leaned down and sniffed with her pretty human-looking nose, then settled down on her haunches, her scaly wings pressed flat against her back, her tail curling up into a point behind her head. Hadn't been darts she'd flung at me, but spines, and poisonous ones at that, if the stories were anything to go by. I kept my eye on that tail.

"I only shot at you when I thought you were an ally of the wizard-human," she said. "I do not care for the taste of girl-humans."

"Oh. All right." I stood up, slow and careful. The manticore followed me with her eyes, which were the color of pressed gold.

"Perhaps you can help me," she said.

Well, that stunned me into silence.

"Do you have a way off the island?"

It took me a minute to find my voice, and even when I did all I could do was stammer out the most drawn-out "no" in the history of time.

The manticore looked disappointed.

"What do you need to leave the island for?" I asked, mostly in a whisper.

"I'd like to go home, of course," she said. "The wizard-human had kept me imprisoned for almost three life cycles. I made my escape four days ago."

She licked at her paw. My stomach twisted around and I stumbled backward, one foot splashing into the spring.

"And how . . ." I said. "How did you—"

"I ate him."

She said it all matter-of-fact, like we were bartering trade in a day market. Sweat prickled out of my skin.

"I told you, girl-human, I do not care for the taste of your sort's flesh." She sniffed. "If you do not have a way off the island, why did you come here at all?"

"We were marooned." I hadn't meant to tell her, but I was so unnerved it spilled out anyway.

"We? There is another human?" She smiled, which was terrifying, her mouth all full of teeth. "A girl-human or a boy-human?"

I didn't want to answer that. So I changed the subject.

"I may be able to get you off the island," I said, quick as lightning. "But you'll have to wait."

"You said you had no manner of escape."

"I don't. But a friend—a girl-human, like me, she might be bringing a ship and crew."

The manticore's face lit up. She fluffed out her mane. "And this friend-girl-human would be able to take me to the Island of the Sun?"

"Sure." I'd heard of the Island of the Sun. It's in the west, not lined up with any of the major shipping ports so not much use to anybody. Except, apparently, manticores. Papa's crew always said it was a wasteland. "But you'll have to wait till she gets here, like I said. And I don't know when that'll be."

"That is acceptable." The manticore stood up and arched her spine, wings fluttering. Her tail curled above her back. "I shall accompany you back to your dwelling."

Naji. My stomach twisted again. Hopefully he hadn't come back yet, and I could find a way to warn him. At least I didn't seem to really be in danger—that would keep him from swooping in to save me.

"It's small," I said. "It'll remind you of your prison, I'm sure of it. You'd be better to live out in the woods . . ." I swept my hand around and the trees rustled.

"Don't be absurd, girl-human. You will leave me when the friend-girl-human comes. Show me the way."

My brain spun round and round. All I could think about was Naji skulking in front of the fire, unaware that I was bringing in a monster keen on eating him. Was this how it all ended? Me not being able to out-talk a manticore and Naji winding up as its dinner?

"Why do you dally?" The manticore's voice echoed through my skull.

"Uh, I need to get some clean water. Hold on." I felt around in the underbrush for the water bucket. The manticore regarded me with her big gold eyes. I dipped the bucket into the spring, and watched as the water flooded in. Every now and then I dipped the bucket so the water flowed back out again, blocking the manticore's view with my back while I did it. All the while I scrambled to come up with some way out of this mess. Could you strike a deal with a manticore? Stories always made 'em out as monsters, teeth and claws and nothing else.

"This is taking too long," the manticore said.

"Sorry." My heart pounded. I let the bucket fill completely and then stood up. "Look, you gotta promise me something if I'm gonna help you off the island."

"A promise?" The manticore smiled again, teeth flashing. I regretted my words immediately.

"Look, if we're gonna help you, me and my friend, you can't run around eating every man—uh, every boy-human—we come across, do you understand?"

"No," the manticore said. "You would starve me?"

"Of course not! But you'll have to be, ah, selective."

The manticore unfurled her tail, the tip of the spine glistening. "I'm always selective with my meals," she said. "I only ate the wizard-human out of desperation. I have never cared for the flavor of his sort. Much too stringy."

"Uh, that's not exactly what I meant . . ."

The manticore curled up her lip into a toothy little sneer.

"Why don't you just ask me before you eat anyone? In exchange for getting you off the island?"

"I can agree to those terms."

"And you have to *not* eat the guy if I say no."

For a moment the manticore pouted. Then she licked a paw and ran it over her mane. "We shall see."

Good enough. And if she didn't like the taste of the Wizard Eirnin, maybe she wouldn't have no interest in eating Naji, neither.

We walked side by side back to the shack on the beach. I sure as hell wasn't letting her walk behind me, though she didn't seem to much care one way or the other. She moved real quick, even considering her size, though branches snapped, and leaves and pine cones showered over us every time she knocked into a tree. She made more noise than me or Naji ever did.

When we came to the shack, I smelled fish and wild onions frying on the hearth. I stopped. He came home, found me gone, and started cooking?

And then my heart started pounding again, 'cause now I had to find a way to warn him.

The manticore stopped outside the shack. "You are correct," she said. "This is much too small for me."

I prayed to Kaol and every other goddess I knew that Naji would stay inside. "Let me go in first, let him know—"

"Him?" One of her eyebrows arched up. She ran her thin pink tongue over her perfect lady's lips.

"You promised you'd ask," I said, and then I bolted inside, slamming the door shut. Naji looked up at me.

"I really expected you to do that sooner," he said.

"What?" My breath was coming too fast, and I tried to rein it so he wouldn't think nothing was wrong.

"Run off. I didn't think I could truly keep you locked in the shack." He went back to stirring our meal. "I assume you went to get water? It seems like it was an uneventful trip."

He looked at me again, and I could only stare back at him, stricken.

He frowned, and his eyes darkened. "What's wrong?"

I set the water down in its place beside the hearth and tried to come up with the words. Course, I didn't get the chance, 'cause the manticore bounded into the shack, damn near knocking the door off the hinges.

Naji was crouched in fighting stance with his knife drawn before I even saw him move.

"Ananna," he hissed. "My *sword*."

I picked the sword up from where it was propped up against the wall and tossed it at him, but I kept my eyes on the manticore. "You *promised*," I said.

Naji whipped his head around at me.

"Yes, but you did not tell me you had a Jadorr'a in your stone-nest."

She said "Jadorr'a" the way I might've said "sweet lime drink" or "sugar roses."

"Ananna, what have you done?" Naji asked me, his voice low. He sounded angry, which if he was like any other man meant he was scared.

The manticore let out a little grumbly noise and crouched low like a cat about to pounce.

"Kaol, couldn't you just eat some fish like a normal cat?" I shouted.

But both of 'em acted like I hadn't said nothing.

And then the manticore's pretty human face twisted up in a grimace. "Jadorr'a!" she said. "You've been cursed."

Neither me or Naji moved.

"You hide the smell well, but . . . there, there it is again." She shook her head, mane flying out in a big golden puff.

"You can't eat him if he's cursed?" I said.

"Of course not! It taints the flavor of the meat and will pass on to me, and besides which, from the smell of it, this is not a curse I want to possess." She sniffed the air again.

"So, you're not going to eat him?" I said.

"Not until the curse is lifted." She sniffed once more, her nose wrinkling up at the brow. "Three impossible tasks," she said. She turned to Naji. "I shall help you."

Naji looked at a loss for words, which might've been funny in any other circumstance.

The manticore sat back on her haunches. "It's very warm in your stone-nest."

"We have a fire going," I told her.

Naji shot me a dirty look.

"You promise you ain't gonna eat him till his curse is lifted?"

The manticore shuddered. "I told you, I cannot abide the flavor of cursed flesh. It tastes half rotted."

Naji stayed in fighting stance.

"Girl-human, you were correct in assuming that I would find your stone-nest too similar to the walls of the wizard-human's prison. I shall make a nest nearby. Is that acceptable?"

I didn't dare look at Naji when I answered "yes."

The manticore nodded and backed out the door, the snap and stomp of her footsteps drifting through the cracked stone walls.

Naji finally let down his knife and sword. He turned toward me. Kaol, I wanted to run out onto the beach and dive into the cold black sea. Anything to get away from the expression on his face.

"What—"

"She bullied me!" I said. "She asked if I knew a way off the island and I was trying to keep her from finding you and—and *eating* you and—"

Naji held up one hand.

"You don't have a way off the island."

"I will when Marjani shows up. Look, she doesn't eat women, all right? And she won't eat you 'cause of the curse, and we can't break that till we leave. So Marjani takes us to the Island of the Sun and we drop off the manticore and then we fix your curse."

Naji stared at me. "My curse is unbreakable," he said.

"That ain't true." Sadness washed over me, and I wondered what would happen if I kissed him right then, and showed him at least one of the tasks wasn't impossible.

"It is." He sighed. "At least I know I won't die in the jaws of a manticore. Although I can't believe you brought that creature here."

"I didn't have no choice! What the hell was I supposed to do? She kept shooting spines at me."

Naji looked at me sideways. "She wasn't going to hurt you."

"Yeah, but how I was supposed to know that?"

Outside, the manticore roared, and it sounded like a trumpet announcing the winner of the horse races in Lisirra. Naji tossed his sword onto the table and looked defeated.

CHAPTER TWO

I was sick to hell of eating fish. Even on board Papa's ship we never ate this much fish. There'd be dried salted meats, and fresh seabird, if we were close to land. But here on the Isles of the Sky it was nothing but fish, flaking like paper and just as tasteless.

"Then go hunting," Naji told me one evening when I complained. "I'm sure your pet manticore will be happy to accompany you."

"She ain't my pet." I flung a piece of fish down to the strip of tree bark we used as plates. In truth I'd thought about hunting before, 'cause I'd seen flashes of these graceful horsy animals through the dappled light of the trees, but I didn't know the first damn thing about hunting game. If I had a pistol, maybe I could do it.

I didn't tell Naji none of that, though, 'cause I knew he'd make fun of me. He was still sore about me bringing the manticore around.

"Finish your meal," he said, like I was some little kid.

I glared at him and shoved the food away, sending the fish splattering across the floor.

"Finish it for me," I said, and stomped out of the shack.

I walked down to the shore edge to calm down. I made sure not to get too close to the signal fire, but I could see it glimmering off in the distance, golden swirls twisting up toward the sky. And the smell of it was strong too, on account of either the breeze or the island shifting us downwind: it wasn't so much like wood burning at all, but like blood.

"Girl-human, I am in need of your assistance." The manticore came ambling down the beach, flicking her tail left and right. That tail still gave me the shivers.

"What do you want?"

"There's a burr in my mane." The manticore shook her head. "A great tangle. Would you remove it for me?"

I stared at her.

"The hell would you do if you were on the Island of the Sun?" I asked. "Take it out yourself."

The manticore growled. Growls I didn't mind, but you best believe I had my eyes fixed firmly on the poisoned tip of her tail.

"I would command one of my servant-humans to remove it for me," she said. "And she would remove it without complaint, singing all the while."

"Servant-humans."

"Yes. We fill our palace with your kind and they do our bidding and offer themselves as food whenever we are hungry."

I wasn't sure I believed her. She had a lot of stories about the Island of the Sun, and its great red-sand desert and the great wealth of her family and what an *honor* I'd give them, one they would certainly thank with a *boon*, if only I delivered an uncursed Jadorr'a to their eating table. She trotted over and sat down beside me, tucking her massive paws underneath her body, sticking her head close to my lap. There was a snarl in her mane, a big knot where something'd gotten stuck.

"Fine," I said. "But I ain't singing."

She sniffed like she wasn't too happy, but then she stuck her chin on my knee. The weight of her head was a lot more than I expected.

I combed my fingers through her mane, which was surprisingly soft, plucking out around the tangle. I moved slow and steady 'cause the last thing I wanted was to pull too hard and have those big white teeth of hers slice through my leg. Ain't no way it was a burr in that huge mass of fur—a burr's too small—but I felt around with my fingers and I realized she had a pine cone stuck in there.

"This may take a while," I said.

The manticore didn't answer save for that trumpeting sound she made whenever she was content. Everything about her voice sounded like a musical instrument. Even her full name—Ongraygeeomryn—kinda sounded like a bell chiming when she said it. I couldn't say it, which was why I just called her the manticore and left it at that.

When I had the pine cone about halfway untangled from her mane, my stomach growled, and I thought about the fish I'd flung at Naji.

"Hey," I said, plucking at her fur like it was a guitar string. "Would you go hunting with me?"

The manticore lifted her head a little, enough that I got a face full of her mane.

"Hunting?"

"Yeah." I leaned back, wiping her fur from my mouth. "I'm sick of eating fish."

"Fish is not food."

"It is for people. Look, could you help me or not? I just want to bring down one of those horse animals I've seen in the woods."

"Caribou. That is what the wizard-human called them."

"Fine, the caribou. Could you bring one down for me? Don't use your stinger," I added. "I want to eat it, remember."

The manticore laughed. "To bring down such a clumsy creature will be easy. 'Tis a shame there are no more humans on this island."

I didn't say nothing to that, just tugged at the pine cone, hoping it'd come free. It didn't.

"If I bring you a caribou," the manticore said, "will you groom me whenever I ask?"

I stopped. "Groom?" There I went, making deals with a manticore again.

"Aye. Brush my mane and coat, and pull the thorns from my feet."

"That all? You want me to wipe your ass too?"

"Don't be crude, girl-human."

"I'm just checking on the particulars before I agree to anything."

"No, that service I will not require of you. Manticores bathe themselves."

Well, that was something, at least. In truth plucking the pine cone from her mane wasn't that terrible—kind of relaxing, actually. Took my mind off Naji.

"Sure, I'll groom you. But not for one caribou—for any you catch. And you'll catch 'em anytime I ask."

She made a *hmmm* noise of displeasure.

"Look, it'll take me and Naji a while to get through a whole one of the things."

The manticore sighed. "Yes, I suppose that is true."

"Plus you said it was easy hunting."

I had her there. She got this squished-up look on her face that meant I'd just called her manticore-ness into question.

"I agree to your terms, girl-human. A lifetime of caribou for a lifetime of grooming."

I hope not a lifetime, I thought, but I picked up her paw and shook on it.

The manticore stayed true to her word. I pulled the pine cone from her hair and the next morning I woke to the sound of claws scratching across the shack's door. Naji stirred over in the corner, still asleep. The fire in the hearth had burned down to ash. I stumbled over to the door and opened it.

The manticore sat with a dead caribou at her feet, her face smeared with blood.

"Here is your caribou, girl-human," she said.

A jagged tear ripped across the caribou's throat, and its head hung at an angle. "You didn't sting it, did you?"

"On the spirits of my mothers, no, I did not." The manticore gave me this solemn look. "Enjoy your meat, girl-human." Then she trotted off, wings bouncing, toward the shadow of the forest.

When I turned around, Naji was lurking behind me, sword and knife drawn.

"Kaol!" I shouted. "How long you been standing there?"

"I was in the shadows," he said. "I didn't want the manticore to see me." He walked up to the caribou and poked it with the toe of his boot. "Why did she bring you this?"

I crossed my arms in front of my chest and didn't answer.

Naji turned around. "Ananna, you have no idea how dangerous that creature is—"

"Oh, come on," I said. "She can't eat either of us."

"She *won't* eat either of us," Naji said. "There is a difference."

I scowled at him 'cause I knew he was right.

"Now answer my question," he said. "Why did she bring this to you?"

I sighed. Naji kept his eyes on me, waiting. And so I told him what happened the night before, with the pine cone and all. His face didn't move while I spoke, though his eyes got darker and darker.

"That was a mistake," he said. "Making a deal with a manticore."

"Well, it got us meat, didn't it? Something that ain't fish." I yanked his sword away from him. "You don't like it, you don't have to eat it."

He didn't say nothing, and I stomped outside and pushed the caribou to its side and stuck the knife into the skin of its belly. I'd cleaned fish before—big fish, too, sharks and monster eels—so I figured a land creature couldn't be much different.

Naji came out and watched me. I could feel him standing there, the weight of his presence. It made my skin prickle up sometimes, having him watch me. Not in a bad way.

"I would still check for spines," he said. "You shouldn't take a manticore on its word."

"Planning on it." I had been, too. I ain't stupid.

It took me close to an hour to skin the caribou and gut it and slice the meat from the bones. I didn't find any spines, and I checked everywhere I could think of — in the stomach and mouth, in case she tried to hide one. Nothing. By then Naji had the hearth fire going, and he roasted some of the meat and we had a right proper meal.

The caribou didn't taste like any meat I'd had before—it was a bit like sheep meat, only wilder and leaner—but it was sure better than another round of fish. Naji ate it without saying nothing, and I figured he was sick of fish too but wasn't gonna admit it.

When we finished eating, Naji told me to start cutting the raw meat into strips.

"Why?" I asked him.

"Because otherwise we're going to wind up with a mountain of rotting caribou carcass," he said. "Which is something I'm guessing you didn't think about when you asked the manticore to hunt for you."

I hadn't, mostly 'cause I didn't realize how much meat was on 'em, nor how dense it was. So I went outside and started hacking at the caribou with his sword. I laid the strips out on some flat stones, figuring Naji planned on drying 'em out but not sure of the procedure for it.

He disappeared with the water bucket into the tree shadows and returned a few minutes later, the bucket full of seawater. He went into the house, then came back out and started gathering up the meat strips.

"What did you get all that seawater for?"

"We need the salt." Naji draped the meat strips over his forearms. "Keep cutting. We'll probably have to sleep outside while the meat is processing."

I frowned at that, thinking about the rainstorms that stirred up the woods without warning.

By the time I finished cutting up the caribou my arms ached something fierce and the whole front of my coat was stained with blood. And I couldn't run over to Eirnin's house and get a spare, neither.

I carted the sword back into the shack and dumped it next to the hearth for cleaning. Naji was scraping salt out of the bucket, this big pile of it glittering on a piece of tree bark like sand. Another kettle boiled and rattled over the fire, and the air smelled like his magic. He'd already hung up some of the meat strips, hooking 'em to the rafters with little bits of vine from the woods. They swayed a little from the breeze blowing through the open door, looking like dancing snakes.

"How'd you know to do all this?" I asked.

"I learned when I was a child," he said. "Did you finish slicing up the carcass?"

I nodded, wanting to ask him about his childhood, wanting to know everything I could about him. But I figured he'd snap at me if I said anything.

"Good. Start hanging the rest of the meat from the ceiling."

I did what he asked. It was satisfying work—we'd pack the strips in sea salt, let 'em sit, and then lash 'em to the ceiling. Plus, I liked working with Naji, being close to him without having to find anything to say or without having to worry about the stupid curse. It reminded me of the way Mama and Papa used to work together on the rigging, in the early parts of the dawn, clambering over the ropes and shouting instructions at one another. I used to watch 'em from the crow's nest and think about how that must be what it's like to love someone.

When we finished the whole shack smelled like meat, and you could hardly walk from one side to the other on account of all the slivers of caribou dangling in the way.

"How long's it gonna take?" I asked. "Till it's all dried out?"

"A few weeks." Naji glanced at me. He was over at the hearth, messing with the fire. "There's a cave not far from here. We should start moving our things."

"The cave!" I said. "The rain'll get in."

"Exactly. It's why we had to hang the caribou up in here." Smoke trickled up from the fire, gray and thick. It made my nose run.

"I know that." I scowled. "Just don't know why we have to live in the cave is all."

Naji stepped away from the hearth. "Would you rather move into Eirnin's house?" He glanced at me. "Spend the next few weeks living side by side with ghosts and magic homunculi?"

I glared at him. He looked like he wanted to laugh. I knew he had me.

I rolled up my clothes and started the trek down to the cave.

CHAPTER THREE

Living in a cave wasn't so bad, despite the way the dampness flooded in every time the skies opened up with rain. This soft, thick moss grew over the rocks and made for a bed more comfortable than my big pile of ferns back in the shack. We kept a fire burning near the entrance and ate half-cured caribou and berries and the occasional fish to mix it up.

After a few days, the manticore sniffed us out.

"Girl-human," she said. "Did you and the Jadorr'a think you could flee from me?"

It was nighttime, the sky starless from the rain clouds, and Naji was sleeping down deeper in the cave, his tattoos lighting up the darkness. I didn't know if he was dreaming or casting magic in his sleep. He'd told me once he talked to the Order sometimes, though he never told me what about. They would've rescued him weeks ago, when we first landed, but they wouldn't have rescued me. That's why he was still here.

And no one else is crazy enough to sail to the Isles of the Sky. Hadn't seen so much as a sail on the horizon the entire time we'd been on the island.

I popped my head out of the cave's entrance. The manticore sniffed at me and flicked her tail back and forth.

"The shack's filled up with meat," I said.

"Caribou is not *meat*," she told me. "Too gristly, too tough. Like tree bark."

I couldn't imagine the manticore having ever actually tried tree bark, but I didn't say nothing, just shuffled out into the woods. The air was damp and cold like always, and I pulled my coat tight around me.

"Do you need something?"

"May I see your new rock-nest?"

I sighed. "It's just a cave."

"It is larger than your old nest."

"Yeah, I guess."

The manticore trotted past the fire and into the cave's main room, her footsteps silent on the moss. Naji's tattoos turned everything pale blue.

For a minute the manticore stared at him, tongue running over the edges of her teeth. I edged toward the sword.

But the manticore didn't lunge for him or shoot a spine. Instead, she turned around on the moss a few times, like a dog, and then settled in.

Well. Looked like she found a new home.

"Brush my mane, girl-human," the manticore said. "In exchange for catching the caribou."

"I thought the caribou was in exchange for pulling out the pine cone."

She shook her head and I didn't feel much like arguing with her.

"What do you want me to use?" I asked. "My fingers?"

"Don't be silly. A brush will suffice."

"A brush?" I laughed. "I don't have no brush." I pointed at my own hair, which was a tangled, knotted mess from the rainwater and the woods and the wind—even if Naji had been halfway interested in me at some point, he sure as curses wouldn't be now. I'd hacked some of it off with Naji's knife, but it was hair. It grew back. "You think I'd look like this if I owned a brush?"

The manticore frowned. "I thought that was merely the humans' way. You will not tend to your grooming unless commanded by a manticore."

"The hell did you get that idea from?"

The manticore looked genuinely confused.

"You know what?" I said. "Forget it. I don't have a brush, but I'll work it through my fingers, all right? Best I can do."

The manticore heaved a sigh like this was the biggest burden to her, worse than getting trapped on a deserted island in the north, worse than having to eat animals instead of people. Not that she shut up about either of those things.

I sat down beside her and started working through her mane, a few pieces at a time. It was pretty tangled—not as bad as my hair, but bad enough that I could see how someone as prissy as her would want it fixed.

It was boring work, but calming. Once I got the tangles out her mane was soft as spun silk, and it reminded me of the scarfs and dresses we'd pull from Empire trading ships, the ones I used to sleep on as a little girl.

And there, in the darkness of that cave, in the cold damp of that island, I started missing Papa's ship real bad. I combed through the manticore's mane and I thought about the open ocean, the hot breezes blowing across the water and the warmth of the sun. I didn't think I'd ever feel warm again.

I moved to the other side of the manticore's head. I could see Naji, curled up on his side. Seeing him made me sadder still, remembering how miserable he'd been on the *Ayel's Revenge*, how comfortable he'd been in the desert.

Even if he loved me back, we were tied to different parts of the world.

"You should kiss him, girl-human."

I yelped in surprise at the sound of her voice, and my fingers caught on a snag in the manticore's mane. She hissed and yanked her head back.

"What?" I said. "Kiss who?"

"Who else is here?" she said. She rubbed against her scalp with the back of her paw. "The Jadorr'a."

"What would I do that for?"

The manticore giggled. It sounded like a wind chime. "To complete the first impossible task, of course."

I froze, my hand hovering near her mane. Ain't no way she could know that I was in love with him. Did manticores even know what love was? I doubted it.

"I ain't his true love," I said gruffly, shoving my fingers back into her fur.

"Aye, but he's yours," she said. "I can feel it when you're close to him, like a lightning storm."

My face turned hot. "That's the island talking," I muttered. "Don't mean nothing."

"Go on," she said. "While he's sleeping. Don't you want to help him?Your friend?" She smiled, teeth sparkling in the firelight. "Your *true love*?"

"Course I want to help . . . *my friend*." I pushed away from her and crossed my arms over my chest. "But you're just telling me to do it so as you can eat him."

"In time," she said. "All tasks must still be completed." Her eyes glimmered. "Just one little kiss. He won't even know it was you."

I looked at her and then I looked at Naji, handsome and disfigured all at once. Maybe she was right. If I kissed him softly enough, maybe he wouldn't even know it was me: it had never, in the past month, occurred to me to kiss him while he was asleep. In the soft, velvety haze of the open air, this seemed like the most perfect idea I'd ever heard.

One kiss, just enough to help him on his way. To give him hope again.

"Go on," she said, speaking into my ear, close enough I could smell the carrion on her breath.

I pushed away from her. Naji kept on sleeping. He lay on his side, one arm slung across the pallet of moss. His hair curled around his neck. The lines of his scar looked like the paths a lover's hand would take as she ran her fingers down his face. They were beautiful.

I knelt down beside him. His breath was slow and even. I could feel the manticore staring at us, waiting.

I leaned forward, holding my breath. He didn't move.

I closed my eyes.

I pressed my mouth against his, and his face against mine was rough and soft like falling leaves.

My whole body swelled with light. I felt a crack, like lightning cleaving a tree in two, like a wine glass shattering on a stone floor.

Something breaking.

And then I was flat on my back, and Naji's knife was at my throat, his knee digging into my stomach.

"Ananna?"

"What the fuck are you doing?" I shrieked. My face was hot and I could feel this weight behind my eyes and I told myself I wasn't going to cry, not over this. The memory of the kiss was sweet as spun sugar on my tongue, but the rest of me burned with humiliation.

He slid back, dropping the knife away. "What did *you* do? I felt someone attack me—"

The manticore started to laugh.

"I was just walking by!" I shouted. "And you jumped out at me."

"Jadorr'a," the manticore said. "The girl-human *kissed* you."

Apparently manticores knew as much about keeping a secret as they did about humans—not a damn thing.

Naji's face didn't change. I wanted to throw up.

"You can feel it, can't you? I know you can. I can smell it, the change in the curse—" whispered the manticore.

"Shut up!" I scrambled away from Naji. He was still staring at me, but now something had changed in his expression. I couldn't read it, didn't want to read it.

He didn't move except to let his knife drop to the floor. The weight in my eyes built and built, and I jumped to my feet and turned and ran out of the entrance of the cave, into the dark rattling woods. It was cold as the ice-islands, but I was so hot with humiliation—I gave him a kiss and he thought it was an *attack*—that I didn't feel it except in my lungs, burning 'em like fire as I ran into the chiming forest.

I tripped on a fallen tree trunk and went sprawling into the ground, wet from the recent rain. The gossamer dust of the leaves coated my palms, and when I sat back and pushed my hair out of my eyes I could feel it sticking to my skin.

The forest was chiming like crazy, as though a storm was on its way, and I let out this scream 'cause it was the only thing I could do. I screamed and slammed my fists into the ground. The dampness crept in through my clothes and I didn't care. I just screamed.

"Ananna?"

Naji's voice was soft and hesitant, blending in with the forest's chiming.

"Go away."

He materialized beside me.

"Go. The. Hell. *Away*."

"No."

I wiped at my face, smearing mud across my cheeks. The powder from the leaves came off on the back of my hand. "Fine," I said, and tried to stand up. He grabbed my arm.

"Look at me," he said.

"Let go."

He didn't, and his grip was stronger than I expected. I tried to wriggle away from him but he held me tight.

"Will you stop it?" he said. "I'm trying to thank you."

That stilled me, the kindness in his voice. I slumped against the ground, and he dropped his hand to his side. My arm burned from where he touched me, and not 'cause it hurt, neither.

"It worked," Naji said. "Your ki . . . what you did. It worked."

I didn't say nothing, just drew my legs into my body and curled up tight like I could disappear into the shadow.

"It wasn't impossible," Naji said.

"Course it wasn't," I snapped. "What's impossible is somebody loving *me*."

He didn't answer. Part of me had been hoping he'd tell me I was wrong, that he'd at least try and comfort me, but when he didn't my chest got tight and painful. I turned away from him and my skin prickled the way it did when the air was full of magic. But there was no magic here. Just another reminder that Naji didn't love me back.

"Thank you," he said after a few moments had passed.

"Whatever." I stood up. He didn't stop me this time. I couldn't stand the closeness to him. I kept thinking about the way his mouth had felt. "I have to go."

"Thank you," he said again, like those were the only words he knew.

I walked away from him, away from the forest and the cave, toward the sea.

• • •

I woke up the next morning covered in sand, my head pounding like I'd spent the night tossing back rum in some Bone Island drink-house. The sunlight, weak as it was, hurt my eyes, and I rolled over onto my stomach and pressed my face against the cold beach.

I thought about Naji. Jackass.

I thought about myself. Idiot.

It took me a while to work up the willpower to sit up. I didn't know where I was. I couldn't see the smoke from the bonfire, which was a bad sign, but one I chose not to dwell on for the time being.

Somebody said my name.

At first I thought it was Naji, that he'd been lurking in the shadows waiting for me to wake up so he could humiliate me again with his thank-yous, but then whoever it was said my name again, and I recognized the ice in the voice.

The Mists lady. Echo.

"Hello again," she said, curling into existence beside me. "I heard you experienced a bit of a disappointment last night."

I couldn't speak. I was too blindsided by her sudden appearance. She slid closer to me, the edges of her body blurred and translucent, as if she wasn't completely in our world, and I skittered backward a little, not daring to take my eyes off of her. She was after Naji at the behest of her lord, who Naji'd stopped from taking over our world a few years ago. The lord wanted revenge for it, wanted to see Naji dead or enslaved or worse. Naji had hidden himself from the Mists, though, so she always came to me instead.

Except Naji had cast new magic when we came here, magic that was supposed to keep me blocked from the Mists too. It was supposed to keep me safe—

Unless he'd dismantled it while I slept last night. Like the thought of me loving him was enough to leave me soft and vulnerable out there on the beach. Like it was worth the pain it caused him.

"What do you want?" I asked, pushing myself up to standing. My legs wobbled and the world spun around me like I was drunk. I didn't want to let on that I was supposed to be hidden from her sight.

"My lord would be willing to extend his offer to you a second time. Power. Wealth. *Magic*." She leered. "All you have to do is hand over the Jadorr'a. It's an excellent arrangement, if you're so inclined."

"I ain't."

I took a few steps backward across the beach, hoping I was headed in the right direction, hoping that my running away would discourage her somehow. But of course it didn't. Echo followed, sliding up close enough that I could feel the cold dampness from her body. I stopped, paralyzed by fear. Echo curled around me, one hand tracing the outline of my profile. But she didn't touch me. I was still wearing the charm around my neck. I wasn't hidden, but I was protected.

"I know what it's like," she whispered in my ear. "To be hurt by a man. It must be hard for you. It's not the kind of hurt you can heal with violence."

A starburst of anger exploded in my chest, and for a moment my thoughts were filled with an irrational white-hot blaze.

And then I whirled around and punched her square in the face, right at that point where her eyes met her nose. Pain erupted through my hand like I'd punched bone, but then my fist slid straight on through her head, and she dissolved into smoke, disappearing completely.

For a long moment I stood there, my anger consumed by astonishment, and waited for her to return. But there was just the waves crashing up against the bottom part of the island, the wind rattling the pine trees. Nothing.

After a while, I set off down the beach, although I did pull out my knife. Just in case.

I walked for a good hour, working off the soreness in my legs and the ache in my head. I'd split open my hand when I punched Echo, but after a while the sting of that disappeared too.

"Girl-human!"

I stopped. The blaze of anger made a sudden, violent appearance. The damn manticore. She'd started this all, hadn't she? All for a meal.

"Leave me alone!" I shouted.

The manticore trotted out of the woods, flicking up little sprays of sand with her paws.

"The Jadorr'a sent me," she said. "He said you were in danger."

"Not anymore." If I needed any more evidence that I repulsed him enough to undo the protective magic, it was right there: he hadn't come for me himself.

"This is all your fault," I said.

The manticore fell into step beside me.

"I know."

I glanced at her. Her face looked strange. It took me a moment to realize that it was 'cause she looked guilty.

"He hurt you," she said. "Soul-hurt."

I kicked at the sand.

"As opposed to body-hurt."

"Yeah, I got it. I ain't stupid."

The manticore stopped and nuzzled my shoulder like she was an overgrown cat. "I thought he returned your affection. Humans seem to care about happiness. I wished to gift some to you. In exchange for combing my mane."

I scowled. "You had me do it so you could eat him."

"Well, yes, that too."

I didn't say nothing.

"One does not negate the other," she added.

"Well, you just made things worse." Not exactly the wounding insult I'd hoped for, but I was too tired from everything to be clever.

"I know," she said.

And then she knelt down in the sand. "If you would like, I'll allow you to ride me."

I stared at her. "Is this a trick?"

She peered up at me through the frame of her fur. "No trick, girl-human. It is a great honor to ride a manticore."

"Are you gonna stab me with your tail once I get up there?"

"If I wished to poison you, I would shoot the spine into your heart from here."

That was probably true.

"Come along, girl-human. We are far from your rock-nest, and I will not kneel like this all day."

I looked at her, considering. My body ached and I was sick of walking. And it would be something to say I got to ride a manticore.

Besides, she still looked kinda guilty, and I realized I actually believed her: that she thought she had been helping—at least up until we cured the rest of the curse and she got to snack on him.

"All right," I said.

I swung my leg over her shoulder and settled myself between her leathery wings. She straightened up, tall as a pony. I wrapped my arms around her neck, leaning into her soft mane-fur, which smelled clean, like the woods after a rainfall.

"Do not fall off," she said.

"Ain't planning on it."

And then she took off in a gallop, moving like liquid over the sand. A cold wind blew off the sea and pushed my hair back from my face. She let out this great trumpeting laugh that echoed through the woods, stirring up the birds, and after a minute I started laughing with her. The anger washed out of me, and the sadness and the fear and the humiliation. The wind coursed around us like we were flying, and it stripped Naji right out of my mind.

The manticore got me that gift of happiness after all.

Course, it didn't last. We had to arrive back at the cave eventually, and as the manticore slowed to a trot, I could see Naji pacing back and forth across the beach. He was wrapped up in his black Jadorr'a robe and he looked like a smear of ink against the impossibly wide sky.

"You must disembark," the manticore said, kneeling. I climbed off her and gave her a pat on the shoulder.

"Thanks for the ride," I said.

"It was my gift to you."

Naji had stopped pacing and he stared at me, his hair and cloak blowing off to the side. I trudged across the beach toward him, sand stinging me in the eyes.

"Why did you undo the protective spell?" The wind caught my voice and my question rose and fell like it belonged to a ghost. "The one that's supposed to keep me safe from the Mists?"

"Have you gone mad?" Naji stared at me. "Why would you think I'd do that?"

"Because Echo showed up. That's why I was *in danger*."

Naji's face went pale beneath his scars.

"I didn't hand you over," I said. "Obviously. But it was a pretty crap thing for you to just—expose me like that."

"I told you, I didn't undo the spell."

"Then why did Echo find me?" I shouted, the wind ripping my question to shreds.

A peculiar expression crossed over Naji's face. It almost looked like pain, like guilt or sorrow or even worry, but I knew better. "I would never do something to put you in danger."

"Yeah, just to save your own skin. I imagine you were willing to put up with a headache if it meant getting back at me."

"I had more than a headache." Naji's voice was low. "I would have come myself, but I didn't think you wanted my help. I would gladly offer—"

"You're right," I snapped. "I didn't want your help. I can take care of myself. You're the one with the problem here."

"I don't want you to think I put you in danger," Naji said. "It was . . . The magic must have weakened more than I thought—"

His words wounded me. "So you did weaken it, then."

"No." He shook his head. There was that peculiar expression again. "No, absolutely not. It was an . . . ah, emotional weakening." He took a deep breath. "Intense emotional reactions can sometimes interfere with magic. It will sort itself out, I swear to you. But to have you so upset with me, my magic wasn't as powerful . . ." His voice trailed off.

I focused my gaze on him, sharpening it. Anger built up in my chest again. "Upset with you?"

"Yes, when I, um, didn't reciprocate—"

"Kaol, stop talking!" My hands curled into fists and I thought about pulling my knife out and stabbing him in the thigh, the way I had the night I met him. "Guess I just ruin everything, don't I? Not like I fulfilled one of the tasks for you or nothing."

"I told you I was grateful for that," Naji said quietly, but he didn't look at me.

I whirled away from him. I couldn't look at him another damn second. My whole body was shaking. This was why I hadn't kissed him for so long. Because I knew this would happen. My kiss was so repellent that it shut down all his damn spells.

"Maybe I'll just leave," I said, speaking to the sea, my back still turned to him. "Maybe that'll make things easier."

"Ananna—"

I didn't let him finish. I walked away from him, past the manticore and into the woods. He didn't follow.

I slept outside that night, in a nest of pine needles and fallen tree branches that the manticore had stacked up deep in a clearing in the woods, not far from the shack. I could smell the smoke from the hearth. Naji'd been tending the fire the last few days, making sure it smoked proper and didn't go out. I didn't know if he tended it tonight. I didn't care, neither.

I fell asleep early, after eating some berries and caribou, and curled up along the manticore's massive shaggy side. Her heart beat against the walls of her chest, slower and heavier than a human's heart. There was something comforting about it, like a drum beat setting time to a story.

I woke up in the middle of the night.

The manticore was still sleeping and the forest was quiet as death, which set my nerves on end. Forests ain't never quiet, not even in the middle of the night.

I peeled myself away from the manticore and scanned the darkness. I was still wearing Naji's charm even though I'd wanted to take it off—but the thing had kept Echo from touching me enough times that I figured that was the kind of stupid Mama would've slapped me for. And as I crouched there in the shadows, I was more grateful for it than I cared to admit.

"It really doesn't seem fair, don't you think?"

Echo.

My blood froze in my veins, and I leaped to my feet, all the muscles in my back and my arms tensing up. Her voice was coming from all over the place, like she'd melted in with the forest.

"It doesn't seem fair," she said, "that you can strike me in the face, and I can't even touch you."

"Seems plenty fair to me," I called out, managing to choke back the quiver in my words. Echo laughed. The trees rustled a response. I beat my hands up against the manticore's side, but she didn't move.

"I'm afraid that won't work, Ananna. We hold sway over the beasts of your world."

"The manticore ain't no beast."

More laughter. I shoved up against the manticore and kicked at her haunches. But she just slept on.

"This is growing tiresome," Echo said.

"I know," I told her. "Suggests you ought to just move on, don't it?"

Something flashed behind my eyes, and next thing I knew I was standing on the beach, in the cold open wind, next to the bonfire.

This was the closest I'd been to it since the day Naji set it to burning. It was bigger now, the figures writhing in its flames more defined. I could make out the features of their faces. Those faces weren't something I wanted to see.

"This is much better, don't you think?" Echo stepped into the hazy golden light. It shone straight through her so she glowed like a magic-cast lantern. "Easier to see each other."

I kept my eyes on her, even though the fire flickering off to the side made me want to turn my head. Both times we'd gotten rid of her involved hitting her unawares: Naji with his sword, me with my fist. So I did the first thing that came to my head. I lunged at her.

She glided out of the way, and I landed face-first in the sand behind her. I didn't waste no time feeling sorry for myself—a sucker punch don't work more than once that often—and twisted around so I could see her again. She floated there beside the fire, her arms crossed over her chest.

"What do you want?" I said. "You know I ain't gonna hand over Naji."

She sighed. "I really wish you would stop saying that."

She kept on sizing me up, and I knew there wasn't nothing she could do or else she would've done it already.

"We just gonna stand here till the sun comes up?" I asked. "You wanna place bets on what side of the island it'll be? I bet it's over that way." I tilted my head off to the left. "Ain't seen it rise over that half of the island in a while. Figure we're due."

"That wasn't my intention, no," Echo said. And she gave me this hard cruel smile that I didn't like one bit and gestured at the fire. "This is lovely. The assassin's handiwork, yes? I've seen this sort of magic before. It's rather unstable."

She glanced over at the fire. "You don't spend much time here, I've noticed, watching the flames. They're quite remarkable. I'm sure my lord could teach you to do this sort of thing, if you were so inclined. Our world is the world of magic, did you know? It's the place all your magic is born."

"I already know one way to build fires," I said. "I don't need another."

"This isn't a fire," she said. "It's far more dangerous."

That was when I looked. I tore my eyes away from her and looked at the fire. It'd been tickling there at the edges of my sight all that time, like an itch I wanted to scratch, and I finally turned my head and looked.

It swallowed me whole, all that golden light. Sparks and a warmth like the bright sun at home. The pale northern sun didn't even compare. And here: Naji'd brought a piece of that familiar sun here, he'd set it to burning on the sand.

The bodies in the flames swirled and danced and called me over.

Echo was up close to me, whispering in my ear, and the fire burned away the coldness of her breath. "You can create that yourself. He'll never teach you. But we can. I can. You can carry that light with you everywhere you go."

I stared at the fire, my hands tingling. I tried to tell her I couldn't do magic. But maybe I could, if I was part of the Mists.

"Who wants to be a pirate when you can be a witch? The most powerful witch the world has ever known. You won't just control the seas, you'll control the pulse of life. That pulse is what makes these flames burn. It is what gives power to that silly trinket around your neck—"

That brought me out of myself. She wasn't offering power, she wasn't even offering magic. She was after Naji. Always had been.

And the fire, for all its beauty, for all its magic, was still fire. It would only burn me if I got too close. Just as it had done Naji.

I dipped forward and yanked a stick out from under the fire. It was hot, but I didn't drop it; no, I spun around and flung the stick and the lick of flame at Echo, and her eyes went wide with surprise and then with anger, and then the stick sliced straight through her and she turned to mist and disappeared.

I collapsed on the sand. My hand stung. In the golden light I saw the place where the stick had touched my skin, saw the red line it left there.

The beach stayed empty. The wind howled and the waves crashed down below. I forced myself to stand up, legs wobbling, and began to pick my way across the beach. I didn't realize I was heading for the cave till I got there and found myself swaying outside its entrance, the dim, flickering light from the campfire casting long uneven shadows.

Inside the cave, Naji groaned.

"Naji?" I stepped in, leaning up against the damp stones for support. Naji was curled up in front of the fire, his hands pressing up against his forehead. He stirred when I said his name.

I shuffled forward and knelt beside him. Prodded him in the shoulder. He lifted his head.

"What did they do to you?" he rasped.

"Nothing." I leaned back, didn't look at him. I was too tired to be embarrassed. "Tried to get me to hand you over. I didn't, course, even though—" I decided not to finish that thought.

Naji stared at me. "What?" He pushed himself up. He was pale and ashen, his scars dark against his skin. His hair hung in sweaty clumps into his eyes. "Wait, you mean the Otherworld . . ." He collapsed back down on his back, looking up at the ceiling.

"Of course I mean the Otherworld. Who else would be chasing after me?"

"The flames," he said. "I felt them. The heat . . ."

I kept real quiet. My hand started stinging again, and I had to look at it. A thick red line cutting diagonal across my palm.

"We were by the fire," I said. "Echo took me there."

"Oh, of course." Naji closed his eyes. "She can't hurt you, you know."

"I know. The charm."

Naji looked at me, looked at the charm resting against my chest.

"So why in all the darkest of nights did you touch the flames?"

"What?" I slipped my hand behind my back. "The hell are you talking about?"

"The flames, Ananna. The *fire*. I know you touched it. It struck me down so hard I couldn't even come save you."

"I don't need you to save me." I stood up. "And it's not like you want to save me anyway." Naji didn't move, his eyes following me across the cave as I scooped up the cooking pot we'd filched out of the Wizard Eirnin's house. I set water to boiling on the fire.

"You still touched the flames."

"Do I look like I touched any flames?"

Naji got real quiet, and his eyes darkened, and he tilted his head so his hair fell over his scar. I felt suddenly sheepish.

"I didn't touch no flames," I said. "But I yanked out one of the sticks to send Echo back to the Mists."

Naji glared at me.

"Had to use something," I said. "Didn't have your sword." The water was boiling. I poured it into one of Eirnin's tin cups and dropped in the flat green leaves Naji used to make tea. Some herb that only grew in the north. I didn't know its name.

"That was very stupid," he said.

"It was just a stick!"

"It burned you."

He said this more gently than I expected, but I still shoved the tea at him, sloshing a little across his chest. He glanced down at it like he'd never seen a cup of tea before, but after a few seconds he wrapped his hand around the cup and drank.

"Not bad," I said.

"What?"

"It didn't burn me bad." And I showed him my hand.

"Would a stick pulled from any other fire have burned you at all?" he asked.

I scowled at him. "You only care 'cause the burn hurt you. But it ain't hurting no more, right? So could we just drop it?"

"It's not about the burn hurting me—"

"Oh, shut up."

"Ananna—"

"Shut up!" I was regretting coming back to the cave now. I should have just trudged back to the manticore. The damn beast probably slept through the whole thing, but at least she wouldn't nag me about getting burned by magical fires or look at me like I was this big disappointment 'cause I was the one in love with him and not some pretty little river witch.

Naji didn't try to say nothing else to me, which was a relief. I curled up on a pile of moss near the entrance to the cave, where I could hear the trees and the ocean, and pretended to fall asleep.

CHAPTER FOUR

I woke up the next morning to the manticore licking my face.

"Stop it!" I shouted, rolling away from her. "Feels like you're skinning me alive."

"Girl-human," she said. "The Jadorr'a asked me to fetch you."

"Again?" I twisted my head around and squinted up at her. Sunlight shone around her big glossy mane. "I ain't in no danger."

"He said it was urgent. I told him I wouldn't do it, that I am not his personal servant, but . . ." Her tail curled up into a tight little coil at the base of her spine.

"Urgent?" I asked. "Is it the Mists?"

"Oh no. He said it wasn't a matter of danger."

"Then what is it a matter of?"

She blinked her big golden eyes at me. "I don't know."

Figures. Still, I roused myself up, taking my time 'cause it was the worst thing I could do to Naji, making him wait. Me and the manticore strode side by side down to the beach, where the smoke from the bonfire bloomed up against the sky, dark gray on light gray.

I crossed my arms over my chest. "Where the hell is he?"

"He said he would meet you here."

I sighed and scanned over the horizon. Nothing but emptiness. Except—

There were two people standing beside the fire.

I'd gotten so accustomed to the aloneness of the island that the sight of two human figures at once startled me. One of 'em was definitely Naji, 'cause he stood farther back from the flames, wearing some dark cloak I didn't recognize, one that wasn't tattered beyond repair. And the other—

I leaned forward, squinted. "Marjani!" I shrieked.

"What is that?" asked the manticore.

"Remember how I said a friend was coming to pick us up from the island? Well, she's here!"

"We can leave?"

"I hope so."

The manticore reared up on her hind legs and let out a string of trumpets and then raced toward the fire before I could stop her. I pounded along in the sun, the wind cold and biting, my breath coming out in puffs. Marjani stared at us. She was wearing a bright red fur-lined cloak that I gotta admit I wanted. It looked warmer than anything I'd nicked from the Wizard Eirnin's house.

"What the hell?" she said.

The manticore skittered to a stop a few feet away from her. I snuck a look at Naji—he had his arms crossed over his chest, his face dark with intensity. "Don't get too close to the flames," he said.

"I won't," I said. The sight of him twisted my stomach up into knots for a few seconds before I shoved it all away.

Marjani's voice interrupted my thoughts. "Is that a—"

"Oh! This is the manticore," I said, like I was making introductions.

The manticore lowered her head, all deferential and polite like she was meeting a lady. She must've wanted off the island more than I realized.

"My name is Ongraygeeomryn, and I am most grateful for your assistance."

"You never talked that nice to me," I said.

"You never had a water-nest."

Marjani stayed calm, although the longer she looked at the manticore the deeper her frown became. I ran up to her and threw my arms around her shoulders and she laughed and hugged me back.

"I am so glad to see you right now," I said. Now that I was across the beach I could just make out some big white sails way off in the distance. It was a bigger ship than the *Ayel's Revenge*, probably a warship, though I couldn't tell from that far off.

"They wouldn't come any closer," Marjani said.

"How'd you get on land?"

"I climbed." She jerked her head over to the place where the beach dropped off, and there was a hook wedged into the sand.

"That held?" I said.

"Barely." She smiled.

"You came back," I said, 'cause part of me still thought it was hard to believe. I knew it wasn't the easy thing to do. Hell, probably wasn't even the most honorable, what with Naji being a murderer and a mutineer and all. At least she didn't know about what I'd done to Tarrin of the *Hariri*, about how I'd had to kill him in self-defense. I didn't like thinking about it.

"Of course I did," she said. "Besides, I need your help. His too."

Naji glanced at her, his eyes all suspicious. "Help with what?"

"I'll explain once we're on the ship. I don't imagine the crew's gonna be too happy about sitting out this close to the Isles of the Sky for much longer." She turned to the manticore. "Naji told me about the, ah, arrangement you made with Ananna. I'll allow it, but you should know I'm not taking you aboard if you intend on eating any of the men on that ship."

"What?" The manticore bared her teeth and hissed.

"Sorry." And Marjani pulled out a pistol and pointed it at the manticore's heart. The manticore drew back, not quite into a cower. She kept her teeth out, though. "You'll stay in the brig for the entire trip. I'd muzzle you if I could."

"But you'll let her on board?" I asked.

Marjani sighed. "I'm not about to double-cross a deal you made with a manticore."

I wondered if Naji'd told her about the three impossible tasks as well. Probably. But I doubted he'd tell her about the kiss. Hoped he wouldn't.

"Get your things," she said. She threw me a second pistol and a pouch of powder and shot. "And keep that damn manticore in line."

The manticore hissed, crouching low to the ground.

It didn't take long for me and Naji to gather up our clothes and Naji's weapons. I didn't talk to him, didn't even look at him, but as I walked out of the cave he put his hand on my arm and said, "We should take the caribou."

"Don't touch me."

Naji didn't say nothing for a few moments. Then: "It hasn't quite finished drying out yet, but perhaps we can find a place on the ship. Payment for bringing a manticore on board."

He was right and I knew it, even though the thought of spending another minute alone with him, remembering everything about what happened the last few nights, the good parts and the horrible parts both, made me want to throw up.

"Fine," I said, dumping my clothes on the ground.

We wrapped the meat in his old assassin's robe. There was so much we only took half the strips, leaving the other half there to rot or feed the noisy creatures of the island.

I hated every minute of it. I kept waiting for him to say something about the fire or even about the kiss, but he never did.

Marjani was waiting for us by the fire once we finished, sitting on a piece of driftwood with her pistol pointed at the manticore. The manticore was curled up on the sand, eyes full of hate.

"I didn't look at it once," Marjani said as Naji and me walked up. "But you're insane if you think I'm going to forsake a fire in all this coldness."

Naji scowled and didn't say nothing.

"I do not like this friend-girl-human," the manticore said.

"Well, she's the one with the boat." I stopped in front of Marjani. "We got dried caribou to give to the crew."

"They'll like that. Half of them are from the ice-islands."

I carried my stuff up to the beach's edge, next to the place where Marjani had thrown her rope. Something about the edge of the island made me dizzy, like it was the place where the world cut off.

I peered down. A rowboat bobbed in the water. I tied me and Naji's clothes up together and tossed them down, then tossed down the caribou meat too. Both landed right in the middle of the boat. A useful trick, Papa'd told me when he taught me. Never know when you'll need to toss something.

"Are we gonna climb down?" I asked.

"I can't climb," the manticore said.

"I'll take you." Naji cut across the beach. "All of you," he added, when the manticore opened her mouth.

I remembered the day we arrived on the island, how close he pressed me into his chest. And it was weird, 'cause the last thing I wanted in the world was for him to hold me—but at the same time, it was the only thing.

Instead, he asked me if my hand hurt.

"What?"

"Your hand. That you burnt last night."

Thinking about it made my skin tingle, but it didn't hurt none at all. "No, it doesn't. Told you it was fine."

Naji gave me a hard look. I stared back long as I could. "I'll bring the manticore and Marjani down to the boat one at a time," he said. "Don't start rowing out to the ship yet."

"I know that."

Another dark look and then: "Don't leave me on the island, either. You know what would happen if I stepped out of the shadows on that ship. The crew won't trust that sort of magic. I'd be tossed overboard."

"I ain't gonna leave you!" It took every ounce of willpower not to smack him hard across the face. "I ain't cruel, Naji. I ain't *you*."

He glowered at me. I glowered right back.

"Good," he said, and then he grabbed me by my uninjured hand and the darkness came in.

Marjani's ship was a big Qilari warship called *Goldlife*, and it didn't belong to Marjani but to a skinny, mean-looking captain named Chijal who had a jagged white scar dividing his face clean in half. Nobody so much as glanced at Naji's face when they hauled the rowboat up on deck—and though she didn't say nothing I had a feeling Chijal was the reason Marjani had bartered her way onto this particular ship.

The crew was rowdy and loud, drunker as a group than the crew on the *Revenge*, and even more lewd. The first day I had to hold my knife to some guy's throat to keep him from grabbing at me.

When night fell, and we'd cleared out of sight of the Isles of the Sky, Marjani took me and Naji down to the brig. Nobody was down there on account of the manticore, though she seemed more preoccupied with trying to lick every spot of brig-sludge off her coat.

"Girl-human!" she bellowed when I dropped off the ladder. "I demand my release at once!"

I pressed my hands against the bars. I felt sorry for her, I really did, but even I wasn't about to let her free on a ship full of men.

"If I let you out, you'll eat half the crew," I said. "And a ship this size, we need 'em to get you back to the Island of the Sun."

She pouted.

"Yes," said Marjani. "That's what I wanted to talk to you about."

I turned to look at her. Somebody'd strung up a trio of magic-cast lanterns that swayed with the rhythm of the boat, casting liquid shadows across Marjani and Naji.

"We're not going to the Island of the Sun," I said.

The manticore hissed. So did Naji.

"You realize that manticore wishes to eat me, correct?" he said, sounding like snakes.

"No, we definitely are dropping off the manticore," said Marjani.

The manticore hissed again, and I turned and shushed her.

"We're just not doing it with this boat."

Me and Naji both stared at Marjani, and she gave us this wry little smile.

"This is about that favor you want from us, isn't it?" Naji asked.

"It won't be difficult," she said. "Certainly not for you . . ." She looked at me when she said that bit. "The *Goldlife* crew are gonna help us steal a merchant ship, and then we're gonna sail her into Bone Island and get her a crew."

"And then you'll take me home?" the manticore asked. "Will you cure the Jadorr'a's curse first?"

Nobody answered her.

"Who's gonna captain?" I asked. "One of Chijal's men?" The thought of it turned my stomach. The officers were just as loutish as the crewmen.

"Oh, absolutely not," said Marjani. "We'll captain her. Me and you together."

Naji looked relieved, but I just stared at her.

"That'll never work," I said. "Ain't no man'll sail under a woman—"

Marjani held up one hand. "That's why I needed both of you."

"No," said Naji. "Absolutely not."

I looked from him to Marjani and back again, and in those sliding soft shadows I saw her plan taking shape: put Naji in some rotted old Empire nobility cloaks and he'd look the part of captain sure enough. A mean one, too, what with the scar.

"You won't actually captain nothing," I said. "Right? We'll use him to book a crew."

"Exactly," said Marjani. "Captain Namir yi Nadir. I started spinning tales about him while I was looking for a ship to bring me out here."

"What!" Naji asked. "Why?"

"So men'll want to sail with you," I told him. "What kinda captain is he?" I grinned. "Brutal and unforgiving, always quick to settle a dispute with the sharp end of a blade? Knows how to whisper the sea into a fury anytime a man disobeys him? A real *monster* of a captain, right?"

Naji was glaring at me, his eyes full of fire. Seeing him angry like that soothed the hurt inside me. Not a whole lot, mind, but enough that some of the sting disappeared.

"Of course not," Marjani said. "I want men to sail with us, not fear us." She turned to Naji. "I put out stories about you sacking the emperor's city with a single cannon and a pair of pistols and another one about you seducing a siren before she could sing you to your death."

The anger washed out of Naji's face. "And people believed that?"

"People'll believe anything, the story's good enough. I also put out word that you pay your men fair, you offer cuts of the bounty even to the injured, and you'll sail with women."

"I do all that?" Naji frowned. "I'm not even a pirate."

"No, you're an assassin," I said.

The anger came back again, just a flash across his eyes, but it was enough.

Marjani gave me a look that told me to cut it out.

"All of this is moot until we get a ship," she went on. "So, Ananna, I'd like to see you arm yourself with more than a pistol and a knife. Naji . . ." She gave him a half smile. "Well, your Jadorr'a skills may be required."

Naji scowled.

"This is the only way we'll be able to complete the rest of the tasks," Marjani said, and my face went hot, 'cause I knew then that he'd told her everything, about the curse's cure and my kiss. "You'll never be able to convince Chijal to do it, that's for certain."

And then she walked out of the brig before Naji had a chance to answer.

We sailed for four days and didn't see another soul, just the gray expanse of sea and sky. It was colder on the boat than it had been on land, the wind sharp against the skin of my hands and face, like it could flay it from my bones. One of the crewmen, a boy from the ice-islands named Esjar who had white-yellow hair and looked about my age, gave me a pair of sheepskin gloves.

"For the *lady*," he said with this weird flourish I realized was meant to be an Empire bow.

I took the gloves and stared at them. Papa'd always told me to treat the ropes with my bare hands. *Ship gets pissy otherwise*, he said. *Rope'll slip clean away from you.*

"They stop the cold." Esjar spoke Empire, but he had the same hissing accent as Eirnin. "We ain't in Empire seas anymore. Out here, you need them, same as you need that pretty red cloak."

I glanced down. Marjani'd let me have her cloak once we came on board—she had another one, dark blue, that she said she liked better—and I had to admit it kept me warmer than any clothes I'd ever owned. So I slipped on the gloves.

They helped. Yeah, the ropes slipped out of my hands more often, but at least my fingers could move.

Esjar and I became friends after that, chatting sometimes as we were working the ropes. He'd actually heard of the Mists—most of the ice-islanders had, in fact, which surprised me, seeing as how they ain't so well known in the south. Esjar explained to me that the boundaries between worlds are thinner up at the top of the world, and most ice-island children learn early on to look out for flat gray eyes and cold mist.

"Which is tricky," he said, looping the ropes into a sheet knot. "'Cause mist is all over the place in the north, and gray eyes ain't too uncommon either. So you learn to pay attention to the differences."

"The differences?"

"Yeah." Esjar nodded, tugging the ropes tight. "Nothing from the Mists is human, and you can tell that, when they're creeping around. Something's off about them. Like they don't got a soul."

I nodded, remembering my encounters with Echo and the others back in Lisirra. "But you don't really notice until it's too late."

"That's the trouble with them." Esjar started knotting the next two ropes together. "The whole thing with them is that they want to get to our world, 'cause our world's more stable. Not so much magic."

I laughed at that. "There's magic all over the damn place."

"Sure, but not like in the Mists! Those floating islands we just picked you up from—that's what the Mists are like, only worse, much worse. They're built out of magic, see? And a little bit seeps through to our world and the magicians can make it work. But in the Mists magic is everywhere. So they want to come here and take over 'cause it's safer."

I shivered. Esjar hunched over his work, face scrunched up in concentration. I remembered the story Naji had told me, about how he'd stopped a lord of the Mists from crossing over permanently. That was why they were after him now, and it'd never made much sense to me, how persistent they were. But the Isles of the Sky, especially before Naji worked his spells to keep us safe, had been awful—not just 'cause of the cold and the rain, but 'cause everything was so uncertain.

And living in a world like that, only worse? I'd be trying to cross over too.

"What else do you know about them?" I asked. Esjar tied off the last of his knots and looked at me.

"Not much," he said. "Why you asking?"

"Just curious, is all." I grinned as if that would prove it. "It's creepy, you know, like the stories of the dead my old crew liked to tell."

Esjar grinned back. "In the south you fear the dead. In the north we fear the Mists." He squinted out at the horizon line. "Not much else to tell, truthfully. Their magic is dangerous, 'cause they're so seeped in it. My papa told me a story once about a cousin who faced down a man of the Mists, and his skin turned to tree bark and he rotted into the soil before anyone could save him. Supposedly he was alive for the whole thing—people could hear him screaming and begging for mercy and whatnot."

My whole body went cold.

Esjar looked at me and frowned. "But my papa was known for

bullshitting," he said quickly. "So it probably wasn't that bad."

The sails snapped around us, the wind cold and biting, and I forced myself to believe him.

One evening the crew all gathered up on deck for drinking and singing and storytelling. I went too, even though it meant having to listen to stupid jokes all night—I noticed Marjani made herself scarce.

I hadn't been out there an hour when Naji slunk up, sword hanging at his side, rubbing at his head like something must've kicked up his curse. Probably from some of the crew leering at me all night.

"I don't need your help," I hissed at him, dragging him over to the railing. The sea was a churn of black and stars.

"I'm not here for you," he said. "Though you really should be more careful. Those men aren't . . . they aren't honorable."

I crossed my arms over my chest and glared at him. "You think I've never been on a ship full of drunk pirates before?"

"They could still overpower you—"

"I thought you weren't out here for me."

He didn't say nothing, just turned his face toward the sea. I stalked away from him. Fine. Let him slash at any asshole who tried to grab at me. Get us tossed into the ocean, he would.

I huddled up near the fire some crewman had got going for warmth. Esjar was sitting over by the fore mast, playing a tune on this beat-up old Qilari guitar. I glanced over my shoulder at Naji—he was watching me, one hand on his sword hilt. Conspicuous as hell. But at least he'd see what I was about to do.

I walked over to the mast. "Hey, ice boy," I said.

He stopped playing and looked up at me. "Hey, sun girl."

I shifted my weight from one foot to the other. I ain't never been any good at flirting, but Esjar looked at me with these heavy-lidded eyes and said, "See you're still wearing my gloves."

"Oh." I held up my hand to show him, even though he'd obviously already noticed. "Yeah. You're right, I needed 'em."

He laughed and started plucking out a Confederation tune on his guitar. I didn't say nothing—I wasn't too keen on letting him know who I was, since the Hariri clan almost certainly still had a watch out for my head, despite all the time that had passed—but I did sit down beside him. His fingers moved deft and sure over the guitar strings.

Naji was still watching us.

I was sweating underneath my cloak and the cold sea air, nervous. Esjar finished up his song and set the guitar off to the side.

"So what's your story?" he asked me. I was surprised; for all our conversations, we'd never really talked about ourselves before.

"Ain't got one."

Esjar kinda smiled at that, but he didn't ask no more questions. We sat side by side for a few minutes, not talking. I scooted closer to him. He put his hand on my knee.

"I don't got much of a story, either," he said.

We sat in another few moments of awkward silence while I tried to figure out what my next move should be. I was aware of Naji standing at the railing, turned sideways to us, like he was watching us out of the corner of his eye. I was about to ask Esjar if he wanted to go down below, but then a couple of crewman struck up an old Empire song, bright and cheerful.

"Hey, sun girl, you know this one?" Esjar asked.

"Sure do. It's got a dance that goes with it. I can show you if you want." When Esjar nodded, I stood up and held out my hands. He laughed and grabbed both of them and I pulled him to his feet.

I looked over at Naji, trying to be casual about it. He was frowning at us.

Least your head ain't hurting no more, I thought bitterly.

I led Esjar to the center of the deck and showed him the basic steps. In truth, I didn't know the dance all that well—I'd watched people do it whenever I made port in Lisirra with Mama and Papa, and I'd followed along with the steps once or twice. But I knew enough to show Esjar: mirrored steps, back, right, forward, swinging your hips all the while. He took to it quickly enough, and we swung over the deck, laughing and whirling while the rest of the crew stomped out a beat.

When the song ended, the crew burst into applause, and Esjar pulled me into him and kissed me.

It surprised me, but I liked it too, and I kissed back, tasting the seasalt on his lips. Part of me wanted to see how Naji was reacting, but part of me just wanted to kiss Esjar until the sun came up.

We pulled apart. I couldn't help myself this time, and I glanced over at Naji, who was watching us with his face shrouded in shadows.

Then the crew started another Empire song, and Esjar whooped and pulled me into the dance again, and for the first time in months, it was almost like Naji didn't exist.

The next morning, I got a couple of water rations from the galley and then headed down to the brig, where I found the manticore, curled up in the corner and mewling like a kitten.

"I brought you some water," I said.

"I want meat, girl-human!"

"You'll have meat tonight." I picked the lock with my knife and let myself in, skirting around the neat pile of crushed pig bones. The crew kept some livestock on board, and they gave her the bits nobody wanted to eat, plus fish, which she apparently ate despite claiming it wasn't food. "Once me and Marjani have our own boat I'll make sure you get real food."

"Manflesh?" Her head perked up. Her face was dirty, her mane matted even though I'd worked through the tangles a few days earlier. The sight of her twisted my stomach.

"I'll see what I can do. Here." I dumped the water in her bowl and she knelt down and lapped at it. I sat beside her, stroking her side, listening to the *drip drip* of seawater coming through the boards.

Footsteps on the stairs. I prayed to Kaol that it wasn't Naji.

Marjani's head appeared in the doorway. "Brought you something," she said. "Oh, Ananna, you're down here."

"Where else would I be?"

She shrugged, then grinned at me. She had a burlap sack with her, the bottom stained red. The manticore lifted up her head and sniffed.

"Animal meat," she grunted.

"Yeah, well, I keep hoping some of those barbarians'll hack each other to bits, but they just . . . don't." Marjani pushed open the cell and dumped out the contents of the burlap sack: fish heads and a pair of shriveled up old pig's feet, more than a little moldy.

"Best I could do," Marjani said.

The manticore returned to her water.

Marjani gestured for me to get out of the cell. I sighed, patted the manticore's shoulder, and stood up. I knew the manticore would eat the food Marjani brought her, but she'd only do it alone. Pride. And I couldn't much blame her.

"Heard you had a good time last night," Marjani said.

"Yeah? Who'd you hear that from?"

"Half the crew. And Naji," she added, giving me this disapproving look I didn't like one bit.

I wasn't gonna ask her what he said. I wasn't going to ask her if he seemed angry about it or annoyed or sad. Mostly 'cause if she told me he didn't care, I was pretty sure I might die.

"We just danced," I said.

Marjani laughed. "And kissed. A couple times." She paused. "Do you know how to make the moon tonic? The cook should have all the ingredients."

I blushed and nodded. Mama had shown me how to mix it up when I turned fifteen.

"I doubt he'll know what you're making," she added gently. "The cook isn't exactly well informed on the matters of women."

"I told you, I don't need it! We didn't do nothing!"

"For the future, then." She smiled. "Anyway, that's not actually what I need to talk to you about." She peered out the brig doorway, and then turned back to me. "Those . . . people . . . who are after Naji. They're here."

My stomach turned to ice, but then I realized we were still sailing along, no magic erupting out behind us, no soldiers of the Mists crawling over the deck. But Marjani looked skittish, almost scared. I grabbed her by the hand and led her over to the bench built into the wall.

"What happened?" I said. "Tell me everything."

She took a deep breath. "I was in the navigation room last night, checking our progress. Alone. And then all of sudden this woman was in there with me. I didn't hear the door. She was just . . . *there*." Marjani shivered.

"Echo," I said.

"What?"

"That's her name. She was kind of smoky, right? Like she's not quite in this world?"

Marjani frowned. "Sort of. When I refused to take her to Naji, she fought me."

"What! You mean she could touch you?"

"Yeah. Can she not touch you?" Marjani tilted her head, studying me, like she was trying to work out all the pieces.

"No, she can't—" And then I remembered the charm around my neck. "Oh," I said. "You don't have Naji's protection."

"Protection?"

I lifted my charm out from my shirt collar and showed it to her. "I can't take it off," I said. "It'll flare up Naji's curse otherwise. But whenever I'm wearing it, she can't touch me." I slipped it back inside my shirt. "I'll tell him to make you one, once we get to land. We probably don't have the ingredients on the boat."

"I'd like that." Then Marjani gave me a quick, nervous smile. "Although I did beat her back easily enough last night. I don't think she was expecting me to be carrying a loaded pistol."

"You killed her?" I thought of the lone pistol shot I'd been given when the *Ayel's Revenge* captain marooned me and Naji on the Isles of the Sky. I'd used it to start a fire that went out in the rain. If only I'd saved it—

"No, she billowed out like dust and disappeared." Marjani sighed. "Why the hell are they coming after me? You've got the curse, so you're at least . . . *magically* tied to him." She looked at me closely then. "And maybe more than magically, right?"

I looked down at my lap. "That ain't important. They're after you because you know him. They can't get to him, see, because he's hidden himself with his magic—"

"So they go after the next best thing. I get it." Marjani shook her head. "He just keeps bringing around trouble, doesn't he? The magic on board the *Ayel's Revenge*, and now this." She laughed.

I couldn't disagree with her. "He's nothing but trouble," I said. "Although he was trying to save the ship, during that mess with the *Ayel's Revenge*. He just did it in a . . . Naji way."

Marjani laughed at that. But when her laughter faded she took on a serious, intense expression.

"How dangerous do you think she is?" she asked. "Without the protection charm."

It was a reasonable question, and I wanted more than anything to give Marjani a reasonable answer. But I didn't have one. I'd never fought Echo. She whispered pretty words in my head and I had to remind myself where my loyalties lay. Maybe they were misplaced, setting 'em with Naji.

"She's dangerous when she talks," I finally said. "'Cause it ain't death she's dealing. If a pistol shot'll send her away, that should be enough to keep you safe until landfall. But just—be careful if she tries to talk to you."

Marjani looked at me for a long time. "I understand," she said. Then: "I'll let you know if I see her again."

"Have you told Naji about this?"

Marjani shook her head. "I wanted to hear what you had to say about it. Naji's a little . . ." She waved her hand through the air like she could catch the right word. "A little intense. He reminds me of the academics I met at university. So focused. You can see the bigger picture."

I beamed at that.

"I should still mention it to him though, shouldn't I?" Marjani ran her hands over her hair. "It's got me spooked, I have to admit."

"I'll go with you," I said, even though I didn't particularly want to see him just yet. "We can ask him about the protection spell too." I stood up and turned to wave good-bye to the manticore. She'd fallen asleep. "And if you want me to go to the navigation room with you, next time, I can do that too."

"Thanks." She grinned at me, although I could see a bit of nervousness in her eyes.

We left the brig together.

CHAPTER FIVE

I was up in the rigging a week later when the alarm went up. Somebody'd spotted a ship.

I immediately slid down a nearby rope and scurried down below to grab my sword out from the little corner where I'd stashed it. The quartermaster had given it to me when we first boarded, but I never liked carrying a sword around when I was working the ropes.

Marjani was up at the helm, talking to the first mate, her arms crossed over her chest, her expression serious. The ship was a flurry of men and their swords and pistols as the crew scrambled for their battle stations. Somebody was pounding on the drum, and cannons were wheeling across deck. The ship was a bright smear of red and gold on the horizon. The colors of the Empire.

Naji appeared beside me, and put his hand on my arm. I jumped and yanked it away.

"What's going on?" he asked. "Are we under attack?"

Marjani called us over to the helm, waving her arm wide. "It's an Empire sloop," she shouted over the din of battle preparations. "We're gonna have to fight for her."

Naji gave me a sideways glance and set his face in stone.

"I don't need your protection," I told him.

Naji frowned and didn't say nothing. Marjani jumped down from the stern deck and pulled out her own sword and her pistol and nodded at me. "Captain's lending us Tavin, Ajim, and Gorry," she said.

"And his weapons. Otherwise, we got to take the ship ourselves."

It's best to take a ship without violence. You ride on board with your fiercest looking men, fire off a couple of shots, hold a knife to the captain's throat. But you don't kill nobody. Merchants' ships are the easiest for that. The crew don't value their cargo more than their lives.

But this wasn't a merchant ship, it was Empire standard, and I could bet they were loading up their cannons and singing their battle songs as we waited. I bet they had their blood-drop battle flags raised and at the ready. Empire soldiers ain't no merchants. They'll die for their ship.

And then I had an idea.

"I'll be back," I told Marjani. "I ain't running. Just . . . I'll be back."

"No!" she said. "They'll be here—"

"Give me five minutes," I said. "I'll be back."

And then I took off, scrambling down the ladder to get to the brig.

The manticore was pacing in her cell, tail curling and uncurling. She looked up at me when I came in, her face wan and pale.

"I got somebody you can eat," I said.

Her lips sneered back. "Don't lie to me, girl-human."

"I ain't lying," I said. "I got lots of somebodies, in fact. We're about to board an Empire sloop, to take her. There'll be fighting, but—"

She ran her tongue over her lips, though I could tell from the darkness in her eyes she still didn't believe me.

"I'm gonna let you out," I said. "But you gotta swear—swear on our friendship, and I know we got one—that you'll only go after a man in Empire uniform. You know what that looks like?"

She shook her head. Her teeth were like daggers.

"Red," I said. "They wear red with a gold snake on the chest. Tie up their hair in red scarves. You got that? A man's got on red and gold, you can eat him."

"If you are lying to me," she said. "I will fill you full of poison and drop you to the bottom of the sea."

"Fair enough." I yanked out my knife and picked the lock on her gate, swung it open. She bounded out, snarling and hissing, and then stopped right beside the doorway. She looked at me over her shoulder.

"Once I have eaten," she said, "You may ride me. For your battle."

"Fine." I pushed her toward the doorway. I didn't have the heart to tell her sea-battles don't work that way.

We ran side by side through the lower decks, men screeching and drawing swords as we passed. "She ain't gonna hurt you!" I shouted, waving my pistol around, afraid somebody was gonna shoot her before we got to battle. "She's got a taste for Empire men!"

As many ice-islanders were in that crew, I figured they'd like the sound of that, and it didn't take long before the crew was cheering us instead of shrinking from us, calling out they hoped she'd rip them Empire scummies to pieces and eat their intestines. I blamed the battle fever. Sends men into such a frothing rage they forget to be scared of a manticore.

Marjani glared at me when we got up on deck.

"I was really hoping that's not what you were going to do," she said.

"She's *starving*," I told her. "You expect me to keep her locked away while we're piling up dead men out here?"

Marjani crossed her arms in front of her chest.

"It's an Empire ship! They won't come peaceful and you know it."

She did know it. She nodded at me, and then turned to Naji,

started telling him the protocol for boarding a ship. He stared at her, face blank.

I wondered if he was as scared as I was.

The manticore growled. "Where are the red-and-gold men?" she asked me, her breath hot against the side of my neck.

"There." I pointed out to sea with my sword. The Empire ship was coming closer, her red bow veering in for us. Dots of light flashed on her deck. Empire swords. "We're gonna board her," I added, 'cause I figured the manticore was wondering.

And then Marjani's hand was on my arm. She pushed me toward the rowboats that hung off the side of the ship. "You want the manticore, you get to take her across the water."

"You got rope?" I asked.

"What?" said Naji. "You're going to send her out there . . . no. No, absolutely not. It'll completely incapacitate me—"

"Then go with her!" Marjani shoved Naji at me. "I'll take the *Goldlife* crewmen and swing across. You don't have much time before they start firing. *Go*."

For a second Naji and me stared at each other and I knew I couldn't let him get to me, not now. An Empire man'll die for his ship. I wasn't gonna die for my broken heart.

"Come on!" I climbed into one of the boats, the manticore at my side. She trumpeted—not the way she had when we were racing across the beach. This sounded like a damn battle horn.

The *Goldlife* crew let out a cheer, all throaty with bloodlust.

And then the Empire fired its first volley of cannons.

Naji let out a shout and jumped into the boat beside me. Marjani swung her sword through the rope and we crashed into the water, the air thick with black smoke and the scent of cannon fire. The manticore wasn't trumpeting no more, but flattened down in the center of the boat, one paw pressed over her head, whimpering.

I grabbed hold of the oars and pushed off toward the Empire ship, trying to ignore the booms and thuds echoing overhead.

Naji flung himself on top of me, his weight pressing me into the manticore.

"What you doing?" I shouted. I could taste the gunpowder in the air.

"Protecting you," Naji snarled. He was already covered in sweat; it must be hurting him, us being out on the water.

"Then help me row!"

He grabbed one of the oars and we pushed off together, the Empire ship looming tall in front of our little rowboat, sunlight making the water sparkle. Debris showered down on top of us, bits of wood and sail and metal and probably blood and bone, though I couldn't think about that. Naji screamed, the muscles bunching up in his arms, and he kept shouting, "The shadow! The shadow!" and I didn't know what the hell he meant at first, 'cause all I could think about was getting us out of the water. And then I realized the Empire ship was casting a long dark shadow across the sea, and once we got there he could slip us on board so we wouldn't have to scamper up the side of the ship.

I rowed harder. Water splashed over the side of the boat, soaking me through. I could hear men screaming up on the ships, both of 'em, and pistols going off, and the cannons, booming and booming and booming like never-ending thunder.

And then we crossed the shadowline. Naji wrapped his arm around my shoulder and shoved his hand in the manticore's fur, and all the noise fell away.

It was nice in the shadow, quiet and cool, with Naji's body pressing up against me like maybe we were lovers after all. And I floated there in the darkness like I was underwater, and I didn't want to come out, I didn't—

We slammed onto the deck of the Empire ship.

The *Goldlife* hadn't fired on her yet, of course, 'cause we were looking to take her, not steal from her, but those Empire soldiers were firing off their cannons quick as they could, and the deck was thick with the residue from the powder. Nobody noticed us at first, not in the fury of the battle, but then the manticore reared up on her hind legs and roared so loud the wood vibrated.

Everything stopped.

I pulled out my sword and pistol. Naji lifted his sword over his head.

All those Empire men turned from the stations and stared at us, a Confederation pirate and a Jadorr'a and a hungry manticore.

I'd never boarded a ship during a battle before. I'd always stayed with Papa's boat and fought alongside Mama. But I heard the stories from the crewman who'd come back, bragging up their fighting, and all those Empire crewman were staring at me like they were expecting something.

"We're here to take your ship," I said, and I'm proud to say my voice didn't waver none at all.

The manticore roared again, and then she lunged forward, knocking down this poor Empire soldier with her great sharp claws, burying her face in his belly. Blood splattered across the deck.

I looked away, my stomach clenching.

And then all those Empire men started screaming—I didn't blame 'em one bit—and shooting at the manticore. She lifted her head out of her meal, blood smeared all over her face, teeth gleaming in the sun, and hissed.

Spines shot out of her tail, impaling soldiers in the heart, in the head, in the belly.

Naji yanked me down to the deck, slapping his hand over my head. "I think this is one battle where we're not needed," he said.

"They're gonna kill her!" I squirmed away from him, lifted my head up enough to see a soldier running up to the manticore with his sword outstretched. I shot him.

"Ananna!" Naji hissed my name like he did when he was angry. I ignored him, just jumped to my feet and launched into a crush of soldiers, slicing at them with my sword to keep them off the manticore. Her spines whizzed past my head but none of them ever hit me.

And then Naji was fighting alongside me, his sword spinning out in a flashing silver circle. He moved like a shadow, darting between soldiers, keeping them off me as I kept them off the manticore.

Where the hell is Marjani? I kept thinking, 'cause I'd no idea how to take a ship. I knew in theory, but here in practice all I cared about was keeping me and Naji and the manticore alive. So I poured all my concentration into fighting, and I didn't feel no pain or fear, just my heartbeat and my breath.

Dully, I was aware of the manticore taking down another soldier, his screams echoing out across the sea, the scatter of soldiers rippling backward across the deck as he fell.

I fought.

And then the fighting stopped.

I wanted to keep going, all that blood rushing through my veins, all that blood soaking into my skin, but Naji got me in a lock and pulled me still. The Empire peace horn was blowing, long and low. The Empire men had all thrown down their weapons.

Marjani was standing up at the helm, a knife pressing into the captain's neck, two *Goldlife* crewmen at her side.

The manticore was eating.

"It's over," Naji told me, his mouth close to my ear. "We have the ship."

I felt like I'd woken up from a fever dream, everything

distorted and strange. The sunlight was too bright. The blood on the deck too red.

The peace horn died away.

Marjani dropped her knife from the captain's throat, and Gorry and Ajim took him by the arms, dragged him away from the helm. Marjani leaned forward.

"This ship is under the control of the Pirate Captain Namir yi Nadir." She jabbed her finger toward Naji, who tensed his arm. "Any man who wishes to join our crew may do so and no harm will come to him. Those of you who wish to die for the Empire . . ." She turned to the manticore, who was still hunched over the remains of the soldier. "You will have that chance as well."

Goldlife pirates were streaming on board, but nobody moved to stop them. Tavin hoisted up the boat's new colors, some flag Marjani had sewn before she picked us up at the Isles of the Sky: a black background and a dancing skeleton stitched in red silk. It snapped and fluttered in the sea wind and for a second the scent of blood and fear got wiped away, and the ship was almost silent.

Silent. Peaceful. And all I wanted to do was lie down and sleep.

I slept in the captain's quarters that night, after stripping away my bloody clothes and swimming in the cold ocean to wash the blood from my skin. There was a real bed in there, big enough that two people could share. Naji let me and Marjani sleep in the bed while he hung a hammock from the corner and slept there. I fell asleep easy enough. I woke up in the middle of the night, the cabin dark and shadowy and unfamiliar.

I listened to Marjani and Naji breathe for a while, their breaths soft and out of synch, and when I realized I wasn't gonna fall back asleep I rolled out of bed and pulled on one of the Empire captain's gold cloaks and went up on deck.

Nearly all of the Empire men had chosen service over capture—Empire don't train 'em as well as they think, I guess—but we were still headed for Bone Island, on account of Marjani not trusting a ship full of ex-soldiers. I didn't blame her. We'd dump 'em there and let 'em find their own way back to their lives, then pick up a crew of our own.

But for now, we had 'em running the night shift, and they all shrunk away from me when I came up, turning back to their ropes and riggings. I ignored 'em, just walked up to the bow and leaned over the edge to feel the cool salt air on my face.

"Girl-human."

I turned around. The manticore padded up to me, her face cleaned of blood, her mane brushed and shining—some poor Empire sap had been assigned to tend to her grooming needs.

"What are you doing up here?"

"I do not like the underneath," she said. We hadn't locked her up in the brig, but I'd asked her to stay down below in the hold on account of her presence making the men jumpy.

I didn't say nothing and she added, "It stinks of human filth."

"Hard to take a bath on a ship," I told her.

"You're surrounded by water!"

I didn't have nothing to say to that.

The manticore sat beside me, wings tucked into her sides, her tail curling up along her back. We didn't speak for a long time.

"Thank you for allowing me to eat." She sounded sincere, too, and kind of sad. "I had been very hungry before."

"I know." I stroked her mane and she nuzzled against my hand like a pet.

"I will not eat any men without your permission."

It still creeped me out a little, that she ate humans, but part of me knew it was just the way things were, like me having to eat fish and sheep and goat. It wasn't her fault that she ate people.

And I'd killed more men than she could eat that afternoon, all 'cause they were trying to kill her, but I tried to put it out of my mind the way Papa told me to, 'cause dwelling on it can turn you dark. But it was hard.

She gave me one of her sharp smiles and turned back to the sea. "It is strange, living with humans. But I am growing used to it."

"I thought you lived with humans on the Island of the Sun."

The manticore flicked her tail. "That's different. They are our servants, girl-human, our slaves. Here, we are equals." Another flick. "Or as equal as human and manticore can be."

"Oh, is that so?" I leaned over the railing and looked down at the black ocean water skimming up along the side of the boat. "So tell me, how was it a human managed to kidnap you?"

The manticore let out one of her low, quiet hisses. "He was treacherous and dishonest. Not like you, or even the Jadorr'a." She licked her lips and looked up at me. "You should not trust wizard-humans, as a rule."

"I'll keep that in mind."

"It was my parents' fault," she went on, like I hadn't spoken. "His water-nest crashed onto our beach. We were going to eat him, of course, but he had magic, and my parents were willing to strike a deal."

That caught my attention, since everybody'd been warning me about the dangers of striking a deal with a manticore. Looks like it got Eirnin killed.

"Did he double-cross them?" I asked. "Your parents?"

"Of course he did, girl-human! We traded him his life for some of his spells and potions, but during the trade he cast a great smoke-cloud and paralyzed me. I do not know how he dragged me back to his water-nest, but I learned quickly that it hadn't been broken at all. It had been a ruse, designed to ensnare me."

"Why?" I said. "It's not like he tried to sell you or nothing—"

"Sell me! If only he had tried. No, he planned to cut me open and use my heart for some foul wizardry or other. Every morning for those three life cycles he taunted me with his knife. The morning that I escaped was the morning he was to kill me."

I stared at her in the moonlit gloom. Her human-looking face was lovely in that silvery-white light, but she looked sad and lonely—or at least as sad and lonely as a manticore could. I draped my arm around her shoulder and leaned up against her mane, and she let out a little trill that sounded almost grateful.

"If I'd known you were there," I said, "I'd have cut you loose myself."

"I do not blame you for the not-knowing," she said. "He hid me behind a veil of magic."

"Well," I said, pulling away from her. "You don't have to worry about it anymore. We'll get you home soon."

"Yes," the manticore said, and she let out a sweet ringing chiming call. "I know."

The next morning, me and Naji and Marjani met up in the captain's quarters to talk about what we were gonna do after we got our crew sorted.

"Drop off the manticore," I said.

Marjani stood staring out the porthole, gazing, I suppose, at the sea. A beam of sunlight settled across the bridge of her nose. "I already told you, I'm not letting that manticore stay on board my ship longer than I have to." She turned to Naji. "What were the two remaining tasks? Finding a princess—" Her voice trailed off, and she had a strange, troubled expression.

"Starstones," Naji said. "Find a princess's starstones and hold them against my skin."

Marjani stared at him. "Yes," she said softly, "I remember now."

"And the other was to create life out of an act of violence," I said. "Whatever the hell that means."

Marjani frowned. "Riddles."

"Of course." Naji said. "It's a northern curse."

"And what the hell's a starstone anyway?" I asked.

"Magic," Marjani said, and she turned back to the porthole, her face blank.

"They're rare," Naji said, although he sounded distracted and uncomfortable. "And honestly, I'm not too keen on chasing after them—"

"Why not?"

But Naji and Marjani both ignored me.

"Well?" I said, annoyed. "Why not?"

"It's dangerous," Naji said.

"Easy answer."

"Perhaps we could go to one of the universities," Marjani said. "The scholars might be able to help you." She was still staring out the porthole. "The university in Arkuz is excellent . . ." But her voice wavered a little, and I could tell that whatever had sent her off to a life of piracy in the first place still lingered back in Jokja. I had a feeling it was more complicated than what Chari, the old pirate I'd befriended back on the *Ayel's Revenge*, had told me, about her not wanting to marry some nobleman—but I didn't much want to pry, either.

"Lisirra would be better," Naji said. "I have more ties there."

Marjani looked at him. "I suppose that makes sense." I could hear the relief in her voice.

"What do you think, Ananna?" Naji asked.

I glanced over at Marjani. She wasn't staring out the window no more, just leaning up against the wall with her arms crossed over her chest. It was clear to me she didn't want to go back to Jokja. I thought about Lisirra, the sunny streets and the water wells and the sweet-scented gardens. The exact opposite of the Isles of the Sky.

"Lisirra sounds good to me."

And so it was decided. The pirate ship *Nadir*, formally a nameless Empire sloop, would load up a new crew, drop off a manticore, and sail to the universities of Lisirra.

It only took a day to sail into Bone Island, faster than should've been possible. We had favorable winds, and the ship was quicker than any sloop in the Confederation, though Marjani said the Jokja navy had built some rumored to sail even faster. She sneered at a knot of Empire sailors as she told me, like they'd stolen the ship plans from Jokja themselves.

But I suspected Naji might've had something to do with the speediness of our trip—he stayed in the captain's quarters most of the time, the way Marjani told him to, and when I took him some food at Marjani's request I saw spots of blood on the writing desk.

The day we pulled into port was bright and sunny and shot through with the first warmth I'd felt in months. As the crew prepared to make port, I marched into the captain's quarters.

Naji was stretched out on the bed, staring up at the ceiling. He lifted his head when I came in. We'd hardly spoken since the battle.

"You look like an Empire commander," he told me. I was still wearing that gold cloak and had taken to knotting my hair back in the Empire style, 'cause it did do a better job of keeping my hair out of the way.

"You look like a Port Iskassaya drunk." I hadn't meant to sass him, but I couldn't help it, he was so bedraggled. "We're gonna have to clean you up before we take you in to sign up a crew."

"Marjani has already informed me."

We stood in silence for a minute longer. Then he lifted his head. "Did you need something, Ananna?"

I stared at him.

"Thank you for calling down the winds," I finally said. "To get us here faster."

His face was blank as always, but something glittered in his eyes, some flash of appreciation. I left the captain's quarters before he could say anything more.

Bone Island had always been my favorite outlaw port of call when I was a kid, 'cause it's big enough that it almost feels like a real city, and there are merchants selling clothes and silks and fancy Qilari desserts, instead of just whores and weapons, like at some of the other pirate islands. And it's always mild there, never cold and never too hot, and the water in the beaches is pure bright blue, the same color as the sky. Even the rains are warm.

Marjani put me in charge of prettying up Naji and making him look like a captain. I didn't want to do it—I wanted to stay on board the boat with the manticore. But when I said something about it Marjani didn't even glance up from her maps and notes.

"The manticore," she said, "will not get us a crew."

I knew she was right and I knew she was my captain now too, not in name but in action. I didn't talk back.

Naji was waiting for me on the docks, his hair brushed out and combed over his scar—otherwise he was filthy. It almost hurt to look at him.

"I want a bath," he said. "I don't care if it won't make me a believable captain. *I want a bath*."

"Already planning on it."

I took him to the Night Porch, a whorehouse down near the beach that was attached to the nicest bathhouse on the whole island.

Led him round back so I wouldn't have to see him staring at the whores all draped out in the main room in their silks and jewelry, all of 'em prettier than me.

The baths were as nice as I remembered, clean and misty and smelling of aloe and basil. We stood in the entryway, steam curling up Naji's hair, and he said in this voice like a sigh, "Civilization."

"Not exactly," I said. "But close enough." I jutted my head toward the main room. Men's laughter boomed out with the steam. "You can go in there." I tried not to think about the women they kept on hand to slough men's backs and wash their hair. "I'll be in the secondary room there."

Naji frowned. "They separate men and women? In a pleasure house?"

"No," I said.

Naji opened his mouth, but I whirled away from him before he asked me some question I didn't want to answer. The thought of him seeing me naked next to all those perfect whores made my skin crawl.

"It'll be difficult for me to relax if we aren't in the same room," Naji called out behind me. "The headaches—"

I stopped, one hand on the doorway. I could hear water splashing, the low hum of women's voices, and I wondered why he was bothering to mention that to me. I knew about his damned headaches, and I also knew there wasn't any danger here. Part of me wondered if maybe he just wanted my company—but no. I knew better.

"Too bad," I said.

The secondary room is the one where the whores go when they ain't working, and men don't usually venture in 'cause there ain't no one to wash 'em and flirt with 'em and make 'em feel wanted. I stripped over in the corner where no one would pay no attention to me, and then I slipped in the soft warm bathwater, bubbling up from some spring deep in the ground. It was my first proper bath in ages and I stayed in for longer than I normally did, dropping my head below the water and watching all the ladies' legs kicking through the murk. Nobody said nothing to me, which was exactly how I wanted it.

I met Naji in the garden after my bath. He came out with his hair wet and shining in the sun, his dirty clothes out of place against his gleaming skin. I was sitting underneath a jacaranda tree that kept dropping purple blossoms in my hair.

He sat beside me.

His presence still gave me a little thrill. We sat in silence for a moment, and I enjoyed it, his closeness and the warm sun and my clean skin. Felt nice.

"Do I look like a pirate captain now?" he asked.

"No." I didn't look at him. "You need new clothes."

"Ah. Of course."

I leaned forward, resting my elbows on my knees. I didn't quite know how to go about doing this. It wouldn't do to have word spread around about some man going shopping, then turning up in those same clothes at the Starshot drinkhouse as the Pirate Namir yi Nadir. Cutthroats are a gossipy bunch. Gotta be; it's how you find out the best schemes and stratagems. Nobody wants to get caught unawares.

It was hard to think out there in the warm sun, all clean and bright, with Naji sitting beside me, but an idea came to me anyway, a big flash of an idea.

"I know what we can do," I said, straightening up.

"Shopping?" Naji asked. "Or stealing?"

"Neither." I stood up and led him out of the garden, away from the whorehouse and the fresh steam of the baths. Paid a carriage driver a couple pieces of pressed copper to take us out of town, down to the rows of little ramshackle shacks that sprouted up along the oceanline like barnacles. Naji didn't say a word the whole time. I figured he wanted out of those rotted clothes more than he was letting on.

The house looked the way I remembered it, a little wooden shack with banana trees out front, the backyard sloping down to the ocean. I jumped out of the carriage. Naji stared at me.

"What are we doing?" he asked.

"Getting you some clothes. Come on."

He stepped out of the carriage like I was setting him up for some kind of con. I stomped through the soft seagrass in front of the house and rapped my fist against the door.

"Where are we?" Naji asked.

"You got a headache?"

"No."

"Then you know I ain't in danger. Stop asking questions."

He frowned and I thought his eyes looked kinda wounded, but he didn't say nothing.

The door swung open, and Old Ceria, my old sea-magic teacher, stuck her head out, squinting in the sunlight. She looked at me and then she looked at Naji.

"What happened to his face?" she asked. "Looks like what happens when you let Lady Starshine in charge of the roast at the dry season festival. Charred on the outside, bloody on the inside."

Naji turned to stone, his eyes burning with anger. Before the kiss, I might've warned him.

"He got hurt a long time ago," I said. "Ceria, we need to borrow some clothes, if it's not too much trouble."

"You mean *take some clothes*." But she held the door wider and let me and Naji step inside. It was dark in there, with heavy curtains pulled over the windows. Dried-out seaweed hung from the rafters, and all manner of sea creatures lay out on the cabinet—or the shells of 'em did, anyway. The smell was the same too, stale and salty.

Old Ceria was a seawitch, like Mama, and Mama would always bring me to see her when I was a little girl, to try and extract magic out of me. Ceria lived on Bone Island 'cause she couldn't abide Empire rule, but she didn't have no love for the Confederation neither—for pirates in general. She barely tolerated Mama, truth be told, but she was willing to put aside differences as far as magic was concerned.

I hadn't seen Ceria in years, but she looked the same as she did when I was younger, as dried out as her seaweed and her dead crabs.

"He the reason you ran off from the Hariri clan?" Ceria asked me, jutting her head toward Naji.

Shit. I didn't think she would've heard.

She gave me a narrow, sharp-toothed smile.

I didn't answer her, didn't even move my head to shake it yes or no. I could feel Naji staring at me, staring at her.

"Oh, don't worry," she said, grinning wider. "You think I care about Confederation politics? Just asking 'cause it ain't never wise to give your heart to a blood-magician."

I went hot at that.

Old Ceria chuckled and even though she was an old woman and I knew that meant she deserved my respect, I kinda wanted to hit her.

"You two wait here," she said. "I take it you want the clothes for him? You're looking awful dapper in that Empire cloak." A little curl of her lip when she said *Empire*.

She disappeared into the back of the house. Naji and me stood in silence, and I listened to the waves rolling in to the beach behind us. Naji was still fuming over Ceria's comment about his face—I could see it in the way he kept balling up the rotted fabric of his shirt in one hand.

I tried to work up the nerve to apologize to him.

Naji said, "Captain Namir yi Nadir will cover his face."

"Marjani won't like that."

"Marjani can dress up as a man if she wants a captain so badly. I'm covering my face."

Old Ceria came into the room, a tattered brocade coat tossed over one arm, some trousers and shirts tossed over another.

"I should be getting you a scarf, then," she said.

Naji sneered at her and she threw the clothes at him.

"Ain't scared of you, blood-magician. Got nothing but sea-water in these veins." She nodded at me. "You best watch out, girl."

"He won't hurt me," I said.

"Seems to me he already has."

Naji stalked outside with his new captain's clothes, but I stayed in the house for a minute or two longer, staring at her, thinking back to those horrible afternoons as a kid, digging up sand on the beach for her spells.

"How'd you know?" I asked.

"I'm a witch, darling," she said. "I saw you coming two weeks back. I know his story too, the curse and all. The kiss." She winked at me.

I scowled at her, then jumped up and pushed out of the house before I said something I'd regret. With a jolt, I wondered if she would tell the Hariris that she saw me, but then I remembered she'd always hated the Hariris more than other pirates. Maybe she'd just tell Mama.

Still, it was a reminder that I wasn't in the north anymore—I was back in the parts of the world where the Hariri clan had plenty of eyes, and no doubt they'd still be looking for me, even if I'd mostly forgotten about them over the last few months, seeing as how I had bigger problems on my mind. I'd have to come up with some excuse for not dawdling in port. Threaten to feed some

Empire man to the manticore. I felt sorry enough for her as it was, having to eat fish bones and sea birds again.

Naji stood at the side of the road, pulling his hair over his scar, the clothes lying in a pile at his feet.

"You're getting 'em all dusty!" I shouted.

"Who cares?" Naji asked. "They're just going to rot once we make sail."

I picked up the clothes and shoved them at him. He yanked them away from me, his hair hanging in curls across his face.

"Why did you bring me here?" he asked.

"To get you clothes."

"You knew she would—" His face twisted up with anger. "You knew she would say something. You wanted her to."

I looked away from him, cheeks burning.

"Why?" The question was sharp and painful as a knife. It cut into me and I knew I deserved it. "Why did you do it?"

"You should change," I muttered. "Before we go back into town."

He glared at me.

"I'm sorry. I didn't think . . . I didn't do it on purpose." I still couldn't look at him. "And your face doesn't look like a half-roasted pig anyway."

Silence. The wind blew in from the ocean, stirring up sand and dust.

"You have no idea what it's like," Naji said.

I kept my eyes on my feet and listened to his footsteps crunch over the road and then rustle into the grass. And when I glanced up he was over on the side of Old Ceria's house, half hidden by the banana trees, pulling his new shirt over his head.

CHAPTER SIX

Marjani had already set up at the Starshot drinkhouse, claiming a table in the back, away from the singer warbling some old Confederation tunes. I threaded through the crowd, Naji behind me in his captain's outfit. It suited him, I thought, especially the brocade coat. Before he'd covered up his face—with a scarf I nicked for him off one of the carts outside—he'd been so handsome my chest hurt to look at him.

When she saw us, Marjani folded her arms over her chest.

"Take it off," she said.

"No," I told her, before Naji could say nothing.

She flicked her eyes over to me.

"It makes him look more formidable," I said.

"I'm not leaving my face uncovered," Naji said.

Marjani sighed. "No one's going to say anything—"

"Yes," Naji said. "They will."

I stepped in between the two of them and said, "We should probably do this fast. Manticore's gonna get hungry out on that boat. Don't know how long she'll be able to avoid temptation."

Marjani sighed. "Yes, I'd thought of that myself. You stay here and get the drunks. I'll go out in the street and look for the desperates."

And then she was out the door.

It didn't take long for word to circulate that the Pirate Namir yi Nadir was in port and that he was signing up men for his new crew.

Probably helped that an Empire warship flying pirate colors was waiting out in the docks, but mostly it was the fact that pirates can't keep their mouths shut for longer than five minutes. It occurred to me that leaving port early probably wasn't gonna be good enough—I needed to keep my face covered too, before some Hariri ally or wannabe-ally or plain ol' asshole who wanted to kick up a fight spotted me and kidnapped me back to Lisirra.

All that time on the Isles of the Sky, with no company but Naji and the manticore, had left me soft. Not wary enough, like the Mist woman had said.

So I snuck out back and slipped down the street till I came to a shop selling scarves and jewelry. I bought a pair of scarves and covered my face the way Naji did and wrapped my hair up in the Empire style, though with a black scarf instead of a red one. The cloak hid my chest well enough. I figured I could pass for a man.

"And who the hell are you supposed to be?" Marjani asked when she came back in with some men she'd picked up off the streets.

"The rat who got Captain Namir yi Nadir the ship," I said.

She frowned. I could tell she didn't approve. Messed up his reputation, having a ship handed to him on account of subterfuge.

"A prisoner?" I said. "Who agreed to sail under his colors? And by allowing me my freedom we can see the extent of his mercy?"

"Better," Marjani said. "And the mask?"

"A show of solidarity."

She didn't push that none, neither. I don't know why I hadn't yet told her about the Hariri clan. Felt bad about lying in the first place, I guess. And she'd had this all planned out—it was the reason me and Naji weren't still stuck on that frozen floating slab of rock after all. I didn't want to be the one to throw a kink in her plans.

I'd just keep my face covered, and we'd be fine.

It was mostly Marjani who did the recruiting anyway. She'd

done it before, I could tell. Even now that she was back in the drinkhouse, she didn't just sit down and wait for men to come to her—she wove through the place, Naji trailing behind her like a puppy, dodging whores and serving girls and the worthless outlaws who came out here not knowing one whit about sailing a ship. She had an eye for the ones that would know what they were doing, and she knew how to catch 'em at their drunkest, when they would slap an *X* on anything you stuck in front of 'em.

She left me in charge of the table, in case anyone came asking. I leaned back in my chair and sipped from my pint of beer and tried not to think about Naji.

"Excuse me? This where I sign up to sail with Captain Namir yi Nadir's crew?"

The voice was speaking Empire all posh and educated, and when I dropped down in my chair and looked up I saw one of the soldiers we'd cut free when we made port.

"What you want to sail with us for?"

"Are you the manticore's trainer?" The soldier reached over and plucked at the mask. I slapped his hand away.

"I ain't her trainer. And we ain't taking on mutineers."

"I'm not a mutineer." The soldier sat down at the table. "Where are you sailing?"

I crossed my arms over my chest.

"Well?"

Marjani had given me some story or another, but most of it had slipped out of my head due to drink. "Captain's sailing after treasure."

"All pirates sail after treasure," the soldier said. "What in particular is he looking for?"

I fixed him my steeliest glare. "Gotta ask him yourself."

The soldier looked me right in the eye. "I will. Once I'm on board your ship. What about that manticore? She sailing with us too?"

That, at least, I could answer. "At least as far as the Island of the Sun. She and I made a deal, and now I'm making good on it and taking her home."

The soldier arched his eyebrow. "You made a deal with a manticore?"

I shrugged.

"Well," he said. "That if nothing else has convinced me." He grabbed the name sheet and the quill Marjani had left with me. I tried to snatch it away from him—no luck. "There isn't an Empire general alive who could make a deal with a manticore and survive." He scrawled his name across the sheet. *Jeric yi Niru*. The *yi* gave him away as nobility, I knew, and I knew too his nobility was real, since no Empire soldier would lie about his status the way a pirate would—the way, for example, Marjani had lied about the status of the pirate Namir yi Nadir. I scowled at the sheet.

"I'll feed you to the manticore first sign of trouble," I told him.

He gave me a smile. He was older, with streaks of gray in his hair, although his skin wasn't as weatherworn as it would've been had he spent his whole life at sea.

"The Empire look suits you," he said before turning away and heading off toward one of the serving maids. I don't trust handsome people, and he wasn't handsome in the slightest. I decided to give him the benefit of the doubt.

"Hey!" I shouted. "Snakeheart!"

He looked over at me. "I'm not an Empire soldier anymore. I'm afraid the epithet no longer fits."

"We set sail at sunrise tomorrow. You're not there, we're leaving you."

He gave me a nod.

"And I ain't kidding about the manticore!"

He just laughed, which pissed me off. I wanted to shout something back to him, but he was talking to the serving girl again, leaning in close to her, and I figured he wasn't gonna pay me no mind.

Marjani and Captain Namir yi Nadir came back about thirty minutes later. I hadn't gotten anybody to sign up save for Jeric yi Niru, who seemed to have stashed himself in a corner with a pitcher of ale. Marjani handed me her logbook, folded open to the first page. There were names spelled out in her neat, tidy handwriting down one side, a row of mostly *X*s cascading down the other, mixed in with the occasional signature.

She tucked my loose sheet of paper, with its one signature, back in the logbook. "Our crew, Captain."

"Stop calling me that," said Naji.

"Just getting you used to it," she said.

Naji turned to me, his eyes big and dark over the edge of his mask. "Are you my decoy?" he asked.

"What?"

He ran his fingers across my scarf. I could feel his touch through the fabric, on my lips, and my whole body shivered.

"No." I stood up, pulling myself away from him. "I need something to drink."

He didn't say nothing more, though Marjani watched us close, eyes flicking back and forth, until I turned and melted into the crowd.

The crew we signed up turned out decent. Not as good as Papa's crew, but better than the *Goldlife* bunch. A handful of 'em were Confederation drifters, men who got the tattoo but don't stick to one particular ship, but most were unaffiliated sailors from the Free Countries in the south. A crew like Papa's, which is bound to one particular ship and captain, aren't so keen to sail with outsiders. It's an honor thing, though Mama used to tell me it was really just plain ol' snobbery, the way Empire nobility looks down on the merchants. But the drifters aren't so particular, probably 'cause they're used to a crew like Papa's looking down on 'em for jumping from boat to boat, and our crew blended together without much trouble.

I kept my face covered the first few days, but got sick of it soon enough, the cloth half smothering me in the humid ocean air.

"Finally," Marjani said. I'd taken my hair out of the Empire scarf, too. I was still wearing the cloak, though I kept it open at the neck on account of the heat. "I was starting to hear rumbling about how you and Captain Namir yi Nadir were the same man."

"What? That don't make no sense. They've seen us together before."

She waved her hand dismissively. "They thought he could copy himself, be in two places at once."

"They thought I was Naji? I don't look nothing like him!"

"I told you," Marjani said. "People will believe anything."

In truth, I could see how the crew might've gotten that idea about Naji. He kept to his captain's quarters most of the time and let Marjani do all the captaining. She got me to be her first mate—second mate, she called it—and at first I wasn't quite sure how to act. I'd seen Mama plenty, of course, so I tried to act like her. I kept my back straight and my head high and I carried a dagger and a pistol with me everywhere I went. Got real good at whipping out the dagger and holding it up to some back-talking crewman's neck too.

Besides which, I didn't keep the manticore in the brig.

"They're scared of you," Marjani told me one morning, the sun warm and lemony, the wind pushing us toward the south, toward the Island of the Sun. We were up at the helm, the crew sitting in little clumps down on deck, not working so hard 'cause they didn't have to. The manticore was sunning herself over at the stern, her tail thwapping against the deck as she slept. "They are?"

"Sure. It's a good thing, though." She leaned against the ship's wheel, squinted into the sun. "Because you're a woman. If they're scared of you, they'll listen to you."

"That's how it works with men too."

Marjani shook her head and laughed. "Not always. Men have the option of earning respect."

The wind picked up, billowing out the sails. The boat picked up speed. One of the crewmen hollered up in the ropes. Probably Naji's doing, that wind. There was something unnatural about it.

"I always wanted to captain a ship," I said after a while. "When I was a little kid." I didn't mention that I'd still wanted it when I was seventeen years old and about to be married off to Tarrin of the *Hariri*. "Used to fancy I could dress up like a boy and everyone would listen to me. I never thought about getting some man to stand in as a proxy."

Marjani squinted out at the horizon. "Dressing up as a man can get you in trouble."

"What do you mean? Always figured it'd be nice. I could never pull it off proper, 'cause of my chest."

Normally Marjani might've laughed at that, but today she just ran her hand over the wheel and said, "I used to dress as a man to visit someone I loved. It was a sort of game. I met her when my father sent me to university, since I split my time between my studies and court, like a half-proper lady." Marjani laughed. "When she came of age she'd complain about suitors constantly—this one was too skinny, this one was too old, this one talked too much about politics." Marjani kinda smiled, but mostly she just looked sad. "And so I decided to surprise her, and show up as a suitor."

"Did it work?"

"For a little while. I didn't fool *her*, of course, and she loved it, but I fooled her parents. One of the noblewomen figured it out, though, and I spent some time in prison for lying about my identity."

"Is that why you left Jokja?" I asked. "Why you took to piracy?"

All the emotion left Marjani's face. "Yes."

We stood in silence, the unnatural warm wind blowing us toward the Island of the Sun. I knew she'd told me something important, something secret. And I felt even worse about keeping the Hariri clan from her.

I tried to tell her. I did. I started forming the words in my head. But then one of the crew called up to her about trouble in the galley over some sugar-wine rations, and she leaped over the railing to deal with it, and the moment was lost.

A few days passed, and we got closer and closer to the Island of the Sun. One afternoon I went down to the galley to get some food for myself and some scraps of meat for the manticore. There wasn't a whole lot there, though. Fish parts and some dried sheep meat. I kept the sheep meat for myself, started dropping the fish into a rucksack.

"Still wearing my captain's old uniform, I see."

At the sound of Jeric yi Niru's voice I almost dropped the sack of fish. I whirled around. He lounged against the doorway, a trio of seabirds hanging on a rope from his belt.

"What do you want?" I narrowed my eyes at the seabirds. "And where the hell did you get those?"

"Shot 'em down." He slung the birds over the table. "I trained in archery before I was a sailor. We must be nearing land. The manticore's island, I hope?"

"You hope?" I shoved another fish head in the sack. "What do you care? She ain't bothering nobody on this boat."

"She's hungry."

I scowled. "You don't think I haven't noticed?"

"I appreciate you not feeding any of us to her."

I didn't say nothing.

"Here." He slid one of the birds off the rope and handed it to me. I stared at it, at the black empty beads of its eyes, the orange triangle of its beak. "For the manticore," he said.

I lifted my head enough to meet his eye. He gave me another one of his easy smiles.

"Thanks," I said.

"Always willing to help the first mate."

I froze. "You mean navigator."

He winked at me. "No," he said. "I don't."

I yanked out my knife and lunged toward him, but he was faster, and he grabbed my arm and twisted me around so he had my back up against his chest. I struggled against him but couldn't break free, and my heart started pounding and I was scared, but I knew I couldn't let him know.

"I wouldn't do that," he whispered into my ear. He plucked the knife out of my hand. "You're going to need me."

"Need you?" He dropped my arm and I stumbled away from him. When I turned around, he was examining my knife. Hell and sea salt.

"Yes," he said. "To find the starstones. That is what we're looking for, isn't it? After we leave the Island of the Sun?"

My whole body went cold. I didn't even bother to lie. "How do you know that?"

Jeric tapped his ear. "I pay attention. Even when I'm held prisoner aboard a pirate ship, I pay attention. You do realize starstones aren't the sort of treasure the crew is expecting, don't you? Even the more educated among them has never heard of a starstone—they'll think you're chasing after magician's treasure." A slow grin. "Fool's treasure, is how you pirates would put it, yes?"

I did my best Mama impression. I kept my face blank and my eyes mean. It didn't seem to work.

"You'll have a difficult time keeping the crew," he said, "once you tell them what you're after." Jeric tilted his head. "And you'll have an even more difficult time if I were to let slip what I discovered about the captain and *her* first mate—"

I snarled and leaped forward and grabbed the knife from him. He let me have it without a fight.

"What's to stop me from killing you?" I said, shoving the knife up at his throat. "Got a hungry manticore and—" I almost said *Jadorr'a*, but stopped myself in time. "I could feed you to her right now."

Beneath the mask of his smirk, Jeric's face went pale.

"Or I could wait," I said. "And feed you to her on the Island of the Sun. Her whole family could feast on you." I smiled.

"You don't know what you're dealing with," Jeric said softly. "Chasing after starstones."

I shrugged. "Don't screw with me. Or my captain. And maybe you won't wake with a manticore's spine in your belly." I grabbed the seabird off the table. "Maybe."

I stalked out of the galley angry and shaking. I didn't know nothing about starstones. I'd never even heard of 'em before the Wizard Eirnin had rattled them off as part of Naji's cure, and as far as I knew Marjani and Naji hadn't talked about them in detail. But I guess I was wrong, if Jeric yi Niru had managed to pick up on it. Ship walls leak secrets.

I went back up on deck. Marjani wasn't nowhere to be seen—some old Confederation pirate was handling the helm. She was probably in the captain's quarters. Maybe she could find some excuse to toss Jeric in the brig and I wouldn't have to worry about it no more.

The manticore was stretched out over on the starboard side, her head lying on top of her paws. I stopped by to drop off her food.

"Hello, girl-human," she said. "We are close to the Island of the Sun, yes? I can smell their sands on the air."

"Yeah, we're close." I dumped out the fish and the seabird. She sniffed at 'em, didn't say nothing. No surprise there.

"You'll get to eat all the humans you want soon," I said.

"Yes," she said, sounding glum. "I had hoped the Jadorr'a's curse would have been broken—"

"You want to stay on the boat?" I said. "You can stay. Munch him all you want once we've cured him."

The manticore looked at me with horror. "No more boat."

I smiled. "I figured."

She leaned forward and swallowed a fish head with one gulp. "You wouldn't bring him back to the island?" She looked at me, fish scales glittering on her lips. "Even after he soul-hurt you?"

"That's not a good reason to kill a man."

"You aren't killing him," she said. "You're feeding me. His energy would live on." Her eyes were clear and golden, like water filled with sunlight. "For us to eat a man, it is a great gift."

"Dead's dead," I told her. "Sorry."

She blinked like she didn't understand, and I ran my fingers through her mane and left her to her meal.

I walked over to the captain's quarters and banged on the door.

"Open up!" I shouted. "It's me."

Naji answered, his face still covered. I don't know why he bothered when he locked himself away in his quarters all the time.

"Hello, Ananna," he said, and the fact that he hadn't come down to the galley when Jeric was threatening me lingered on the air.

"Marjani in there?"

Naji held the door open wider and stepped back. Marjani was leaning over the navigation maps.

"Oh good," she said when she saw me. "My navigator."

"We need to talk," I said.

She thrust the sextant at me. "Check our course," she said. "You needed to do that this morning."

I looked down at the map. An emerald brooch was stuck in the Island of the Sun, a lady's hairpin stuck in the southern coast of Jokja. Shouldn't it be Lisirra? But I didn't say nothing about it; I had bigger concerns at the moment.

"You know that Empire soldier we signed up?" I said.

"Not Empire anymore," Marjani said.

"He threatened me."

That got her attention. She lifted her head, eyes concerned. "What?"

And so I told her what had happened in the galley, about him being onto our ruse with Naji, and knowing we were chasing after the starstones, all of it. Marjani listened to me and the lines in her brow grew deeper and deeper the longer I talked.

"We should be able to hold him off until we arrive at the manticore's island," she said when I finished. "We may have to leave him there." Though I could tell that didn't sit right with her at all.

Naji had slipped over beside us while I spoke, and he looked at her above his mask, and he said, "Don't."

"Don't what?"

"Leave him with the manticores." Naji hesitated. "We may need . . . he may prove useful."

There was this long stifling silence.

"Oh?" Marjani asked. "You've decided to play captain now?"

I'll give him credit; Naji didn't even flinch. "Marjani," he said. "Have you ever *seen* a starstone?"

Marjani glared at him.

"Neither have I," he said. "But when I asked the Order about them . . ." his voice trailed off. "If the man has knowledge, it may come in useful."

"Absolutely not. He'll stir up a mutiny if we leave him on board."

"She's right," I said. "An Empire soldier learns how to be a weasel from boyhood. He wants something from us—"

"Then give it to him."

Marjani and me both looked at Naji in surprise, but he didn't seem to notice. He pulled the mask away from his face, and even though I didn't want it to, my breath caught in my throat.

"I want rid of this curse, and I'm not taking any chances," he said. "Keep him alive, this Empire soldier. Keep an eye on him, and keep Ongraygeeomryn near you, but don't kill him."

He glanced at me out of the corner of his eye. "What's his name? This soldier? Do you know it?"

"Jeric." I hesitated. "Uh, yi Niru."

"Oh," said Naji, frowning. "He's a noble."

"Yeah, which means he's doubly untrustworthy."

"Just keep him alive," Naji said.

Marjani shot him another dark look, but he pulled the mask back over his face and turned away. I leaned back over the navigation map and set up the divider.

Then the warning bells rang.

Another ship was approaching.

CHAPTER SEVEN

We ran out on deck, swords and pistols drawn. The crew were lined up against the starboard side, their voices a low murmur.

"The hell are you doing!" Marjani screamed at them. "Get your asses to work!"

They turned around, and when they saw Naji with his sword and his mask, they took off scrambling across the deck. Something glinted out on the horizon. Smoke trickled into the air. Fear clenched in my belly.

Marjani grabbed the spyglass off the helmsman and peered through it.

"Holy hell," she said. "They're Confederation." She laughed.

Naji slunk up behind me and put a hand on my arm. I didn't try to shake him off.

"What clan?" I whispered.

"Dunno." She peered through the spyglass again. "Red background, black skull—"

"With a crown?" I could hardly breathe. "A skull wearing a crown?"

"Looks like it, yeah."

"The Hariris," I said.

Naji pulled me close to him. My heart jolted in my chest like lightning was running through my body. "Go down below," he said. "And stay there. Take the manticore with you."

"What?" Marjani looked from him back to me. "Why? They'll see us flying pirate colors and let us—"

"They're after me."

Marjani's face went dark.

"I'm sorry, I shoulda told you—"

"Why in hell is the Hariri clan after you?"

"Ananna," Naji said. "Please. Go."

"No," Marjani said. "Don't you dare move from that spot. What do the Hariris want with you?"

My voice shook when I spoke. "I was supposed to marry Tarrin—Captain Hariri's son—and I didn't want to . . . and then I killed him . . ."

This time, Marjani's face turned ashen.

"You killed a captain's son?"

I nodded.

"For Kaol's sake, Ananna, why?"

"He was gonna kill me—"

She shook her head. "No. Explain this to me later." She clanged the attack bells, deep and ominous and so loud they hurt my ears.

"Arm the cannons!" Marjani shouted. "Prepare for battle!"

"Please, Ananna," said Naji. "Please hide."

"No!" I jerked around to face him. "This is my fault. I ain't gonna go cower in the brig while you and Marjani and everybody fights for me."

Naji's eyes looked sad, and for a half second I thought maybe he was worried about *me* and not about the pain of the curse.

I pulled away from him and raced across the deck toward the manticore, who had stood up, her tail curling and uncurling.

"This noise, girl-human," she said. "Are we close to land?"

"'Fraid not." I stood face to face with her. "You see that speck of light out there . . ." I pointed to the horizon. "It's a ship full of men you can eat."

Her eyes lit up.

"In exchange for a meal," I said, "may I ride you? Into battle?"

"With the other ship?"

I nodded. "They're after me, and I bet they try to board." I took a deep breath. "I need you to protect me."

She scowled. "Do I look like the Jadorr'a?"

"Please, Ongraygeeomryn." I know I mangled her name 'cause it came out sounding like a blood-cough and not like bells at all, but she still smiled without showing her teeth. "It would do me great honor to ride you into battle."

She dipped her shoulder, and I climbed on. Her wings rose up around me like a shield.

"Where should I go?" she asked.

"The helm, the helm!" I pointed with my sword. Men were stopping their work to stare at us, but I ignored them as the manticore bounded across the deck, leaping up beside Marjani.

Naji didn't say nothing at all.

"Bring the ship around starboard!" Marjani shouted. The men scrambled up in the rigging, moving the sails. She grabbed the wheel and yanked it hand over hand. The manticore trumpeted and dug her claws into the wood as the ship tilted and turned.

Naji's eyes began to glow.

"I wouldn't—" Marjani said.

"You are not me." Naji crouched beside the manticore, his eyes fixed on the *Hariri* as she loomed larger and larger.

"Do they have another assas . . . another Jadorr'a on board?" I asked him.

"No." He pushed his coat sleeves up to his elbow and drew the knife over the swirl of one of his tattoos. Blood welled up in thick shining drops. He dropped it over the deck, and when it struck the wood it began to glow pale, pale blue.

The manticore licked her lips. I yanked on her mane. "You'll be eating soon enough."

Naji ignored both of us.

At the helm, Marjani screamed, "Keep working! Get those cannons lined up! Ral, I don't want to see you looking over here. The *Hariri*'s your concern now! Move! Go!"

My heart pounded up near my throat. Naji knelt down at the splatter of his blood and began to chant.

The *Hariri* got closer and closer.

I threaded my fingers through the manticore's fur.

The wind was warm and the air was clean and Naji's voice hummed with my heartbeat.

And then the *Hariri* fired her cannons.

The *Nadir* jolted, sending me and the manticore skittering backward. Naji slammed forward on the deck but didn't stop chanting. Marjani brought the ship around, side by side with the *Hariri*.

"Fire!" she screamed.

A chunk of the *Hariri*'s side blew out across the water. Smoke curled up in the air.

And then I saw it.

The machines the Hariris had out in the desert, the ones that glinted metal and glass: they had them on the boat too. That glint of light flashing off the surface of the sea—it'd been their machines.

"What in hell?" asked Marjani.

"Oh no," I said, my body shaking.

Naji glanced up, his eyes bright and empty-looking.

One of the machines unfolded itself from the deck of the *Hariri*, looking like some golden insect. With a long, whining shriek, it leaped up into the air, metal wings beating into a blur, heading straight for the deck of the *Nadir*. The men screamed and scattered.

Naji said something in his language.

The machine froze in mid-flight, its wings stilled. For a second, it hung there, shining like a piece of jewelry.

Then it crashed down into the sea, water sloshing in a great wave over the side of the boat.

Silence and smoke.

"Keep firing!" Marjani shouted.

The men listened to her. Cannon fire erupted across the side of the *Hariri*.

More machines lifted up off her deck. They were like wasps, like spiders, like stinging scorpions. Only all of them could fly, and all of them were big enough to hold a pair of grown men.

"What are those things?" Marjani yelled.

"Metallurgy." Naji's voice shook.

The machines buzzed through the air. Ten of them. Fifteen.

"We can't turn the cannons up," I said.

"Fire!" Marjani shouted out to the crew. "Use your pistols!"

Shot blasts erupted all over the deck. The machines moved forward.

Naji chanted. One of the machines sputtered and crashed into the water. Another. Another. But his voice was fading, turning scratchy and old-sounding. They were closer, closer—one of them began to spiral out, and it spun and spun and then slammed into the side of the *Nadir*. The whole boat tilted.

Naji collapsed across the deck.

I leaped off the manticore and knelt beside him. His breath came out raspy and weak. I yanked the mask away from his face and he sucked in air. His skin was pale, his brow lined with sweat. But he sat up.

"I couldn't breathe," he said softly.

"Don't wear your mask." And I flung it aside, just as the machines landed across our deck.

"Get on the manticore." He shoved me away and stood up, his movements shaking but strong. I clambered onto the manticore's back.

"I can't eat these creatures," she said to me, and for a minute I thought she sounded scared.

"You'll eat what's inside of 'em," I said.

The largest of the machines groaned and split open. Captain and Mistress Hariri sat beneath the shield, both of them dressed for battle and armed with a trio of pistols each.

"We're here for Ananna of the *Tanarau*," said Mistress Hariri, her voice like death. "She murdered our son. By the rules of the Confederation, you must hand her over."

The men lined up along the edge of the boat, pistols pointed at the Hariris. Half of them were Confederation, and they knew better than to fire.

"We aren't flying Confederation colors," Marjani said. "We don't have to adhere to Confederation rules."

"Where's the captain?" asked Captain Hariri. "Captain Namir yi Nadir? Where is he?"

Marjani didn't answer. She just pulled out her pistol and cocked it back.

"Here." Naji stepped forward.

Captain Hariri looked at him for a long time.

"You're not a pirate," he said. "You're a—"

Then Naji spoke in his language, and light erupted out from the lines of his tattoos and the splatters of his blood on the ship's wood, and it arced across the ship and slammed into Captain Hariri's machine. The machine shot across the deck.

Both of the Hariris jumped out of the way, nimble as cats, and everything started again.

The rest of the machines roared open. *Hariri* crewmen poured out. That knocked our own crew out of their stun, and they launched forward in melee, pistols blasting and swords ringing.

"Ongraygeeomryn!" I shouted, pulling out my sword. "Now!"

"Ananna, no!"

But I wasn't listening to Naji. We flew off the stern deck, the manticore trumpeting loud and perfect. She landed square on the chest of some poor Hariri clansman and his blood spilled across the deck. I caught sight of Captain Hariri in the blur of pistol smoke and fighting and got off one shot and missed. He disappeared behind one of the machines.

"Manticore, this way!"

She lifted her head and hissed. Nobody was coming anywhere close to us, which probably made Naji happy if it weren't for the occasional bullet whizzing past my head. But I needed to get to Captain Hariri. It was the only way to end this.

"Come on!" I shouted. "Time to eat later!"

She leaped to her feet and then galloped across the deck. I swung my sword out against a *Hariri* crew man and tried to find Captain Hariri in all the confusion.

"The machines!" I shouted, pointing with my sword. The manticore hissed again, but she slunk up to them, her ears pressed flat against her head. I felt like I was in the chiming forest again, all that sunlight bouncing off the spindly metal legs.

We crept slowly, cautiously.

A shot fired off and zipped past my head. I crouched down and buried my face in the manticore's mane while she reared around and sent a pair of spines zinging through the air. I heard a man scream.

The manticore skulked forward, the muscles in her back and shoulders tensed and hard. She sniffed at the ground.

For a moment, the smoke cleared, and there was Captain Hariri, reloading his pistol.

I yanked out my second pistol, took aim—

A blast of Naji's magic echoed across the boat, bright blue and smelling of spider mint. Everything tilted. My head spun. The manticore snarled and leaped out of the way of the falling machines; Captain Hariri disappeared, knocked out by the force of Naji's blow.

Magic showered over the side of the boat, staining the water that icy Naji-blue. The *Hariri* smoked and glowed she had moved closer to us, her cannons firing.

Another blast of magic.

This one knocked me off the manticore, and I slid across the deck, my body smearing with salt water and blood. All over the ship, men were fighting best they could in the daze of magic, swords swinging sloppy and wide. I caught sight of Jeric yi Niru drawing his blade across the stomach of a *Hariri* crewman. When the crewman fell, Jeric dragged me to my feet.

"First mate," he said. "Your captain is dying."

"What?" I took him to mean Marjani, but when I turned to the stern deck she was still spinning the wheel one-handed, her pistol cocked and ready in the other. Not dying at all.

"No," he said. "The fake captain."

"Naji!" I pulled away from him and raced across the deck. I could hear the manticore behind me, the soft snapping squelch of her jaws on some crewman's neck. Men's screams. I didn't look back.

Naji was sprawled out on the bow, his arms soaked with blood, his face drawn, his skin almost blue. I knelt beside him, and he turned toward me. Pressed one hand against my face. His blood was hot and sticky against my skin.

"I can't do it anymore," he said, his voice like broken glass. "I'm sorry."

"Did someone hurt you?" I felt around for a wound. "Where are you hurt? I can fix it—"

"Ananna, you don't understand . . . I need blood . . ."

The magic. Nobody had cut him or shot him, it was the magic.

"Mine," I said. "You can have mine."

He shook his head, but I didn't listen to him earlier and I wasn't listening to him now. I drew the tip of my sword down my arm. The sting of it took my breath away.

"Here," I said, and there were tears in my eyes and I hoped he'd think it was from the cannon smoke. "What should I do with it?"

"No . . ." He closed his eyes. "I don't want . . . Not from you . . . It'll connect us . . . It's invasive . . ."

"What are you talking about? We're connected already! We need to kill Captain Hariri. His wife, too. I can't find 'em in all this! Can you do it?"

He didn't answer.

"Can you track 'em? Naji! You have to pull 'em out! I'll kill 'em, all right? But it's the only way they'll stop."

The boat lurched. Marjani screamed orders from the helm, but my head was spinning from the blood seeping out of my arm. "Naji!" I said.

He took hold of my bleeding arm. I braced myself against the deck as the boat tilted farther. Men were scrambling up in the riggings, trying to get her righted.

"Hurry!"

He ran his hand up my arm, blood oozing between his fingers. I ground my teeth together so I wouldn't scream at the pain of it. He began to chant, and his words rolled over me and then I didn't feel the pain no more.

His voice strengthened. He gripped tight on my wrist. My blood rolled in rivers down the length of my arm. He sat up. The shadows underneath the machines started to wriggle and squirm, and men were screaming and moaning.

He leaned close to me, and put his mouth on my ear. "I

won't make you kill them," he whispered. "I know it hurts you."

It stunned me, that sudden burst of kindness, that suggestion that he might care for me, might care for my well-being.

The fact that he knew it hurt me, when I hurt people.

"Thank you," I murmured.

He stood up. The glow in his eyes brightened, and for a second I felt this weird tingle in the arm I'd cut for him, this hum of magic rippling across my skin. And then the tingle was everywhere, sparking up the air, the way it gets before a lightning storm in the desert. Naji was close to me, his body and his mind both, and I felt a surge of warmth from him. A feeling of things being *right*. And then I got the sense of all these hearts beating, every heart on that boat, the blood and the life of every crewman who hadn't gotten tossed down to the deep.

I wondered if this was how Naji felt all the time.

He spoke. His voice echoed inside my head, that secret rose-petal language, like I was hearing his thoughts and his words both. A connection.

The shadows billowed up like smoke, thick enough to rip the *Hariri* machines into shreds, into long glinting metal ribbons. Men flung themselves against the side of the boat. The *Hariri* fired off another volley of cannons. And then in all that confusion, all those glints of metal, all that smoke, all that splintered wood, I knew where Captain and Mistress Hariri were.

I didn't see them.

I just knew.

They were on the bow of the ship, cutting their way through *Nadir* crewman.

I jumped to my feet. Naji grabbed my arm, turned his glowing eyes toward me.

"I know where they are," I said.

"I know." He blinked and I felt a surge of worry. "Ananna, I can protect you."

"You don't have to protect me!" And I wrenched my arm free, despite the strength of his magic—the strength my blood had given him. I leaped off the helm and followed the trail of the shadows, listening to the beating of those two hearts that wanted me dead.

"Girl-human!" The manticore galloped up behind me. I glanced at her over my shoulder. Her entire face was covered in blood. Her teeth shone like knives.

"You smell like Jadorr'a," she said. "But I will not eat you." She dipped her shoulder down. With Naji's magic inside me, I swung myself onto her back.

"To the bow!" I wound my fingers in her mane and pressed myself low against her back. We pressed on together, the shadows sliding over us like water.

I still couldn't see the Hariris, but they were there, I *knew* it, I could feel the proximity—

Off in the distance, a *pop*.

Warmth spread across my belly. Pain. Warmth and pain. I looked down.

Blood.

The smell of smoke and metal.

Someone was laughing. A woman. Shrill and mean. I recognized it—

"Girl-human! You are body-hurt!"

"She shot me," I said, 'cause I couldn't believe it.

"Yes, Ananna of the *Tanarau*," said Captain Hariri. He lifted up his pistol, pointed it at me. The barrel loomed huge and dark. "She shot you."

Lightning arced across the boat.

The Hariris both crumpled like rag dolls.

I blinked.

"Lightning doesn't move sideways," I said. The world was spinning round and round. The pain in my stomach was dazzling.

I wasn't gonna scream. I wasn't gonna cry.

And then I heard a voice like roses and darkness, and I smelled mint and medicine, and strong sure hands wrapped round my chest, and I was tumbling, tumbling, tumbling into the warm soft sea, but I was safe. That I knew.

I was safe. I was protected.

CHAPTER EIGHT

I woke up in a room made of light.

I blinked and rubbed at my eyes and slowly things started moving into focus: a big open window lined with gauzy fluttering curtains, the kind you use to keep bugs out. A table with a water pitcher. A bed, which I was in.

Otherwise, the room was empty.

When I tried to sit up pain exploded through the lower part of my stomach, and I fell back, gasping. I put my hands on my stomach. I wasn't wearing my Empire robe no more, but some kind of thin dress, and through the fabric I could feel the thick weight of a bandage.

I remembered the *pop* of Mistress Hariri's pistol, the swell of pain. Had the Hariris captured me? No, they were dead. Lightning had cut them down . . . No, that wasn't right, either—

"Hello?" I nudged myself up on one shoulder. That didn't hurt too bad. "Anybody around?"

No answer but the wind rustling the curtains. It smelled of the desert.

I lay back down. Stared up at the ceiling. It looked kinda like the clay they used in Lisirran houses, only it was red-orange, like a sunset.

Footsteps bounced off the walls.

"Hello?" I tried to sit up again, grinding my teeth against the pain.

"Ananna? What are you . . . ? No, lie back down." Naji darted up next to the bed and pressed me gently against the soft downy pillows. "You shouldn't move yet."

He wasn't covering his face, and in the room's bright sunlight the twists of his scars made him look concerned.

"Where am I?"

"The Island of the Sun." Naji straightened up and walked over to the table, covered with scraps of parchment with brownish-red writing and vials of dried plants. He set something on it—another vial. "You woke up earlier than I was expecting. That's good."

"Did I die?" I asked. I couldn't remember nothing about what happened after the battle. How far had we been from the island when the Hariris struck? Not far: Jeric yi Niru had shot down sea-birds . . .

"No." Naji sprinkled some of the plants onto one of the scraps of parchment and folded it into a package, the ends tucked inside themselves. "You came close, very close, but . . . I pulled you back."

He slipped the paper package underneath my pillows. "With magic?" I hesitated. "Blood-magic?"

"Yes." He sat down on the bed beside me, leaned up against the wall. "Medicine wouldn't have saved you."

"Oh." I paused. "Did it . . . did it hurt you bad? When I . . . when she shot me?"

Naji turned to me. "Yes," he said, but his eyes were soft, like he hadn't minded. "And I worked to save you, and that made the pain go away."

"I'm sorry."

He looked at me long and hard. "Don't apologize."

Then he brushed his hand over my forehead, pushing the hair out of my eyes. His touch startled me, the cool dry skin of his palm.

"Rest," he said. "I'll be back to check on you."

"Wait," I said. He stopped. "How long we been here?"

"We sailed in yesterday evening." His face hardened. "It seems your manticore is the daughter of the island's pride leader, so our plan for a quick getaway would be distressingly rude. They want to give us a feast when you're better."

My expression must have told him something, 'cause he said, "They swore they will not force us to engage in cannibalism. Still, most of the crew have opted to sleep on the boat."

I kinda smiled at that. No wonder the manticore had been so demanding of me. Wasn't a manticore thing, it was a *royalty* thing. Well.

"When you sleep," Naji said, "the dreaming will help you heal faster."

"Oh." I frowned. "I didn't think blood-magic could save people—"

"Blood-magic can do whatever I will it to do."

I didn't say nothing to that, and Naji gave me a nod. I expected him to leave, but instead he walked over next to the window and pushed the curtains aside and looked out. I watched him for a little while, as the curtains fluttered around him like butterflies. The wind blowing in was hot and dry and smelled of clay. It made me sleepy. Or maybe it was the spells he cast, the little packet of dried herbs under my pillow.

It didn't take long before my eyes refused to stay open, and I curled up on top of the blankets and the dreams came in like the wind.

They were dark and strange, those dreams, and I was back in that black-glass desert, only this time I wasn't scared. Nobody was searching for me. I just wandered across the desert, the glass smooth and strangely cool beneath my bare feet. I wore that same dress I'd had on when Naji and me crossed the desert together after I saved him, on our way to the canyon that was supposed to hold a cure to his curse. Sometimes I thought I saw creatures made out of ink and shadow. I'd turn to look at 'em and they'd dart out of my line of sight, but they left dark streaky trails in their wake, and when I touched them my fingers came back sticky with blood.

When I woke up again it was dark outside and my stomach didn't hurt no more. Torches flickered pale gold against the walls. Naji was gone.

This time I was able to sit up, but it exhausted me, and I leaned against the wall and took deep gulping breaths while my heart pounded against my chest. The bedside table was still littered with Naji's parchments. I picked one up. It was in his language, and I didn't recognize the alphabet, couldn't match the letters to the sounds.

And yet I could hear his voice inside my head, gruff and throaty, chanting the song that had saved me. I couldn't read the parchments, but I could understand it.

Weird.

"Ananna?"

It wasn't him, it was Marjani. I dropped the scraps of parchment, and they fluttered across the top of my bed like flower petals.

"Naji said you had woken up—"

"Yeah." I gathered up the parchment, my movements slow and heavy, like I was underwater. "He told me there's gonna be a feast."

"Don't remind me." Marjani rolled her eyes. "They've already begun preparations. I've had to reassure them about fifty times that we don't mind eating 'servant food.'"

I grinned.

We sat in silence for a little while, the shadows sliding across the floor. I thought about the shadows in my dream, the shadows that had led me to the Hariris.

"How's the boat?" I asked.

"Got us here." Marjani sighed. "Still working on repairs, although it shouldn't be much longer. A day or so." She paused. "Jig's up on Captain Namir yi Nadir, by the way. Crew figured it out during the battle. Good news is they don't seem to mind."

"So Jeric yi Niru doesn't have nothing on us no more."

"I suppose that's true. He's still an eavesdropper. Untrustworthy." She sighed. "Only lost about ten men, all told. A few more were injured. I'm going to give them a higher cut for it. Next time we do some honest pirating, anyway."

"So you're the captain now?"

"That's what they've been calling me." She smiled at me, a real smile. "Naji makes them nervous now that they know about his magic, although I think they'll tolerate him being on board on account of him blasting those damned metal bugs out of the sky."

She looked at me, then, and I knew she was looking for the story, about the Hariris and who I really was. Marjani knew subtlety. I'd warrant she'd won the crewmen over long before the battle—why else would they've listened to her when the Hariris attacked?

She'd won me over a long time ago too.

So I finally told her everything. I told her about running away from Tarrin of the *Hariri*, and I told her how Naji was supposed to kill me, and that I saved his life and that in turn saved me—she already knew most of that already, just none of the details. And I told her about how I killed Tarrin in the desert.

And the whole time she kept her eyes on me, not moving or speaking, just watching me and listening.

When I finished, I expected her to do something, to yell at me for putting the *Nadir* in danger, or for not trusting her enough with the truth. But all she did was nod.

"I'm glad you told me." She stood up. "You still want to be my first mate?"

"You ain't pissed?"

"Don't be ridiculous. We all have secrets. Mine probably won't attack us with a swarm of flying machines, but . . ." She shrugged. "It's over now, right?"

"It's over." I pressed my head back against the wall and closed my eyes. "The Hariri clan'll disband now. Anybody comes after us for the captain's death, I got the right to go after him for revenge, or to send someone after him—doubt anyone'll bother."

Marjani looked amused. "I never understood the Confederation rules for revenge."

"Trust me, ain't no one in the Confederation understands 'em neither."

She laughed. Folded her arms over her chest. "I should go. Naji said sleep would help you get better—so, please, sleep for as long as it takes. I don't want to stay on this island much longer."

"Sure thing." I smiled. "Captain."

The manticores scheduled the feast for two days after I got up and walked around the manticores' palace garden. Naji took me down there, one hand pressed against my back as he led me out of the bare servants' quarters and across the island's dry red sands. As we walked, I kept thinking I heard him talking to me. But when I asked him what he wanted, he only shook his head and told me he hadn't said nothing.

"You're still in the process of recovering," he said stiffly. "Things will clear up for you soon enough."

As it turned out, the manticores' palace wasn't really a palace; it was big pile of red and yellow rocks surrounded on all sides by flowering vines and fruit trees and soft pale grasses. The human servants took care of the garden—I saw 'em working as I stumbled over the paths. My sunlit room was actually in the servants' quarters, which were a series of little clay shacks lining the edge of the garden. The manticore had explained to her father that sleeping inside was a human preference, and then he explained to me that these shacks were the best they had. I didn't mind. Better than sleeping in the grass.

Naji led me into the shade of a lemon tree and helped me sit down. The palace of rocks loomed up huge and tall against the cloudless blue sky.

"That ain't a palace," I said.

"Manticores don't live inside." Naji sat down beside me. "They think it's barbaric."

"How do you know that?"

"I found myself trapped in conversation with Ongraygeomryn's father after we landed."

I looked out over the garden. The plants swayed in the hot desert wind. One of the servant girls walked alongside a row of ginger flowers, spilling water over each one from a bucket that came up almost to her knees.

I didn't see any servant boys.

"Do they all want to eat you as badly as she does?"

"Oh yes." He blinked. "For the first time, I find myself *grateful* for the curse."

I didn't know if it was all right to laugh, so I just kinda squinted at him and nodded. He had covered his face to walk me out to the gardens. I wanted to tell him he didn't need to do that, that he was handsome even with the scars, that the scars made him more beautiful than any untrustworthy pretty boy lurking in some Empire palace.

I didn't, though, 'cause I knew if I did he would leave. And he only saved my life 'cause of his curse, but out there in the garden, the scent of jasmine heavy on the air, it was easy to pretend otherwise.

For those two days before the feast, Naji wouldn't let me go any farther than the gardens—he said I still wasn't strong enough—and every day at sunrise and sunset he came into my room and slipped another packet of blood-spells and dried herbs underneath my pillow. Sometimes he sang this song in his dead-rose language and I'd fall asleep and dream of the black-glass desert and a dry wind full of starlight that would blow me across the landscape and cradle me gentle as a lover.

Sometimes, even when I was alone, I'd hear him singing. I'd hear him *thinking*. I figured it must be leftover from the magic.

The manticore came to visit me too. The first time she came trotting up to us while Naji led me through a maze of thorny red flowers in the garden.

"You lead her well, Jadorr'a," she said. "You've only taken one wrong turn so far. You'll arrive at the maze's center soon."

Naji gave her this annoyed stare, and I knew, suddenly and without explanation, that his magic showed him the way through the maze, and he hadn't taken a wrong turn at all.

"Girl-human," she said to me. "I am glad to see you have not died."

"Yeah, me too."

The manticore looked different now that she was home. Her mane shone like copper, and her coat was smooth and silky. Her eyes were ringed in red powder that made her look feral and haunted all at the same time.

"The servant-humans have promised you many delicious items for the feast," she said. "Fruit and fish and honey." She wrinkled her nose when she spoke.

"My father is most grateful that you have returned me," she went on. "Even though you could not bring us the Jadorr'a uncursed—"

Naji sighed.

"Still, he would like to meet with you, to thank you personally, and to offer you a boon."

"She isn't well enough," Naji said.

The manticore looked at me with concern. "But you are walking through our gardens!"

"A walk through the gardens isn't quite the same thing as a meeting with the pride leader." Naji stepped in front of me like he was protecting me, even though I wasn't in danger from the manticore.

She didn't seem to notice, though, just tossed back her mane and pawed at the ground. "At the feast, then. He is anxious to meet with you."

"At the feast." I nodded. "Looking forward to it." I pushed Naji aside. He stayed close, though. He'd been staying close a lot lately. Closer even than when we'd been stranded on the Isles of the Sky and had to stay close 'cause we were the only two humans around other than Eirnin.

"The feast!" the manticore cried, chiming with delight.

The night of the feast, Marjani and Naji and me all walked from the servants' quarters to the garden together, along with the braver crewmen—including Jeric yi Niru, who Marjani didn't want to leave on the newly repaired boat alone. The manticores' servants brought us clean clothes, soft cotton robes dyed the color of pomegranates and saffron, and they gave us steam baths and lined our eyes with red powder, the way the manticores did.

Naji had his face wrapped up in a scarf. I wondered if he really thought the manticores cared about his scars.

The feast was in the garden, with long low tables set up beneath the fruit trees. We sat down in the grass, lining up on one side of the table, and waited.

"The pride will join you soon," said one of the servants, who tilted her head when she spoke and never looked any of us in the eye.

The sun was just starting to set, and the light in the garden was purple and gold and turned everything into shadow. A trio of servants began to strum harps and sing in a language I didn't recognize, and soft pale magic-cast lanterns blinked on one by one up among the trees.

"Why're they making us wait?" I asked Marjani. Marjani shook her head. "I don't trust manticores."

"They won't do anything," Naji said. He leaned forward on the table, drumming his fingers against the wood. "As many deals as Ananna has made with Ongraygeeomryn, there's no way they'd risk killing her now."

"What? Why?"

"Their elaborate system of boons and favors." Naji looked at me. "You're lucky," he said.

I knew he wanted to say more, but a loud, reverberating trumpet cut through the thick air.

All the servants scrambled to line up behind us.

The music twinkled on in the background.

The manticores marched into the garden.

It was the entire pride, I guess, 'cause there were about fifteen manticores in all. They walked one after another in a long procession. Ongraygeeomryn came in toward the end, flanked by an older lady manticore and man manticore. They sat at the center of the table, right across from me.

The man manticore reared back his head and trumpeted, and this was the loudest trumpet I'd ever heard. It seemed to echo out for miles.

The music stopped playing.

"Girl-human," he said, turning his golden eyes to me. "Do you have a name?"

The silence in the garden was so thick I thought I might choke on it. All the manticores stared at me expectantly.

"Yes," I said. "Your Grace."

"Don't call me that. I am not a human king." He leaned forward, sniffed the air. "What is your name?"

I glanced at Naji. Should you tell a manticore your name or not? He must've known what I was thinking, 'cause he kinda nodded at me like it was all right.

"Ananna of the *Nadir*."

Ongraygeeomryn smiled at me.

"Ananna," the manticore leader said. "I will gift you a boon in exchange for rescuing my daughter from the foul Wizard Eirnin."

The other manticores trumpeted and flapped their wings and furled and unfurled their tails. I saw Marjani shrink down out of the corner of my eye, but nobody let loose any spines.

"You will receive the boon tonight, after the feast." He nodded at me. "It is rude to divulge the nature of the boon in public, but Ongraygeeomryn told me what you would like most in the world, and I am confident in her judgment."

That got my suspicions up a bit, 'cause much as I liked the manticore I wasn't convinced she knew what I wanted most in the world. Mostly 'cause I didn't know what I wanted most in the world. I used to think it was being a pirate captain, but I wasn't so sure of that anymore.

Still, I knew better than to say something. When it comes to dealing with people who think of themselves as important, it's usually best to keep your mouth shut.

"You will find the boon most satisfying," Ongraygeeomryn told me. "I am certain of it."

I nodded and plastered on a smile that I hoped came across as polite.

"Servant-humans!" bellowed the manticore leader. "Bring us food!"

The servants disappeared into the gardens and then reappeared with heavy stone platters laden with fruits and little savory pies and bottles of Empire wine. They set them down first, and I could see all the manticores trying to act like it didn't turn their stomachs.

Then the servants brought out more stone platters covered with slabs of raw meat, pink and glistening in the candlelight. I knew it wasn't sheep.

"We thought this would be more comfortable for you," Ongraygeeomryn said to me, nodding her head at the piles of meat.

"Yes," said her father. "Normally we catch them alive."

Marjani and I glanced at each other.

"We appreciate your thoughtfulness," Marjani said, though her mouth twisted up when she spoke.

Naji didn't say nothing, just slipped his mask into his lap and picked up a lemon-salt fish.

I'd never been to a proper feast before, just the big drunken parties that pirates call feasts. Nobody got up and danced on the table, or groped any of the servant girls—even the crewmen we had with us seemed too terrified to do anything but pick at their food. The music playing in the background was soft and fancy. The conversation was polite and didn't say nothing of any substance. The only thing that made me realize I wasn't up in the palace with the Emperor was the way the manticores ate: they leaned forward and tore chunks of meat off with their teeth, and red juices streamed down their faces and tangled up in the manes.

After dinner, the servants came around with cloths and wiped the manticores' faces clean. One of 'em came at me with a cloth but I declined polite as I could. So did Marjani, though she sounded like a right proper lady—"I don't require your services tonight, thank you." The servant kind of smiled at her. Then she turned to Naji, his scars shadowed and deep in the dim light. He scowled at her until she shuffled away.

When all the platters of food had been cleared, all us human stared at the manticores like we expected something bad to happen. I didn't think they were going to eat us or nothing, but I was still a little concerned about the boon.

"We would be most honored if you would share a dessert wine with us," said the manticore leader. "Ahiial. It is a delicacy from the northern part of our island, and a very precious nectar indeed."

"What's it made of?" I asked. Somebody had to say it.

"It's derived from the pollen of the ahiiala flower," said Ongraygeeomryn. "The only plant we consume."

"The stories say it has magical properties," said a lady manticore with pale white dappling on her coat.

Marjani and me both looked at Naji.

"It's fine," he said.

"Of course it's fine!" boomed the manticore leader. "Servant-humans, bring us the wine!" He smiled, and he only showed the points of his teeth. "You will not be able to drink any of that human swill after tasting ahiial."

Naji shrugged, and I got the sense that he'd had it before.

The servants trotted up to the table, half of 'em holding shallow porcelain bowls and the other half holding rough-hewn stone goblets. They lined 'em up on the table. Then another row of servants marched out, this time carting huge carved pitchers. They made their way around the table, slowly pouring a bit of ahiial for each guest.

The ahiial was pale gold, the color of morning sunlight and a manticore's fur. It smelled sweet, like honey, like a man's perfume.

We all waited till everybody's cup or bowl had been filled. Then the manticore leader lifted one paw.

"To Ananna of the *Nadir*," he said. "Who saved my eldest daughter, the heir to my pride. I am indebted to you."

Naji squirmed beside me. I remembered what he'd said to me back on the Isles of the Sky—*You made a deal with a manticore?* And the way he said it, too, like I'd just confessed to killing my own mother. I could just about see him remembering it himself.

Well, too late now.

The manticore leader bowed his head and lapped at his wine. Even Marjani, who knew as well as I did how rude it was, hesitated.

But I also knew poison wasn't how a manticore killed—not poison in a glass of wine. If they wanted us dead they would have shot us full of spines or launched across their table with their mouths wide open, showing us all three rows of teeth. So I picked up my glass and drank.

It was sweet, sweeter than honey, and the taste of it filled my mouth up with flowers.

When I didn't keel over dead, or jump up, bewitched, and start clearing away the table like a servant, the rest of the crew followed suit. Jeric yi Niru knocked it back like a shot of rum. Marjani sipped it like a lady in a palace. Naji finished his off in a trio of gulps.

"What do you think?" the manticore leader asked me.

"Delicious," I said. And stronger than a barrel of sailor's rotgut. The whole garden was filled with light. All the flowers were glowing. Overhead, the stars left bright trails across the black sky. I laughed, suddenly full up with mirth, the way it happens when I get drunk under good circumstances, with a boat full of friends and the ocean stretching out empty and vast before us.

"Wonderful," the manticore leader said. He nodded his head and the music struck up, some bawdy song I recognized from whenever Papa's crew made port. "Servant-humans!" he called out. "Bring us more ahiial!"

They did, and we drank.

CHAPTER NINE

I sprawled out on my bed, music still drifting in from the garden through my open window. The manticores had proceeded back into their palace of rocks, and the rest of the crew had come crawling off the boat to flirt with the servants and drink ahiial and rum, which was when I decided to slink back to my room. My injury left me too tired to deal with a true pirates' feast.

Every now and then laughter exploded into the nighttime, drowning out the music. Men's laughter, women's laughter. The ahiial left me so happy I didn't even feel left out.

Somebody knocked on my door.

"Who is it?" But I felt a wriggle in the back of my brain, and I knew—

"Naji."

I sat up. "Ain't locked or nothing."

Naji pushed the door open. He had his mask on but his hair was all tousled from the wind. He hadn't been dancing after the feast, I remembered. Just sat on the sides and watched.

"You need to change the . . . the spell that was making me better?"

He shook his head and stepped inside. Came up right close to me, close enough that I could smell him: honey and medicine. He kept his eyes on me.

It was weird, and it confused me, but my heart pounded loud and fast from the way he looked at me.

Like I was Leila. The river witch. His old lover.

"Can I ask you a question?" he said.

I was too nervous to speak. I shrugged.

He took off his mask, yanking it hard away from his face. He let it drop to the floor.

"Do you remember when you told me I wasn't ugly?"

I stared at him. I couldn't get past the light in his eyes.

"You don't, do you?"

"Of course I do," I said, and my voice came out real small.

"Did you mean it?"

"That I don't think you're ugly?"

He nodded.

I couldn't think straight. All I knew was my heart slamming against my chest and his eyes drinking me up like ahiial. How many times had I thought about the answer to this question? How many nights had I spent trying to figure out the exact way to tell him what I thought of him, what I thought of his face and his hair and his body?

Too many to count.

"Of course," I said, voice hardly a whisper again. I swallowed. "I think . . . I think you're beautiful."

His face didn't move. "I thought you don't trust beautiful people."

"Not beautiful like that. I mean . . . I don't ever want to stop looking at you."

The funny thing is that I couldn't actually look at his face while I said that 'cause I was so embarrassed, and so I looked at his throat instead, at the little triangle of skin poking up out of his shirt. He'd taken off the pirate coat.

For a minute I wondered why the hell he was asking me this anyway.

And then he was kissing me.

I ain't kissed many boys before, but Naji knew what he was doing better than any of 'em. He put his hands on the sides of my face and pressed himself close to me, and the whole time it was like he and I were the only people in the world. My hands kept crawling over his chest and shoulders, trying to memorize the lines of his body, and I was dizzy, but in a good way, the way you get when you swing through the ropes on a clear sunny day. That was what kissing Naji was like: the best day at sea, warm sunlight and cool breeze. Happiness.

Kissing Naji was happiness.

When he pulled away from me he smoothed my hair off of my forehead. I was too stunned to do anything but stare at him.

"Is this all right?" he asked.

"Uh. Yeah." I frowned. He kissed me again, and I worked up the nerve to press my hands against his hips. He wrapped his arms around my waist and pulled me close, and the smell of him was everywhere, and I swear I could feel his blood pulsing through his veins. The closeness of his body was so distracting, so wonderful, that I forgot to be nervous.

He lay me down on the bed, still kissing me, and my thoughts were a jumble of confusion and excitement and desire—his desire and my desire both, like two pieces of silk braiding together. I couldn't believe this was happening, couldn't believe he was gazing at me like he wanted me.

"Why are you doing this?" It came out wrong, kinda accusatory. He stopped.

"You said it was all right," he said.

Oh, now you've gone and messed everything up, I thought.

"It is." I reached out, tentative, and cupped the scarred side of his face in my hand. He jerked at my touch, but didn't pull away, and for a moment he looked as vulnerable as I felt. "I mean, I just don't understand . . . why now . . . ?"

He traced the line of my profile, one finger running over my forehead and my nose and finally my lips.

"I should have done it sooner," he said. "I should have done it on the Isles of the Sky." And he kissed me before I could say anything more. I got lost in it, the kissing. It went on for a long time. My lips thrummed, and my body was hot and distracted.

After a while, he pulled away, just a little, and we lay in silence, looking at each other.

I touched his scar, the skin rough and slick at the same time. He flinched away. I dropped my hand.

"I'm sorry," I said.

"No," he said. "No, I just . . . no one's ever . . . before."

"Oh."

Another long silence, and then I lifted my hand and touched him again. This time he only blinked.

"I like it," I said.

He didn't answer. His face was so serious, like always. Except for his eyes, which were gentle right now. Almost kind.

"Why don't you ever smile?"

"What?"

I traced a line from the unscarred skin of his brow down across the folds in his flesh to his chin. "I've never seen you smile."

"You don't want to."

"You don't know that."

"Yes, I do."

He pushed away from me. A coldness settled over me: he was going to leave.

"Wait," I said. "I'm sorry. I just . . . Ain't you happy right now?"

"You don't want to see me smile."

"But I do. Ever since . . ." There was no point. His eyes had gone cold and stony again. I'd ruined everything.

And then something dislodged itself in my brain.

I thought about him showing up at my room for no reason.

I thought about the kissing.

And a realization lit up bright and blazing as the sun.

"Oh," I said. "Oh, Kaol. You ain't happy at all."

He looked at me, pained, like he wanted to protest.

But he didn't.

"This isn't you," I said, and the words turned to panic in my throat. "This isn't . . . you wouldn't on your . . . the boon."

Naji looked stricken. Confused. He didn't deny nothing.

I felt like I was spitting out poison. I shoved myself off the bed. Heat rose up hot and angry in my chest. "It's the boon!" I shouted. "From the manticores!"

Kaol, why hadn't I stopped him when he first came in? Why hadn't I *known*?

"Ananna, no, you don't understand." His words shook. "The magic, it's—"

"Shut up!" I drew my robe tight over my body—it had slipped off my shoulders before. "I can't believe . . . I'm so sorry . . . I actually thought you wanted me—"

"I do." Naji rubbed his head. He still looked confused. "I do want you—"

"Get out!" Part of me didn't mean it. Part of me looked at Naji and thought about how he'd cared for me after I was shot, how he walked me around the gardens and stayed close to me even though I wasn't in any danger. But I couldn't run the risk of letting him hurt me. Not again.

"Get out of my room!" I shouted.

Naji stumbled out of the bed. He seemed drunk. *The ahiial*, I thought. They stuck something in his wine.

What you want most in the world. The manticore must've thought it was Naji.

"This isn't how I wanted things to happen," Naji said, still watching me with that pained, befuddled expression.

"It ain't how I wanted 'em to happen neither!" I yanked my sword out from its hiding place under the bed and brandished it at him. I couldn't decide if I was angry at him or at the manticores or at myself. "So get out now."

He stared at the sword and looked sad. "I do want you," he said.

Blood rushed in my ears. I remembered us standing in the sunlight of the garden, his hand on my arm, the scent of flowers heavy on the wind. I remember him looking at me, flush with happiness.

Naji turned and walked out the door.

I couldn't sleep. The bed smelled like Naji.

I left my room and followed the hallway through the servants' quarters, one hand trailing along the powdery walls, dust kicking up behind my feet. The quarters were silent and still, but the air was stuffy out in the hallways. No windows. So I went outside and sat down underneath a palm tree, leaning up against the trunk.

The desert swirled around me, cold and sad with the nighttime.

I wasn't going to cry, and I wasn't going to remember.

"What are you doing awake?"

It was Marjani. She came walking from the direction of the desert, her robes stained with dirt at the hem.

"Where the hell were you?"

"Thinking." She folded her arms in front of her chest. "You look like you had too much ahiial."

"I left when you did," I muttered.

"I know." She sat down beside me. "What's wrong?"

"Nothing."

She folded her legs up against her chest and tucked her chin on her knees. "You got that boon yet?"

Kaol, she had to ask that, didn't she? I spat in the dirt.

"I'll take that as a no."

"Take it as a yes." I glared off into the darkness. "And I don't want to talk about it so don't ask."

Marjani blinked at me and then lay her cheek against the top of her knees. We sat in the dusty quiet until I couldn't stand the sound of silence no more.

"When we leaving?" I asked.

Marjani lifted her head. "Tomorrow, I imagine. Later, though. After the crew've all slept off their hangovers."

"We got a course laid out yet?"

Marjani hesitated. I peered at her, wondering what she was keeping from me. The mystery kept my mind off other things.

"We aren't going to Lisirra," she finally said.

"What? Why?" I dropped my head against the palm tree. "Another damn delay? Marjani, you've no idea how much I want to get rid of Naj . . . of the curse."

Marjani gave me a weird look, but all she said was, "We're going to Jokja. I know of starstones there."

"You didn't think that might've been important to mention *before*?" But then I remembered seeing that brooch stuck in the map at Arkuz. It hadn't registered at the time, but— "Kaol, how long have you been planning this?"

"Since Bone Island." Marjani's expression didn't change. "I shouldn't have kept it from you, but—I had my reasons."

I glared at her.

"I wasn't sure I wanted to . . . go back."

Something about her voice softened me. "Is it dangerous for you?"

"Probably not," she said softly. "The king died three weeks ago. I received word when we were on Bone Island."

"The king? You got banished on orders of the *king*?"

"The king had a . . . personal connection to the affair." It took me a few minutes to realize what she was saying.

"You tried to court the Jokja *princess*?"

Marjani blinked at me a few times, eyelashes fluttering against her cheek. Then she laughed. "I never thought about it that way before."

"But it's what you did! Merciful sea, Marjani, that's a hell of—" I stopped. "Wait, so she's the queen now? Your, ah, your friend? That's how it works in Jokja, yeah?"

"Yes."

"She ever pick a suitor?"

Marjani shook her head.

"That's the real reason you want to go back, ain't it?"

Marjani looked away, out toward the desert. "Saida's family has owned a pair of starstones for several generations. I remember hearing about them from the court storyteller. And the condition of the curse required a princess, if you recall . . ." She laughed, shook her head. "It's really quite perfect."

Almost as perfect as me falling in love with him 'cause of helping him find his cure.

I was back in that bedroom, Naji kissing me and touching me and *looking* at me all 'cause of some manticore sorcery—

"Ananna? Are you sure you're all right?"

I scowled.

Marjani tilted her head in a way that reminded me of Mama, bending over to lay cool rags on my forehead whenever I had a fever. "It's about the boon, isn't it?"

"I told you I don't want to talk about it!"

"It might help you, though." Marjani eyes were wide and clear. "It helped me. Talking."

I stared at her and didn't say nothing.

"What did they give you, Ananna?" And her voice was soft like she was speaking to a child.

I hesitated.

"Ananna—"

"Naji!" I shouted. "They gave me Naji."

That was met with silence, like I figured it would. Then Marjani said, "Not as a meal, I hope—"

"No." The palm tree was leaking sap, sticky and cool against the skin of my back.

"Then wha . . . Oh."

I didn't say nothing.

"How'd they—"

"I don't know!" I slammed my fist into the ground. "Poisoned him or something. Magic. I don't know."

"Manticores with love spells," Marjani said. "Well, that's awfully terrifying."

"It ain't funny."

"No," she said. "It's not." She leaned forward, put one hand on my knee. "Sweetness, how do you *know* it was the boon?"

"Because there ain't no way he could want me on his own!"

Marjani frowned.

"And I asked him to smile and he wouldn't do it, and then he acted all confused, like he was coming out of a fever. Plus I can just *tell*, after spending every damn day with him."

"It might've been the boon," Marjani said. "But that sort of magic always builds upon latent desires—"

"Don't try to make me feel better!"

"I'm not." Her hand dropped off my knee. I thought about the way he held me close as he kissed me. All that manticore trickery. "I knew someone back in Jokja who studied magic. She explained how those kind of spells work, and she said you can't make anything happen if it's not there to start with it."

I'd heard that too, but this was manticore magic, and it was probably different.

Marjani and I sat in silence for a few moments longer, and then she said, "Was he at least any good?"

I looked up at her. Then I burst into laughter, relieved that she was here, that I could talk to her about this.

"Why would you ask me that?" I asked, still laughing.

"I'm just curious." She grinned. "A Jadorr'a . . . I always thought they sublimated their desires. You know. Abstinence so that their magic can work. Closeness to death and all that."

"He had desires," I said carefully. "And his magic still works."

She laughed, her voice breaking against the wind.

"And we didn't . . . didn't do everything," I finally said. "I figured out what happened before . . . before we could . . ."

At that, Marjani stopped laughing. She made this sympathetic clucking sound and stuck her arm around my shoulder, pulled me in close for a hug.

"I mean I've done it before. But it was never a big deal. It was always just . . . *weird*. And with Naji I thought . . . thought it might be special."

"Oh, sweetness."

"The others were just . . . boys I met. You know. And I was kind of hoping that I'd get to see what the big deal was."

"The big deal?"

"You know." I didn't know how to put it into words. "How it's supposed to feel really good, and you just . . . fall away . . ."

"Oh, that." Marjani laughed again. "You know you don't need Naji for that. Or anyone."

I frowned.

"Did you really never . . . All right, listen." And then she leaned close to me and told me about my body, stuff nobody'd never told me before, like I was supposed to just *know*. I felt like some stupid little kid, listening to her, my eyes getting big and wide, but she didn't sound like she thought any less of me for not knowing.

"That's what I mean," she said when she had finished. "I know you think you're in love with him—"

"I don't just think!" I said. "The curse—"

"Oh, never mind the curse. You can't let that dictate your life." She paused. "You don't need Naji to give you pleasure, and you don't need Naji to make you happy."

Right now, it didn't feel like that, but I knew better than to say something to her.

"You killed the son of Captain Hariri," Marjani said, "one of the richest pirates in the Confederation, before he could kill you. You helped win a *sea battle* against the Hariri clan. You struck a deal with a manticore and lived. Why do you care what Naji thinks of you?"

I didn't have an answer to that.

She stood up and dusted the sand off her robes. "When we set sail for Jokja tomorrow, I don't want to see a single misty-eyed glance his way, do you understand? You have a ship to navigate and a crew to help command, and I have neither the patience nor the inclination to put up with a heartsick child."

"I ain't a child."

"Then act like it." She held out one hand and I took it and she pulled me to my feet. "Do you want me to command it? 'Cause I will, if that'll get you to stop mooning over him."

That got a grin out of me. "No, Captain."

"Captain." She laughed. "We'll see how long they call me that." She put her hand on my back. "Come on," she said. "I'll walk you inside."

I let her. And for a minute, forgetting Naji didn't seem totally impossible no more.

CHAPTER TEN

The manticore came to see me before we set sail the next day. I was up on the boat, screwing around with the rigging 'cause half the crew was too hungover to be of much use. One of the manticore's servants crept across the deck, and I damn near tossed a pile of ropes on her.

"Mistress," she whispered, keeping her eyes downcast. "Ongraygeeomryn would like to speak with you."

I'd kinda been hoping I wouldn't have to see the manticore before we left, 'cause I was still sore on account of what happened with Naji, even though I was trying real hard not to moon over him.

But I figured this was my chance to prove that I was strong and that I didn't need him, the way I'd proved it last night, underneath the thin rough blankets of my bed.

"Tell her she can come talk to me when she's ready," I said.

The servant trembled. "Mistress," she said. "The manticore doesn't wish to come aboard . . ."

"Oh hell." Figures. "She on the beach, at least?"

"Yes, mistress." The servant pointed a trembling finger off to the side. "My rowboat is in the water. She doesn't wish to be kept waiting—"

"Of course she doesn't."

I rowed me and the servant back in to the beach, and sure enough, the manticore was stretched out on a quilted silk blanket on the sand, another servant standing beside her with a palm leaf.

"Girl-human!" she cried. "Did you enjoy your boon last night?"

"You mean Naji?"

"Of course! Such an easy one to enchant. Almost no convincing necessary at all." She looked closer at me. "You did want him still, yes? He is your true love."

Never mind the curse, I thought. But I didn't say nothing. The manticore looked so damned pleased with herself.

"He was very . . ." I glanced off in the direction of the palace, hoping he wouldn't show up while I was talking. "Skillful."

The manticore looked puzzled for a moment. "Is that a good thing?"

"Uh, yeah."

She beamed at me. "That is excellent news! We do not describe our matings as skillful; I shall remember that."

Part of me wanted to ask her how she did it, if it really had been the ahiial, or some other manticore spell, maybe drawn out of the red desert sand. The sand-charmers in Lisirra could do that; I remembered from my trips to the night market. But what would be the point? It had happened, and not 'cause he wanted it.

Something else was bothering me, though.

"So he isn't . . . he isn't gonna keep bugging me after this?" I asked. "I've heard about love spells, and they always . . . persist, if you know what I mean."

"Persist?" The manticore frowned. "No, girl-human. Love does not persist! It is allotted to us once a life cycle."

Oh. Like cats.

"The boon was only for one love-period," the manticore said. Her eyes dimmed. "I could ask my father to recast it in perpetuity—"

"No!" I held out my hands. "No, it's fine. Once was . . . once was enough."

"Spoken like a manticore!" She smiled big and bright at me. "I knew you were of a superior mind to the servants."

"I'm gonna miss you, Ongraygeeomryn," I said, stumbling over the last syllable.

And even with the boon, I still meant it.

"When the Jadorr'a is free of his curse, you are always welcome to return him to us. Remember, it would do him a great honor."

I just looked at her, although I thought about how easy it would be to cart him back here.

Easy, but not *fair* and wrong to boot. Dishonorable. Even if he had soul-hurt me a million and one ways.

No. I promised Marjani I wasn't gonna moon over him.

So I threw my arms around the manticore's neck and gave her a big hug. She nuzzled me back, her mane tickling my nose.

"You are always welcome on the Island of the Sun as a guest," she said. Her tongue swiped across my cheek and left my skin stinging. "With or without the Jadorr'a. You are always a friend."

Jokja was two weeks' sail from the Island of the Sun, through water bright and green as glass. It was an easy voyage. Once Naji found out where we were headed and why, he called down favorable winds every morning, and we had plenty of food. The best bit of all was that the crew listened to Marjani and called her captain. They didn't even grumble about chasing after starstones, since our chase was taking us into Jokja. Plenty of treasure there if you know where to look.

Some afternoons I'd sit up in the riggings, whenever there wasn't nothing else to do, and remember how I used to dream about captaining my own ship, knowing all along it was as impossible a dream as marrying into the emperor's family or becoming as powerful a witch as Mama. But Marjani had managed it easy enough. Maybe I could too.

The only trouble with the voyage was Naji. I did my best to avoid him after what happened. He and Marjani slept in the captain's quarters, same as before, but I couldn't stand the thought of sharing the cabin with him. So I dragged a hammock down to the crew's quarters and cleared out a spot of my own in the corner. It was as awful as you'd expect, but better than having to spend my nights so close to Naji. Sometimes when I was close to him I felt like his thoughts were trying to crowd into mine. I hated it.

Daytime, it was easier to avoid him. He rarely came out on deck, despite everyone knowing he wasn't really Captain Nadir, and so I just made sure not to go to the captain's quarters. Marjani didn't like it, but she put up with it, sending word through one of the crew to come meet her at the helm whenever she needed me.

One afternoon I was sitting up in the rigging, watching the waves break up against the side of the boat. Wasn't much work to be done that day; the breeze was just enough to glide us along. The ropes cradled me as I leaned back and blinked up at the bright blue sky.

Everything was beautiful enough for me to forget my troubles.

And then I felt a tension in the ropes. A tug.

"Who is it?" I called out. My shift wasn't over till sunset, but it could've been one of Marjani's messengers. The ropes tugged again, and then I knew who it was. I couldn't say how. I just *knew*.

Naji climbed up onto the yard, his dark hair appearing first, and then his mask, and then his dark clothes. My heart started pounding, but I didn't say nothing, just watched him climb. When he finished, he tottered back and forth, one hand clinging to the mast, watching me.

We sat in silence for a long time, the wind whistling around us.

I could hardly stand it. Everything up here in the rigging was bright—the white sails, the sunlight. And then Naji had to show up, a dark imperfection.

"You sure you should be out of your cabin?" I asked, hoping if I said something he'd go away. "Not really Captain Nadir's style, you know."

Naji shifted his weight, looking uneasy. "I'm not Captain Nadir." He took a deep breath. "Ananna, I'd like to speak with you."

I shrugged.

"About—" He edged forward on the mast, moving closer to me. I pulled myself in like I could disappear.

He stopped.

"We still have two more tasks to complete," he said. "And you clearly can't stand the thought of my company."

I looked away from him, out to sea.

"If this is what you want," he said, "to sleep down below, and to spend your days in the rigging—then it's fine, for our time on the ship." His voice wobbled when he said *fine*, like he didn't mean it. I looked at him, not sure what I expected to see. What I found was an intensity in his expression. A hopelessness, maybe.

Love spells build on existing desires.

"But when the time comes for us to disembark, we're going to have to be in close proximity again. You know I can't leave you alone in the city, especially not with the Mists still a factor." He leaned up against the mast and looked exhausted. "You're going to have to speak to me eventually. I'm sorry . . . sorry about what happened, and I want you to know that it isn't how it seemed—"

"Yeah," I snapped. "That was the whole problem."

"That isn't what I meant." Naji scowled. "If you don't want to make amends, fine. But I need to know you aren't going to run off the moment we make port. That will kill me. Do you understand? It will kill me."

My skin felt hot. Of course I knew it would kill him. That was the whole reason I'd agreed to help him in the first place, that night in Lisirra.

"I ain't gonna run off," I said. "And if you need me to travel with you, then I guess I'll have to do it. But we're on the boat right now, so it ain't much of a problem, is it?"

He stared at me with that same intensity as before, and I could feel him burning through me. I shook my head. "Is that all you want?"

He didn't move. The wind blew his hair across his forehead and dislodged his mask enough that a bit of scar peeked through, brownish-red in the sunlight.

"Well?" I asked.

"Yes." He turned away from me. "Yes, that's all I wanted."

The day we arrived in Arkuz was hot and bright, the sun an unblinking eye overhead. The docks were busy and close to full, but Marjani sweet-talked our way into a slot near the marketplace. I'd been to Jokja before, but always on Papa's boat, and we always sailed along the coasts to plunder, 'cause Jokja's got a lot of wealth, like all the Free Countries do. They have access to the mines in the jungle, which everyone from outside the Free Countries is afraid to travel through 'cause of all the magic there, plus some of the fastest and best-equipped ships on the seas. Jokja's navy is the one navy a pirate, Confederate or otherwise, doesn't want to cross. The Empire navy might be bigger, but Jokja's got technology on their side. Fast ships and quick cannons. Papa was brave to sack the Jokja coast, all things considered.

Anyway, I'd never much had a chance to just wander around Arkuz the way I did in Lisirra, and I was looking forward to it, to seeing the acacia trees and tasting the chili-spiced fruit Marjani was always going on about.

After we'd docked, Marjani ordered the crew to take shifts watching the ship. As she was sorting 'em out, Jeric yi Niru slipped out from down below and grabbed me by the wrist. I had my knife out before he could say nothing. Naji wasn't nowhere to be seen. I wondered if it hurt him and he was just respecting my wishes not to see him, or if Jeric yi Niru had no intention of harming me.

"Still chasing after fool's treasure?" he whispered.

"Let go." I wrenched my arm free of his grip, though I kept my knife leveled at his throat. "What do you want?"

"You really think you'll find the starstones here? Jokja's a land of science, not magic."

"Magic's everywhere, Snakeheart. And what do you care anyway? You'll still get paid."

"With what? Starstones?" He laughed again. "Do you even know what they are, first mate?" He leered at me and I pressed the knife up against his skin, not enough to hurt him but enough to draw blood. He didn't even move. "Have you ever seen a starstone before?"

I didn't answer. Off in the distance, I could hear Marjani shouting at the crew, but I didn't dare take my eyes off Jeric yi Niru's face.

"I'll take that as a no." He laughed. "I have. They're awfully pretty. Like the stars fell from the sky. That's where the name comes from, did you know that? There's a story, an old Empire story. The nobles like to tell it. A man was pursuing a woman, the most beautiful woman in the Empire. She told him she would marry him, but only if he fit a starstone into a ring for her to wear. He spent years seeking one out, and when he finally found it, do you know what happened?"

I pressed my lips tight together and kept my knife at his throat and didn't say a word.

"He scooped it up in his bare hand and all the life fell out of him. The starstone sucked it right up."

"He died?" I hadn't meant to act like I cared, but it came out anyway.

"Yes, first mate. He died. His life flowed into the stone. That's what makes them so beautiful, you know. All that human life trapped in such a small space."

Find the princess's starstones, the Wizard Eirnin had said, *and hold them, skin against stone.*

Skin against stone.

I scowled, though I eased up on my knife a bit. I'd be damned if I let Jeric yi Niru know what I was thinking. "Sounds like Empire trash to me. Let me guess: The woman in the story was above his station and the man had to be punished for chasing after her? Half the Empire stories I've heard end like that."

"No," Jeric yi Niru said, "that isn't it at all."

"Jeric!" Marjani's voice cut across the ship. "Ananna! What the hell are you two doing?"

"We were talking, Captain," Jeric yi Niru said.

Marjani gave him the iciest glare I'd ever seen her take on. "Nothing's ever just talking with you, Jeric. If I hear one word of trouble from you, you can stay behind in Arkuz in your Empire robes when we make sail."

That shut him up. The people of the Free Countries don't take too kindly to Empire soldiers milling around their cities, even a turncoat like Jeric.

Once the boat was secure enough for Marjani's liking, she led me and Naji off the docks and through the hot bright streets of Arkuz. I kept a big space between me and Naji 'cause it seemed easier that way, but the whole time I was thinking about that stupid story Jeric yi Niru had told me. The task was impossible not because starstones are rare, but because touching 'em killed you.

I glanced at Naji out of the corner of my eye, but he stared straight ahead, his face covered with a desert mask that drew more looks from the Jokjana than his scar would've. It marked him as Empire, since there are no deserts in the Jokja. I wondered if he'd ever heard that story. Probably. He'd been pretty quiet on the subject of the starstones. It was mostly Marjani plotting everything out, bringing us here to Jokja. And I knew that didn't have nothing to do with Naji's curse or rocks that can destroy you at the touch.

My thoughts churned around inside me like a sickness.

We walked on and on, far enough that I lost the scent of the ocean and caught instead the rainy damp scent of the jungle. Arkuz reminded me of Lisirra, 'cause it was big and sprawling and crowded with street vendors selling spiced fruit and charred meat wrapped up in banana leaves, and shops full of spices and jewels and fabric dyes and precious metals. And everybody looked like nobility, the women in these long fluttering dresses, their shoulders bare and their wrists heavy with bangles, and the men in tailored slim-cut cotton shirts.

I speak a bit of Jokjani, enough to understand the vendors trying to entice me to come buy something from them, but not enough to have any idea what Marjani said to the guard at the entrance to Azende Palace once we finally arrived. He used a different dialect than I was used to, and Marjani matched it. For a while it didn't look like he was gonna let us pass—he was courteous enough to Marjani but kept glancing at me like I was some street rat trying to make off with his palace-issued bronze dagger, and he was obviously trying his best to not even look at Naji.

Marjani was getting more and more annoyed, I could tell, her hands clenching into fists. The guard kept shaking his head and saying something in Jokjani that I knew wasn't *no* but sounded close. Then Marjani took a deep breath, closed her eyes, and told him her name. Her full name, her old name, not Marjani of the *Nadir* but Marjani Anaja-tu. A noble's name. I'd never heard her say it.

The guard's eyes widened.

"Do you recognize that name?" Marjani asked. Her voice trembled a little, and I tensed up my arm, ready to grab my sword if anyone made a grab for her.

The guard answered with something that sounded like another name, and this time it was Marjani's eyes that got wide.

"Really?" she asked. Then she straightened her shoulders and said something I couldn't catch. The guard responded. I got *you* and *palace* and something about time and nothing else. Marjani didn't look upset though, which was a good sign. Then she said, "Take us to her."

The guard scowled and gave her this insolent little bow.

Naji frowned. "Was that true?" he asked Marjani in Empire.

"Every word," she answered in Jokjani. "Don't speak Empire here."

Naji glared at her. I wondered how much of that courtship story got related to the guard.

The guard led us through the palace gate and then through a garden laden with flowers and vines and palm fronds, like the royal family thought they could corral the Jokja jungle for their own use. The air smelled sweet and damp, and women in thin silky dresses looked up from their books and paintings as we walked past. All of 'em were pretty the way nobility always is—it's a prettiness that's painted on, not in-born, but it still made me nervous, the way they watched us with their polite, silent smiles.

The palace was open-air, the scent of the garden drifting into the room where the soldier left us waiting. "I'll alert the queen to your presence," he said to Marjani before he turned on his heel, footsteps echoing in his wake. Naji and me both sat down on the big brocade-covered chairs set up next to the windows. Marjani stayed standing.

"Are they going to arrest you?" I asked.

"What?" Naji asked.

Marjani didn't answer.

"That is what you told him, right?" I asked. "That story about what you told me—"

"No," Marjani said. "I didn't tell him the story I told you." Her fingers twisted around the hem of her shirt.

"Then what—"

"If you spoke better Jokjani," Marjani said, "you'd know."

That stung.

"Arrest her?" Naji asked. Marjani ignored him, and he turned to me, which made my heart pound for a few annoying seconds. "What do you mean?"

"Nothing," I snapped. "My Jokjani ain't good enough for me to know anything."

Worry lines appeared on Naji's brow.

The door banged open, and the sound of it echoed across the huge, empty room. A pair of guards came in—these had different uniforms from the one at the gate, and they carried swords instead of spears. Marjani straightened up. She didn't say nothing to me or Naji, just stood there smoothing her hands over the fabric of her shirt, all wrinkled up from where she'd been clutching it.

The guards walked across the room and stopped and turned to the door. And then two more guards walked in, and then a trio of pretty young attendants and then this graceful woman with dark brown skin and a halo of black hair. Figures she'd be beautiful.

"Saida," said Marjani, her voice husky.

The woman stopped. She lifted one hand to her mouth. "Jani?" she asked. "No, it can't—"

Marjani nodded. I realized her hands were shaking. The woman—Saida, the woman from the story, the princess, the *queen*—rushed forward, the soles of her shoes clicking across the floor.

The guards didn't even move.

"I thought you were dead!" She threw her arms around Marjani's neck and buried her face in Marjani's hair. Marjani scooped her arms around Queen Saida's waist and her eyes shimmered. When she blinked a tear fell down her cheek.

Naji looked back and forth between the two of them and then over at me.

Queen Saida kissed Marjani, and they stayed that way for a long time, like they'd forgotten what kissing was like. When they pulled apart, their hands stayed touching. "You're queen," Marjani said, her voice full of wonder. They were speaking a Jokjani dialect I had an easier time understanding.

"I am." Queen Saida gave this little bow like it was the other way around, like Marjani was the queen and not her. "Were you so far away that you couldn't hear news from Jokja?" She smiled. It made her light up like she was filled with stars.

"No, I heard. That's why I came. But I just . . . I couldn't quite *believe* it."

"You knew I'd inherit."

"I know, but it's one thing to hear about, another to actually see—" She shook her head. "And I've been in the Empire so long, I'd forgotten—"

"The Empire!" Queen Saida exclaimed. "What's that like? Have they invaded the ice-islands yet?"

Marjani rolled her eyes. "Surely the queen of Jokja would know if the Empire had made a move for the ice-islands."

"I know they've been trying." Saida tilted her head. "Are you sure you were in the Empire? Because you look like a pirate."

"Well, I was doing that, too."

Queen Saida burst into laughter, though she covered her mouth up like a lady. Which I guess she was.

Marjani gave her a smile, small and sad.

And then Queen Saida turned to me and Naji. He pulled the mask away from his face, rose up from his chair, and gave her this handsome bow. Then he hauled me up by the arm.

"Saida, I would like you to meet Ananna of the *Nadir* and . . . Naji."

"Just Naji?" asked Saida.

"I am Jadorr'a."

Queen Saida's polite smile didn't waver once. "It is a pleasure to meet you," she said to Naji. She pressed her hand to her heart. Naji did the same and bowed again. Then she turned to me. "And you, Pirate Ananna." I gave her a bow 'cause I liked that she treated me and Naji like we were visiting nobility. Wouldn't expect that from somebody so beautiful.

"I'll arrange for rooms in the guest quarters," Queen Saida said. She looked at Marjani. "Would two suffice? One for each of your companions?"

The air was heavy with the scent of flowers. Marjani nodded slowly. Nobody said nothing about Marjani's room.

"Wonderful. I'm afraid I have business to attend to . . . I wasn't expecting you—"

"I'm sorry," Marjani said.

"Don't apologize. I'll let the cooks know you're here. You can join me for dinner."

She dipped her head again and then turned on her heel, skirts swirling around her legs. When she left the room, a scent like spice and flower petals lingered in the air.

One of the guards stayed behind.

"I can see you to the atrium while your rooms are being prepared," he said, in that stiff formal way soldiers get sometimes.

Marjani looked dazed. She didn't answer him, just stared at the door where Saida had disappeared.

"That would be fine," said Naji.

The guard glanced at him real quick and then averted his eyes.

The atrium turned out to be an enormous room filled with sunlight that overlooked the jungle. There was a guy there telling a story to some little kids, half of 'em looking like nobles and the other half looking like servants, and a table laid out with food, fresh fruit and sugared flowers and spicy herbed cheese, plus a sweet sugar-wine that reminded me a little of rum.

There were some guards too, near the door, keeping their eyes on everything. I was in half a mind to try and steal something just to see if I could.

Marjani collapsed on a pile of cushions near one of the windows. Sunlight sparkled across her face. She pressed her hand to her forehead and looked out at the jungle, green and undulating like the sea.

"You didn't ask her about the starstones," Naji said.

My stomach clenched up. I should tell him what Jeric had said. But not here, surrounded by stories and sunlight, even though I knew I'd have to tell him eventually: I didn't want him to die, no matter how bad he hurt me.

"The starstones aren't going anywhere," Marjani said. "I'll ask her tonight."

Naji frowned, and for the first time since I met her, I felt a sudden flash of irritation at Marjani.

The storyteller finished up, and the kids all burst into applause and started begging for another one. I slumped down next to Marjani.

"I didn't think I'd ever come back here," she said out of nowhere. "It's funny. This room—we used to listen to stories together right over there." She jerked her head to the corner with the storyteller. "And she'd bring in musicians sometimes and teach me how to dance. I'd never learned at home, 'cause Father was so keen on me becoming a scholar." She smiled again, and this time she looked wistful, which I guess was better than bitter. "I used to think about it sometimes, watching you dance on the deck of the *Ayel's Revenge*."

I blushed. "I don't dance like a queen."

"Neither did she."

We sat in silence for a few minutes longer. Naji seemed real intent on the surface of his wine.

Marjani turned her head back toward the jungle, and I wondered how best to tell Naji that the thing that could cure his curse would kill him in the process.

CHAPTER ELEVEN

My room was beautiful, with a soft canopied bed and windows that faced the jungle, and a huge porcelain washtub that the servants filled with cool, jasmine-scented water when they brought me into the room. First thing I did was take a bath. Sea baths will keep you clean enough, but nothing beats fresh water to slough all the salt off your skin.

The servants brought clothes, too, a thin cotton dress and a narrow gold belt that I cinched around my waist. I combed my hair out and sat on the window ledge and looked down at the wash of green roiling up against the city's walls. Papa'd told me once that he knew a man who had crossed the Jokja jungle and came out the most powerful sorcerer either the Empire or the Free Countries had ever seen. I'd never decided if I believed him or not.

For a minute, I wondered what Papa was doing. Had the Hariris gone after him first, back when I was crossing the desert with Naji? That wasn't usually the way of things, but you never knew with a clan so enamored of the land. Or had Papa and Mama even heard about what I did, to Tarrin, to his parents? Mama hadn't used her magic to track me, at least not that I could tell, although I might have been too far away from them for it work. Or maybe they just didn't care.

The wind blowing in through the windows changed. I noticed it as a prickle on my skin. The hairs raised up on my arms. A chill crept into the room.

I fumbled around on the bed, trying to find the knife I'd tossed there while I was taking my bath. The wind blew harder, and then a mist crept in—a northern mist, nothing I should have seen in Jokja.

I touched the charm around my neck.

"Ananna," Echo said.

I whirled around, knife out, heart racing. She stood beside the window, and she was dressed like a Jokja lady. But she had the same mean starry eyes and the same cold voice and the same swirl of mist where her feet should have been.

"Get out of here," I said.

"Still protecting him?" Echo drifted forward, bringing the cold damp in with her. "You've come up in the world since last we spoke."

I readied my knife.

She floated over to my bed and sank into it.

"But your affection for the assassin appears to be waning."

I glared at her, tensed my fingers against my knife.

She smiled hard and cold at me. "The offer still stands," she said. "Take us to him, and we'll grant you a thousand boons."

"Why?" I said. "Why do you want him so bad? Just 'cause he bested your lord?"

She looked at me, calm and implacable. "That's exactly why. My lord was humiliated by that particular defeat. We don't like being defeated, particularly by humans." She narrowed her eyes and wrinkled her nose in disgust. "And we don't like being humiliated either."

"Yeah? So you're just gonna let Naji keep defeating you every time you show up?" I jabbed my hand at the door. I didn't think this was about defeat at all. It was about wanting a place in our world, like Esjar had told me. "You just floated in here like there wasn't a door or walls. Go find him yourself. Or *make* me do it, you want him that bad."

"But I can't touch you," she said. "Because of that *thing* around your neck." She tilted her head. "Even after all the hurt he's caused you, you still wear it?"

"Apparently."

"So coy." She smiled again. "And as point of fact, the assassin has not defeated me. He's merely hidden himself with some silly human charm. It took three years by your reckoning to find him before—without anyone having to betray him, even. So don't think your refusal will actually save him. It only delays the inevitable." She laughed. "And rest assured that when I find him without your help—and I will—you will not be granted a thousand boons. And not even his pathetic human magic will protect you."

I waited for her to laugh again, or give me that infuriating mocking smile of hers, but she didn't. She just stared at me with a calm, placid expression and I thought about how he'd refused to smile for me like kissing me was the worst thing that could happen. I thought about how I didn't let myself think his wanting me was the result of a spell, *how it didn't even cross my mind* when it should've.

I thought about how he made me stupid.

"You're considering it," she said. "I can see it in your eyes."

"I ain't considering nothing." No, I'd been thinking about the manticore, and how dangerous everyone said that was, making a deal with her, and yet I'd managed to get away with my life intact.

I didn't want to hand the world over to the Mists, but maybe I could still hand over Naji, and save the world myself.

The door to my room slammed open, and there stood Naji with his sword and pirate's coat. He gave me a look so full of dismay it was like he could read my mind.

I jumped to my feet, heat rushing to my face.

Echo stiffened. She sniffed at the air, jerked her head around the room.

"I can smell him," she hissed. She didn't sound like nothing human. "He's here."

"No, he ain't," I said.

"Don't lie to me!" She slid forward, growling and spitting. "I told you, Ananna, I've found him before and I'll find him again."

Naji streaked forward and sliced her clean in half with the sword. She dispersed into mist. The room was so cold my teeth chattered.

Naji sat on the edge of my bed, his eyes staring at the space where she had been. I wrapped my arms around my chest. Slowly, the cold leaked out, the warmth came back in.

"You were going to betray me," Naji said.

"What!" My face got hot. "No, I wasn't." But the lie turned to ash in my mouth and I didn't try to deny it again.

Naji looked up at me. I expected anger but his expression was flat and empty. "Yes, you were. I could . . . tell."

"You could tell? How the hell could you tell?" I shook all over, staring at him. And then his voice was in my head.

Because we're connected.

I shrieked and jumped back, slamming my hands over my ears. Naji's mouth hadn't moved. He hadn't spoken. But I heard him.

I'd been hearing him, on and off, speaking when he wasn't speaking. I'd caught glimpses of his feelings. Not all the time. Just little enough that I thought it was my imagination, that I thought I was feeling my own emotions.

"Do you understand what happened during the sea battle?" Naji asked.

"I got shot through the belly." My voice trembled.

"Before that."

I closed my eyes. My arms tingled where I'd sliced open my skin.

"Yes," Naji said. "You gave me your blood. I tried to tell you . . ." His voice dropped, and I remembered. He was dying on the deck, choking out that my giving him blood would connect us. And I hadn't understood, because we were already connected, because of the curse, because I loved him.

"When you gave me your blood," he said. "That magic . . . it drew us together. It's ack'mora, not northern magic like the curse." He took a deep breath. "You wanting to betray me is like me wanting to betray myself. I had to fight . . . to fight from—"

"Stop," I said, because I could hear the rest of that sentence echoing in my head. *Fight from handing myself over to the Mists.*

Naji leaned up against the bedpost like he was trying to catch his breath. He peered up at me through the tangle of his hair. I could hardly breathe: I kept thinking about the moments I felt warmth from him when he was with me. Happiness. Comfort.

"When you shared your blood, it created intimacy," he said. "And the magic joined us together. It was like sex—"

His voice trailed off.

I glared at him, humiliated. "Wouldn't know," I snapped. "I figured the boon out before we let it get that far, remember?"

He stared at me, his mouth open like he wanted to say something. I could feel his thoughts, his emotions, crowding at the gates of my mind, but now that I knew what they were I shoved them away. I didn't need him inside my head.

"That wasn't my fault," Naji said.

I turned away from him, still flush with embarrassment. He was right, of course, but I wasn't gonna let him know that.

"Maybe you should leave." I glanced at him over my shoulder. "I'm not sure I want to talk to you right now."

"The boon wasn't my fault," Naji said. "But you were going to turn me over to the Otherworld. That was your choice." He looked sad, even though his words slashed at me like they were full of rage. I wasn't going to let him know I felt guilty about that, either.

"I was only thinking about it," I said. "She raises some good points."

His mouth hardened.

"I asked you to leave and you're still here."

He stood up. Grabbed his sword. But he didn't leave. He came and stood real close to me. The exact opposite of leaving.

"They lie," he said. "When they try to strike deals. You'll be in thrall to them, if you help them, if you—"

"I ain't gonna help 'em!" I shoved him away. "Get out of my room. And stay out of my head!"

"I'm not in your head," he said. "You've blocked me."

"Seems fair, given how I can't get in your head."

Naji gave me a long look. "Yes, you can," he said. I knew he was right. "You've been doing it all this time. You just don't seem to want to control it."

Anger flashed white-hot behind my eyes. "Don't tell me what I don't want to do!" I swung my fist at him, sloppy with rage. He caught my arm, and at his touch I saw a flash of that night after the manticore's feast, only it wasn't me looking up Naji, it was Naji looking down at me, his thoughts flushed with desire and . . . and affection.

I yanked away from him.

"There," he said. "You went inside my head."

I turned away from him, sucking in deep breaths. That desire, that affection—that wasn't from the boon. I felt it. It was from *him*.

"I know about the starstones," Naji said. "I know about your conversation with Jeric yi Niru." A pause. "I know you . . . worried."

"Oh, shut up!" I jerked away from him. "I did not."

Naji watched me.

"I have to try," he went on. "With the starstones. I've been communicating with the Order. I have to try—"

"Of course you have to try," I said. "It's the only way I'm going to get rid of you."

He recoiled, and something flashed across his face that I couldn't identify. I didn't bother peeking to see what it was; it might have been hurt. But then his eyes narrowed and he said, "You're never going to get rid of me. Not as long as your blood flows through my veins."

I scowled. "Get out of my room."

"I'm only warning you."

"Get out!"

"If you try to call down the Otherworld," he said, his voice low and dangerous. "I'll know. Don't ever forget that."

"For Kaol's sake, Naji, I ain't gonna call down the Otherworld. I just want you to leave me alone!" I whipped my knife at him without thinking. He slid away in a blink. The knife thrummed into the wall.

"That was unnecessary," he said.

"Get *out*."

He gave me one last hard cold look before melting into the shadows. I leaned up against the wall and dug the heels of my hand into my eyes, trying to stop the tears from flowing over my cheeks, and failing. I concentrated, trying to see if I could feel him hiding in the room, if I could slip into his thoughts the way I did earlier. But there was only emptiness, a blank space where he'd been.

I let out a deep breath, and I realized I was shaking.

The sun room was filled with the orange and pink light of the sunset by the time I dragged myself up there for dinner. The windows were all open-air and gauzed with fine white netting. Flowering vines traced along the walls, growing out of carved stone pots. There was a table in the center of the room stacked high with food:

charred meats and fresh fruits and crusty fried breads, along with more bottles of that sweet sugar-wine.

Marjani and Naji were waiting for me when we walked in, but there was no Queen Saida yet. Naji sat up straight in his chair and didn't look at me. Marjani seemed distracted.

I sat down at the table and poured a glass of wine.

"You shouldn't start yet," Naji said. I glared at him.

"This isn't a formal feast," Marjani said. "It's dinner. She can have a glass of wine if she wants."

Naji gave her one of his looks, but she didn't notice, just kept staring at the door. I drank my wine down, poured another glass.

We hadn't been waiting long when a pair of guards marched into the room, and then another pair, and then Queen Saida, fluttering behind them like a flower. Her attendants weren't anywhere to be seen, but I guess she couldn't ditch her guards that easily. She smiled at each of us in turn and then sat down at the head of the table and plucked a mango slice off a nearby platter.

"Eat," she said cheerfully. "The cooks have been slaving away since this morning, I'm sure. I'd hate to tell them their efforts were wasted."

Didn't have to tell me twice. I scooped up a big pile of carrot salad and a lamb chop and took to eating. It wasn't quite like carrot salad in the Empire—they used some different sort of spice I didn't recognize—but it was still delicious.

For the first part of dinner, Queen Saida asked me and Naji a bunch of polite questions about our "journey," like we'd been on board some passenger liner and not a pirate ship. She asked about the manticores like they were Empire nobility. When I told her about the Isle of the Sky, she sat there with her pretty head leaning to the side, her eyes on me the whole time I was speaking. I was halfway through talking about drying out the caribou meat when I realized I'd just spilled half my life story to this beautiful woman.

I took a big bite of lamb to shut myself up.

"And you, Naji of the Jadorr'a," said Queen Saida. "How did you come to know so much about . . . what was it called, caribou? Caribou preservation?"

Naji took a drink of wine. "I had a different life before I joined the Order."

"Of course." Another polite smile. I frowned. She was just so easy to trust.

I snuck a glance at Marjani. She'd stuck a lamb chop on her plate and pulled some of the meat away from the bone, but I could tell she hadn't eaten hardly any of it. She kept her eyes on Queen Saida the whole time, following the movement of the queen's graceful hand as she lifted spoonfuls of cream pudding to her mouth.

I wondered if Marjani was ever gonna ask about the starstones. Probably not. Probably Queen Saida didn't even *have* them, Marjani just wanted to come see her now that she had a ship and a crew that'd listen to her—

Queen Saida set her spoon down beside her plate.

"All right," she said. "What is it?"

"What is what?" asked Marjani, though she flinched.

Queen Saida smiled. "You've been coy all day, dearest. You want to ask me something."

Naji took a long drink of wine. His face had turned stony.

"I don't know how you do that," Marjani said. Her expression was serious and concerned, but her eyes lit up like she thought it was funny.

"Intuition. Now spill it."

Marjani sighed. She tugged on the end of her locks.

"We need to borrow your starstones," I blurted out. "Naji has to touch them."

Naji let out a long sigh.

"My starstones?" Queen Saida laughed. "Is that why you sailed halfway across the world to see me?" She rested her chin in her hand and gazed at Marjani, who looked down at her lap like she was embarrassed.

"Don't be absurd," Marjani said.

"It's for Naji," I said. "He has a curse."

"Are starstones a cure for curses?" Queen Saida turned to Naji. "I'm afraid I don't know much about magic."

"They are for this one," Naji said.

"I thought starstones were dangerous, though? The court wizard never let me near them."

"Your court wizard was correct." Naji glowered, his scar turning him menacing.

"Oh." Queen Saida frowned, and Kaol help me if it didn't make her look even lovelier than when she smiled. "Well, I would be glad to help you, but I'm afraid I don't have them anymore."

The room got so quiet and so still I swore I could hear everybody's hearts beating.

"You don't have them?" Marjani said. "But they're priceless—"

"They were stolen!" Queen Saida threw up her hands. "By members of your lot, in fact. Pirates."

"They are *not* my lot—"

"Oh, I was teasing, dearest." She looked back at Naji. "I'm truly sorry. Father kept them in the armory and during the last sacking . . . Well, that's always the first place pirates go."

"How could they take them?" Naji's voice had gone quiet and angry. "What pirate would possibly possess the knowledge—"

"Why were they in the armory?" I asked, 'cause I didn't feel like listening to Naji rant about the idiocy and unworldliness of pirates.

"Because Father thought of them as weapons." Queen Saida looked at me and I felt myself blushing under her gaze. "Not that he or anyone else could ever figure out how to *use* them as such. Not even the wizards would touch them without special gloves."

"Oh yes," said Marjani. "The gloves. I remember now . . . What was that lord's name, the one who always paraded around with them . . . ?"

Queen Saida laughed. "The Lord of Juma. That was his title, anyway. I don't remember his proper name. But he was always showing off." She laughed again, and Marjani glowed. If the two of them were gonna be like that the whole time, we'd never get nothing done.

"What pirates stole 'em?" I asked. "Were they Confederation?"

"Confederation?" Queen Saida furrowed her brow. "I'm not certain. They were pirates."

I frowned. "You didn't see their colors?"

"She means the flag," said Marjani.

Queen Saida shrugged. "I didn't see them. I get whisked away at the slightest hint of danger—you can ask the captain of the guard." She smiled at me. "Are you going to track them down, like in a story? I've heard some of the Empire stories about the starstones. You ought to be careful."

"Naji needs those stones," I said.

Naji looked up at me from across the table. I turned away.

"Gero!" Queen Saida called out. A man in bronzed armor detached himself from the wall and bowed. "I know you heard the question. No need to pretend in front of me. What do you remember about the ships that stole the starstones?"

Gero nodded again before he started speaking. "They were Confederation, my Light," he said.

"I still don't know what that means," Queen Saida said.

"Confederation pirates sail under common laws, although individual ships and fleets remain independently captained," Gero said, which wasn't quite true, but I didn't feel like correcting him. "I don't remember the flag, however. I'm sorry. It wasn't one I recognized."

"Who would you recognize?" I asked.

Gero turned to me. "The Lao clan," he said. "And the Shujares. The Hariris. The Liras."

The clans most prone to attacking the Free Countries.

"That at least narrows it down," I said. "Thanks."

The guard kinda squinted at me then, like he wanted to say something about me recognizing all those pirate clans. But he didn't. He just turned to Queen Saida and bowed and then pressed back against the wall.

"Well," said Queen Saida. "I'm truly sorry that wasn't more helpful." She looked at Naji while she spoke. "I'll see if I can find out more information for you, and when you make sail, I'll lend you some ships and crew from my own fleet."

"Saida, you don't have to—" Marjani leaned forward over the table and pressed her hand against Queen Saida's arm.

Queen Saida held up her own hand. "Of course I don't have to," she said. "It's not a matter of what I *have* to do; it's a matter of what I want to do."

"Thank you, my Light," murmured Naji. He dipped his head, and emotion flickered through me—despair, creeping in like the cold northern sea, and anger like the fury of the Empire sun. Not my emotions at all.

He was in my head or I was in his: it didn't matter. I saw past his blank assassin's face, and I knew his hopelessness.

And for a moment, my own anger relented.

CHAPTER TWELVE

For the next few days, I hardly saw Marjani at all; she spent all her time with the queen, or shunted off in the queen's apartments on the edge of the garden, doing Kaol knows what. I realized pretty quick that I was the one who was gonna have to check on the boat.

Naji went with me, dressed like a Jokja nobleman save for the scarf wrapped around his face. I hadn't told him I was planning on going; he just showed up at my room and said, "You know how much it hurts me for you to wander off on your own."

"Only if I'm in danger."

He didn't have nothing to say to that, but there was no point in fighting with him. I didn't say a word to him as we walked through the city.

The *Nadir* was still docked at port, Kaol be praised, and she didn't look too worse for wear, neither. A handful of men were sitting around on the deck playing dice when me and Naji came on board. Fewer than I would've liked.

"Where's the rest of you?" I asked.

"Whoring," one of the men said. It was Jeric yi Niru. He squinted up at me. "Have you found the starstones yet? Given both of your life's light is intact, I would assume no."

I scowled at him. "She don't got 'em. Got nicked by some Confederation pirates a while back. We'll be setting after the stones once we know more."

"Ah," said Jeric yi Niru, giving me that smug nobleman's smile of his. "What is it with pirates? Does the threat of death engender an item with more value?"

"You're the one that joined up with the Empire navy. You tell me about threat of death."

The rest of the men laughed. Jeric frowned at me and then nodded at Naji. "The captain's look never suited you," he said. "I like this better."

"So do I." Naji's voice was cold and mean, an assassin's voice, and it shut up Jeric yi Niru fast. The other men stopped smirking too.

I made a quick check of the boat and her stores—some of the rum was missing, and half the bottles of ahiial had been drained and piled up in a corner of the galley. The crew worked fast. But all the weapons were in the hold, and the chest of pressed copper and silver that'd been on board when we took the ship was locked away in the captain's quarters, protected not just with steel chains but with a bit of Naji's magic as well.

I slumped down on the captain's bed so I could listen to the waves slapping up against the ship's side. There's something about a boat that ain't moving. It feels empty. Hollow. Almost better to be on land.

Naji appeared in the doorway. He slid the mask away from his face but didn't bother to come any closer.

I got flashes of things in my head as he stared at me—worry about the starstones, some dull ache I now understood was part of the curse—and I rubbed at my eyes until they went away.

"Cut it out," I said.

"Cut what out?"

"Letting me see your thoughts."

"I'm not *letting* you. You just can. I explained this—"

"Well, stop it!" I scowled. "Is it gonna be like this for the rest of my life?"

"I told you it would. Don't you ever listen?"

He sounded like Mama for a minute there, scolding me for not being able to work magic proper.

"Apparently not," I said, which is what I always told Mama when she asked me. Then: "You're scared about the starstones."

I wanted to see if it would bother him, me knowing what he was thinking. The way it bothered me. But he just gazed at me across the captain's quarters and said, "Yes. The task's impossible for a reason."

There was this silence after he spoke, a place where I should've said, "The other one wasn't." But I kept my mouth shut.

"It has occurred to me," Naji said, "and to the members of the Order I've spoken to, that the only way to escape the curse may be to die." He shrugged. "And if that's what I have to do—"

A coldness struck me in my heart, a hand come out to squeeze the life away from me. Naji felt it too. I could see it in on his face, the way his expression softened as he looked at me. It pissed me off. I didn't want to care if he lived or died.

"We should get back," I muttered, and I pushed past him and made my way back on deck.

We stayed in Arkuz for near a month, waiting for Queen Saida's messengers to bring word of the starstones. One day I finally went to see her in her sun room, surrounded by guards and nobles and Marjani.

"Not yet," she said, courteous and smiling. Marjani gazed at me apologetically. She looked different in a noblewoman's clothes, her hair woven with ribbons and shells, her eyes lined with pale green powder. Like a right princess.

"You'll be the first to know as soon as I hear something," Queen Saida said. She took one of my hands in her own. Her skin was soft as silk. "I have twenty of my best men out looking for those stones."

"You know I can captain the ship myself," I said. "And leave Marjani here."

Marjani jerked her head up toward me but didn't say nothing. Queen Saida gave me a long, appraising look.

"I don't lie," she said. "My best men are looking for the stones."

That made me blush. She didn't even sound angry or nothing. Just a little disappointed in me, like I'd reminded her I wasn't a noble after all. And it actually made me feel kinda bad.

Afterward, I wandered around the gardens, sneaking past the guards and servants and ladies sitting in the sun. I could hear birds singing to one another out in the jungle. You wouldn't think you were in the city, there in the palace gardens.

I found a shady spot beneath some flowering bushes to sit and think. I was tired of hanging around Arkuz, waiting for something to happen. We were losing crewmen, too. You stay in a place long enough, they start thinking they like that place better. Especially a place like Arkuz. I couldn't much blame them.

The thing was, I didn't know if I wanted to find the starstones, not if it meant Naji would die. And the third task, the one about life coming out of violence—that didn't even make any sense. Knowing magicians, it was probably just some roundabout way of saying he had to kill himself on the starstones.

Ananna, you think too much about things that don't concern you.

I yelped and scrambled out from under the bushes, my knees and hands covered in dirt. Nobody was about but a sleepy-looking guard leaning up against his spear.

Stop worrying about me.

It was Naji's voice, and it was coming from inside my head.

"Naji!" I whispered. "I told you to stay out of my head!"

He didn't answer. I clenched my eyes shut and concentrated

real hard, and I saw a window looking out over the jungle, and a bed draped with sheer curtains. He was in his room.

I stalked out of the garden and into the palace and right up to his room and pounded on his door until he answered.

"Ananna," he said. "Always nice to see you in person."

"Stay out of my head!" I shouted. I launched myself at him, aiming both of my hands for his chest, figuring I could at least topple him over. He grabbed me by the waist and swung me off to the side.

"You're such an ass," I told him.

He laughed. "Why? Because you couldn't knock me down?"

"'Cause you tossed me around like a rag doll. Good thing I didn't have my pistol on me."

"Yes," he said. "Good for us all."

"Oh, shut up."

"I did want to tell you," he said, his voice serious and eyes bright, which made me want to punch him, "that I do appreciate your concern for me—"

"What concern?" Even though I knew he knew.

"Thinking you could set sail on your own and find the starstones for me—I'm sure there'd be a great sea battle involved, lots of cannon fire and swords and whatnot."

"Isn't that what you want?"

"Don't be absurd. You couldn't even imagine the headache it would give me—" He stopped. "Actually maybe you could now. You haven't been in sufficient danger for us to find out."

"That ain't what I meant. You want the starstones. So you can touch 'em and kill yourself and not have to deal with *me* no more."

Naji blinked at me. "No," he said. "That isn't what I want at all."

I could tell he meant it, his sincerity hanging over me like a storm cloud, but whatever it was he did want I couldn't see.

Off in the corner of the room, I heard this soft thumping noise, like a rug being beaten. And when I tore my gaze away from Naji I actually screamed, Kaol help me, 'cause standing next to the open window was the biggest damn bird I'd ever seen.

It let out a big screeching *caw*.

"The hell is it?" I shouted, going for my knife. Naji didn't move.

"An albatross."

"A what?" But I knew it was a seabird, one of the big white ones Qilari sailors think signal luck—good or bad, I can never remember.

"There's something tied to its foot." Naji leaned forward and snatched something from the side of the bird's leg. It was a little mother-of-pearl tube with a glass stopper. Naji pulled out the stopper and then drew out a second tube, this one made of paper. The bird cawed again and flapped its wings, stirring up the hot humid air.

"You think it's for the queen?" I asked.

"The Jokja don't communicate via albatross," Naji said.

The bird cawed again. Then it pecked at Naji's hand, the one holding the paper. Naji frowned.

Another caw.

"It wants you to read it," I said.

The bird lifted up its wings and hopped on the bed.

"See!"

Naji gave me a dark look, but he unrolled the paper, smoothing it out along his thigh. The writing on it was curved and ornamental, decorated with drawings of seashells and ocean waves. I leaned over his shoulder to read.

> *We hope this message reaches you with ease, Naji of the Jadorr'a. I am the scrivener of the Court of the Waves and am writing to you at the behest of the King of Salt and Foam.*

The king would like to speak to you personally as soon as possible. He extends an invitation for you to visit the Court of the Waves. Regards, Jolin I.

"What?" I said. "The Court of the Waves? The hell is that?"

"I don't know." Naji slid the map out of the mother-of-pearl tube and unfurled it. The bird cawed—the sound of it made me jump—and then flapped its wings and lifted up into the air and out the window. I watched the bird fly away for a moment before turning back to the map. It showed the western stretch of the Green Glass Sea between the Island of the Sun, where the manticores live, and the Empire continent. There was a place marked in the middle of the water.

The mark was labeled: WE SHALL POST SENTRIES TO HELP YOU FIND YOUR WAY.

"This is very strange," Naji said.

"I don't trust it."

Naji frowned. "I don't either. I shall ask the Order about it. Perhaps that will give us some insight."

I didn't think the Order had much of value to say on anything, given its track record, but I knew Naji was gonna do it regardless. Still, I studied the map, tracing my finger across its width. I thought about staring at the maps on board the *Nadir*, navigating our path to the Island of the Sun—

"This mark is where we fought the Hariri clan." A coldness gripped my blood, and the scar on my stomach ached.

"How can you possibly tell?"

"'Cause I'm the damned navigator. And I know—"

"Ananna," Naji said gently. "The Hariris are dead. I killed them."

I pushed the map away. My hands were shaking. "We shoulda checked that bird," I said. "I bet it was metal, like those machines they've got . . ." And the more I thought about it the more convinced

I was that the feathers had glittered in the sun, and it had left a streak of smoke as it flew off into the air.

Naji set the map and note on the bed and pressed his hand against my shoulder. I barely felt it. "You know I'm not going to put you in danger," he whispered.

But this wasn't danger; it was fear. It was the memory of a bullet tearing into my gut. It was Mistress Hariri laughing in the moments before I almost died—before I would've died, if Naji hadn't been around. If he hadn't decided I was worth saving.

When we finally made sail, a week later, it wasn't to chase after starstones or to return to the place where I'd nearly died. It was to visit the Aja Shore, down on the southern tip of Jokja. Queen Saida's idea.

She and Marjani sailed out on this lovely schooner, the wood painted orange and marigold and pink, the sails dyed the color of grass. It looked like a floating garden. Queen Saida, always gracious, offered me and Naji a spot on board, but I wasn't skipping town without the *Nadir*.

"Good," Marjani said when I told her, though she seemed distracted. We were ambling around the perimeter of the palace, next to the fence that kept the jungle from pushing in on the royal lands. "I really didn't want to leave her here." She crossed her arms over her chest, and all the bangles on her wrists tinkled like bits of glass. "You can captain her, if you'd like."

"What?" I stopped. "She's your boat!"

"We captured her with your manticore," Marjani said. "She's as much yours as she is mine."

"I can't captain a boat."

Marjani glanced at me over the top of one bare shoulder. "Of course you can," she said. "If I can do it, you can do it."

"You're smarter than me."

"Smarter doesn't necessarily make a good captain." She shrugged. "Clever does. And you're plenty clever."

I didn't know what to say. All my life I'd wanted to captain a ship, but lately it hadn't seemed that important to me anymore. I was distracted by that bird and its map and its weird note, afraid the Hariris weren't really dead. And I was afraid Naji would be, if we ever found the starstones.

"Besides," said Marjani. "It's just along the coast. A day and a half's journey. Think of it as practice."

Practice. Ha! Well, maybe I'd take off with her boat and her crew, see how she liked it then. Not that I knew where I'd go.

I ain't no mutineer. But I toyed with the thought for a few seconds anyway, the way I toyed with handing Naji over to the Mists. And I felt just as guilty about it afterward.

"We're leaving at dawn tomorrow morning," she said. "Saida really does want you to come. Naji, too. She likes talking to him."

Naji and Saida had swapped magic stories at dinner, spells gone wrong and so on—she said she didn't know much about magic if you asked, though that was a right lie from hearing the way she talked. Naji stuck to discussing earth-magic. I wondered what Queen Saida would think if he told her about me spilling my blood on the deck of the *Nadir* so we could win the fight against the Hariri clan. Probably wrinkle her nose and reach for a piece of flatbread.

So that was how I came to captain the *Nadir* for a day and a half. Wasn't much to it, of course, 'cause we just followed behind Queen Saida's ship, the colors bright against the blue sky and the blue water. Crew was lazy on account of the smooth waves and the favorable winds. I wandered up and down the deck shouting every insult and curse word I knew, the way Papa always did, trying to get 'em off their asses.

"First mate!" Jeric yi Niru called out while I was making one of my rounds. I stopped and glared at him. He was up in the rigging.

"What do you want?" I shouted. "If you say the word *starstone* to me, I swear on Kaol and her watery birthbed that I will shoot you in the heart." And I pulled out my pistol like I meant to use it.

Jeric yi Niru laughed and came dropping down to deck on a line of rope. "You sound like an Empire captain," he said. "They like to threaten the lives of their crew too."

I shoved my gun back into the waistband of my pants. "What is it?" I asked.

"The crew," he said. "I want to apologize for them. You dragged them away from one of the wealthiest cities in the world. The dice houses here—" He shook his head in fake disbelief. I wanted to hit him. "And the women."

I rolled my eyes. "I'm taking 'em to the Aja Shore," I said. "There'll be whores and gambling aplenty there, too."

"Tell them that," said Jeric yi Niru. "I realize to a pirate captain's daughter the life of a captain is nothing but orders given and orders followed, but in truth it's an exchange."

I hate to admit it, but he had my attention. "An exchange?"

"Yes. Like your relationship with that manticore. It was built on favors, yes?"

I didn't say nothing. I wished to the deep blue sea I knew how he got his information.

"You tell the crew we're sailing to the Aja Shore at the lovely Queen Saida's request, but what do they care of Queen Saida? What do they care of *you*? All they care about—"

"Is pissing their money away at the dice houses. I get it."

Jeric yi Niru gave me one of his insolent Empire smiles. But he was right. I'd played the manticore and the manticore had played me and we'd wound up friends. Even if her boon hadn't turned out how she intended.

So I climbed up on the helm and rang the warning bell till I got the crew's attention.

"What is it, Lady Navigator?" one of 'em called out.

"I wanted to let you know!" I said. "That we'll be spending close to a week along the Aja Shore."

The crew all stared at me like I'd just turned into a kitten.

"I know the lot of you have already lost half your earnings to the gambling houses in Arkuz."

"Most of us more'n that!" somebody called out, and some of the crew laughed and some of them grumbled under their breaths.

"That's 'cause you were gambling in Arkuz," I said. "They take one look at your clothes and see an Empire scummy who don't know how to hold on to his money." I paused, looking out over them. "They *cheat*, is what I'm saying."

The crew clapped and stomped and hollered in agreement.

"But on the Aja Coast," I said, "they play nice and fair. You boys want to earn your pressed gold back? Now's your chance."

I had no idea how accurate any of this was, but the crew was hollering again.

"And the *whores*," I added, not knowing the slightest how to build on that. Apparently it was enough, though, 'cause the crew hooted and stomped and nudged one another. I guess just saying the word *whores* is enough to get them excited.

"So I want you boys to think about those Aja women and those Aja dice houses," I shouted. "While you're climbing up in the rigging and steering us forward. I ain't sailing on Queen Saida's command, I'm sailing to give the lot of you a little taste of paradise."

They actually cheered me. Not like a crowd cheering a champion in the fighting ring, mind, just some yelling and hollering and whatnot. Still felt good.

"Now!" I shouted. "Get back to work!"

And no one was as surprised as me when they did.

The Aja Shore reminded me of Bone Island, only cleaner and full of nobles and rich merchants instead of cutthroats and pirates. Queen Saida kept a private island set a ways off from the shore, with a big house filled with servants, who, far as I could see, got to live there all year and only had to work when Queen Saida decided she wanted a vacation.

We didn't bother making port at the dock, just dropped anchor out in the open sea off behind Queen Saida's island, the *Nadir* looking big and hulking and monstrous next to her pretty little garden ship. I let the crew row in to the mainland to go chasing after the gambling I promised them. Then Naji and me made our way to Queen Saida's house. It was like being in the palace. Her private guards hung around trying to look inconspicuous, and the servants gave me weird looks before leading us up to our rooms. They seemed to give Naji a pass, probably 'cause every time he opened his mouth he sounded like a noble.

"We're preparing your midday meal now," the servant told us as she wandered around my room, pulling down sheets and drawing the curtains away from the open windows. The sea glittered in the sunlight. "The house bell will chime when it's prepared." She nodded at me and slipped off into the hallway.

I sank down on the bed and sighed. The warm wind blowing in through the windows made me sleepy, though at least it smelled like the sea, like home, instead of the jungle. It didn't take long before I drifted off to some breezy dream. Marjani was there, and Queen Saida and the manticore. No Naji. It was nice.

In the dream, Marjani knocked on wood, looking at me expectantly. She knocked so loud it woke me up, and I realized someone was knocking on my door. The little whisper in my head told me it was Naji.

"What do you want?" I called out.

He pushed the door open and stood there staring at me.

"Well?" I asked. "Ain't no Mist lady in here."

"I can see that," he said.

I had half a mind to go sifting through his head, but I didn't much feel like putting forth the energy.

"Seriously," I said, "did you need something?"

Naji shook his head silently and just kept staring at me. I sighed and rolled over onto my back, looked up at the ceiling.

"I spoke to the Order about this Court of the Waves," Naji said. "There's no record of such a place in any of our histories. Saida's librarian had never heard of it either."

I sighed. "Well then. I *really* don't trust it."

Bells started ringing.

"Well, that's proper timing, isn't it?" I sat up. "Food's always better than magical killing rocks."

"Wait," Naji said.

"What? They said they'd ring the bells for lunch."

Naji shook his head. "They aren't coming from the house."

I froze, listening. He was right. The bells were caught on the wind, blowing in from the sea—

And then I heard the faint boom of cannon fire.

That got me to my feet. I rolled off the bed and darted over to the window. I couldn't see nothing but the sparking sea, but the smell of cannon fire smoke, acrid and burning, was on the air.

Naji grabbed me by the arm, yanked me back. "My room," he said.

He dragged me down the hallway. His room looked the same as mine, but the thud of cannons was louder. I ran over to his window, which faced land.

The Aja Shore was burning in patches. A Confederation ship sidled up along it sideways. Another volley of cannon fire. I leaned out the window, ignoring the sudden pain in my temple, straining to see what colors she was flying—but the smoke was too thick.

The city bells clanged against my skull. Naji tried to pull me out of the window.

"No!" I shouted. "I gotta see which ship. If it's some Hariri allies—"

"Ananna, you're hurting me."

The pain in his voice startled me enough that I loosened my grip on the windowsill and went tumbling backward. He caught me before I could hit the floor. My headache evaporated.

"They aren't here for you," he said. "They're sacking the town."

"Yeah, looking for me!" I wrenched away from him and was halfway to the door when he had one hand on my shoulder, one arm wrapping around my chest, drawing me into an embrace that startled me into stillness.

"Please," he whispered into the top of my head. "Please. It hurts me even more now. Now that I—"

I pulled away from him. Whatever he almost said, I didn't care. And besides, I didn't have any other choice. I needed to get out to sea. It wouldn't take long before they made it to Queen Saida's island, before they saw our boat floating out in the water—if they hadn't already. We didn't have the colors up—I ain't stupid—but any pirate worth his salt would see that the *Nadir* was a gussied-up Empire boat. And if these were Hariri allies, they would know what that meant.

"I ain't safe here, neither," I finally told him, pulling out one of my pistols. "And if we lose our ship, then we lose everything."

And then I bounded out of the room.

CHAPTER THIRTEEN

Marjani caught me in the hallway. She had her sword in one hand and her pistol in the other, though she was still dressed like a princess.

"Do you know who it is?" I asked.

The smell of smoke was everywhere.

"Not any of the Hariri allies that I know about."

I slumped with relief, dropping my sword to my side. "They're here because of Saida," she said. "The Aja merchants always bring out the best jewelry and silks when she comes to visit." Marjani took a deep breath. "Her guards have taken the queen's ship. I told her we'd take the *Nadir*."

"As privateers?" I frowned. "Are we gonna have to swear allegiance to Jokja and all that?"

Marjani scowled. "Does it matter? And not officially, no." She jerked her head in direction of the shore. "Those pirates are going to try and take the *Nadir* once they've finished sacking the shore anyway."

That was probably true.

We didn't have much crew on the *Nadir*—most of 'em were on shore, and so we just had the few scoundrels who got stuck with the second shift. Jeric yi Niru was one of them, though, and lo and behold he'd gotten them to ready the boat for battle. When me and Marjani came on board and saw the crew packing the cannons and readying the sails, he gave us both a bow and a tip of his Qilari hat.

"Captain," he said. "I imagine we'll need to fetch the rest of our soldiers for the battle."

"They're my crew, not soldiers," Marjani said. "But yes, you're right." She took the helm. I stood beside her, my heart pounding in my chest. The sky was black with smoke, and I could hear screaming and pistol blasts coming from the mainland. The queen's ship was ahead of us, her green sails bright against the haze. My head ached some, from being separated from Naji, but it wasn't too bad. If I concentrated I could make it disappear completely.

"Ananna!"

It was Naji. He stepped out of the shadow of the mast, clutching a sword and a knife, his eyes glowing.

"I have to protect you," he said.

I didn't say nothing.

Marjani glanced at him. "Oh good, you're here. We're going to need all the help we can get."

Naji frowned at her, and then put his hand on my arm. His skin was warm through the fabric of my shirt. "Please," he said to me. "It's not your fight."

"It's my boat!" I said. "Marjani said so. The *Nadir*'s as much mine as she is hers. I ain't gonna let some Confederation scummies steal off with her."

The skin crinkled around Naji's eyes. He pulled out his sword.

"Hold steady!" Marjani shouted, leaning against the helm. We were close to the Confederation ship, close enough that they had to have spotted us—

They had. Their cannons were rotating.

"Fire!" Marjani screamed, and the whole boat rocked backward as the cannons fired, adding more smoke to the thick air. I braced myself against Naji. The Confederation ship shuddered, but we'd managed to knock half their cannons off the line of sight.

The men cheered. Marjani didn't; she just set her jaw straight and hard. "We haven't won yet."

I jumped down to the deck, figuring they'd need as much help in the reloading as possible. I ignored Naji following me as I worked on one of the cannons, the gunpowder making my eyes water.

The Confederation ship fired on us. I skittered backward, limbs flailing. Naji caught me even though I knew I'd slid past him in the explosion—his lightning-quick assassin dance again. He looked relieved.

I pushed up to my feet.

A wind blew in from the open sea, sweet and clean, and for a few quick seconds it cleared away the smoke.

I saw the other ship's colors.

A blue field. A gray skeleton, dancing the dance of the dead.

The *Tanarau*.

Mama. Papa.

"Stop!" I screamed. "Stop firing!" I was half talking to the crew and half talking to the *Tanarau*, even though I knew it was madness to think they could hear me across the water. "Stop! It's me! It's *me*!"

"What in the darkest of nights are you doing?" Naji grabbed at me but I wrenched free. I raced up to the flagpole and yanked on the rope. Our colors dropped.

"What in the holy hell!" Marjani leaped over the helm. "What do you think you're doing?"

"We have to surrender!" I shouted.

"What?"

I didn't answer, just pulled hard on the rope and caught the colors in my arms. One of the crewmen was on me with his sword, and I swung around and caught him, blade to blade, before he could cut me.

"I know that ship!" I shouted, but he didn't care. He just wanted to fight. The sound of our swords rang out across the deck. I tossed the colors aside, lunged at him. More cannon fire from the *Tanarau*, and the boat lifted up and slammed back down. I managed to stay on my feet.

Then Jeric yi Niru stepped in, nimble as a dancer, wedging himself between me and the crewman so that the crewman hit his sword instead of mine.

"Go on, first mate," he called out over his shoulder. "Hoist up the surrender flag."

Where the hell is Naji? I thought, and then I saw—Marjani'd gotten a couple of the bigger fellows to hold him down. And she was coming after me herself.

"It's my parents!" I screamed.

She froze in place. "Are you sure?"

"Course I'm sure. I sailed under those colors for close to two decades." I fumbled around on the deck for a scrap of sail. Yellow-white, but it would do. "Once we get them to stop firing I can go over and have them let us be."

"And how do you know that will work?" Her voice was quiet and cold, but she'd dropped her sword to her side.

"How'd you know it'd be safe for you to come back to Jokja?"

Her jaw moved up and down like she was trying out responses. Nothing came out. She gave me a curt nod, and I tied the scrap of sail to the flag rope and hoisted it up. Jeric yi Niru had knocked the crewman out and nobody else tried to stop me. The *Tanarau* stopped firing on us once the sail was halfway up, the way I figured she would. Papa always heeds calls to surrender.

Naji shrugged away from his captors.

"Let me do the parley," I said to Marjani.

"You bet your ass I will."

"No," said Naji. "If they harbor ill will because of the Hariri affair—"

"They won't." I was already readying the rowboat. I had my sword and my pistol and my heart was beating faster than it did before any battle. I called over Jeric yi Niru.

"Drop me down," I told him. I know it's crazy, but I trusted him more in that moment than I did anyone else, on account of him helping me call surrender.

"Aye-aye," he said, eyes glinting like he was making fun of me.

"Wait!" Naji flashed across the deck and reappeared beside me in the boat. I didn't have time to protest before Jeric yi Niru cut the line and we crashed into the water.

I rowed us over to the *Tanarau*. The closer we got the slower I rowed. What if Naji was right? What if they were still sore about me running off on my wedding day? What if they pledged some sort of allegiance to the Hariris, and this was all a Hariri trap after all?

"You're right to worry," Naji said, staring straight ahead, looking grim.

"Shut up!" I said. "It's my family. They ain't gonna hurt me."

"You don't know that," Naji said, and he tapped his finger to my forehead. "Can you see what I'm thinking right now?"

"I don't got to. I know you think this is a bad idea."

We were almost to the *Tanarau*. I pulled the oars in and let the waves knock us up against her side. A few seconds later, the ropes dropped down.

Two *Tanarau* men hauled us up. One of 'em I didn't recognize, but the other was Big Fawzi, and when he saw me he squinted and then widened his eyes.

"Hey," I said.

"Ananna? What the hell? We thought you were dead."

"Not yet."

And then I heard Mama's voice, sweet as a song, asking the men what the hell was going on. I jumped out of the rowboat, the feel of the *Tanarau* firm and familiar beneath my feet. The sails flapped and snapped in the wind, and the sound was different from the sails on the *Nadir* and the *Ayel's Revenge* and the *Goldlife*. The rigging hung different. It was like I never left.

"Ananna!" Mama pushed through the crew. She was decked out for battle in men's clothes, her belt lined with pistols, but when I saw her all I could think about was the way she'd looked when she wore her worn silk robe as she rocked me to sleep back when I was a little kid.

"Mama!" I raced forward. She caught me up in her embrace. The pirate in me thought back to Tarrin of the *Hariri*, reaching for his knife as he lay dying. But the daughter in me just wanted to be hugged.

"I never thought I'd see you again." She pulled away and I saw the smudges in her kohl where she'd started crying. Mama never lets you see her cry; she can stop a tear before it falls down her face. But if you know how to look for the signs, you can still spot it. "I'd heard the Hariris sent an assassin after you."

"They did."

Mama frowned, and before she could say anything, Papa's voice boomed across the ship.

"And what the hell kinda parley is thi—"

He stopped when he saw me. For a moment nobody moved. We all just stood there in the smoke and the sea breeze.

"Nana," he said. He threw off his sword belt and his pistols and then rushed toward me, scooping me up like I was a kid again. "You were dead," he said to me, leaning close. "You were dead. The assassin—"

"He's here," I said without thinking.

Everybody on the damn boat pulled out a weapon. Swords and pistols and daggers all threw off glints of light in the sun.

Naji slumped against the railing and sighed.

"No!" I said. "You don't understand. He didn't . . . he can't kill me, all right?"

"That him?" Papa jerked his chin toward Naji.

Naji looked back at him warily. "I won't allow any harm to come to your daughter."

"That right?" Papa stared at him for a long time. Naji hadn't pulled his sword, and his tattoos were all covered up, and he was still dressed like a pirate. Nothing about him, except maybe the scar, suggested that he was an assassin.

"I've protected her this long," Naji said.

Another long pause, and then Papa roared with laughter. He turned to me. "You've turned into a right princess, you need some shield-for-hire following you around. Like those foppy Empire nobles." He laughed again.

"I didn't hire him!"

Mama scooped her arm around me and pulled me close. "Throw up the peace flag!" she shouted. "And make sail for the open sea before the Jokja authorities show up."

That set the crew to scrambling. The queen's boat wasn't attacking no more, but it wouldn't be long before the queen's navy arrived. And I doubted Queen Saida would give amnesty to anybody who'd just burned half the Aja Shore, even if they were my parents.

When the *Tanarau* took to the water, the *Nadir* was right behind her. But not the queen's ship. Mama must've had somebody send word to Marjani. I wondered if she still thought we were in parley.

A pirate ship is outfitted to go faster than even the Empire's little sloops, but Papa had us sail out past sunset, to be sure. They stuck me and Naji up in the captain's quarters, like I was still five years old and liable to get underfoot. Though in truth I was grateful for it, 'cause I was tired, even though it hadn't been much of a battle.

Naji and me sat side by side on the little trundle bed. We didn't say much. I didn't even feel him inside my head. I think it was more under his control than he'd let me believe. Or maybe he'd just put it under his control.

Once we seemed clear of an attack, Mama and Papa came back into the cabin.

"I think you got a story to tell us, girl," Papa said. He pulled a jar of sugar-wine out of his cabinet and slid down in his big brass chair. Mama leaned against the wall. Both of them looked worn out.

The boat tipped back and forth from the winds and the speed on the water.

"I guess I do," I said.

Papa drank the sugar-wine straight from the bottle and slammed it down on the navigation table.

"Why'd you run off?" Mama asked.

"I didn't want to get married."

She frowned at me, but I could see Papa get a hint of a smile.

"Heard you killed the Hariri boy," he said.

"He was gonna kill me." But that wasn't the part of the story I wanted to tell, and I wrapped my arms around my stomach and took a deep breath. Naji glanced at me and frowned.

"She was saving her own life and mine," he told Papa. "They attacked us with . . . machines . . . out in the desert—"

"Sandships," Papa said. "Heard about 'em. Never seen 'em." He took another swig of wine and handed the bottle to Naji, who shook his head. I grabbed it instead, which made Papa laugh.

"So why didn't you kill her?" Mama asked Naji. She pulled her pipe out of her jacket pocket and a pouch of grayweed and took to packing it in tight.

Naji blinked.

"You're an assassin, yeah? That's what she said up on deck." She snapped her fingers and flames danced on top of her fingertips, and she lit her pipe. Another snap and they were gone. The sort of thing she used to call "courtier's tricks" back when I was trying to learn magic.

The scent of her smoke made me dizzy with homesickness, even though I was home.

"I am a member of the Jadorr'a," Naji said. "And yes, Captain Hariri hired me to . . ." His voice trailed off, and I almost took his hand in mine. Stopped myself just as my fingers grazed across his knuckles.

Mama must've seen 'cause she arched an eyebrow and said, "Didn't think you had it in you, Nana."

"What are you talking about?" I asked, scowling. And then before she could answer I blurted out the whole story about the snake and the curse and the Wizard Eirnin and the Isles of the Sky and the *Nadir* and the starstones. The whole time Mama and Papa listened, and the only time either of them moved was when Mama puffed on her pipe.

"Starstones," Mama said when I'd finished.

"Yeah," I said. "We gotta go find the sons of whores who stole 'em, but Marjani doesn't want to leave Jokja."

Papa squinted. "Well. That is a conundrum."

"You ought to just take her boat," Mama said.

"I ain't no mutineer."

They both laughed at that.

"It ain't funny!" I said.

"Well, she promised you starstones and then didn't deliver," Mama said. "I think that's reason enough to take her boat."

I could feel myself getting hot with anger, and I balled my hand up into a fist and thought about hitting somebody. The truth was my distaste with mutiny had nothing to do with it. I owed Marjani my loyalty for the rest of my life. After all, she came back to the Isles of the Sky for me.

Papa drained the last of the sugar-wine.

"Or we could stop screwing around with you," he said.

"What?" The anger flared up. Maybe it was mine, maybe it was Naji's. The blood-connection made my emotions confusing.

Papa chuckled and stood up. "Come down to the holding bay, I'll show you."

Mama smiled at me through the cloud of smoke.

And I got this thought in my head, like maybe they'd aligned themselves with the Hariris after all, and this was all a trap.

"Naji, come with me."

"Of course." When I stood up, he stood up. Mama shook her head.

"Never seen a pirate with a bodyguard," she said. "Thought I taught you to do your own fighting."

"He ain't my bodyguard!"

"Enough." Papa's voice boomed out in full-on captain's mode. "Sela, I know you're still sore about the marriage, but it's over with now. Ananna." He turned to me. "I ain't gonna hurt you. Blood ties are stronger than any Confederation law."

Mama huffed in the corner.

"I'm just a daughter," I said.

"You're my daughter, sure. Ain't no *just* about it."

I looked at him, unsure of what to say.

He clapped me on the back. "I'll let you follow, if it'll make you and your assassin feel better. Sela! Up here."

"Don't boss me," she said, but she joined him, and together we wound through the belly of the *Tanarau* to the holding bay. Some idiot part of me wanted to press close to Naji, but instead I clutched the hilt of my sword and kept my eyes out for an attack.

When we got to the holding bay, Papa undid the lock and kicked the door open. "Have a look," he said.

I could smell Empire spices and the faint briny seaweed scent of the charm Mama used to stop bugs from eating holes in the silks. It reminded me of sleeping down here, pretending I was a child of the desert and not the water.

I stepped inside.

"What am I looking for?" I asked, folding my hands over my chest. "It's just treas—"

Naji's sword clattered to the floorboards.

"Ah," Papa said. "He knows."

"The starstones," Naji said.

I felt like all the air'd been let out of me. Naji rushed forward, pushing me aside. He knelt down in front of a pile of Jokja cotton—and a trio of smooth white pebbles. I hadn't paid them any mind. I figured they were there to keep the cotton from sliding around. I was more concerned with the box sitting beside them, carved and jeweled in the Jokja style.

Naji reached out one hand. Stopped. He was trembling.

"I wouldn't touch 'em," Mama said.

"I know that." It came out in a hiss. I knelt beside him. The stones didn't look like nothing special. Just river rocks that'd been worn smooth by the water.

"You sure this is them?" I asked.

Mama snorted. "You shoulda seen 'em when Kel took 'em out of their box. Lit up all of down below, they did." There was something in her voice that sounded sad, and I knew Kel, whoever he was, was gone. I wondered if Mama and Papa had known what the starstones were when they brought them aboard.

"Can't you feel it?" Naji's eyes glowed. "The magic in them?"

"No."

Naji grabbed my hand and squeezed it between both of his palms. I jolted at his touch, and at first I thought it was just me being moony—but then I realized it was something else, some power coursing through him, seeping out of his skin. Not his blood-magic, which was like death curling her cold soft hands around your heart. This was ancient. This was the towering trees growing out of the cold damp ground of the ice-islands. This was the darkness of caves and the richness of desert sand. This was the emptiness of the night sky.

"They aren't actually weapons, you know." Naji said, his voice soft. "People want them to be, because of their strength . . ." His hands trembled against mine.

"They're the source of all magic," Naji went on, so soft I was pretty sure only I could hear him.

"What?" I stared at him. Behind us, Mama took a few steps closer, leaning in like she wanted to hear.

"You felt it," Naji said, looking over his shoulder at her. "The power. When your crewman died—"

"I don't want to talk about that."

Naji actually shut up. I guess Mama's sharp voice can even scare a Jadorr'a. Or maybe it wasn't Mama he was scared of.

"What's going to happen to you?" I said. "When you hold them?"

He looked at me. "You already know."

I shook my head. "It ain't right. I mean, think about what happened when I . . . you thought the other thing was impossible, and it wasn't at all."

Naji's eyes loomed dark and empty. Then he turned back to the starstones. I didn't let that stop me.

"There's gotta be something about you," I said. "'Cause you're Jadorr'a, 'cause you can't die, it's in all the stories."

I knew I was babbling; I knew Mama and Papa were giving each other looks over in the corner. "None of the tasks are impossible, that's the thing. You only *think* they are. It's like how I thought it was impossible for me to do magic and then I *did*, and I saved your life on the river, and—"

He lifted his head. The glow in his eyes illuminated the tears streaked across his cheekbones.

"Naji?" I whispered, 'cause all other words had left me.

"I hope you're right," he said, and then he reached out with his bare hands and scooped up the stones.

Magic flared around us, bright white and stinging like the edge of a flame. Naji screamed. The stones filled with light. For a dazed second, I thought that Jeric yi Niru was right, that they really did look like the stars plucked out of the sky.

And then I heard Papa shout, and I was aware of him and Mama both drawing their pistols, and Mama saying something like *not again*. And Naji stared at me with hollowed eyes and a gaping mouth, the stones growing brighter and brighter. I realized I could see the outline of his bones beneath his skin.

"Drop them!" I screamed. "You've done it! Skin against stone! Drop them!"

The faint presence of Naji's thoughts evaporated out of my head, leaving me empty and alone.

The stones clattered against the floor.

And then so did Naji.

CHAPTER FOURTEEN

I bounded on board the *Nadir*, screaming Marjani's name. Tears streamed down my face. I couldn't stop shaking.

"What is it?" She appeared at my side, one hand holding her gun, the other wrapped around my shoulder. "Where's Naji? Dammit! I knew we shouldn't have surrendered—"

"No!" I shouted, before she could call up the crew to arms again. "It wasn't . . . Where's Jeric yi Niru?"

Marjani blinked at me.

"Where's Naji?" she asked again.

"He held the stones," I said. More tears welled up behind my eyes. "He held the stones and now he's . . . now he's—"

"The stones?" Marjani shook her head. "Ananna, what are you talking about?"

"The starstones!" I shouted. "My parents had the starstones!"

"What?" Marjani stared at me. "And he . . . Oh, Ananna . . .is he . . ." She swallowed. "Is he dead?"

I shook my head.

Marjani closed her eyes and let out a long relieved sigh.

"But there's still something wrong with him. He won't get up. Jeric yi Niru!" I wiped at my eyes, suddenly ashamed of the tears, and turned toward the deck. "Where *is* he?"

"Here, first mate."

He slunk up behind me. When I glanced at him his face twisted up into a mask of sympathy and he said, "Oh, my dear,

I'd offer you a handkerchief, but it seems—"

"Stop it." I dug the heel of my hand into my eyes. The salt stung. "What else do you know about the starstones?"

Jeric gave me his slow, easy grin. "I believe you're in need of an Empire magician, not an Empire soldier."

I slapped him.

"Uncalled for," he said.

"You're a noble," I said. "Nobles don't sign up with the Empire's navy unless they get to be officers. But you ain't no officer."

The smile vanished from Jeric's face.

"Right now I don't give a shit what you did that got you condemned to sea. But I've half a mind to think it might got something to do with starstones." I pulled out my pistol and pointed it at his chest. "Am I right?"

"Will you shoot me if I say no?"

I curled my finger around the trigger.

Jeric grinned again, although this time it wasn't so easy. "You're cleverer than I gave you credit for."

"What else do you know about them?"

"You said the assassin is still alive?" Jeric's eyes glinted. "I've heard of people surviving this long after touching the stones, but I've never met one. Of course, I've also heard that they never come back the same."

Fear prickled cold and sharp down my spine, ice in the heat. I didn't know if Jeric yi Niru was lying to me or not.

"Could you help him?"

Jeric shrugged.

"Come with me," I told him. Then I turned to Marjani. "I'm going to bring Naji back on board and you need to tell Queen Saida to let my parents go."

Marjani opened her mouth.

"Just this once. They'll be back. I know Papa. She can do whatever she wants to them then. But please. Just let them go today."

Marjani got real quiet, and then she gave me a short little nod, and that's how I knew for sure that the queen's fleet had been following behind us as we gave chase, all set to interrupt our parley and take my parents prisoner.

I grabbed Jeric yi Niru by the arm and dragged him to the rowboat. He stumbled along with me and didn't say nothing as we climbed in, just gave me that steady stare of his—though this time it was shot through with wariness. My pointing the pistol at him had been a bluff; it was just as likely he got sent out to sea for seducing some courtier's wife. Sometimes you gotta take a gamble.

The boat splashed down, cold seawater cascading over my lap. I didn't care. I didn't care about nothing except getting Naji back on board the *Nadir*, and then to someplace that could give him care.

"I'm putting you in charge of the stones," I said. "We're bringing them back with us."

"Mercy, why?"

"My reasons are my own," I snapped. It was because of the curse—I didn't know if Naji touching them this time had worked or not. I wanted to cover all my bases.

"And how exactly do you plan to get them on board the ship?"

"They've got a box. Papa's crew was able to transport 'em fine that way."

"I imagine it's safe to assume they're not in the box now."

I glared at him.

"I'm sure you know what my next question is." He paused, eyes glittering. "How do we get them in the box?"

"I don't know. That's why I brought you."

Jeric settled back and didn't say nothing.

Naji was still stretched out when we got to the *Tanarau* holding bay. Mama was sitting over him with a bucket of seawater and the big pink conch shell she used on fevers and nightmares. She had peeled his shirt away and set the shell on his scattershot scar.

His tattoos glowed.

The starstones were glowing too, although they were dimmer now, casting long, pale shadows. Mama looked up at me when I walked in, her face foreign-looking in the light of the starstones. Her eyes flicked over to Jeric yi Niru.

"If those stones knock you out, don't expect me to treat you," she said to him.

Jeric didn't respond, not even to give her one of his mocking smiles. I knelt beside Naji and pushed the hair out of his face. I concentrated real hard, trying to see if I could peer inside his thoughts, to see what he was feeling. But I couldn't.

His skin was cold to the touch, but when I pressed my fingers against the side of his neck I could feel his pulse fluttering soft and light.

"Do you know if he'll get better?" I was afraid I would start crying again.

Mama didn't answer, just handed me a little silk bag filled with the glass vials she kept her spell stuff in, the bits of coral and the sand from Mua Beach and the dried seaweed harvested off the coast of the ice-islands.

"I mixed up some salts," she said. "Lay them under his nose twice a day. Maybe it'll work."

Not maybe! I wanted to scream.

Behind me, Jeric yi Niru cleared his throat.

"I don't want to hear your opinion on the subject," I shouted. "Grab the damn stones and take them to the rowboat."

"I wasn't going to say anything." He paused. "And I'm afraid I can't just *grab the damn stones*."

"Find a way."

He sighed. Then he looked at Mama. "What's the thickest fabric you have on board? A carpet would be best."

She gave him a dark look.

"I'm not taking the carpet with me. We just need a way to set them back in their box."

"Of course," Mama said stiffly. Then: "Anything you see in the holding bay, that's the best we got." She pointed off to the corner. "Got some Empire rugs there, that thick enough?"

"Ah," Jeric said, winking, "a pirate with taste."

"Shut up, Jeric." I threaded through the treasure and peeled one of the rugs away from the stack—a small one, the sort they lay in front of shop entryways. Jeric took it from me and slid it under the first starstone like he was scooping up a spider. When he lifted the carpet off the ground, he sucked in his breath and clenched his teeth, and his eyes widened with strain. The starstones pulsed, twinkling like stars.

When he was done he slammed the lid down over them, blinking out their light. Then he collapsed against the wall, breathing heavy.

"Don't ask me to do that again," he said.

Mama got one of the big *Tanarau* fellows to carry Naji to the rowboat. I followed behind with the box of starstones. It was lighter than even an empty box of that sort should be, as though it held negative space. Naji was limp as a rag doll in the crewman's arms, his head lolling back. Papa's crewman took Naji over in a *Tanarau* rowboat and I stayed close by in my own, not letting Naji out of my sight.

Jeric yi Niru didn't say a word as we crossed back over to the *Nadir*.

• • •

Naji slept for seven days.

He didn't move, didn't roll over, didn't moan like he was having nightmares. He just lay there, tattoos glowing. Queen Saida put him up in one of the garden houses, which she said were always used for convalescence—I let her 'cause she called off her fleet when we headed back to Arkuz, and Papa and Mama and the *Tanarau* went free. And when I insisted, she brought in one of her palace wizards to hang the garden house with protection spells, just in case the magic cloaking Naji from the Mists weakened while he was sleeping.

The garden house was one big empty room full of sunlight and the scents from the garden. Sheer curtains hung over the windows to keep the bugs out, and at night I could hear noises from the jungle, the rackety screeching of animals, and noises from the palace, too: music and laughter, women's voices trailing out into the night.

I did what Mama said, and put the salts under Naji's nose. Still he slept on. Queen Saida sent in a physician and then a wizard. The physician showed me how to drip water into his mouth so he wouldn't die of thirst, and the wizard told me it wasn't necessary.

"The magic's keeping him alive now," he said.

"That don't make sense."

"Of course not," he said. "It's magic." He sighed and pressed his hand against the scar on Naji's chest, the scar that covered his heart.

I stared at him, my face blank, still not understanding. "Magic is tied to the human body. Some people have a little, some people have a lot."

"Some people have none at all," I said.

The wizard smiled. "Fewer than you would expect." He sighed. "The stones make the magic inside us swell up, multiply. It chokes out everything else, all the light of life." He paused. "Your friend is quite strong. Most blood-magicians are. But even so, his survival is . . . unusual."

"Will he ever get better?" My voice quivered like I was about to start crying but I told myself: *No, no you will not cry in front of strangers. In front of anyone.*

"I don't know, sweetness." The wizard leaned forward and looked at me real close. He was old and wrinkled, but his eyes were bright and kind. "I'll read through my books, and see if I can find anything, all right?"

I nodded, even though I knew he wouldn't find nothing.

After a while I took to laying my hand on Naji's heart the way the magician did, so I could feel it beating faint and far away. I sang old Confederation songs to the beat of his heart. The song for lost love. The song for strength and for health. The song to stave off death.

For seven days, I didn't leave the garden house. Marjani brought me food and sat by my side, unspeaking. Queen Saida paid her visits and offered condolences. The magician returned with books and scrolls, none of them with any information to help.

Jeric yi Niru came on the fourth day, stepping into the garden house without knocking. I mistook him for Marjani at first, confused by worry and sleeplessness and the fuzzy sunlight pouring in through the curtains.

"The hell do you want?" I said when I realized my mistake.

"To come see," Jeric said. "I spoke with the palace magician. In all my studies, I never heard—"

"Get out!" I hurled a leftover breakfast plate at him. My aim was off. It banged against the wall and clattered to the floor. "He ain't some experiment for you to poke and prod."

Jeric yi Niru lifted his hands in the air. "I never thought a *pirate* would let her emotions get in the way—"

I sent a coffee cup flying through the air. This one shattered across the floor into pieces.

"Get *out*," I shouted.

"Don't you understand?" Jeric asked. "The starstones were my treasure. I studied them for years at the courts, long before you were even born. The magic in them—the *power*—if the assassin was able to survive their touch, I may be able to—"

I was on my feet, my knife in my hand, my hand at his throat. Jeric yi Niru stopped talking, just stared down at me.

"You want to stop this line of thinking," I said.

Jeric yi Niru didn't say nothing even though I could tell from the expression on his face that he wanted to.

"I ain't interested in helping develop Empire weapons, which I'm assuming is what you're after—"

Jeric sneered. "I don't care about the Empire. Why is that so hard for you to understand? The Empire banished me to service on the sea. I don't want to help them. I only wish to examine Naji to help myself."

I glowered at him and dug my knife a little deeper into the skin of his neck. Three drops of blood appeared, and Naji's magic suddenly flooded through me. I hadn't felt any connection with Naji since he fell, but now there was a rush of coldness in my thoughts, a black-glass desert, a song in a language like dying roses, calling out for help.

I dropped the knife and stumbled backward across the room. Jeric laughed at me, but when I fixed my glare on him his laugh dried up like saltwater in the sun.

"I'm not letting you touch him," I said, shaky.

"I can see that." Jeric lifted his hands like he was surrendering. "I only thought I'd ask."

"The answer is no. Now get out."

He didn't. He just watched me from across the room. I forced my concentration on Jeric, trying to ignore the terrifying, icy rush of Naji's thoughts.

"When you're older," he said, slowly and carefully, "you'll understand what it is to have a life's devotion."

I stared at him, taking deep breaths.

"You were right, by the way." He gave a short nod. "I was sent to sea because of the stones. There's a Qilari merchant who made his home in Lisirra. He owned a pair. I befriended him just so I could study those starstones. But studying wasn't enough. I wanted to own them."

"They really were your treasure," I snapped. "Thief."

"You have no room to talk, Ananna of the *Nadir*. No room at all."

He was right about that. I took a deep breath, bracing myself against Naji's thoughts, wishing Jeric would just leave.

"But you're right. I did steal them. It didn't take long before the authorities captured me." He sighed, wistful. "I was sentenced, and here we are. I never once touched the stones directly. I was too afraid. And I never thought I'd have the chance again, until I heard you and the captain speaking about them after you captured my ship. That's the entire reason I joined with your crew in the first place."

I stared at him. For once he didn't look mocking or smug.

"That's mad," I said. "Look at Naji! Look at him." I jabbed my finger at his body, unmoving on the bed. Jeric gazed at him without expression. "You want that to happen, go chase down the *Tanarau*. I'm sure they'll be happy to oblige a snakeheart in his suicide attempt."

"I don't want that," Jeric said.

I glared at him. But he didn't say nothing more, just turned and left.

I closed my eyes, relieved to be alone except for Naji. Even though Jeric's fresh blood was gone, Naji's thoughts still swirled up with mine, cold and shadowy. I could feel him, distant, indistinct. But alive. Alive.

I curled up beside him on the bed until the thoughts bled away.

On the seventh day, the assassins came.

There were three of them, all dressed the way Naji had been when I first saw him in Lisirra. Black robes, carved armor, swords glittering at their sides. They didn't cover their faces, though. "Who are you?" one of them asked in Empire when they walked into the garden house.

"Who the hell are you?" I shot back, even though I recognized their clothes. Still, I grabbed Naji's cold hand and squeezed it tight.

The first assassin narrowed his eyes at me. He was from the desertlands, like Naji, though he didn't look like Naji at all. Older and not as handsome and no scar. The other two looked Qilari.

"You aren't saving him, keeping him here," the desertlands assassin said. "He needs our magic."

"And you shouldn't care if he lives or dies," one of his companions added.

I didn't let go.

The desertlands assassin stepped up to me. My breath caught in my throat, and I kept my eye on his sword even though I knew if he wanted to use it I wouldn't be able to get away. But he didn't attack me. He kept his movement slow and steady, and put a hand on my forehead like he was feeling for a fever. I jerked away at his touch, but he grabbed me by the arm with his other hand and held me in place.

"You're scared of me? I'm no different from him." He leaned in close, looking me in the eye. I didn't turn away. I bet he could hear my heart.

He dropped his hand, pulled out a knife. I jerked out my own knife and pressed myself against the wall. One of the Qilari assassins laughed.

"This isn't for you," the first assassin said.

He picked up Naji's hand and cut a line down his arm. A thin trace of blood appeared on Naji's pale skin. I got another rush of thoughts that didn't belong to me—black-glass deserts and cold cold winds. The assassin glanced at me.

"Don't worry, little girl. This wound will heal." Another smile. He dipped his finger in Naji's blood and then licked the blood away, neat like a cat. He closed his eyes.

"Oh," he said. "He failed to mention that."

The Qilari assassins stirred. "Mention what?" one of them asked.

"He blood-bonded." The first assassin looked over at me, still cowering against the wall like a little ship rat. "With this one, it seems."

The Qilari assassins exchanged glances.

"Ah," one of 'em said. "That explains her unnatural devotion."

"My devotion ain't unnatural!" I shouted, in spite of myself. "And besides, I'd be helping him even if we hadn't shared bl—"

The desertland assassin held up one hand and my voice left my throat and I was filled up with silence. "There's no need to explain yourself. I know about the curse and the foolishness with your kiss."

Something heavy landed in my chest. I didn't say nothing. "And I know *this* foolishness was one of the tasks." The assassin sighed. "He certainly dawdled long enough."

"What?" I stepped forward, whole body tensed. "What do you mean, *dawdled*?"

The assassin looked at me. "Ah, the joys of dealing with the uneducated—"

"I know what the word means. I don't understand why you—"

"I commanded him to break the curse," the assassin said. "I

thought he did well, managing the first task so easily." He sneered at me. I sneered back. "Unfortunately, the cause of the first task resulted in him taking too long with the others."

The sneer disappeared from my face, and the assassin laughed. The cause of the first task? My kiss? I understood what the assassin was implying, but I didn't believe him. Naji didn't love me back. This assassin was making fun of me. I was certain of it.

I lifted up my knife and lunged at him.

A blur of shadows and the two Qilaris had me pinned to the floor and the desertland assassin had my own knife at my throat.

"You knew that wouldn't work," he said.

"Get off me!"

He lifted the knife up off my skin by a fraction. "You need to step outside now," he said. "My associates and I have work to do."

"Are you gonna kill him?" I asked.

"A true Jadorr'a welcomes death."

"I ain't a Jadorr'a."

"Yes, but Naji is." He pressed the flat side of the knife against the left side of my face—the same as Naji's scar. The metal was cold, colder than ice. "Although I'm not going to kill him. He still has work to do." He dropped his knife. "Now leave."

The assassin grabbed my arm and yanked me back, hard enough that my feet lifted off the ground. He put his mouth against my ear. "You shouldn't care for him so."

"Let me go, you Empire ass."

The other two drew their daggers. I stopped struggling. "Love is a wound," the assassin said. "Neither life nor death."

I wanted to tell him to shut up, but I figured I better hold my tongue. He smiled at me, showing all his teeth.

"Whatever you're thinking, girl," he said. "Speak. I won't hold it against you."

"Love is a wound?" I said. "Sounds like something a killer would say."

"So you must understand my metaphor well."

His words slammed into me, and for a moment I faltered, thinking about Tarrin bleeding in the desert. Then I kicked him, hard, in the shin. He laughed and dropped my arm, and the two Qilaris lifted me off my feet and dragged me, kicking and struggling, out of the garden house. I slammed my feet into one of them, right in the hip, before the door swung shut and I landed face-first in the soft grass.

"Are you all right?" The voice was speaking Jokjani. I spit out dirt and looked up. One of the palace soldiers, his eyes wide with fear. "They wouldn't let me go inside. I tried—"

"Ain't your fault."

The soldier pulled me to my feet. I smelled mint.

A few moments passed, and the smell grew stronger, drowning out the rainy scent of the garden. Bright blue light seeped out of the house's windows. The soldier positioned himself between me and the house, gripping his dagger tight, and I wanted to tell him he didn't have to do that for me, but I was too tired to try and get the words right. Plus it reminded me of Naji, and I was afraid if I spoke then I would cry.

A chill crept into the air.

I stepped away from the garden house and sat down beneath a banana tree. I kept seeing Naji stretched out on the bed, unmoving. I kept hearing his faint, slow heartbeat. And then the scent of mint flooded through the garden. It plunged me backward in time, till I was facing down Naji that first night, when he could've killed me easier than a bug, but he didn't.

Don't cry, I told myself. You're a pirate. Don't cry.

But I did anyway. The palace guard came and patted me on the shoulder like I was noblewoman crying over a suitor. I snarled at him until he went away.

The assassins stayed in the garden house for a long time, long enough that the afternoon rains came and went, that the sun sank into the horizon and turned the sky orange, that the soldiers changed places, the first one scuttling off into the palace and leaving another man, older, more grizzled-looking, in his place.

I didn't move from my spot beneath the banana tree.

The assassins came out of the garden house one at a time, their robes swirling around their feet, the armor gleaming in the thick orange light. They ignored the soldier and walked up to me.

"We need your help," the desertlands assassin said.

I glared at him. "Need my help how?"

"You don't seem to understand much of anything, do you?" he asked. "Perhaps if I inserted more profanity—"

"Just answer my damn question! What do you need my help for?" My heart was pounding. "Is Naji dead?"

"Your blood-bond." The assassin looked like he'd just swallowed a scorpion. "It seems we have use of it."

"What?"

He grabbed me by the wrist and pulled me up close. "It's not a difficult concept to grasp. We were unable to pull Naji out. We may be able to do so with your blood. It seems your bond was helping keep him alive."

I stared at him.

"I'm not explaining all this to you, girl. I saw he had enough of you in his blood when I cut him—I was testing for the curse but got *that* nasty little surprise."

"Not so nasty," I snapped, "if it means you'll get to save him."

The assassin scowled at me and dragged me back into the garden house. I let him. I didn't think it would work, but I let him.

"Stand here," he said, lining me up at the foot of Naji's bed. The floor was covered in rust-colored markings, and the air smelled like blood. One of the Qilari assassins bolted the door shut and they both stood behind me. I could feel their eyes on the back of my neck.

The desertlands assassin pulled out his red-stained knife. "Hold out your arm," he said.

I was shaking. I didn't want to let him cut me, but I didn't want Naji to die, neither.

"I know you want him to wake up," the assassin said, sneering a little. "I saw it when I cut him."

"Are you going to kill me?"

"Would you let yourself die to save him?"

"Ain't nobody wants to die," I said, and I knew it wasn't a proper answer.

The assassin moved up close to me in a blink. Another blink and he'd stretched my arm out over the bed. I thought maybe I should struggle.

Another blink and he cut me.

The cut was long and deep and this time Naji's thoughts flooded over mine so deeply I stopped being in the garden house and started being in the black-glass desert. It was empty except for the wind. I shivered in my thin Jokja dress and called out Naji's name. My voice echoed out across the emptiness. I took a hesitant step forward, and my knee slammed into something invisible, and invisible hands grabbed my arms and pulled me back.

A voice whispered on the wind. Not Naji's. It belonged to the desertland assassin. *Look for him*, he said. *Stop shouting. It won't do any good.*

"I can't look for him!" I shouted, struggling against the invisible hands. The Qilari assassins. I knew it and didn't know it, all at once. "I can't move."

With your mind, girl.

I stopped struggling. The wind swirled around me, icing over my bare arms and my bare cheeks. My bones rattled in my skin. The cold was worse than the Isle of the Sky had ever been. But I forced myself to concentrate, to reach out with the fingers of my mind.

I found him.

I found his thoughts, warmed by blood, thin blood, weak blood. He was thinking about food and water. He was thinking about me.

The invisible hands yanked me so hard my head spun round and around and then I was back in the garden house, sagging between the two Qilari assassins. The desertlands assassin was leaned over Naji, tracing blood—my blood, I knew—in patterns over the scar on his chest. My blood was all over the bed. It dripped down my arm, stained my clothes.

"He was thinking about me," I said, dazed.

"Shut up, girl." The desertland assassin didn't even glance up at me from beside Naji's bed, and the two others dragged me over to the corner. I slumped down on the floor, still dizzy and confused. In my head was an image of myself, standing on a boat, looking out over the ocean. And I was beautiful somehow, like all my insides had turned to light.

He was thinking of me as he lay dying in a world between worlds.

And it was real. I could feel it. I *knew* it.

I leaned against the wall, taking deep unsteady breaths. The Qilari assassins were singing, the desertland assassin was chanting. Their eyes glowed pale blue in the darkness. My spilled blood steamed and smoked, and it smelled like mint and the ocean.

After a while I couldn't see much of anything but the blue of the assassins' eyes and the ghostly trace of magic-smoke.

And then I heard someone say my name.

The singing and the chanting stopped. The smoke lingered

in the air. I could feel the walls of the garden house shifting and squirming just outside my vision.

And then a warmth flowed into my thoughts, familiar, barely there—

"Ananna?"

"Naji!" I pushed myself up to my feet, tottering in place. All three of the assassins turned and glared at me.

"Not yet, girl," hissed the one from the desertlands.

"No," Naji said, his voice rough and faint. "No, it's fine, I'm here—"

The assassin turned back to him. The glow faded from the Qilaris' eyes. I stumbled forward, my arm aching, my head spinning. "Naji," I said. "You're all right—"

"Not exactly."

I knelt beside the desertland assassin, who made no move to send me away. He just stood there glaring. Naji was stretched out on the bed the way he'd been all week, but now his eyes were open and his fingers fluttered against the sheet.

"Naji," I said, because I couldn't say what I wanted to. I buried my head into his shoulder. The scent of medicine and magic lingered in the room, and although the smoke was drifting away the air still seemed thick. Naji laid his hand on top of mine.

"You're here," he said.

"I had to save you. These buddies of yours ain't worth a damn." I blinked, trying not to cry. I was aware of his hand touching mine. "Besides, where else would I go?"

"I don't know. I thought you might take off with the *Nadir*, plundering."

I tried to laugh, but it came out strangled-sounding. "Thought? How could you think anything? You were . . ." I didn't know what to call it. Dead?

"I was trapped in between here and the Mists," he said. His hand was still on mine. "The Order found me, sent Dirar to bring me back." He glanced over at the desertland assassin and nodded. "Thank you."

Dirar scowled. "It was lucky the girl was here."

I didn't say nothing.

"Yes," Naji said. "I suppose you'll be alerting the Order of my blood-bond."

Dirar huffed and crossed his arms over his chest and didn't answer. Naji chuckled. I didn't understand what was going on. I wasn't sure I wanted to.

"By the way," Naji said. "It worked."

I stared at him for a long time.

"One more," Dirar said. "I suppose you plan on taking another four months with this one? Or maybe you'll just go for another four years. Why not?"

Naji's eyes took on that brightness that replaced his smile. "It worked," he said again. "Can you feel it?"

"No," I said, except as soon as I spoke I did: a lightness in his presence I hardly noticed. Missing weight. Missing darkness.

"You do," Naji said, his eyes still bright. "Come here."

"What?"

"Lean close," he said. "I have something to tell you."

Dirar stomped over to the garden house door with the other two assassins. All three of 'em stared at us. But I leaned over anyway, tilting my ear to his mouth. He put one hand on my chin and turned my face toward his.

"It worked," he said, and then he kissed me on the mouth, his lips dry from sleep.

CHAPTER FIFTEEN

I kept watch over Naji for two weeks, long after the other assassins left. We had to move him to a room in the palace, because the garden house was destroyed by the magic-sickness, its walls turning into thick ropy vines, the bed transforming into an enormous moon-colored flower. I stayed away from the place where the garden house had been.

But tucked away in the palace, Naji did get slowly better. The color returned to his face. His tattoos stopped glowing. He ate every bite of food Queen Saida had brought to him.

Sometimes he kissed me.

Some days I would lay my head on Naji's chest, the way I had when he was asleep. I listened to his heart beat strong and sure. He let his hand drift over my hair and down the length of my spine. It was nice. I was afraid to say something about it, though, afraid that if I opened my mouth it would all disappear.

When he felt good enough to stand up, I walked with him around the perimeter of the palace garden, the way he had with me on the Island of the Sun. He pointed out flowers to me, identifying them by name, telling me what sorts of magic properties they had, but all the while his hand was on the small of my back, and I didn't remember one word of what he said.

Jeric came to visit. He knocked on Naji's door while I was there, and when I answered, he scowled at me and said, "I'd hoped you'd be gone."

"Go away," I said.

"No." Naji's voice was bright behind me. "No, Ananna, it's fine. He can stay."

Jeric gave me a smug smile and pushed into the room. Naji was sitting on the bed, the sunlight making his hair shine. Jeric gave a scholarly little bow and said, "That one"—he pointed at me—"gets overenthusiastic. I only wanted to ask you about the starstones."

Naji nodded. I was all prepared to chase Jeric away, but when he started asking questions Naji didn't seem to mind answering them. I guess it was Naji's university background, and all the studying he had to do for the Order. He told Jeric what it felt like when his skin touched the stones, and his theories about how they had affected the magic in his body. Jeric nodded all the while, scratching notes down in a little leather-bound book, and after they got to talking both seemed pleased with themselves. I sat in the corner and listened, because it was interesting, even if I didn't always understand the technicalities of what Naji said, even if the thought of the starstones scared me a little, still.

Jeric only visited once, but he became a lot easier to deal with after that. Like Naji'd given him a gift.

One afternoon me and Naji went to see Queen Saida in her sun room. Marjani was there, dressed in a long golden dress that suited her, her hair woven with ribbons and shells. Saida looked a proper queen in Empire silks, Jokja metals in the bangles on her wrist. She stood up when me and Naji walked in.

"You've recovered!" she cried out. "Marjani told me the news, but I'm so glad to see you walking about." And she actually crossed the room to greet us. She kissed both of Naji's cheeks and beamed at him.

"Thank you, my Light," Naji murmured, bowing his head.

Queen Saida turned to me. "And I heard you were most instrumental," she said. "The Jadorr'a told me about it when they thanked me for my hospitality. I told them no Jokja has ever feared a Jadorr'a." She laughed. Naji's eyes crinkled into a smile.

"And what about the third task?" Marjani asked from her seat by the windows. It was raining, gray-green light pouring in around her. "Have you figured out what that means yet?"

"Ah yes!" Queen Saida said. "The third task. I can ask the palace magicians to look into it for you, if you'd like."

I thought about how worthless her palace helpers had been when it came to finding the starstones, but Naji only nodded and said, "Yes, I would appreciate that. Thank you."

Afterward, me and Naji walked together in the garden, the way we usually did. I linked my arm in Naji's and he didn't say nothing about it, so I figured it was all right. I'd been refraining from dipping in his head ever since he woke up. It had been startling to see myself in there, beloved—though I was still afraid of what might happen if I didn't find myself at all.

The rain had slowed down to a slow shimmering drizzle. The sun came out and refracted through the drops, filling the air with diamonds. Me and Naji sat down at one of the pavilions near the fence. The jungle was quiet from the rain.

"Why'd you tell her to help you?" I asked.

"So I can cure my curse."

"You want to get rid of me that easy?" I tried to keep my voice light, but it trembled anyway.

Naji looked at me with eyes as dark as new moons. "No."

I looked down at my lap.

"Surely you'd like to run off and have your adventures," he said, "without having me tag along complaining about the vagaries of the ocean."

"What's a vagary?" I said. "And I wouldn't mind none anyway. Having you with me." With that last part, I blushed and slurred my words on purpose.

Naji leaned over and kissed me, one hand cupping the side of my face. "I wouldn't mind either," he said softly, "but I prefer not to feel as though I'm dying every time you loosen the sails."

I laughed at that, and his eyes lit up. I'd been seeing that more and more. It got to the point that I could fill in the blanks, and every time he did it was like his whole face was smiling. Funny that I hadn't seen the crinkle back on the Island of the Sun. When I thought about it, I knew it had been there.

Naji kissed me again.

Something squawked over in the garden.

"What the—" I pulled away from Naji and sure enough there was that big white seabird that'd flown into his room before we found the starstones. Another note was attached to its foot.

The bird cawed and flapped its great white wings.

"It's that bird again," I said.

Naji took my hand in his. "I saw it," he said. "When I was under."

"What? Really?"

The bird hopped forward and stuck out its leg. Naji slipped off the canister and dropped out the note and the map, the same as before.

> *Naji of the Jadorr'a:*
>
> *I never received a reply to our last missive, although Samuel assures me that you did read the note. I plead you not to dismiss this one as well—we are not seeking your harm. Nor do we have interest in your skills as a murderer-for-hire. The King of Salt and Foam merely wishes to thank you. That is all. If you are concerned, you may bring guards and weapons,*

magic or otherwise, as you see fit. I guarantee you will not have use of them. Regards, Jolin I.

Naji lay the note down in his lap.

"What do they got to thank you for?" I asked. "You sure nobody knows nothing about them?"

Naji sighed. "I told you, they're completely unknown to the Order and to Saida's scholars—I asked about the court and about this Jolin I both. Nothing." He hesitated. "However, I did see that bird when I was trapped in the liminal space, circling the sky, over and over, dropping down sheets of parchment . . ." He turned to me. "Ask one of the palace clerks for some ink. I'm going to send them a response."

"You don't even know who they are!" I snatched the note off his lap and flapped in the air. "This could be the Mists. A trap—"

"It isn't." He pulled the note away from me. "I'll fetch the ink myself."

I scowled at the bird, who just cawed at me.

Naji disappeared into the palace. Part of me wanted to follow behind him and find some way to stop him, but I just sat there glaring at the seabird to see who would blink first—me, as it turned out. Whatever Naji knew, whatever Naji thought—some of it was seeping into my brain. Not all of it, but enough that I let him be.

Naji emerged twenty minutes later with a pot of ink. When he saw me staring at the seabird he laughed.

"Write your damn note," I told him.

"Ananna." He sat beside me and pulled his black quill out of his shirt. It occurred to me that despite everything that had happened to us he'd never once lost that quill, and then I thought about how thin Jokja cotton was and I wondered just where he kept the quill at all, 'cause I'd never seen it.

"Naji," I said.

"I want to visit this . . ." He glanced down at the note. "This King of Foam and Salt. Things don't appear in the liminal space unless they're important."

I sighed. "You want me to sail you to . . . to wherever. The middle of nowhere. The place where Mistress Hariri shot me."

He touched my cheek with the back of his hand. "This has nothing to do with the Hariris."

"Fine," I said. "But I don't know if I can convince Marjani to come with." I gave him a sly smile. "Maybe you can be Captain Namir yi Nadir again."

"I doubt it." He stared at me, his eyes all dark and intense. He was gonna get himself killed.

The way he almost did picking up the starstones.

But that was different. That was the *curse*. This was just some nonsense he saw while he hovered between worlds.

I listened to the *scritch scritch scritch* of his pen against the back of the seabird's note. When he finished he slid the parchment back into the tube and then slid the tube back onto the seabird's leg. He kept the map, at least.

Then the seabird spread out its wings and dipped its head down low, almost like it was bowing, before taking off into the gray-blue sky.

I knocked on the door to Marjani's bedroom. A guard stood nearby, gazing at the wall in front of him in such a bored way that I knew really he was keeping tabs on me. Don't know why: Queen Saida was off in some diplomatic meeting, according to the whispers around the palace, and it's not like I was up to any mischief.

The door swung open. Marjani blinked when she saw me.

"I need to talk to you," I said.

She pushed the door open wider so I could come in. Her room was bigger than mine, with lots of open windows and expensive-looking furniture and a bed that looked like it had never been slept in.

"Is the ship all right?" she asked, soon as the door was shut. "The crew?"

"What? Oh yeah, they're both fine. Crew all came back from the Aja Shore and picked up their work shifts right where we left off."

Marjani smiled. "I'm glad to hear that."

"Actually, I kinda wanted to talk about the ship."

"You want to leave."

That gave me pause, the way she knew right away, and for a moment I just stared at her. She didn't look like Marjani much anymore, with her pretty dresses and the makeup around her eyes, but I realized it was just that she didn't look like the Marjani I knew, and that she had been *this* Marjani long before she met me. I wondered if she thought the same thing about me. I hadn't been in men's clothes much since we came to Jokja, either.

"Yeah," I said, "I want to leave."

She gave me a quick smile.

"Do you?"

The smile disappeared, and there was this long pause as she looked out the windows. "I don't know," she finally said. "I miss it, you know, but when I was sailing I missed all this."

I knew she really meant that she had missed Queen Saida, but I didn't say nothing.

"Where do you want to go?" she asked.

I took a deep breath. "We got coordinates to someplace out in the ocean. Naji—he's got some *feeling* about them, though—"

"You don't agree," Marjani said. "You don't want to go."

"Yeah, but . . . the thing is, I looked at the coordinates and they're . . . well, they're about the same place where we had that battle with the Hariris."

She stared at me. "Violence," she said. "It's a cure for his curse."

"It's the middle of the ocean!" I said. "More likely it's some Hariri trick."

Marjani tilted her head at me. "Do you want me to go so you can stay here?"

"No! I ain't no coward. I just . . . it's your ship, you're the captain—"

Marjani's face changed. Just for a second, when I called her captain. I got the feeling she missed it all more than she let on.

"Besides," I said, "if we do gotta fight the Hariris, I need to have you around. Don't think I could lead the ship into battle the way you could."

She laughed. I could tell it was 'cause she was flattered. "Well," she said, "how can I say no to that? Not that I think you're going to have to fight the Hariris."

"We won't be out long," I said.

"You say that." She shook her head. "I'll go. I do miss it terribly. Saida may not be too pleased to hear it, but . . ." Her voice trailed off and she toyed with the end of one of her locks.

"Tell the queen I'll bring you back safe," I said. "Pirate's honor."

Marjani looked at me and laughed, but I knew I had my captain back.

We made sail three days later.

Queen Saida'd had her navy repair the boat after our trip to the Aja Shore, but Naji was still too weak to do magic, so we had to sail the old-fashioned way, with no guarantee of favorable winds. In truth it was nice, 'cause it gave the crew something to do besides sitting around on deck drinking sugar-wine and playing dice. And I didn't have to deal with Jeric begging for more information about the starstones—Marjani kept him busy down in the armory, tending to the pistols and ammunitions and making sure everything stayed dry.

A storm blew through a week in, threatening to knock us off course. I crawled up in the rigging myself, to help keep the sails straight. Ain't nothing like it, swinging from rope to rope while the water soaks you to the bone. It ain't pleasant, but it was something I'd missed.

The whole time Naji was up near the helm, a rope knotted round his arm so he wouldn't get tossed overboard, and whenever I glanced at him he'd be staring straight at me, his eyes flickering in and out, his face twisted up in pain. I'd locked him out of my head for the time being, but seeing that expression hurt me in a way that had nothing to do with my body.

That storm was the only one we faced, though, and for the rest of the trip the seas were smooth as glass, the winds brisk and warm. Two weeks passed. I checked the navigation every day and compared it to the map the seabird had left us. But it was hard as hell, 'cause the map just led us straight to the middle of the open ocean.

"You sure this is correct?" Marjani asked me one afternoon when she was up at the helm. I had the maps spread out on the deck beside her, pinned down with rum bottles and sea rocks.

"Sure as anything," I said.

Marjani frowned. She'd been in good spirits when we started out, but now that we were out on the open sea she was constantly gazing off to the east. Off to Jokja.

"Does Naji know anything?" she asked.

I shrugged.

"Go ask him."

"He probably ain't well—"

"Go ask him." She gripped the wheel a little more tightly. "I trust him more than I trust that map of yours."

I couldn't much blame her for that, seeing as how the map had been given to us by a bird. I left her to her steering and made my way down to the captain's quarters, where Naji was laid up recovering from my swinging around the rigging. I knocked but didn't bother to wait for an answer, and when I walked in he was stretched on the bed, his hands folded over his chest.

"Marjani wants to know if we're going the right way," I said.

He turned his head to look at me, his hair falling across his face.

"Are you navigating?"

"Course I am."

"Then of course we're going the right direction."

I scowled at him, though inside my whole heart lit up like a bonfire. "Yeah, but we ain't sailing to land. Some tiny spot in the middle of the ocean . . . that ain't easy to get to. You know she's talking about using magic."

"I know what she's talking about." Naji sat up and patted the bed beside him. I stared at him for a few seconds.

"I want you to sit beside me," he said.

"What for?"

He laughed, one of those short sharp Naji laughs. "We aren't lost," he said. "I've gone to Kajjil, to follow our path on the underside of the world. We're quite fine."

I blinked at him, confused.

"My trances," he said.

"Oh."

"It's how we learn things in the Order. Come, sit."

I sighed and sank down on the mattress beside him. He put his hand on my knee. I glanced at him and he flicked his head away real fast. The air crackled with something like magic.

He kissed me. I was starting to get used to his kisses, but this one went on longer than usual, and his hands trailed down over my shoulders, and tugged on my shirt, tugging it up over my shoulders.

"Oh," I said, pulling away from him, flustered and embarrassed, sure he would take one look at me and call the whole thing off.

"Are you on shift?" he asked. "You said you had taken the mornings—"

"Yeah," I muttered. "I was helping Marjani out some, but it wasn't my official time—"

He kissed me again.

We sank down to the bed. I wrapped my arms over my stomach, afraid *now* would be the moment that he left. But he didn't leave. He slipped out of his own clothes, and his tattoos were flat and dark against his skin, tracing all over his chest and down to the tops of his thighs. The scar from the spell fallout was red and new-looking, not like the scar on his face.

He climbed into the bed with me. I couldn't believe it was going to happen, but when I let myself peek at his thoughts I felt only this hot red flush, and I knew he wanted me.

He kissed me all over, on my neck and my jawline and my shoulders. He touched me in that certain way and I felt him everywhere, the movement of his body and the warmth of his breath. It hadn't felt like this the other times I'd been with someone. I hardly felt nothing before; now, all I had was feeling.

Naji buried his head in my shoulder, his breath hot on my skin, and dug his fingers into the blankets. Afterward, he kissed me long and deep and rolled over onto his back.

My chest filled with this warm honeyed feeling. And I knew it wasn't gonna go away. I could feel his thoughts bumping up against mine, telling me it was for real, it had always been for real.

I kissed along his chest and asked him what we were looking for. I figured he'd know from his trances.

"Sentries," he said.

"You just got that out of the letter."

"Well, of course, that's what I'm working off here."

I rolled on top of him, pinning him to the cot. He gazed up at me. "I thought you saw them in Kajjil," I said. "Or the seabird. Or something."

"I saw the albatross when I was under," he said. "It didn't speak to me. And Kajjil doesn't work that way. I don't see people. I track them."

I sighed. "I still think it's a trap."

Naji pulled me down and kissed me, his hand running up and down my spine.

"Stop it." I pushed away from him. He frowned. "You're distracting me!" I said. "Marjani's probably pissed enough right now—"

"Do you really care?"

I glared at him. He knew I did, although not enough to leave. My thoughts were spilling out of me.

"We're just gonna sail around in circles till the crew has the doldrums and we've eaten up all the food and then the Mists is gonna *attack*—"

"It's not the Mists," Naji said. "I know that for certain."

I looked at him long and hard. He was telling the truth. Or what he thought was the truth.

"Who posts sentries in the middle of the ocean?" I asked.

"Someone who lives in the middle of the ocean," Naji said, and he drew me close to him and kissed me again. This time I let him.

CHAPTER SIXTEEN

Next morning, I was up at the helm, guiding the *Nadir* through those smooth glassy waters. I'm not crazy about steering on the best of days, and that morning I was tired and distracted with thoughts of Naji. Plus the morning sun was hot and bright in my eyes. All I wanted was to be down below, my clothes in a heap on the floor, Naji's mouth at the base of my throat.

Old Sorley came bounding up to the helm with his hat in his hands.

"The hell do you want?" It came out a lot gruffer than I meant.

"Madam First Mate," he stuttered, looking down at his feet. He'd been some kind of servant before he got nicked off the street and forced onto an Empire boat. "You told us to come to you if we saw anything odd."

I tensed my hands around the helm but kept my eyes straight ahead. "Yeah? You see something weird?"

"Yes, madam."

A pause.

"Well, what is it?"

"It's . . . well, it's probably nothing . . ."

I glowered at him.

"Sharks!" he squeaked. "It's sharks!"

"Sharks?" I squinted out at the horizon, light flashing up into my eyes. "Don't let anybody fall into the water, it'll be fine. Not like we're in danger of sinking."

"No, you don't understand . . ." He crushed his hat into a tight little ball between his hands. "They ain't normal sharks. I can't . . . it's a bit hard to describe, madam, I'm sorry—"

I felt bad for him. "Show me."

He nodded. I called off for Jeric yi Niru to take the helm. He came over no questions asked, the way he usually did these days, though he gave me one of his insolent little nods. Some habits you just can't break.

I followed Sorley across the deck to the port side. Sunlight was everywhere, bright and glittering.

"There," Sorley said, pointing with his crumpled up hat.

I didn't have the words for it.

There were sharks, to be sure. About sixteen of 'em, lined up four by four, swimming alongside us without breaking formation.

And they were wearing *clothes*: vests made of seashells, all strung together so that they looked like scaled Empire armor. The sharks skimmed across the water, tails switching back and forth in time.

"What the hell?" I said, 'cause what else do you say? Then I turned to Sorley: "Go get the captain." I thought for a moment, then added, "And Naji."

He didn't hear me, though. He was leaning over the railing, waving that stupid hat around. "Hey!" he called out. "I brought her! The first mate! Captain's not on duty."

"What are you doing?" I grabbed at him. He ignored me. I glanced over my shoulder—a bunch of the crewmen had gathered behind us. They were all spooked.

"The hell's going on?!" I shouted. "One of you, go get the captain." Nobody moved. "Now!"

They scattered, as though "one of you" meant "all of you." When I turned back to the railing, Sorley was staring at me, and down in the water, one of the sharks had broken formation.

"Pardon me!" the shark called out. "But does this boat bear Naji of the Jadorr'a?"

I screamed. Kaol help me, but I screamed liked I'd just been sliced through with a damned Qilari blade. The shark dipped its head in the water and splashed around foam.

"A thousand apologies, my dear, I didn't mean to frighten you—"

"Why are you *talking*?" I screamed. I turned to Sorley. "Why didn't you *tell* me?"

He looked cowed. "I didn't think you'd believe me."

I took a deep breath. A talking shark. I leaned back over the railing.

"Are you from the Mists?" I asked, watching closely for a spray of smoke or a smear of light.

"No, I'm from the waters," the shark said. "I am Lorens, member of the Eighty-Seventh Guard Infantry, sentry to the Court of the Waves and sworn protector of the King of Salt and Foam."

My mouth dropped open a little.

"We were sent here to guide you to the rendezvous point. Assuming you are, in fact, carrying Naji of the Jadorr'a. The young gentleman said you were." He splashed water in Sorley's direction.

"Are you gonna kill him?" I asked. "Naji?"

The shark looked affronted. "Madam, never! We are in his *debt*, you must understand—"

"Ananna?"

I stepped away from the railing and whirled around. Naji came barreling across the deck, Marjani close behind. "What's wrong?" he asked, putting his hands on my face and pulling me close. For once in their lives the crew didn't hoot and holler when he did it.

"What's going on?" Marjani asked.

"Sharks," I said.

She stared at me like I'd gone mad. "Sharks," she said. "*Sharks* have got the crew off the sails?" She frowned. "It's like they've never been at sea before."

I tried to figure out a way to explain it to her without sounding mad, but I couldn't. Naji stepped up to the railing. Turned around again.

"They want you," I said. "They can, uh—"

"They what?"

"This is getting absurd," Marjani said. "Ananna, just tell me what's happening."

"I'm not—"

"Are you Naji of the Jadorr'a?"

It was the shark again, his rough rasp of a voice calling up out of the water. Marjani shrieked and stumbled up against me, one hand on the butt of her pistol. Naji, though, leaned over the railing. "I am!" He sounded unconcerned, like he spoke with sharks all the time.

"We are in your debt," the shark said.

"Why?"

"What is going *on*?" Marjani whispered.

"I ain't got no idea."

Marjani shoved me toward the railing. The other sharks were all facing us now, their heads bent low into the water. The head shark hadn't bothered to answer Naji's question.

"You must come down below!" the shark said.

"Below what?" asked Naji. "The water?"

The shark nodded.

"I'm afraid that isn't possible, not if you'd also like to speak with me. I won't be able to breathe—"

"We've made arrangements."

I grabbed Naji's arm. "Don't do it," I whispered. "It's a trap."

Naji wrapped his arm around my waist. "May I bring some companions?" he asked.

"What?" I hissed.

"Of course." The sharks all bowed again, splashing water.

"Are you insane?"

"We shall send the device to the surface shortly," said the head shark. "You may bring down as many of your crew as you like. In shifts, of course."

Naji waved his hand. "No need." He squeezed my waist again. I scowled at him.

The sharks disappeared beneath the water.

"What are you *doing*?" I shouted, smacking him in the chest. "You're gonna get us both killed!"

"Yes, I agree." Marjani stepped forward, hand still on the butt of her pistol. "I'd prefer you not get my navigator *eaten*, thank you."

"I'm proving to you—to both of you—how undangerous I think it is," Naji said. "Ananna, I want you to go with me."

I peered up at him. He really did think it was safe; I could feel it creeping into my own thoughts. But that didn't mean I agreed with him.

Naji's eyes glazed over, like he was thinking. "Something about this," he said. "It feels . . . right. Pieces falling into place."

I wanted to hit him.

"You can come too," Naji added, turning to Marjani. "If you're truly concerned about Ananna's safety—"

"That wouldn't be wise," Marjani said quietly. Behind her, the crew shuffled and mumbled to each other. She was probably right. Captain and first mate disappearing beneath the waves with a bunch of talking sharks? Hell, I'd be hightailing it out of here too.

Frothy bubbles appeared on the surface of the water, followed by a low whining noise that reminded me of the Hariri clan and their machines. I yanked out my knife. The boat began to rock.

"All hands to stations!" Marjani screamed. "Keep her steady!"

The crew scrambled to attention.

Sea foam sprayed over the railing. Naji stepped in front of me.

Ha, I thought. *Showing me how safe it is.*

And then there was a hiss like the biggest snake you ever heard, and a big glass box erupted out of the sea, showering the *Nadir* with water and sea foam. Me and Naji and Marjani were soaked through.

For a minute the box floated in the open ocean, glittering a little in the sunlight. Then the top of it popped open.

"Naji of the Jadorr'a!" shouted the shark, who'd showed back up without his sentries. "You and one other must come inside the transport."

Naji pressed himself against the railing. "Will we be able to breathe?" he asked.

The shark nodded. "We tested it on air-breathers. There are some among our number."

Naji turned to me. "Air-breathers," he said.

"Does he mean other humans? 'Cause I don't breathe water."

"I doubt it. There are certain sea creatures who only live half in the water." His eyes sparkled. The closest he ever came to smiling. I figured he'd gone and lost his mind. "Please, Ananna," he said. "Come with me."

"Course I'm gonna come with you." I eased my knife back into my belt. "Just don't expect me to be happy about it."

"Me, neither," Marjani said. "If you let her die, I'll kill you."

We were both soaked already, so me and Naji just dove into the water and swam over to the box. My heart pounded the whole time, 'cause I couldn't quite shake the notion that the Hariris or the Mists were behind this somehow. Plus the thing kept hissing and groaning and the water around it bubbled like it was boiling.

Once we climbed in, I had Marjani toss me my gunpowder. That left me a couple of shots on my pistol, plus my sword and my knife, and Naji's sword and knife, and his magic too.

The lid lowered down onto the box.

"You want to kill me." My voice echoed weirdly against the glass walls.

"I want no such thing."

"You know what's going on, then." I looked at him. "But you won't tell me."

"I honestly don't. Which you know, because . . ." He tapped his head.

"Still like hearing you say it out loud."

There was a big hiss and the box began to lower into the water. I braced my hands against the glass and waited for the water to come rushing in and drown us. It didn't. Just slapped against the outside of the box, blue and green and filled with sunlight.

"I have my intuition," Naji said. "It's surprisingly fine-honed."

I thought about all the times he'd known the Mists was trying to seduce me. All the times he showed up at the last minute to save me from more worldly deaths. All the times he knew exactly what to say to piss me off.

His intuition. Yeah, I guess I could give him that.

We sank lower and lower. The water got darker and the air got colder, but at least we could still breathe. The shark swam alongside us.

"It didn't strike you as weird they wouldn't tell you what's going on?"

Naji glanced at me. "It's a little strange," he said. "But not nearly as strange as a talking shark."

I sighed.

Deeper and deeper. It was dark as night now, no sunlight to speak of, just the endless black press of the ocean.

And then a light glimmered off in the distance, tiny and bright.

"What's that?" I asked, leaning forward. I was afraid to touch the walls of the box, afraid they'd shatter into a thousand pieces.

The light brightened and expanded.

It swelled, looking for all the world like the moon on a cloudy night. A big bright circle amidst all that watery darkness.

The box hissed and screeched.

And then we got close enough and I could see—it wasn't just a ball of light.

It was a city.

"Kaol," I said, my words forming white mist on the glass. Even Naji wasn't so unconcerned no more. He pressed his hands against the side of the box, his eyes growing wider and wider.

The box slipped through the water, churning up bubbles behind us. I could see the buildings were made out of broken-up shells and something rough like sand and what looked to be glass. A fuzzy algae that glowed like a magic-cast lantern grew over everything, hanging off the edges of buildings like moss. And the buildings didn't look like the buildings anywhere on land, 'cause they twisted and curled out of the ground like sea-bones, and they merged together and split apart without no definite order. Sea creatures flitted past us, some of 'em wrapped in strips of seaweed that flout behind 'em, and some of 'em were decked out in the same shell armor as the sharks.

Naji and me didn't say a word to each other. I got flashes of his thoughts: wonder, confusion, a little bit of fear. Or maybe it was my thoughts. They were all mingled together.

The box came to a tunnel, encased in shining shells, with words spelled out across the top in a language that didn't look nothing like anything I'd seen before. The tunnel sucked us down to a sort of dock, and the box lifted up, water streaming over the sides. We weren't underwater no more.

"What's happening?" I asked.

The box lid hissed open. Air rushed in, damp and musty.

Naji looked at me and I looked at him, and then he climbed out.

"It's fine!" he said. "There's air, a place to stand—"

"I can see that," I snapped, since I could spot him, a little wavy from the cut of the glass, but definitely standing. I climbed out too, though I kept one hand on my pistol as I did so.

We stood in a hallway as big and empty as the desert. It was all made out of glass too, except this one didn't flood with sunlight and rainbows. It didn't flood with nothing, thank Kaol, although every time I thought about all that ocean water crushing in on us I took to shaking.

Naji and me stood on the platform and waited. Our box bobbed in the strip of water that flowed in through an opening in the wall, and I could feel the magic sparking around us.

A shark's fin appeared in the water. Part of me wanted to grab for Naji's hand, but I grabbed for my pistol instead.

A shark lifted his head up out of the water. It wasn't the same one that brought us down, and he wasn't wearing no armor, neither, just a circlet of sea-bone around his neck.

"Follow me," he said. "Along the walkway."

I couldn't stand it no more: I took Naji's hand in mine. Like a little kid, I know, but swords and pistols can't save you from drowning.

Naji dipped his head politely and together we followed along with the shark, our footsteps bouncing off the glass. When we came to the end of the hallway, the shark said, "You may open the door. Preparations have been made for your arrival."

I murmured an old invocation to the sea, one Mama'd taught me years ago, while Naji pushed open the door.

No water. Just air.

It opened up into a big round dome, the way I'd always imagined a nobleman's ballroom to look. Only the floor opened up here, too, a ring of cold dark seawater. The shark's head popped up.

"Our soothsayer will be here soon," he said. He disappeared into the darkness.

"What do they need a soothsayer for?" I muttered.

Naji wrapped his arm around my waist and buried his face in my hair. I was too startled to react, so I just stood there and let him touch me. "Thank you for coming with me," he whispered, and his gratitude rushed into my thoughts, turning all my fear into a weird sort of happiness.

"Thank you?" I laughed. "I thought this was proof that it wasn't dangerous."

"That too."

It's funny, 'cause even though we were at the bottom of the ocean with only a layer of glass between us and the deep, I still couldn't get enough of his hands on me. I leaned against him, his body warm and solid and reassuring, and thought about giving him my blood the day of the battle. It wasn't so bad, being in his head now and then. It was the whole reason I knew he cared about me.

Water spilled across our feet.

"Naji of the Jadorr'a!" The voice boomed through the big empty room. "Is this your companion?"

I pulled away from Naji. An octopus bobbed in the water, its tentacles curling around the edges of the floor, its skin a rich dark blue, bright against the water's black. He wore a row of small white clam shells strapped to one tentacle.

"Yes," said Naji. "This is Ananna of the *Tanarau*."

"Of the *Nadir*," I corrected.

The octopus heaved itself out of the water. "How lovely to meet you. My name is Armand II, and I saw you," he turned to me, "in my visions as well, in the swirls and mysteries of the inks." He looked at me expectantly.

"Uh, that's good."

"I'm afraid the King of Salt and Foam is not a two-way creature, like myself." Armand lurched forward, dragging across the floor, his legs coiling and uncoiling. "But we have made preparations."

He opened up one of the clam shells and pulled out a pair of glass vials filled with a dark, murky liquid. "It will not harm you," he said.

I got this slow sinking of dread, but Naji took one of the vials and held it up to the light. He opened it up and sniffed. Looked at me.

"It's water-magic," he said.

"So? You'd expect sand-magic down here?"

Naji brushed his hand against my face, his touch gentle, almost as soft as a smile. "Forgive her," he said, turning to Armand. "Her profession requires a certain amount of wariness."

"As does yours, I imagine."

Naji looked at the vial again. "Less than you might think."

"What's it gonna do to us?"

"You will be able to breathe water," Armand said.

I frowned. Of course. And Naji was right; that was old sea-magic, the sort of thing Old Ceria would know how to do. It wasn't impossible. It was dangerous, I suppose, but then, so's all magic. So's cutting open your arm and giving your blood to the man you love.

"I'll give it a shot," I said. I took off my shoes and my coat, though I figured I shouldn't meet the King of Salt and Foam, whoever he was, in my underwear. I left my pistol 'cause there was no point having it underwater. Then I took the vial from Armand, unscrewed the lid, and shot the stuff back like it was rum. Immediately my lungs started burning, and I gasped and choked and clawed at my throat. Naji pushed me in the water.

Release.

The water filled up my lungs and then pulsed out though gills that appeared on my neck. The lights from the city swirled and bled into one another, bled into the darkness of the sea.

It was beautiful. And I'd never even have to come up for air.

Another muffled splash and then Naji was beside me, barefoot and coatless, his hair drifting up in front of his eyes. I laughed, bubbles streaming silvery and long between us, and for the first time in a long time I wished I could do sea-magic myself, so I could swim through the water undeterred by breath, and Naji could come with me, and we could swim and play and entwine ourselves together.

"This way," Armand said, graceful now that he was underwater. He propelled himself forward, toward the blur of lights, and Naji and me followed with slow easy breast strokes.

The King of Salt and Foam held court in a big curling palace that looked like more bones. Everything glowed with the light of that weird algae.

I've never been to court before. In Jokja, Queen Saida didn't hold court, just met with petitioners in her sun room. Court's an Empire thing, and the Empire don't like pirates. But I bet the Emperor's court had nothing on the Court of the Waves.

It was full up with all manner of sea life, rows of little clams and a whole school of flickering fish that turned to us like one person when we swam in. There were big sharp-toothed predators and slippery sparking eels and the rows of shark sentries, swimming ceaselessly in circles around the room.

And then there was the king.

He wasn't like any fish I ever saw. He reminded me of the manticore, 'cause he had a long curling shark's body and the wide graceful fins of a manta ray and the spines of a saltwater crocodile, all topped up with a human face with pale green-gray skin and flat black eyes and hair like strips of dark green seaweed.

He was coiled around a hunk of coral when we swam in, and as we approached he rose up in the water, his full length taller than any human man. Naji stopped and bowed his head best he could in the water. I figured I should do the same.

"Are you Naji of the Jadorr'a?" the king asked, his voice booming through the water like the blast from a cannon.

"I am."

"And who is your companion?"

"I'm Ananna of the *Nadir*." Water flooded into my mouth when I talked, only to pour back out through the gills in my neck.

"And how do you know Naji of the Jadorr'a?"

I didn't want to talk again, 'cause of the way the water rushing through my head made me dizzy. But everybody was staring at me, especially the king with his flat black shark eyes.

"I saved his life," I said

The king smiled, showing rows of teeth. Exactly like the manticore.

"Well, I am grateful for that, Ananna of the *Nadir*." He swam toward us, his tail flicking back and forth in the water. "I suppose you'd like to know why you are here."

"Yes," said Naji. "Your Grace."

The King of Salt and Foam stopped a foot away from us. I kept picturing his teeth sinking into my arm, into my belly—but no. He was like the manticore, right? He wouldn't hurt us. His shark sentries hadn't hurt us—

"You created this," the king said to Naji. His manta-ray fins swooped in and out, like they were trying to gather the city up in his arms. "All of this."

Naji stared at him.

"It was your magic, the soothsayer told me." The king nodded. "You cast wave after wave of magic into the sea, and from that magic we were born."

"That's impossible," Naji whispered.

"But it isn't," the king said. "Look at all this. Our city, our people. We can feast you in our hall, we can entertain you in our gardens . . ."

I wondered how an underwater city could have gardens.

"All of this came about because of you," the King said. "The soothsayer saw it."

Over in the corner, Armand bowed.

Naji shook his head. "No, no . . . My magic . . . it doesn't create, it destroys . . ." His voice trailed off. He was shaking, I realized, the water bubbling around him. And his skin had gone pale and sickly looking, even in the soft glow of the algae. I pushed over toward him, wound my arm around his, touched his scars.

"You told me blood-magic can do whatever you will it to do," I whispered, 'cause he was wrong, his magic had saved me from a gunshot wound.

Naji shook his head. "No," he said. "No, I never willed—" He stopped and looked at me. His eyes widened. "Your blood," he said.

"What?" Water swooshed through my head. I did my best to ignore it. "What about—"

"Your blood mixed with my blood . . ." His hands were on my face, his touch muted by the water. "We did this. Together. And I think . . ."

Lightness passed over his face like sunlight. He drifted away from me and floated up toward the ceiling, his mouth hanging open in something like surprise. Tiny white bubbles spun around him.

"Naji of the Jadorr'a?" The king flicked his fins at the courtiers and the school of fish flashed forward and swarmed around Naji, brought him back down to the floor. "Is he hurt?" the king asked me. "I don't understand what he's saying."

I looked at Naji out of the corner of my eye, caught up in all those flashes of light and silver. "I helped him," I finally said. "Whatever he did to make all you . . ."

And then I understood too. The battle with the Hariris. The magic we created. That *violence*, it all spilled into the ocean. This was all the magic-sickness. This was clams growing out of the side of the *Tanarau*, this was blood staining the walls of the *Ayel's Revenge*, this was Queen Saida's garden house collapsing into jungle plants in the middle of her garden. All that leftover magic sank to the floor and brought forth this city, this whole civilization, with a king and a court, with soldiers and soothsayers. Life.

The third piece of the puzzle.

Once I understood what had happened, I felt the curse dissolve away. There was a sharp and sudden crack, like what I felt when I kissed Naji back on the Isles of the Sky, and then there was only a lightness, an absence of weight. This was northern magic, after all, unknowable and strange—we might have created life during the battle, but the curse had stayed in place until this moment, when Naji learned, when we *both* learned, that the third task wasn't impossible. Completing the task wasn't what broke the curse, it was learning that the impossible wasn't really impossible at all.

Naji burst out of the school of fish, his clothes and hair fluttering around him. "Thank you," he said to the king. "Your hospitality is most kind." He seemed back to himself. My head was reeling from what I'd just figured out. *It's gone, his curse is gone.*

The king looked confused. "No," he said. "I am thanking *you*."

He lowered himself to the ocean floor, and then so did all the rest of the courtiers, until everyone, every fish and clam and eel in the Court of the Waves, was bowing to me and Naji.

Naji's face was full of light. He wasn't smiling, but he was happy, and his eyes were gleaming, and his hand looped in mine and squeezed tight as we kicked our feet there in the water. I pressed against him and held his hand as tight as I could. Music was pouring through the hall—not like the music up on land, but this soft creeping echo, like the reedy melody of a flute.

"Is it true?" I murmured to him, wanting to feel his body close to mine, wanting to hear him say it even though I already knew for certain, even though I could feel that the weight of the curse had drained away from him. "Is it broken?"

"It's broken." His hand squeezed mine. The king rose back up, solemn-faced and grateful, and the rest of the courtiers followed. The water churned from their movement.

"You're free," I said.

"Yes," Naji said. His hand gripped mine so tightly my fingers ached. "Free of the curse."

The king was smiling at us. Water rushed into my head and out through the gills in my neck.

"We broke it," Naji said. "I didn't know until I understood, but we broke it."

CHAPTER SEVENTEEN

The King of Salt and Foam gave us gifts: sacks of pearls, vials of Armand's potion that granted breath underwater, hard pink shells lashed together into strange clattering sculptures. They were brought in by a school of fish, all those tiny silvery bodies buoying up the gifts as they swam beside the king.

"The art of our society," the king told us. We were in his garden—turned out it was all seaweed and coral and glowing algae, beautiful and haunting. "We shall erect statues of your faces, Naji of the Jadorr'a and Ananna of the *Nadir*. Our children's children will not forget what you gave us."

"I thank you deeply," Naji said, bowing his head low, all serious and respectful. When I tried to do the same thing I almost turned a cartwheel in the water.

"Come," the king said, "swim with me." And then he began to slice through the water in his graceful, fluttering way, bubbles forming at the tips of his fins.

Naji and me paddled along beside him.

"I would like to know the story," the king said.

"The story?" I asked. Naji kicked me, hard and on purpose.

"Yes. The story of how this all came to be." The King stopped and floated in place, his seaweed hair drifting up away from his shoulders. "I know it was your magic—"

"And Ananna's," Naji said.

The king gave him a polite smile. "Armand saw *you*," he said firmly. "He saw the spells you cast into the sea. You were trying to defend your vessel, I know." The king fluttered his fins. "Armand saw that as well. But what we know of magic—it is all intention, yes?"

"Technically," Naji said. "But when a great deal of magic is cast, the way it was when I—when Ananna and I—were working to defend our ship . . . it sometimes takes on a . . . a life of its own."

The king gazed at him with flat black eyes. "Our life," he said. "Our lives."

"Yes." Naji bowed.

"So we really are creatures of magic."

"Magic and the sea," Naji said. "And yourselves, given the time."

That was a nice touch, I thought. You could tell Naji was used to dealing with royalty.

The king nodded. "I don't entirely understand," he said, "but I will set my scholars to studying the phenomenon."

Naji frowned a little, but I thought that was reasonable enough. Why wouldn't they want to know where they came from? 'Sides, the king was a fish. Couldn't expect him to understand everything about the land, just like we can't be expected to understand everything about the sea. Any pirate in the Confederation and any sailor on the up-and-up could tell you that.

"Regardless of our origins, you are welcome back to my kingdom any time you wish," the king said, and he gave one of those bows, deep and sure-finned in the water.

"I will visit as often as I can," Naji said, returning his bow, and I knew he meant it.

Armand appeared at the entrance to the garden, accompanied by a pair of shark sentries.

"Ah," the king said, "it's time."

"Your water-breath will wear off soon," Armand said. "We should wait in the air-hall."

The king turned to us. "Are you certain you wouldn't like to stay longer?" he asked. "You can stay in the air-hall. I'm certain we could provide food for you."

"We need more than food, I'm afraid." Naji smiled, polite as could be. "We can't go long without fresh water—ah, that is, water without salt."

"And we want to make sure our ship's still waiting for us when we get back," I added.

Naji's voice flashed a warning in my head, but the king only nodded. "I look forward to your future visit," he said to Naji. "I will investigate this matter of saltless water. And remember, all you must do is come to these coordinates. We will know it's you."

Armand rippled in the water like he was impatient. "I don't wish to be rude, Your Grace," he said, "but if the water-breath were to wear out here in the open, the effects would be disastrous."

"Ah yes, of course, Armand." The king bowed one last time.

We swam out of the garden and through the city to the big empty hall where that hissing glass box sat waiting for us. The potion kept working all through the trip, and for about five minutes or so after we arrived in the big empty hall. When it did wear off, though, it wore off quick as it had come on. One minute my breath was churning through my head and the next I had that tightness in my lungs that meant I was drowning. I pushed myself out of the water, onto the platform. Naji shot up a few seconds later, gasping. It felt weird to breathe air again. It was so thin and insubstantial, like spun sugar. I felt like I couldn't get enough of it.

Naji and me didn't really talk on the ride up, though he held me close like he was afraid I would disappear. I didn't feel all that different now that the curse was broken, but Naji was filled up with light, like the glow of the algae down there in the depths of the ocean.

Part of me was afraid he'd leave, now that he wasn't bound to me, but I told myself over and over that he was bound to me in other ways. I told myself he didn't have to be bound to me at all in order to love me. And the way he held me on the way up, his face pressing into my hair, water pooling at our feet, it helped convince me that I was right.

The *Nadir* was waiting for us when we surfaced. Thank Kaol.

Naji watched us load up the treasure, crewmen carrying it down to the holding bay—we were gonna split it proper, on account of how little actual pirating we'd been doing. Me and Marjani's idea. Naji didn't seem to care at all, and he watched us load up the cargo in happy silence. The only time he spoke was when he leaned over the railing and thanked the shark sentry.

"No," said the shark. "Thank you, Naji of the Jadorr'a." Then he turned to me and said, "And you, Ananna of the *Nadir*."

The shark and the glass box disappeared beneath the waves. You'd never know there was this whole city down there, full of talking fish and a king like an underwater manticore. Naji slipped off into the captain's quarters, and I moved to chase after him, but Marjani stopped me.

"What happened down there?" she asked. "Naji seems—"

"Cured?" I asked.

Her eyes widened.

"Yeah," I said. "The last part of the curse, remember? Create life out of an act of violence?"

She nodded, and I told her about the city and its inhabitants, the overflow of his magic. I told her how my blood, with its little trickle of ocean-magic, had mixed with his, and that's how everything came together.

"So we're done," she said. "We don't have to sail around chasing after his curse anymore."

I nodded.

"Now what?"

"You're captain," I said. "What do you want to do?"

She stared at me for a few seconds. "You know what I want to do," she said softly.

I got a heavy weight in my chest. A realization. "Yeah."

We stood in silence for a few moments. Then Marjani broke off from me and stood next to the railing. The *Nadir* bobbed in the water, held in place by sea-magic. She was waiting to be set free. I could feel it thrumming through her planks and her sails.

"I had a thought," Marjani said. "A few days ago, actually, sitting in the garden room with Saida."

"Well, I'd hope you'd had more than one thought the last few days."

Marjani laughed. "Saida was playing an old Jokja song on the reed, and I was sitting there listening—I never did care for sitting around listening to palace music, but with her it's different. Anyway, I was listening to this song and thinking. Thinking about the *Nadir* and her crew. And you."

The wind blew across the water, slammed against the frozen sails. Everything tasted like salt. I didn't want to go back to Jokja, I didn't want to live in the palace and smell the flowers blooming in the jungle. I didn't want to watch the rains fall every afternoon. Most things are only nice for a little while. Jokja was one of 'em. The sea wasn't.

"It's your boat," I said, voice small enough that the wind swallowed it whole.

"Not anymore," Marjani said. "It's yours."

I didn't speak, didn't move, I just kept staring out at the ocean.

"That was my thought," Marjani said. "When I was listening to that music from my childhood. The thing is, I became a pirate to run away from Jokja. But I don't have to run away from it anymore. And if anyone deserves her own boat, it's you."

"The crew'll never—"

"The crew'll listen to anyone who takes them up to the Lisirran merchant channels and pays them fair. And they've listened to you before." She smiled at me. "They're as tired of Arkuz as you are."

I didn't bother to correct her; she was right.

Another wind-blown pause.

"Don't let some Confederation scummy blow a hole in her side," Marjani said, "that's all I ask."

I nodded out at the sea, a nervous happiness churning up inside me. "I'll try my best, Captain."

She laughed.

"Lady Anaja-tu," I said, correcting myself.

"More accurate." She paused. "Go plot the course back to Jokja. We'll tell the crew about the trade-off once we make port in Arkuz." Then she pushed back away from the railing and hopped up on the helm and shouted, "Get your asses back to work! We make sail for Jokja and then Lisirra!" She gazed across the deck. "You can all quit your bitching, 'cause it seems we're pirates again."

That got a roar out of 'em.

As they readied the boat to turn back toward civilization, I slipped into the captain's quarters to draw up our route. When I walked in, though, Naji sat up on the bed and said, "Come here."

"Don't have time for that now." I nodded at the navigation maps. "Gotta chart us a new course. We're heading for Jokja and then . . ." I couldn't help myself; I broke out into a grin. "Marjani gave me the ship! So we won't be staying in Jokja no more. I figured we'd make sail for the Empire merchant channels and then head to Qilar. Ain't been that way in a long time, and—"

I stopped. He didn't have a lot of expressions, sure, but I could tell happy from sad. And he wasn't happy right now.

"I know," he said quietly.

"You *know*? How the hell . . . Oh." I frowned. "You were in my head, weren't you?"

"Yes." No apology, no explanation. "Ananna, I won't be able to sail with you to Qilar."

"Why not?" I could feel his thoughts pressing against mine, but I shoved them away.

"Because I will have to stay behind in Lisirra."

The room got drawn and quiet. The curtains hanging over the portholes shimmered in the sunlight as the *Nadir* made her way east.

"Ananna," Naji said, "one cannot just *leave* the Order."

I stared at him. My heart felt the way it had when he didn't smile at me. Like it was frozen.

"But you *did*," I said. "You ain't been a part of the Order—"

"No," he said. "I didn't."

"I don't understand."

He didn't answer right away, and I lunged across the room and made to hit him, though he caught me by the wrist and sat me down on the bed. "I don't understand!" I shouted again. "You haven't been part of the Order for going close to a year now! I ain't seen you take no commissions or meet with any of them—"

"That's not true," he said softly. "You saw me in my trances. I didn't take any commissions, no, because I was cursed. It was a . . . hindrance."

I went limp. All the anger just collapsed out of me and turned to sorrow.

"I'm so sorry." He reached to touch my hair, but I slapped his hand away. He didn't try to touch me again. "I didn't think we'd break the curse, and in truth, some days I didn't . . . I didn't *want* it broken, despite the pain, because I didn't—"

I stared down at my knees, heat rising in my cheeks. "You should have told me."

"I know."

"So now what?" I asked. "You go back to . . . to wherever, to your castle in . . ." I didn't know where the Order was located. Lisirra? Or the capital city? Who gave a shit?

"It's not a castle," Naji said.

"Whatever! I won't ever get to see you again."

"That's not true," he said, and he pulled me close to him. "You're a *pirate*, Ananna, you can sail to wherever I am, and I can come to wherever you are."

I was hot with anger and I thought about how he wouldn't once smile for me and then I thought about how he kissed me like I was the only person in the whole world. I thought about the light in his eyes whenever he was happy. I thought about how he shied away whenever I touched his scar and the way his hands traced the tattoos on my stomach.

"I love you," I said.

He blinked.

I don't know why I said it. It was true, but I was also furious with him. I guess I just wanted him to know what he was leaving behind.

"I love you, too," he said.

My face got real hot, then, and it wasn't just the anger.

"Then don't leave me!"

"I'm not," he said. "I just can't . . . I just can't *stay*."

"What!" I shoved him away. "That's what not staying means, you idiot. *Leaving*."

"Ananna, I'm bound to the Order. If I try to leave, permanently, they'll kill me. A permanent death."

"As opposed to an impermanent one?"

"Yes," Naji said, his eyes serious. "I work blood-magic, remember?"

He reached out to touch me, but I jerked away from him. He said my name again, and it was full of all this sadness and longing, but I refused to look at him. I gathered up the maps and the divider and carried them outside, up to the helm. The air was calm and I could weigh the maps down with some bottles of rum if need be.

Anything to get away from Naji. At least for a little while.

Marjani glanced at me but didn't say nothing when I stretched my maps out on the deck of the ship. The wind blew my hair into my eyes, and I cursed, trying to get the divider to slide across the map.

"I got Jeric to cast the fortune," Marjani said. "Looks like the air'll be clear from here to Arkuz. How long are you thinking it'll take? We had that storm on the way out . . ."

I was grateful to her for giving me the ship to talk about so I wouldn't have to think about Naji. "About a week and a half, looks like." I smoothed my hand over the paper. "We should have enough supplies. I haven't checked the stores in a while. Have you?"

Marjani didn't answer. And I realized with a start that the entire ship had gone silent: there was no creaking of the masts, no thwap of water against the boat's side.

For a moment, my heart froze.

"Marjani?" I whispered, and I twisted around to face her.

A man was standing at her side, one hand grabbing her arm and the other holding a knife under her chin.

The knife looked like it was made out of starlight.

The man's feet ended in mist.

"No!" I jumped to my feet and drew out my sword.

"Ah, that got your attention." The way he talked reminded me of Echo, cold and empty. He kept his knife at Marjani's throat and she stared at me, shivering, although her hand was creeping up to her pistol. "And you know what I want."

He grabbed Marjani's hand and twisted it around behind her back. Marjani let out a muffled scream.

"Let her go!" I shouted. "She don't have nothing to do with this."

"Of course she does," the man said. "She denied my offers as well." But then he shoved her away from him so that she stumbled up to my side. I didn't waste a second: I swung my sword at him. It sliced through his shoulder and came out at his waist. All he did was laugh.

Marjani pulled out her pistol and pointed it at him. He laughed again.

"The ship is mine," he said. He jerked his head toward the crew, who were doing their work all neat and orderly with faces as blank as masks. "They aren't as protected as you—" he jerked his head at me. "Or as knowledgeable as you—" at Marjani. "But I can't *captain* her to the assassin until you tell me where he is."

My heart jolted. *He doesn't know.* Naji's charm was still working. *He doesn't know Naji's on the boat.*

"We don't know where he is," I said. Marjani stayed quiet, just kept her gun trained at his chest.

"Lies." And he reached back his hand and slapped me hard across the face, hard enough that I stumbled back and slammed against the railing. I was stunned that he could touch me. My fingers grasped for the charm. It still hung around my neck. He laughed. "I'm not *Echo*, child. Echo is only a piece of me." He leaned closed. "I can smell him all over you. His *magic*. His filthy little *dirt charm*." He sneered at me. "You don't protect him as well as he thinks."

"Shut your mouth." I darted forward and grabbed Marjani and pulled her close to me. She gripped her hand in mine.

The man slid toward us. His mist curled around my bare legs. One of the maps had blown over beside us and the mist smeared the ink into long unreadable streaks.

"I've sent Echo to you so many times," he whispered. "Both of you." He grazed his fingers against my cheek and his touch burned with cold. When he touched Marjani she flinched away. "Did you not believe her? All those things she offered?"

I spat on him.

He laughed and wiped the spit away. "That's no way to treat a lord, my dear."

"You ain't no lord."

"But I am. Of course you know that. *He* told you." He smiled again, only this time there was something strange in his smile, like part of his face didn't work. The left side. Like it was scarred—

I knew what he was doing. Giving me what I wanted. Showing me Naji's smile.

"Ananna, be careful," Marjani whispered. I barely heard her.

"Stop it!" I screamed, and I sliced my sword through his belly this time, and all that came out of him was mist.

Where's Naji? I thought, and then I remembered. He wasn't cursed anymore; he wouldn't know I was in danger—

Our blood-bond. He knew Marjani gave me the ship, he should know about this.

Maybe he didn't care. Maybe he wanted me to die, then he could go back to the Order and never think about me again—

I didn't really believe that.

The man reappeared right close to me, close enough that I could feel his breath on my skin. "Couldn't tempt you with ships and lovers and power," he whispered. "Couldn't even tempt you with a smile. But there are other ways, of course." And his mist crawled in through my nose and my mouth, crowding into my brain.

"Don't listen to him," Marjani said. Her voice sounded far away even though she was still pressed up against me, her hand in mine. "He's doing something to you. Don't listen—"

The man turned to Marjani. She gazed up at him. I gripped my sword tighter. The mist was still in my head, turning my thoughts cold and hard. She was going to betray Naji. She didn't love him the way I did. It wouldn't even take much. One sentence. *He's on the ship. In the captain's quarters.*

"Don't even try," Marjani said, gritting her teeth.

The man laughed. "Don't you want to see what I can offer you?" And he pressed his hand on Marjani's forehead. She screamed and jerked away.

"I know what you can offer me," she said. "Slavery and imprisonment."

"You're not as easy to fool as your first mate," he said. "She at least let me show her what I had to offer. I believe she even *considered* it, one bright day."

I felt myself turning hot. A pang of guilt pierced through the fog. How could I think Marjani would hand him over? 'Cause he was right. *I* almost had.

"Yes," the man said, turning back to me. My whole body turned to ice. "You did almost give him up once. Because he had hurt you. And he's hurt you again, hasn't he? I can smell it on you." He buried his nose in my hair and breathed in deep and my whole body crawled with revulsion. "He could stay, you know," he said. "Sail with you through every ocean in this world, blowing your enemies away with spells and blood-magic. Never go back to the Order lair again." The man gave me a lazy grin. "He just doesn't want to."

"And could you give me that?" I shot back. "Naji at my side?"

"I could," the man said. "But then I wouldn't be able to take my revenge, would I? Besides, do you really want a man at your side who doesn't love you?"

I trembled. Behind him, Marjani said, "Ananna, don't you dare listen to him. He's spinning a web—"

"Shut up!" The man whirled around and struck Marjani in the stomach. I lunged at him with my sword, which did nothing, and for a moment or two Marjani stared stricken at him, like she couldn't believe he had hit her. And then she pulled out her pistol and shot him through the heart.

The man roared with laughter. "How many times will you two try to kill me? You know it won't work—"

Light flowed across the deck of the ship.

It knocked me and Marjani over, stunned us both. *Naji*, I thought. *He came after all*—

"Yes," the man from the Mists said. "He did come. Hello, Naji of the Jadorr'a."

My whole body turned cold. Marjani grabbed my arm. "Don't be stupid," she said, voice slurring a little. "Don't be—"

I scrambled away from her. Naji was floating above the deck, his body contorted in pain. And the man was laughing.

"Stop it!" I shouted.

The man looked at me. "I knew that would draw him out," he said. "Putting you in enough danger. *Frightening* you enough." He laughed.

"Why didn't you kill him?" I shouted at Naji, who just screamed and writhed in the air.

"Because even the people of the Mists have charms of our own." The man smiled at me. Then he walked up to Naji and pulled out his starlight knife. Naji moaned. My heart damn near stopped beating.

Charms of our own.

"Ananna," Marjani said, her voice faint behind me. "Don't rush into this."

The man dug the knife into the left side of Naji's face. Naji screamed and kicked. Blood splattered across the deck of the ship. Magic surged through me, a rush like the sort you get before battle. Marjani grabbed my hand and pulled me back.

"Think," she said roughly, her mouth close to my ear. "He has a charm. Something the other one didn't have."

"The knife."

"Yes. But it's too obvious. Something on the knife." Marjani jerked her chin toward the man, the man and Naji. More blood splattered across the deck. My stomach lurched. "Look at the hilt. It's wrapped in enchanted silk. I've seen that before."

"You've been to the Mists?"

"Of course not. It's not Mists magic." She shoved me forward. Naji's pain was starting to intrude onto me. It started in my head, but now it was a stinging in my face, a ghost of a wound lining my left cheek. "Get that charm off the hilt."

I ran toward Naji and the man. I didn't let myself think about what I was doing. I just ran forward and plunged my hand through the man's back. A half second of resistance and then it slipped through as easy as it had the day I punched Echo. The man hardly had time to react when my hand shot out the other side and I grabbed hold of the knife.

Naji gasped and landed with a sickening thump on the deck of the *Nadir*.

The man whirled around and snarled at me, his teeth like daggers. A *pop* of a pistol and his chest turned to mist. Marjani. It wasn't enough to disperse him back to the Mists, but it gave me enough time to see that the hilt of his knife was wrapped in stiff silk that smelled of the sap from the trees of the ice-island.

I yanked on the silk, balled it up and tossed it in the sea.

"I beseech your help!" I screamed. "Waters of the ocean! Please accept this gift—"

The man from the Mists growled and snarled again. He looked less and less like a man and more and more like a beast from a temple painting. His eyes glowed with starlight. His skin was gray and pale, the color of mist.

"What are you doing?" he howled.

"Waters of the ocean!" I shouted, tears streaming down my face. "I beseech your help! Take this man away from the *Nadir* and her crew!"

Naji lifted his head and stared at me. His eyes were so dark they looked like holes in his face. His mouth opened and closed. I could feel him—fear and panic and despair. I pushed it all away.

"Waters of the ocean!" I screamed. "Please!"

A shadow fell over the boat.

For a long terrible moment the entire world seemed to freeze. Then the *Nadir* tilted backward, and a dark ocean wave rose up against the bright sky, the water throwing off dots of light.

"Hold on!" Marjani screamed. "Knot a rope around yourself! Ananna!"

I didn't move. The wave wasn't for me. It wasn't for anyone human.

A wall of ocean water crashed over the ship. For a minute all I knew was water and salt and light. I couldn't breathe. When I opened my eyes I saw Naji floating through the murk, his hair streaming out from around his face, his eyes on mine.

I screamed his name. Nothing came out but a stream of golden bubbles.

And then the ocean slipped away.

I slammed down onto the deck. The whole world was lit up

in white sunlight. I squeezed my eyes closed and pressed my back against the wood. Crewman shouted and sputtered, their feet pounding against the wood. The sails snapped, the masts creaked.

"Ananna?" It was Marjani. "Ananna, wake up. Are you all right?"

I lifted my head and blinked at her. She was soaked, her hair plastered against her face. Behind her, the crew scrambled and crawled across the deck, rubbing at their heads.

"Where's Naji?" I asked. "Where's—"

"Over there . . ." Marjani pointed. Naji was sprawled across the deck, his chest heaving. "The man from the Mists is gone." She gave me a short smile. "Didn't know you could work water-magic?"

I pushed myself up. My head spun. The ship was undamaged from the wave; the masts stood straight and true, the sails fluttered in the breeze. Everything was wet. That was all.

Marjani helped me to my feet. My body ached, but I ignored the pain as I limped over to where Naji lay. I wasn't sure if it was my pain or Naji's anyway.

"Ananna," he said when he saw me.

I knelt beside him and pressed my hand against his forehead. The ocean had washed the blood off his face, but the cut was still there, a dark jagged tear that would add another scar to the lines of his features.

"I saved your life again," I said. "I'm sorry."

Naji laughed, though it came out choked and short.

"You didn't catch the curse again, did you? 'Cause I'd feel right bad about that."

Naji shook his head, wet hair flopping over his eyes.

"Good to hear." I stroked his hair, squeezed the saltwater out of it.

"That was . . . impressive," he said.

I shrugged. "Just gotta know what to ask."

His eyes brightened. For a minute a tightness pinched in my chest. I thought about the man from the Mists smiling for me like he was Naji. But he wasn't Naji. Because this was Naji's smile.

"Are they gone for good?" I asked.

"I don't know," Naji said. "But you scared him worse than I ever could."

I laughed, heat creeping up into my cheeks.

Naji lifted one trembling hand and tucked it against my face. "Thank you," he whispered, and then he drew me down for a kiss.

CHAPTER EIGHTEEN

We sailed into Jokja water a few weeks later, on calm seas and high winds. A trio of royal ships were waiting for us, the Jokja flag fluttering against the bright blue sky.

"What the hell?" I asked. Me and Marjani were up at the helm, looking out for the sparkle of Arkuz on the horizon. Marjani smiled.

"Saida," she said.

"You sure? I dunno, I usually see navy ships, I either fire the cannons or run."

Marjani laughed. "I don't think either of those actions will be necessary."

We sailed up alongside the closest of the navy ships. The crew lined up along the railing and shouted and waved. Marjani shouted and waved right back.

The captain showed up, his green sash rippling like the sea. He gave us a wave. "We're here to accompany you back to land!" the captain shouted, his voice rising and falling on the wind.

"Why?" I shouted back. "So you can arrest us?"

Marjani smacked me on the arm.

The captain shook his head. "By orders of the queen!" he shouted back. "She wanted to see you safely returned, and your boat docked with the royal fleet."

When I looked over to Marjani she was glowing.

"Royal fleet, huh?"

"That's why I'm handing her over to you," Marjani said. "I don't imagine this ship sitting well next to a bunch of Jokja schooners."

I laughed at that, but really my stomach was turning somersaults at the thought of Marjani giving me the ship. She hadn't made it official yet, hadn't told the crew or nothing. I still didn't see how this could go too well.

It took another hour to sail to the Azende Palace docks and get the ship tied down. Just as we were finishing up, a pair of palace guards showed up on deck and snapped their blades into a salute the way they did up at the palace.

"Can I help you?" Marjani asked.

"The queen sent us," the older guard said. "We're here to watch over your ship."

"Don't need you," I said. "Some of the crew'll be happy—"

"Ignore her," Marjani said, and she had that glow again. I wondered if that was what I looked like every time Naji came around. I hoped not. "We'll be happy to make use of your services." Then she turned to me. "Go tell the skeleton crew they have free run of the city. But," and she touched me lightly on the arm, "they have to be back here at sunset, same as the rest." She smiled at me, and the rest of that sentence hung unspoken on the air. For the exchange.

I sighed, but I did as I was told. The crew was certainly happy about it.

Marjani was waiting for me on the dock along with Naji and another pair of palace guards.

"Let me guess," I muttered, "more accompaniment."

"Life at court," Marjani said. "You'd get used to it, I imagine."

"It wasn't this bad before."

Marjani shrugged.

We made our way through the palace gardens and into the queen's sun room. She was pacing in front of the big open windows when we walked in, the sunlight setting all her jewels to sparkling.

When she saw Marjani she cried out, lifted up her skirts, raced across the length of the room, and caught Marjani in her arms.

"Jani," she murmured, burying her face in Marjani's shoulder. "The fortuneer said you were drowned—she saw a wave crash over your boat. I sent out men to look for you, but we hadn't heard—and the sentries were only there on the off-chance—"

Marjani cupped Queen Saida's face in one hand and kissed her, gentle and soft. Saida gazed at her, tears sparkling on the ends of her lashes. For a moment, no one in the sun room moved.

"I really thought you were dead," Queen Saida whispered. "And it was like when you left before, only worse, unending—"

"I'm not dead," Marjani told her.

"It's going to be like this every time you—"

"I won't be leaving again," Marjani said.

Queen Saida pulled away, stared at her. "I thought you were a . . . a pirate now."

Marjani smiled. And then she shook her head no. "No, I was never a pirate. Not really." A long breathless pause. "I'm staying."

My guts twisted up when she said that, not 'cause of her making me the new captain, but because I wanted Naji to say those words to me more than anything: "I'm staying," and he wouldn't, I knew he wouldn't. I glanced at him out of the corner of my eye: he stood very still, his face a mask even though it was uncovered.

"You're staying?" Queen Saida trembled. "You're really staying?"

"Really. I'm really staying."

"Oh, Jani, this is marvelous news!" She threw her arms around Marjani's shoulders and kissed her. "I'll tell the kitchens right away. We should have a feast—"

"I doubt the kitchens will be able to prepare a feast in the next few hours," Marjani said. "And even if they could, it would be far too much work—"

Queen Saida ignored her; she just turned to one of her pretty attendants and said, "Send Najala up to meet with me. I want to discuss the menu."

"Of course you do," Marjani murmured, low enough that only I could hear her.

"Aw, c'mon," I said. "Not many of us get feasts thrown in our honor."

"Yes, I suppose that does make the two of us members of a very particular club."

I laughed. Marjani just shook her head.

But then Naji caught my eye, and my good mood evaporated. His expression was like the night sky during a full moon, dark, dark, dark, but in some ways bright enough to cast shadows.

I could feel Marjani looking at me. I knew she knew something was wrong. But she didn't say nothing, and Queen Saida was calling her away for preparations, and I slipped out of the sun room and down to the garden.

Naji knew not to follow.

The feast wound up being postponed, 'cause, like Marjani said, the kitchens didn't have time to prepare everything to Queen Saida's liking. All that meant was that Naji and me couldn't stay for it. He needed to leave, needed to go back to the Order, back to Lisirra. And truth was I didn't much want to stay in Jokja any longer anyway. Partly because seeing Marjani and Queen Saida made me sad, but partly too because of the way I'd missed the sea so bad during all my times on land. Papa used to talk about it with Mama, the way the sea meant more to him as he got older. Mama always said it was because of the sea's magic, that he was finally feeling it.

And maybe I was finally feeling it too. I'd saved Naji with the sea's magic. I'd saved him, just so he would have to leave me again.

I stayed out in the palace garden all afternoon, listening to the jungle creeping up along the other side of the fence, chatting with the guards as they changed positions, taking cover underneath the banana trees when the rains came. Naji never came around. I told him not to, in the whispers that still bound us together by blood and magic. I told him I wanted to be alone for a while, to think. And he honored that.

Although in my thinking I did, at one point, see just how well we were connected. I thought maybe it would come in handy, once he left and I sailed off to the merchant channels or the ice-islands or Qilar. It was during the rainstorm, and I was stretched out in the grass, rain beating against the wide, flat banana leaves. Everything smelled like soil. I closed my eyes and reached out with my thoughts. It didn't take long.

He was in the palace library, pouring over some old Jokja text. I saw him like I was standing in the doorway, but he didn't look up, didn't greet me, at least not in the physical. Instead, I heard his voice in my head.

I thought you wanted to be alone.

I am alone. So are you.

For all I knew he was still reading that stupid book, but when I thought that, he smiled. Just for a second.

Not so alone, he told me. *You're here.*

Not really.

Your thoughts are. It's the same thing.

No it ain't. Except I didn't say it, exactly, nor did I think those specific words. I just . . . disagreed with him.

We can do this across the seas, he went on. *You do know that, right? We won't really be splitting apart—*

Out in the garden, I sat up, knocking my head against the banana leaves. Rain soaked through my hair, though my clothes.

The image of Naji in the library was lost. His voice in my head was a whisper: *Ananna? Where'd you go?*

I shook my head, trying to knock him out. It didn't work. So I focused on the sound of the rain as it pattered across the garden, and in a few minutes I was alone again.

Won't really be splitting apart.

I curled up beneath the banana tree, tucking my chin onto my knees. I knew he was right, but—

I just didn't want to think about it. I didn't want to think about nothing.

At sunset, I walked down to the *Nadir* alone. She was waiting for me in her place at the docks, her sails drawn up tight, her pirate colors fluttering like they were the Jokja flag. In the golden light of day's end, she looked like something out of a dream, like something out of one of Echo's visions.

Almost too perfect for me.

"Ananna!" Marjani leaned over the railing and waved at me. "I was starting to think you wouldn't show up."

"Got lost in the garden."

She laughed. I wondered if Queen Saida was gonna be on board, surrounded by her attendants. If there was gonna be a line of guards watching as Marjani told the crew I was their new captain.

But there wasn't. It was just Marjani standing there in a simple blue dress, and the only person by her side was Naji.

His eyes crinkled when he saw me, and at first I wanted to ignore him, pretend he was just another scummy among the crew. But when he held out his hand I took it, and I let him drew me close and kiss me softly on the mouth. And I knew then that I'd missed his touch.

"All right, men," Marjani hollered. "I made you all come back here for a reason."

"We leaving?" called out Bashar. "Finally sailing off to Lisirra like you promised?"

"*You* are," Marjani said, and the crew whooped and hollered without thinking on what she might've meant by that.

"In fact, you can leave tonight," she said, and the cheers picked up again. "Assuming that's what your captain wants."

That got their attention. Finally.

"And what do you want?" somebody called out.

"I'm not your captain anymore," Marjani said.

Silence. My palms were sweating, and I wiped them on the edge of my dress.

"You saying he is?" Bashar asked, pointing at Naji. "He ain't no captain. He don't know his way around a boat—"

"I'm saying she is," Marjani said.

Every eye on that boat turned to me. The silence was even thicker than before, so thick I choked on it like Otherworld mist. I realized, standing there, that I'd expected to be jeered, but this silence was worse.

And then Jeric yi Niru stepped out from the knot of crewman. "Annoying though she is," he said, "I couldn't imagine a finer captain."

I glared at him.

Still, his words broke some spell, and the crew started cheering the way they had when Marjani said we were setting sail for Lisirra. I didn't quite believe it at first, that they were cheering—well, not for me really, but for the idea of me as their captain.

"So are we setting sail tonight, Captain First Mate?" Jeric asked me.

"Don't call me that." I stepped forward and looked out over the crew, all of them staring back at me, waiting to give an order. And I knew I could order them to take me anywhere but Lisirra, all the way to the underside of the world if I wanted, and Naji couldn't do a thing about it.

Except he could. Even if he didn't blow the ship off course he could slip into the shadows or go through the trance-place and I'd never see him again.

"We'll set sail tonight," I said. I could feel Naji staring at me, but I didn't say nothing. "We'll set sail tonight, and we'll set sail to Lisirra."

Lisirra was as hot as I remembered, that dry baking heat that soaked into my skin and made me feel like I was home. Naji and me walked side by side through the streets of the pleasure district. It was the middle of the day, and everyone was tucked away in the shadowy coolness of the buildings, the way the *Nadir* was tucked into the Lisirran dock under a fake name and the promise of a few sheets of pressed silver.

Every now and then Naji's hand touched mine. Every time it did my body shivered with happiness.

Naji took me to an inn. The Snake Shade Inn. The one we'd stayed at after I'd started up his curse. This time, though, the innkeep didn't recognize him for what he was. When he handed us the key to our room, he looked at us like we were nothing but a pair of pirates.

Upstairs in the room, Naji undressed me slow and soft, starting with my boots and jacket and then undoing my dress with all the precision of a clockmaker. He stood behind me as he pulled my underclothes off me, and then he pulled my naked body close to him and kissed my neck and whispered in my ear, "I'm not leaving you."

I twisted around to glare at him. "I don't want to talk about that."

He gazed at me for a few seconds. Then he tapped his finger against his temple, tapped it against mine.

"That ain't the same!"

"I know," he said softly, "but it's there."

He set me down on the bed and stood in front of me as he peeled off his own clothes. His tattoos gleamed in the light streaming through the windows. The scar on his chest looked a million years old. The scar on his face from the Mists lord's knife did not.

He crawled on top of me and kissed my mouth and neck and my stomach. He kissed every part of me. Every time he kissed me he told me that he loved me, and after a while I knew I had to believe him.

We stayed in the inn room for a long time. The sun dropped in the sky. The light in the windows turned golden and rich and syrupy. I laid my head against Naji's chest and listened to his heart beating.

"I'm not leaving you," he said again.

"Don't." I was gonna start crying. I could feel the weight of it, lurking there right behind my eyes.

Naji rolled over so we were facing each other. Ran his fingers over my lips. "I'm not even talking about reading your thoughts," he said. "Even if we couldn't do that, I still wouldn't be leaving you."

I scowled up at the ceiling.

"Would you want to stay in one place?" he asked.

"What?"

"Say I bought you a house in Lisirra," he said. "The garden district, maybe. And you lived there. And I could travel through the shadows to come see you—"

"Like the Hariris?" I frowned.

"You wouldn't like that?"

"I like being on a boat."

Naji brushed my hair away from my forehead. "I know," he said. "It's part of you. The ocean. The water. You can't stay in one place. Even if you wanted to."

I thought about those first few days after I ran away, how badly I wanted to be back out on the sea.

"I ain't a sea witch," I said.

He laughed hard enough that the bed shook. "Don't you dare try to tell me you still believe that."

I scowled. "It was just 'cause of your blood-bond."

"It was not and you know it." He kissed the tip of my nose. "If ever there was someone who was a part of the ocean, it was you."

I didn't say nothing.

"You have to follow the currents all over the world. It's who you are." He kissed my forehead, my cheeks, my throat. "And I have to follow death all over the world at the Order's command. It's who I am."

I frowned.

He rolled me onto my back and sat up and traced two paths over my belly with both hands. "Here I am," he said. "And here's you."

The two paths crossed each other.

"I can make that happen," he said. "I can make that happen anytime you need me."

For a long time I didn't answer. I just stared at him, at his beautiful face and his beautiful scars.

"I need you all the time," I said.

"You do now." He kissed my forehead. "And so do I. But after a while we won't. And you'll be glad to be rid of me."

"I won't stop loving you!"

"Did I say that?" His face darkened. "I said you'll be glad to be on your own. And you will."

I couldn't imagine it at first, but then I thought about it and I could. I wasn't like Marjani, who could give up a life on the sea in exchange for a life with her love. Because Naji was right: Marjani wasn't a part of the ocean. I was.

And now I had a boat of my own, and a crew of my own. And we'd sailed to Lisirra with no trouble. They listened to me like I was Papa, like I was important. And when you got down to it, that whole trip, Naji'd just been a distraction, really. Keeping my mind away from the boat.

I threw my arms around his neck and kissed him deep and sure.

"Do you really want to see me smile?" he whispered into my neck. "I know the Otherworld lord tried . . ." His voice trailed off.

I hesitated. "I know how you look when you're happy."

"It's not the same as a smile. I know that." His fingers ran over the bridge of my nose. "After it happened," he said, "after the blood-fire burned me, I would spend hours in front of a mirror Leila had given me, trying to find my face." He dropped his head to the side and didn't look at me as he spoke. "And one day I was going through my expressions, trying to find myself again."

He paused, ran his hand over the tattoo on my belly.

"And I smiled. People used to like my smile. Women, you know." He sighed. "And I'd never seen anything so monstrous."

"You're not a monster," I said.

He looked at me.

"I know that now."

I smiled.

And then he did too.

It didn't look like a smile at first. It looked like a snarl. One part of his face twisted up and the other twisted down. His teeth gleamed.

But I looked at his eyes, where the brightness was. And everything changed.

For the first time, I understood the difference between leaving and not staying. It was the difference between a snarl and a smile.

"Thank you," I whispered, and I kissed his scars, those ridges and lines that twisted his face up into something beautiful. I kissed the place where the man from the Mists had cut him. I kissed over the smooth skin of his neck, the soft tangle of his hair, his lips.

When I pulled away, the smile disappeared from everywhere but his eyes.

"We'll see each other soon," he said.

And he was right.

TURN THE PAGE FOR A SNEAK PEEK AT

MAGIC OF WIND AND MIST.

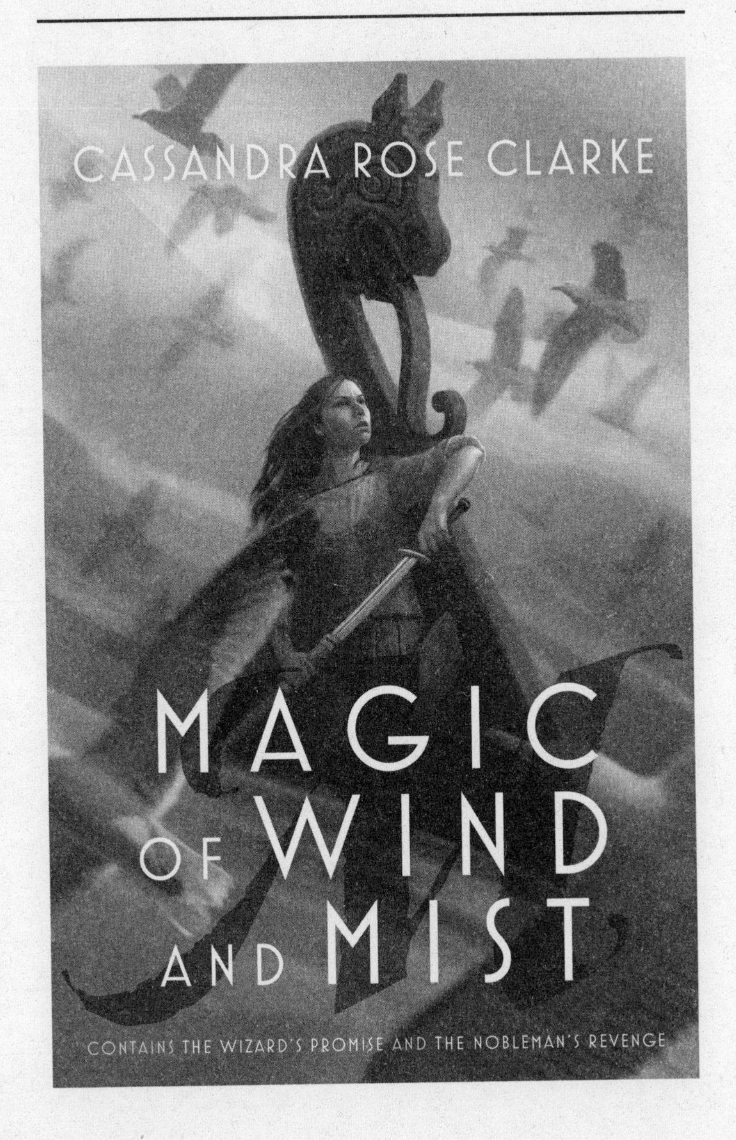

I was picking ice berries for Mama's start-of-spring cake when a spark of magic smacked me in the side of the head. My basket hit the ground and berries rolled out over the mud, and I scowled at the little trail of amber lights darting back and forth through the air.

"Larus!" I shouted. "What do you want?"

The light flickered and coiled in on itself. For a moment I thought it was going to extinguish, since Larus doesn't exactly have the most reliable magic in Kjora. But instead it just zipped off to tell him where I was.

I cursed under my breath and knelt down in the soft, cool earth to gather up the escaped berries. A trail of light from Larus meant one thing—somebody had a message for me. Larus, untalented wizard though he may be, was still the only person in the village who had trained at the academy in the southerly seas and officially been named a wizard by the capital, and thus the only one people ever hired to do tracking spells. He took that job seriously, too, the prig. Like carting weather reports around the village made him important. It wasn't as if he had even trained someplace renowned, like the Undim Citadels.

So someone was looking for me. I knew it wasn't Mama or Papa or my brother Henrik, since they all knew this little road leading away from the sea was the best place to pick late-season ice berries. My friend Bryn never hired Larus for anything after he ruined one of her best dresses with a love charm. And nobody else in the village had any reason to send for me.

Except Kolur, of course. I'd bet my entire basket of berries Kolur was the one looking for me.

I cursed again.

The wind, still sharp-edged with winter's cold, blew through the bushes. I stuck my hand in the brambles and pulled out another handful of berries. This would probably be the last time I'd get to harvest them before next winter, and I wanted to collect as many as I could before Kolur's message ruined my day. That you could still pick the berries this late in the season was why Mama used them in her start-of-spring cakes, since she always said spring was as much a good-bye to winter as it was a hello to summer. Mama liked winter, for some reason. Papa always said it's because she grew up in the south, where heat is dangerous. I could never imagine it.

Larus took a long time following his tracking spell back to me. I'd managed to clear out most of the remaining berries by the time I spotted his tall, gangly figure up on the road. He raised one hand in greeting, the embroidered sleeve of his red wizard's cloak billowing out behind him.

"Hanna Euli!" he called out, as formal as if he were a wizard from the capital. "I have a message for you."

"Yeah, I noticed." I sighed and hooked my basket in the crook of my arm and hiked through the mud to the edge of the road. Larus watched me, his eyes big and blue and round. He wasn't much older than me, although I was still expected to treat him like an adult, given that he was an official wizard. I didn't, though.

"Is it Kolur?" I said. "It's Kolur, isn't it? Couldn't he have let me have a few days of spring?"

Larus cleared his throat and made a big show of pulling a scroll out of the cavernous depths of his sleeves. I sighed and shifted the basket of berries to my other arm. Larus unwound the scroll. It was a short one.

"Get on with it," I muttered.

Larus drew back his shoulders and held his head high. Delivering messages was pretty much the only wizardly thing there was for him to do around the village, so he always took it too seriously. "Kolur Icebreak wishes you to meet him at the village dock at the start of longshadow. He wishes to set sail for the Bathest Chain, as he—"

"What?" I tossed my basket to the side and stalked up to Larus, reaching to grab his scroll. He jerked it away from me and sparks of magic flew out between us, stinging my hand.

"Don't touch the scrolls," he said.

I glared at him and rubbed at my knuckles. I called on the wind, too, stirring it up from the south, but Larus just rolled his eyes like it didn't impress him.

"Tell Kolur I'll sail with him next week," I said. "I've got to help Mama with chores today."

"Let me finish, Hanna." Larus struck his messenger pose again. "For the Bathest Chain, as he's thrown the fortune for the coming weeks and found that the fishing will be excellent for the next few days. He's already spoken with your mother and knows that she can spare you."

I glowered at Larus. He coughed and looked down at his feet. I made the south wind stir his robes, tangling them up around his legs.

"Stop that," Larus said. "You know some child's trick doesn't make you a real wizard."

"Is there anything else?"

"No." Larus pulled a quill out of his sleeve. "Would you like to send a reply?"

"Do I have to pay for it?"

"All messages cost one common coin." He glared at me. "You know that."

"No thanks, then." I picked up my basket. Sometimes you can wheedle a free message out of Larus if he's in the right mood, but I should have known better than to try after teasing him with the wind. He doesn't like being reminded that I'm a better wizard than him, even if I am a girl.

Not that I needed to send a message. Kolur knew I would show up whether I wanted to or not, because I was his apprentice and he was friends with Mama, and between the two of them there was no way I could ever slack off work. I mostly just wanted to send him something rude so it would annoy him.

"Has the message been received?" Larus asked, back to playing the village wizard.

"Yeah, yeah." I ran my fingers over the ice berries, relishing the feel of their cool, hard skins against my fingers. The last crop and I probably wouldn't even get a slice of Mama's cake, since Henrik would eat every crumb by the time I got back. It was always that way, fishing with Kolur. He didn't go out for just one day—no, he had to go out for three or four at a time. Only way he could get a decent haul.

"Well, if there's nothing else," Larus said.

"There's not. Thanks for nothing."

He made a face at me. I didn't bother trying to retaliate, just left him there, making my way down to the road, toward the little stone house where I lived with my family.

When I walked up the muddy path, Mama was out in the garden, tending to the early-season seedlings she'd finished putting in the ground a few days ago. She waved, her hands streaked with dirt. I figured she'd been out here waiting for me, seeing as how she received word from Kolur before I did.

"Did you get the message?" She sat back on her heels. Mama's accent was different from mine and Papa's and everyone else's in the village, since she'd grown up speaking Empire her whole life. Normally I liked it, because it gave her voice this pretty melody like a song, but today even that wasn't enough to sway my annoyance.

"You knew!" I tossed the basket at her and she caught it, one-handed, not spilling a single berry. "Why didn't you just come tell me yourself?"

She smiled. "Oh, I don't like stepping in between your arrangements."

"Larus said he checked with you first!"

"You know what I mean." She stood up and tried to shake the mud from her trousers, although it didn't do much good. "It looks like you have a good crop of berries here."

I scowled.

"Oh, don't be like that." She came over to me and draped one arm over my shoulder. "You know you'd be bored if he hadn't sent for you."

"It's only just starting to get warm! The sun's out"—I gestured up at the sky—"and the south wind's blowing. I was going to practice my magic."

Mama gave me one of her long sideways looks. "You can practice aboard the *Penelope*." She paused. "You know, when I served aboard the *Nadir*, there were no days off, warm sun or not."

I'd heard this story before, and a million like it besides. "That's because the *Nadir* was a pirate ship. Fishing boats have rules. He can't just run me like a slave driver."

"And he's not," Mama said sharply. She lifted up the berries. "Come, let's go make the start-of-spring cake so you can have a piece before you leave this evening."

She strode out of the garden, and I shuffled along behind her, my hands shoved in the big pockets sewn into my dress. It was nice to be back inside, since for all my protestations about the warmth, the spring cold had been starting to get to me, and our house was always warm and cozy from the fire Mama kept burning at all times. Henrik was sprawled out in front of the hearth, pushing his little wooden soldiers around. He ignored both of us, and Mama stepped right over him to get to the tall table where she did all her hearth work.

"Are you going to help me, or you going to sulk?" she asked over her shoulder.

I crossed my arms over my chest and didn't answer. Mama took that as a yes to helping her, the way she always did, and handed me the berries. "Clean those off for me while I mix up the batter."

The basket dangled between us, and she was already pulling the little ceramic jar of flour toward herself with her free hand. She'd hold the basket there all day if she had to. I knew I'd lost. No fisherman's ever gone up against a pirate and won, that's what Papa's always saying. Although in his case, she just looted his heart.

I sat down on the floor next to the fire and started separating the stems and leaves from the berries. Henrik kept on ignoring me, he was so involved in his toy soldiers. Mama hummed to herself as she worked, an old pirate song about stringing up the sails. She'd sailed under one of the greatest pirates of the Pirate's Confederation, Ananna of the *Nadir*, and when she was my age, she was living on board Ananna's ship and sailing to all ends of the earth, fighting monsters and stealing treasure and basically having a far more interesting life than I could ever hope for. Sometimes I tried to imagine what it would be like to sail the seas in search of adventure instead of fish. I wondered about the sort of people I'd meet outside of Kjora, if they'd be as strange and different as all the elders in the village claimed, with antlers growing from their foreheads and cloven feet tucked inside their boots. Mama told me once that was a silly northern story, but I wanted to see for myself.

Mama met Papa when the *Nadir* blew off course and wound up in the waters off Kjora, where she and some of her crew hijacked Papa's fishing boat. Apparently, Papa had been so handsome back then that she'd taken one look at him and decided to stay on the islands—at least, that's how she told it. Papa said the story was a bit more complicated than that, but he never gave me any details.

At any rate, when Mama decided to stay, part of the deal to convince Ananna to let her go was that Mama'd name her firstborn daughter after her. And that turned out to be me. Of course, no one in the village could say "Ananna" right, so the name got distorted to Hanna. I didn't mind. I liked having two names, a fisherman's name and a pirate's name. I took it as a sign that someday I'd do something more with my life than work for Kolur, that I'd sail beyond the waters of Kjora and see the rest of the world and all the excitement it held.

I finished stripping the berries and then carted the basket over to the ice melt we kept next to the stove so I could rinse off the dirt. By the time I'd finished that, Mama had the cake batter all whipped together in a bowl, and she let me stir the berries in before dumping the whole thing in the long, low pan she used for startof- spring cakes. Henrik was still occupying the space in front of the hearth, and Mama had to shoo him aside like a fly so she could stick the cake into the heat.

"Did I ever tell you about the time Ananna and I stole a cake from the Emperor's own bakery?" Mama asked me. She turned to Henrik. "Sweetling, why don't you dry off the bowls?" He sighed and tossed his soldiers aside and did as she asked. I was already stacking the mixing and measuring bowls for cleaning myself.

"Yeah, all the time," I said.

Mama smiled and went on like I hadn't answered. "It wasn't an ordinary cake, of course. It had been enchanted. Anyone who ate even single bite could be controlled by the person who had served it to him. A dangerous thing." She lugged over the bucket of ice melt and set it on the table, and together we set to cleaning. "And worth a fair price, too, on the black market, which is what Ananna wanted with it. Of course, as a cake, we only had a few days to steal and sell it—there was no use trying to go after the Emperor's magicians to try and learn the spell, they're too highly protected. So we had a few of the crew disguise themselves as guardsmen, and Ananna and I dressed up like noble ladies, and we walked right into the Emperor's palace." Mama laughed, plunging a mixing bowl into the ice melt. "We were able to get ahold of the cake easily enough—it was in the kitchen, and the kitchen crew ran scared when they realized we were pirates—but carrying it while being chased through the streets of Lisirra, that was no easy task. The cake wound up falling and melting in the sand." Mama and I lined up the mixing bowls to dry, and I waited for the usual final line. "I supposed it was all for the best. No good could come of magic like that existing in the world."

I nodded in agreement, my expected response. I thought it sounded fantastically exciting, running through Empire streets in a lady's dress, trying not to drop an enchanted cake, but I knew my life didn't have anything like that in store for me.

Mama settled down in her favorite chair to wait for the cake to be finished. "I remember learning how to make start-of-spring cake. Your grandmother had to teach me."

I'd heard this story, too, but I didn't say anything. I liked listening to her stories.

"I gave up on the second try and stomped out of the kitchen, cussing and shouting, just as your father was coming from his fishing. He hadn't caught much that day, either." She smiled again, and the hearth light made her brown skin glow, and I wondered if that was how Papa had seen her that day as he walked in from the gray, cold sea. She must have been a shard of Empire sunlight here in the north. "And he told me it didn't matter to him one whit if I could bake a cake or not, that he had married me for me, and if it was such a problem, then he'd bake all our cakes himself."

I gave the expected titter. Henrik wiped off the wet mixing bowl with a scowl.

"Would you ever make a cake for your wife?" I asked him.

"Wives are stupid." He set the bowl aside.

"Spoken like a man of the Confederation," Mama said gravely. "As it happened, your father was the one who finally taught me how to make a start-of-spring cake, the next year. It was quite the scandal for a few days, a man teaching a woman how to cook." She winked at me. "But I taught him some tricks myself."

I'd heard all those stories, too, about how Mama'd gone aboard Papa's fishing boat and showed his crew a better way to string up the sails so that they could move more quickly through the water. That had generated a scandal for more than a few days, from what I gathered.

We finished cleaning up the bowls. Henrik went back to his toy soldiers, Mama went back to her garden and I went into my bedroom to pack up my things for the fishing run with Kolur. The sweet berry scent of the start-of-spring cake filled the house, and I told myself it'd only be two or three days' time before I'd be back home, ready to practice calling down the wind and finally welcoming spring to Kjora.

I rushed down to the docks, my hair streaming out behind me, a couple of slices of start-of-spring cake dropped in my pockets. It was already past longshadow and the sky was turning the pale purple-blue of twilight. I figured I could give Kolur a slice of cake for waiting.

The *Penelope* was the only boat in the dock, its magic-cast lanterns throwing a pale bluish glow over the water. Kolur waited for me on land, his arms crossed over his chest, the lanterns carving his rugged face into sharp relief.

"You're late," he said.

I reached into my pocket and pulled out a piece of cake wrapped up in a scrap of old fabric. Kolur stared at it.

"I said longshadow," he told me. "Not the middle of the night."

"And it's not," I said. "The stars aren't even out yet. Are you going to eat the cake or not?"

Kolur's pale eyes glittered in the lantern light. Then he plucked the cake from my hand and dropped it in his satchel.

"Get on board," he said. "If we don't leave soon, we'll miss our window."

"I hate night fishing." I sighed. "I've been up since this morning, you know."

"You can sleep once we get to the islands." Kolur gestured at the gangplank. "Go on, then."

I squared my bag on my shoulder and walked aboard. The *Penelope* was small and sturdy, the sails knotted in the pirate style—Papa wasn't the only one Mama taught Confederation tricks. There was a narrow cabin down below where Kolur let me sleep, since he preferred to stay out on deck in case of emergencies. We had a storage room too, and a galley for preparing meals. I went down to the cabin and dropped my bag on the cot, then joined Kolur up on deck, where he was already plotting the navigation that would take us out to the open sea, toward the Bathest Chain.

"Unmoor us," he told me without looking up.

"Aye." I pulled up the gangplank and unlooped the rope tying the *Penelope* to the dock post. She floated free in the bay, the frozen twilight shimmering around us. I called on the wind before Kolur could cast one of the cheap charms he always bought in the capital—it was easy work, since the wind was already blowing from the south, pushing us where we needed to go.

The *Penelope* glided forward, her sails snapping into place. We drifted silently through the moonlit water as Kolur steered from the wheel and I tended to the sails and all our fishing equipment, ensuring that everything was in its place. It was dull work, but at least I got to practice a bit of my magic. Besides, there was something calming about the rhythm of moving through the boat, going step by step to make sure everything was perfect. Like arranging the parts for a spell or a charm. If I used my imagination, I could pretend I was apprenticing for a wizard and not Kolur.

We sailed on toward the northwestern corner of the sky. I dropped the fishing nets at Kolur's feet and then sank down in them, quite prepared to get in a nap before we started fishing. But Kolur was feeling unusually chatty. Just my luck.

"Saw a big school of skrei in the bones," he said, looking straight ahead out at the starry night. "Last of the season."

I pulled out my cake slice and nibbled at it while he droned on about throwing the old fish bones he kept in a pouch around his neck. "Odd to see them this time of year, you know. Usually we're just pulling up ling and lampreys. That's why I wanted to give it a go. Bones told me they'd be gone by next week."

I made a muffled *humph* sound, my mouth full of cake.

"You need to be learning this, if you want to take over your father's boat someday."

He paused, waiting for my answer. I took my time chewing.

"Henrik can take over Papa's boat," I finally said. "I've got other plans."

Kolur laughed. "Taking cues from that friend of yours? You'd be better served learning how to dance than learning how to fish, if you've got your eye on a husband."

He was talking about Bryn, who was quite beautiful and already had a handful of marriage prospects. Good ones, too. Elders' sons and even a wizard from Cusildra, two villages over. Most of the girls in the village planned on marrying, but Mama had pushed me into fishing with Kolur. She said I needed to make my own way. I didn't disagree with her, but fishing wasn't where my future lay, I knew that. I was going to be a witch.

"Nah," I said. "Not unless I can marry someone from outside the village. The boys here are dull." I didn't bother telling him my real plans. Kolur didn't talk about much, and I didn't think he'd understand. All he needed to know was that I didn't want to be a fisherman or a fisherman's wife. Ideally, my future would involve as few fish as possible.

Kolur laughed again. "Ain't that the truth? Glad to see you've inherited some of your mother's good sense." He tilted the wheel, and the *Penelope* turned in the water, splitting open the reflection of the moon. It was full and the stars were out, but the night still seemed too dark, like it was trying to keep secrets.

"Here, take over for a bit." Kolur jerked his chin at the wheel, and I hopped to my feet and gripped the smooth, worn wood while he knelt down on the deck a few paces away, rubbing the space with his hands.

"I just keep going straight?"

He nodded. I tightened my grip and steadied the wheel. Kolur took off his pouch, dumped the bones in his palm and muttered one of the old fisherman's incantations. As far as I knew, this was the only spell he'd ever attempted.

The bones leapt and rattled in his hand, a tinny, hollow sound, as they charged with enchantment.

He tossed them along the deck like dice. And then he gasped.

Now, I'd learned to read fish bones when I was a little girl, hanging around down at the docks while Papa tended to his own boat, the *Maia*. It's easy, easy magic. So I knew what I was looking at when the bones scattered into their preordained patterns. A twist of tail curving out from jawbone: times of strife. A tooth inside a chest cavity: stranger coming to town. And two skulls facing away from each other: romantic troubles.

Not a single thing about the state of the ocean. Not a single thing about skrei.

"What the hell?" I dropped the wheel. The *Penelope* swung out from under me, and Kolur cursed and I shrieked and realized my mistake and jerked us back into position. The bones scattered over the deck. Kolur slid with the boat and gathered them all up in one clean motion.

"Pay attention, girl!" He squeezed his hand into a fist and when he opened it, the bones were jumping again. "I didn't tell you to play fortuneer; I told you to take the wheel. You know what happens when sailors don't do their assigned job? Your mama ought to have made that clear."

"I'm not a sailor," I said.

Kolur threw the bones again. This time, they fell in more common patterns, twists and squiggles that gave us a direction, northwest, and the promise of a good catch.

"Told you," he said. "A school of skrei in the northwest." He pointed at a scatter of teeth that looked like islands in the Bathest Chain. "There's our destination. Getting all worked up over nothing."

"That is *not* what I saw the first time."

"Because the moonlight was paying tricks on you. It's what I saw the first time, until you tilted the damn boat."

"Then why'd you gasp like that?"

"I didn't gasp like nothing." He gathered up the bones again and dropped them back in his pouch. When he stood up, his face had a hardness to it I'd never seen before. A determination. I'd never seen Kolur look determined about anything except the ale down at Mrs Blom's inn.

"Let me take that." He grabbed the wheel away from me, and I knew enough to let go. I was still seething about what I'd seen in the bones. He was lying. Which he did often enough, but it still annoyed me.

"Where are we going?" I glared at him, my hands crossed over my chest.

"Told you, girl, the Bathest Chain. Now go set up the nets before we sail right over the damn things."

He wouldn't look at me. Kolur was already pretty old, older than Papa at any rate, but in the darkness he seemed ancient. Like the capital wizards who have cast so many spells that the magic keeps them from dying.

"Do it," he snapped, and this time I did, because I knew if I didn't, he'd tell Mama and I'd be washing out the outhouse for months. But I wasn't happy about it.

Kolur and I worked well into the night, the *Penelope* slipping through the water with the nets splayed out behind her, the fish glinting silver in the moonlight. The air turned colder, and I was lucky I had one of my old winter coats stashed down below so I wouldn't freeze. Trawling like that was dull work, but with the waters as smooth and calm as they were, it wasn't dangerous. Most of the night, I just sat around on the boat, waiting until Kolur decided it was time to heave the nets aboard and check the catch. We worked together to get the fish on the deck, then Kolur had me cast the charm to keep them fresh for the two or three days we'd be out at sea, sailing a wide circle around the Bathest Chain. When the *Penelope* couldn't hold any more fish, we'd sail back to Kjora, and I'd be free until the next time Kolur decided to drag me away from home.

I thought about home as we sailed through the cold, shivering night. Kolur didn't go in much for talking if he could help it, but he was unusually quiet tonight. Withdrawn. I didn't mind the silence; I'd gotten used to it since becoming his apprentice, but it could get tiresome, being alone with my own thoughts all the time. Bryn would probably have some news about her suitors when I got back—she liked to tell me all the details about their weird habits and conversational topics. Mama'd probably make me help in the garden, and we'd sing old pirate songs as we worked. Papa'd come home with stories about his own fishing trip—all of them dull compared to Mama's stories, even the ones I'd heard over and over. But still, he'd pick Henrik up from the floor and swing him around and then give Mama a big hello kiss. Maybe the sun would even dry up the mud by the time we made it home, and I could go out in the fields and practice my magic without anyone watching.

"Check the nets," Kolur told me from his perch up at the wheel. I pulled myself away from my thoughts and did as he asked.

"Everything's fine." My voice carried with the wind. It was definitely stronger now, the sails snapping and pulling tight on their ropes. I frowned up at them. There hadn't been anything in the fish bones about inclement weather in *either* of the castings, and generally I had an easier time controlling the winds than this.

I glanced up at Kolur. He held the wheel tightly and didn't look at me.

"You think a storm's coming?" I shouted. "You said the weather would be smooth."

Silence. The wind was howling now, cold and sharp as knives, the *Penelope* tilting back and forth in the water. I reached out for it, trying to call it back through me so I could work my magic, but it was as slippery as the ocean.

"Kolur!" I shouted.

This time, he glanced over at me, his dark hair flying into his eyes. "Yes," he said, in an odd, flat voice. "Yes, a storm is coming."

Storms had never scared me much, not even out here on the open sea—I've got my affinity with the wind, and I knew enough protection charms to keep the boat safe. But I didn't like Kolur's behavior at all. It wasn't like him. Normally, when a storm blew in, he'd be fussing and fretting over his precious *Penelope*.

"Do you want me to bring in the nets?" The wind zipped my question away as soon as I spoke it. Kolur looked at me again.

"Yes. The nets. Of course."

Fear gripped me hard and cold. Kolur wasn't much of a fisherman, but he never forgot the nets.

I didn't like this at all.

I pushed my alarm aside and grabbed the nets with both hands and hauled them aboard. If I stood around feeling scared, then that'd be the end of us for sure.

The nets were empty save for the glitter of old fish scales. Ice water splashed over the railing, slapping across the boards and leaving a pale froth in its wake. It was too dark to see anything but the confines of the boat, even with the magic-cast lanterns swaying back and forth. Kolur was still at the wheel. He might as well have been a statue.

I ran up to him and grabbed him by the arm, steadying myself against the podium. "Kolur!" I shouted. "What's going on? The storm!"

He looked at me, and he looked almost normal.

Maybe a little older than usual.

"I'm trying to keep the boat steady, girl. What do you think I'm doing?" He sounded like himself. "Put a charm on her for us."

I nodded, taking deep, shuddery breaths. Maybe the strangeness earlier had just been my imagination. A little bit of fear creeping out to blind me. That could happen.

I rushed down below to gather up the lichen powder and the mortar and pestle. The *Penelope* tilted wildly, and everything slid back and forth. Dark seawater dripped down through the ceiling from the deck and stained the cot. I caught a few drops of the water in the mortar and braced myself against the wall as I sprinkled in the lichen powder. As I mixed them together, I muttered an incantation in the language of my ancestors, guttural and sweet at the same time. Magic thrummed through me. All that power of the islands, all that power of the winds, all that power of the north.

The boat tilted again, lifting up on the starboard side. I cried out and covered the mortar with one hand. For one long and terrifying moment, I thought we were going to flip, and then we'd freeze to death in the black and unforgiving sea.

But then the *Penelope* righted herself, and I cried out in relief and rushed up on deck to finish the rest of the charm.

The winds were worse now and laced through with tiny pellets of ice that struck my bare face. Kolur was still at the wheel, as calm as if the water was flat and the skies were clear. I smeared lichen paste on the masts and the railings, shouting the incantation against a storm. I was so cold, I could hardly think. When I finished, I slumped down next to the small, scattered pile of skrei, trying to steady myself as the boat rocked and the magic flowed out of my veins and into the wood of the *Penelope*. I could feel it working, distantly, like an overheard conversation. We kept rocking and swaying, but thanks to the charm, the ocean no longer washed over the railings, and the water already on deck was no longer frigid. The storm crashed around us but it didn't touch us.

I was exhausted.

Kolur looked over at me and gave a short nod of approval. "You did good," he said. "Kept calm under pressure. Very good."

He turned back to his sailing.

Yes, calm under pressure. He'd been *too* calm. But I was too tired to say anything about it. My limbs ached, and my eyelids were heavy. I pushed myself to my feet, leaned up against the mast.

"I need to rest," I said.

Kolur nodded again, this time without looking me at me. "Figured so. You go on down below, rest off the magic. I'll see us through the storm."

Something tickled in the back of my mind, a phantom thought that maybe I shouldn't trust him. But that was absurd. I'd trusted him for three years, and besides, he was Mama's best friend.

So I went down below and fell asleep immediately.

THE MAD SCIENTIST'S DAUGHTER IS A DEEPLY
ENGAGING TALE BEAUTIFULLY TOLD. CASSANDRA
ROSE CLARKE IS A SUPERB WRITER AND THIS
PELLBINDING NOVEL SHOULD APPEAL TO GENRE
AND MAINSTREAM READERS EQUALLY."

—GRAHAM JOYCE, AUTHOR OF THE SILENT LAND

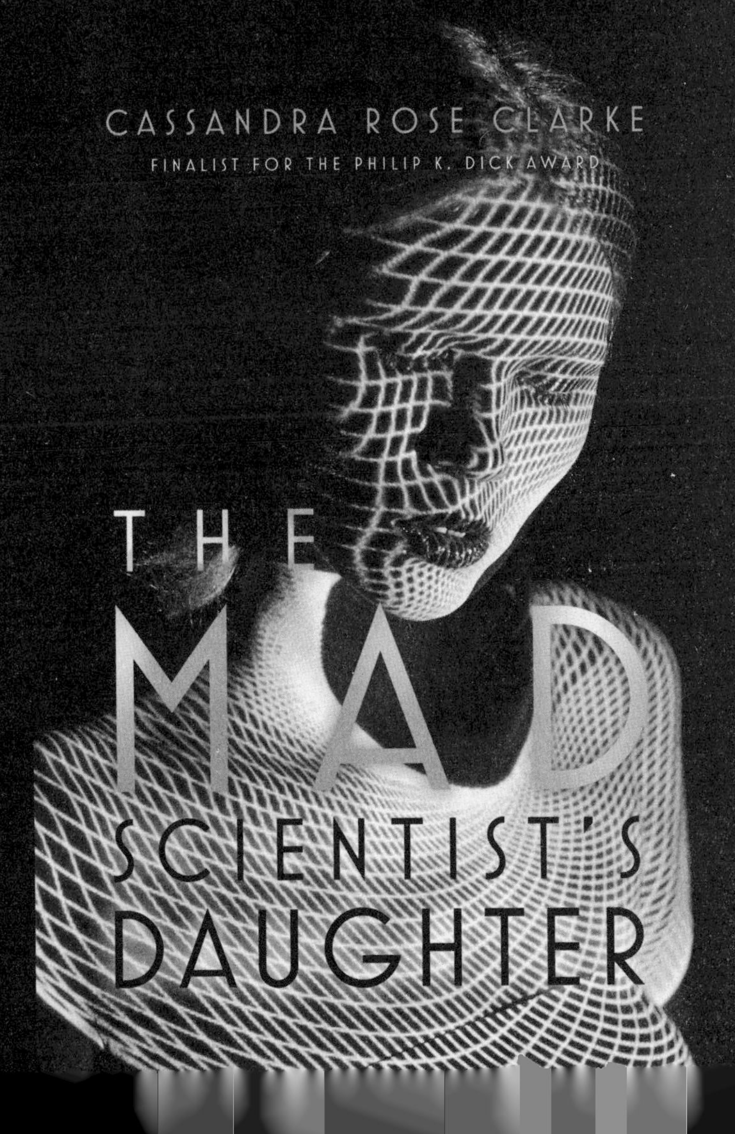